CHASING THE LION

Book One
Of
The Sword of Redemption

Nancy Kimball

Independently published by
Nancy Kimball
Fiction From the Ashes
www.nancykimball.com

Cover design: Alexandre Rito of Design Project www.designbookcover.pt/en/
Cover model: Checotah Knollenberg
Cover and Author Photographer: Robert Johnson
Interior Design and Formatting: Polgarus Studio www.polgarusstudio.com

Dum spiro spero

While I breathe, I hope.

CHAPTER 1 – RUNNING

City of Rome
August 10, AD 82

My mother is a liar. Jonathan's tears added shame to his anger as he ran through the crowded streets. No man of twelve should be fleeing and weeping like a child. The faster he ran through the throng of people and animals, the more the words of his mother's confession snarled behind him.

In his haste to turn from the street corner into the alley, a low stool caught his shin. He tripped onto the poultry seller's table and knocked a plucked chicken to the ground. A dog snatched it and ran amidst the ensuing clamor.

Plucked geese swung overhead. Their cleaved necks dripped blood, the profane rain falling red and wet on Jonathan's arms. Angry shouts from the merchant and a growling dog defending its prize added to Jonathan's ragged heaves. He regained his footing and made a final sprint to his place of solitude. In the alley, he slowed to allow his vision to adjust to the shadows. Instead of the empty oxcart where he could be alone to think and pray, the forms of his tormentors came into focus.

The big one crossed his arms. "Look. It's Jonathan. And he's *crying*." The sneer brought chuckles from the other two boys standing on either side of their leader. "Why are you crying, trash?"

Jonathan stopped and remained silent. He would let them add a hundred bruises to the one now forming on his shin before admitting the reason for his tears.

The skinny one pulled a flint and striker from his tunic. “Let’s burn the oxcart. Without his little cave, he’ll have to find a new place to hide from everybody who doesn’t want him around.”

The shorter boy stepped closer. “Maybe they finally told him who he has to thank for those elephant ears.” He put his hands on the sides of his head and flapped them while he laughed.

They were just words. Like always. Jonathan would ignore them. Like always. He’d heard them all before. If he left now, they wouldn’t make it to the ones that hurt most.

The big one in the center uncrossed his arms, his amused expression turning serious. “Is that why you’re crying? You finally found out who your father is, and he’s a nothing, just like you?”

Today they’d skipped Jonathan’s peasant clothes and skinny legs and gone straight for his deepest wound. A wound their taunts deepened, because today they held truth.

Moments ago, his mother plunged him into the waters of the only taboo subject that existed between them. She knew who his father was. She’d always known. He’d asked why she’d kept it a secret, and why she was telling him now. Her answer had sent him running.

The laughter still spewing from the older boys salted his open wounds.

He punched the skinny one first. The others fell silent. Jonathan whirled and kicked the big one in the knee. Before he could put a blow into the last boy, the coward fled.

Burly arms closed around Jonathan from behind. He clawed at the arm locked around his neck. His feet left the stone beneath them, and he struggled like a netted fish in the bigger boy’s grasp.

The boy he’d hit appeared in front. Hate gleamed in his eyes above his bloodied nose. He punched Jonathan in the stomach so hard the spent air trapped in his lungs shot up through his clamped throat. The gagging sensation only intensified his struggle to breathe.

Another fist to his stomach—harder this time.

Jonathan's vision blurred and pain poured from his middle as he thrashed. He yearned for his mother so much that the echo of her voice penetrated his dizziness. Then the voice boomed, powerful and livid.

The big one dropped him and ran. Jonathan lay on the ground, coughing like his mother in one of her spells. He curled onto his side and cradled his tender stomach, drawing breath in deep gasps. A hand touched his back. A touch he'd known all his life.

Jonathan shifted to sit upright, though his stomach protested the movement.

His mother's gaze went straight to his blood-splattered skin. "You're hurt."

"I'm fine."

She reached for his arm, and Jonathan jerked away. Pain flashed in her eyes, which added to his own. The sight of her kneeling on the filthy stone street, looking as wounded as he felt, cut through his sense of betrayal. Weak and sick, she had still come after him.

Jonathan rose and helped her to stand. She embraced him, the warmth of her tunic pressed to his cheek as when he was a child. He feared tears again. If he allowed them, his pain would become hers, and she had enough to bear. This would be the last night in their home. As much as he wished for a father, he never thought it would mean leaving everything familiar behind.

His mother pulled away to gaze at him with sorrow-filled eyes. "Forgive me."

The breathiness of her words deepened his concern. Chasing him had spent her strength. "We should go home."

He draped her arm around his shoulders and fit himself into her side like a crutch to begin the walk back. The poultry merchant, poised to give threat again by the set of his face, relented at the sight of Jonathan's mother at his side. Jonathan nodded in gratitude when their eyes met.

When he opened the door to their one-room *insulae*, a familiar sight greeted him. Deborah knelt on the floor in prayer. The older woman was like a second mother. Her head snapped up. Relief flooded her features, swallowed by swift indignation as she rose. She swatted him, her hand gnarled like tree bark from age but strong enough to sting.

"What did you think your mother would do when you ran off?"

"It's all right." His mother forced the words between labored breaths. "I enjoyed the fresh air."

"Humph." Deborah frowned. "You sound like it."

His mother grinned at the chastisement as Jonathan lowered her to her blankets on the wooden floor.

"Besides, there's no such thing in this city." Deborah moved toward the one piece of furniture they owned. The small table supported their feather-light coin purse, a clay pitcher cracked near its top, and a single clay cup. "I told you the boy was going off to rail at God and to leave him to it. But no, you insisted on chasing after him. At least you finally know where his stubbornness comes from."

It came from both of them but saying so would be unwise. Deborah poured a cup of water for his mother and brought it to her. She took a long swallow and extended the cup to him.

Jonathan shook his head. "You finish it."

She drained the rest, and his guilt grew with every swallow.

Deborah counted out copper coins from their leather coin purse. "You need to eat to get your strength back, Liv. I'll bring *cena* back for all of us."

"Thank you," he and his mother answered in unison.

Deborah nodded and left. "You better both be here when I get back," she yelled through the closed door.

Jonathan rose and refilled the cup. He took a long draw of the water before handing it back to his mother. A long moment passed, and her breathing slowed to a steady effortless rhythm—at least for now.

"Why can't we stay here with Deborah? When you're—" He couldn't think it, much less say it. Not without the sheltering confines of his oxcart.

"Because to decline your father's request would insult him. Besides, you know Deborah would be unable to provide for you alone."

"What is my..." He couldn't bring himself to say the word *father*. "What is he like?"

His mother touched his jaw. "He is a good man who will love you as I do." Her smile didn't falter, but it disappeared from her eyes.

He knew that look. "What is it?"

She dipped the edge of her sleeve into the cup of water in her hand. Taking his arm, she scrubbed at the dried blood staining his skin. "He does not believe in the true God as we do and requested I not speak of Him in the hearing of anyone at the villa."

"You agreed to this?"

"It wasn't an easy decision. Our deeds, not our words, must win your father to the Lord. Our faith lived out to others should always have hands and feet, even without voice." Her eyes were fierce, even as they pleaded. She took hold of his arm again in a grip firm enough to surprise him. "Do you understand this?"

"I understand."

Her hold on his arm loosened as she sank back against the wall, rustling the straw beneath her blanket.

Deborah returned, carrying three large honeyed fig cakes and a brick of cheese the size of Jonathan's hand. She grinned as he and his mother stared wide-eyed at the bounty. "Our last meal together is a special occasion. I'll hear nothing of the expense, so save your words."

They sat on the floor and reminisced through happy memories, sharing the meal and their single cup. Jonathan didn't chew the cheese. Instead he let it dissolve on his tongue to savor the rich, salty flavor. Deborah told stories of her people that he could recite from memory, but still enjoyed hearing.

His mother grasped Deborah's withered hand. "You know we'll visit as often as we can, and bring whatever gifts we're able."

"None of that, Liv. You know *Jehovah-Jireh*, the God who provides, will see to my needs as He always has."

Night was falling, and their jovial mood faded along with the light from their small window. The last morsels of cheese and honey cake were gone.

Deborah and his mother settled on the straw pallets on their side of the room before darkness cloaked their small home.

Jonathan rested on his pile of straw beneath a threadbare blanket. Each time he moved, the soreness in his stomach reminded him he'd been on the verge of a beating before the older boys fled. Would he ever see them again?

Perhaps his father owned horses and would permit him to ride one. He'd never ridden a horse, but it looked simple. Sit on the animal's back and hang a leg on each side. He would smile down at those wretches and wave from atop the horse like Caesar. Perhaps his father would ride beside him and wave to them too. That would slay the taunts on their tongues before they even left their mouths.

But what if the boys in the alley were right? Would his father find him unworthy as so many others did? Would his father cast him out after his mother— *No.* She couldn't leave him. He wouldn't gain a father only to lose the one person he needed most. So he prayed. *Lord, You healed the lame and the sick, raised the dead, and parted seas like Deborah told us. I know You can heal my mother. Please, Lord. I need her.*

Deborah's whisper in the dark interrupted him. "What did you tell him?"

A long moment passed. "His father is a good man, who will love him as I do."

"Was that all?"

"No."

Silence stretched again. Jonathan strained to hear, even in the small room.

"I told him we must win his father to the Lord through our example, the way you did me when you took me in. You showed me Christ's love when I was starving with nowhere to go."

Straw rustled in the dark. Jonathan imagined his mother and Deborah embracing as they often did.

"You saved my life, and my unborn son. You showed me the way to Jesus." There were tears in his mother's muffled words.

"There, there," Deborah whispered. She would be stroking his mother's back as she had his own whenever he skinned his knee as a child. For a long time, only the soft murmurs of comfort and gratitude permeated the darkness. Then the straw crunched again and all was quiet. A quiet that lasted so long, Jonathan resumed his silent prayer.

Deborah's muted voice interrupted them again. "A senator risks much by claiming Jonathan as a son."

His mother's sigh cut through him like a cold wind.

"I know he does."

"If his father tells him of your past before you do, Jonathan won't understand. He deserves to hear it from you."

"Jonathan knows all he needs to." Sorrow seasoned his mother's whisper. "My life as a slave still pains me too much to speak of it. Especially to my son, for whom I would endure it all again."

"I will pray for both of you, and for his father."

Uncertainty covered him like a second blanket. He didn't know what he was more afraid of. What he already knew or the secrets they were still keeping from him.

Chapter 2 – First Meeting

Nausea kept Jonathan's eyes closed most of the trip to their new home. He'd never been to this part of the city before, or ridden in a litter. The swaying motion didn't bother his mother. She lay beside him on the cushion with everything they owned folded in her blanket between them. After what felt like a full day's journey, she touched his shoulder. "We're here."

The litter stilled, and Jonathan opened his eyes. The men carrying the poles set the litter down, and the curtains on his mother's side were drawn aside.

"Welcome to the *Domus Tarquinius*, my lady. Please, let me take your belongings." The same man who came for them this morning helped her out.

"Thank you, Dionysius." His mother stuck her head back through the parted curtains. "Jonathan?"

"Coming."

Jonathan climbed from the litter and into a vision. That was the only explanation for what he was seeing. The house was the size of their entire insulae building, and as grand as he'd always imagined the emperor's palace. Gleaming white statues of robed men and women lined the walkway to a huge set of wooden doors three times as tall as he was.

"Please, follow me." The man his mother called Dionysius walked toward the doors. The gold threads in the trim of his crisp linen tunic made more sense now that Jonathan saw the house. Even the slaves here dressed like royalty. He smoothed the front of his own tunic. It was clean, but had been too small for months and repaired in more places than he had fingers.

They passed through the doorway, and the vision expanded. Frescoed walls surrounded him with scenes of animals in a forest, nude men and women lounging in clouds, and ships on the ocean. The white stone tiles of the floor shined like new coins. A large fountain pool filled the center of the room.

Someone approached them from further inside the house. The man wore a toga the color of snow, trimmed in the crimson of the senators. His hair was raven black like Jonathan's, except by his ears, where it was an ash gray.

The man's ears stuck out a little too far from his head, just like his own. Jonathan swallowed and felt his nausea return. This was him.

The servant bowed low to the man. Jonathan glanced at his mother to see if he should, but her back remained straight and her gaze steady on the man who approached. She put her hand on the middle of Jonathan's back. Her touch reassured him, but didn't stop his heart from racing.

The servant straightened and clasped his hands behind him. "The lady Livia, my lord, and her son, Jonathan."

The man in the toga stopped an arm's length away. Jonathan stared at the three gold rings on the senator's left hand, wary of meeting the man's gaze.

"Do you know who I am?" The senator's tone didn't threaten or demand.

Yet how was Jonathan to answer? He turned to his mother.

She smiled and stroked his back. "It's all right."

He forced himself to meet the eyes of the man and nodded.

A grin formed on the man's face. Was that good? Jonathan wanted to know what he was thinking. Then again, maybe he didn't. He'd been in this house less time than it took to lace a sandal and already knew he didn't belong here.

"Livia, would you permit Jonathan and me to become better acquainted in the garden? Dionysius will show you to your chambers and obey your every request as if it were mine."

Jonathan wasn't ready to be alone with him. He might never be.

She was going to say yes. He could see it in her eyes. "Thank you, my lord. For everything."

"Do not address me as lord. You are the mother of my son, not a servant in my house. Am I understood?"

The flicker of a smile edged his mother's lips as she dipped her chin.

"Good."

The senator motioned for Jonathan to follow as he turned. Jonathan hesitated, but his mother stroked his hair and then pressed him forward. He took a few steps to follow, but the man turned back suddenly.

"Dionysius, did you inform Manius of the feast tonight?"

The servant glanced at Jonathan. "My lord, I'm not sure you wish me—
"

"What did he say?" There was an edge to the senator's tone now.

The servant turned his back to Jonathan and moved closer to the senator. Jonathan knew he shouldn't listen. His mother wouldn't want him to. But like last night, he did anyway. It was the things people didn't want heard that often held the most truth.

He caught few words of the low tones, but among them were *illegitimate peasant*, *disgrace*, and *no cause for celebration.*

The senator stiffened. "I want to see him when he returns."

"Yes, my lord."

"Apologies my son Manius was not here to greet you both, Liv," the senator said. "He was raised without a mother, but that's no excuse for ignoble behavior."

His mother smiled, but her face remained drawn. Perhaps she'd heard the servant as well.

"Jonathan and I look forward to meeting him to thank him for sharing his home with us. Now please, go on." She pressed Jonathan forward.

The senator seemed pleased by the answer. He opened his mouth as if to speak, but closed it and turned his gaze to Jonathan. "Come with me."

The senator led him through a hall with plaster walls the color of honeycomb that ended at the edge of a great garden. Jonathan passed from the shade of the roof into warm sunlight and stopped. Flowers bloomed everywhere, in more colors than he could count. Hedges shaped like crates surrounded the statues standing guard over the biggest fountain he'd ever seen.

The top tier stood as tall as the house. Jonathan approached and was startled by movement below the surface. Were those fish? Orange and white fish, some as big as his foot, swam to the rim as he stared at them. "Your fountain has fish in it."

The senator came and stood beside him. "It's your fountain too, as are the fish. This is your home now, Jonathan."

Jonathan met the man's gaze. There was something in his expression that told Jonathan not to be afraid.

"Come sit with me."

Jonathan followed him to a bench farther down the pebbled path, and sat as far from him on the marble seat as he could. He glanced sideways, surprised to find the man studying him. Again he wanted to know what the senator was thinking, but retreated to a safer question. "What's your name?"

The senator chuckled, and Jonathan feared he'd insulted him, until he sighed. "Forgive me. It's a good question, but as a *praetor* of Rome, both a judge and senator, not one I've been asked in many years." He grasped his toga at his shoulder and straightened. "Poetelius Tarquinius Cornelius."

That was long and sounded important. Jonathan doubted he should use 'my lord' if his mother wasn't supposed to. "What am I to call you?"

"Father."

Jonathan flinched.

The senator must have seen, because his expression fell.

Jonathan could hear himself say the word in his head but couldn't bring his lips to form it. This stranger was his father. *Father.* For so long, the simple word marked an unexplained absence. The source of the taunts he'd endured for years until sheer repetition hardened him against much of the sting. Before he could call this man father, he must know why.

He met the man's eyes and forced himself not to look away. "A woman said to my mother once that—that I should never have been born. My mother cried for a long time." His voice shook, and his vision blurred from unshed tears, but he could not stop now. Not when an answer was within his grasp at last. "Why did she keep me a secret from you?" He swallowed. "Unless it's true?"

Jonathan closed his eyes, waiting for the answer yet feeling like he dangled from the edge of a great precipice. The longer the silence stretched, the more his dread grew. A hand came to rest on his shoulder, and he opened his eyes in time to see his father speak.

"Never let the thoughtless words of another make you doubt your own worth. You are my son. When the documents are finished, you will carry not only my noble blood, but the Tarquinius name as well. I didn't know, or I would have claimed you at your first breath. Your mother's reasons for keeping you from me were unjustified, but they were rooted in love for you. A love I now share."

Jonathan didn't understand the sensation washing over him. A rift in his spirit began to close with the healing words of his father. He'd wanted him then. He wanted him now. The hand on his shoulder became an embrace. Tears fell unhindered as a lifetime of insecurity crumbled within the arms of his father. The missing pillar of his lost identity rose from the bottom of his soul, erasing every scar from every errant taunt and pitiful glance he had ever endured. He summoned his voice from beneath the unabashed emotion pouring forth to form a single, whispered word. "*Father.*"

Jonathan learned much in the garden. The history of their family, what a praetor does, and how his father's first stag hunt at his age resulted in a broken bow and a wounded servant. His father asked many questions, much about Jonathan's own history, but Jonathan would give the briefest explanation possible and then ask another question of his own. Listening was better than having to speak.

When Jonathan's father eventually led him into a chamber within the house, the air there smelled so good Jonathan wanted to lick it. Cheese, bread so fresh the crust still steamed, and what smelled like a stew from the rich aroma of savory meat lay waiting on a table surrounded by a three-sided dining couch. He'd never seen so much food in one place that wasn't for sale.

"Recline beside me." His father adjusted his toga and nodded to a servant Jonathan hadn't seen until then standing in the corner. The plush cushion felt strange under his side. He'd always sat on the floor or a stool to eat, and he feared spilling anything on the intricately woven fabric.

His mother entered, leaning heavily on the head servant's arm.

"Mother?"

"Livia?" his father said at the same time as they both stood.

"I'm fine," she answered, raising her palm to them. "I'm fine."

She settled near him, and a servant brought a bowl for them to wash their fingers in. Her breathing seemed even, and when she smiled, they both returned to their cushions. Jonathan watched his father to be able to repeat everything he did, including the odd way he held his cup with only his fingertips. The cups were bronze, not clay, and the wine inside them was the best he'd ever tasted.

The servants brought their bowls of stew, and his father took the first bite. Jonathan cringed, unsure now of what to do. His mother grasped his hand below the table, and bowed her head for a moment. Jonathan did the same, and for the first time, she didn't pray aloud. After a moment she squeezed his hand and flashed him the slightest of grins before picking up her spoon.

"Are you finding everything to your liking, Liv?" his father asked.

"Yes, thank you." She brought the spoon to her mouth laden with broth but hesitated. "Are you?"

His father looked at him, his dark eyes crinkling at the corners as a side of his mouth lifted. "Very much."

The scrutiny made Jonathan uncomfortable, and he fished a chunk of meat from his bowl and ate. The flavor as he chewed made him grateful he'd never known what he was missing. His mother and father spoke throughout the meal, but Jonathan hardly heard them. Food this good deserved his full attention. He wished Deborah could have had some, or the boys from yesterday had been here to see his father and this house.

Jonathan waited for an opportunity to ask his father a question. After those in the garden, this one would be easy. "Do you have horses?"

"Jonathan," his mother said sharply.

"It's all right, Liv." His father turned toward him. "I do. Would you like to ride in the chariot this afternoon?"

"I've never ridden in a chariot before. My mother says I was almost run down by one before I was born."

"Well I'm grateful to the gods you both were not. Perhaps your mother will join us. She has always had a way with horses."

"What do you mean? We've never had horses."

"Cornelius, you and Jonathan go. I would like to remain here and rest if you'll permit me." His mother spoke so fast, Jonathan knew the coughing was about to seize her. She covered her mouth with her fist and tucked her head as the violent rasps shook her. She already had a cup of wine, so there was nothing more he could do for her though he wished more than anything there was.

"She'll be all right in a moment," he assured his father.

"How long has she been like this?"

"Since last summer, but it worsened a few weeks ago."

His mother looked up, her eyes glistening with tears from her spell. "Please don't talk about me as—" She pressed her hand to her chest. "As if I'm not here."

"My physician is slated to come tomorrow afternoon. I want him to see you, and Jonathan also."

Why him too? He wasn't sick. And visiting a physician was expensive. Deborah and his mother had sewn extra tunics and blankets by lamplight for weeks to pay for his mother to be able to go to one.

"I've already seen a physician," she said.

"You haven't seen mine. I insist. Now then, Dionysius?"

The head servant appeared from around the corner of the doorway as if he'd been there the whole time.

"Ready my chariot and have the cooks prepare full courses this evening. Salad, sardines and mackerel, oysters if we have them, and pheasant. Second tables can be honey sweetened cakes, figs, and Chian wine. If my son—oldest son—arrives, send him to my study and inform him if he wishes to receive his allowance next month, he'll remain there until I've seen him."

"Yes, my lord."

His father's other son was sounding more and more like the boys in the alley.

The servant left and Jonathan's mother held his hand under the table again. "Please don't allow our presence to burden your son. We could take our meals in my chamber or with the servants."

"Absolutely not. I've made allowances for too many years because I was not the father I should have been after my wife died. By the time I was, he was already grown." His gaze fell on Jonathan. "Which is why I'm grateful for another opportunity."

Jonathan stared down at his lap, afraid the heat in his cheeks would show. If his father expected more from him than he could deliver, he would never be able to bear disappointing him. They ate in silence then, his mother and father exchanging smiles often.

When Dionysius appeared in the doorway, his tunic was less crisp than this morning, with a streak of dirt at the hem near his knee. For some reason, that made Jonathan happy. "Your chariot is ready, my lord."

His father rose, and Jonathan stood and helped his mother to her feet.

"Allow me." His father held his elbow out to her and she squeezed Jonathan's shoulder before letting go and taking his father's arm. Jonathan walked with them to the front of the house, enjoying the way his mother and father looked side by side.

Outside a servant restrained a pair of black stallions. The gleaming animals snorted and pranced in their leather harnesses. Silver embellishments on the straps matched those on the chariot case. Even the wheels were accented in silver atop the bronze overlay of their spokes.

Jonathan trotted ahead to pet them. Their short hair felt smooth and warm, but they were much bigger than he'd thought up close. Perhaps he wouldn't wish to ride astride one after all.

"Jonathan."

He turned and ran back to his mother, who released his father and hugged Jonathan close.

"Obey your father. Be safe, as always." She released him and cupped his cheek.

"Yes, Mother." Jonathan wished she wouldn't treat him like a baby in front of his father. How was he going to earn the man's respect that way?

She let her hand fall back to her side. "I love you."

"Love you too," he mumbled under his breath and ran for the horses again.

He looked back, and his father was saying something to his mother. He was too far away to hear what, but whatever it was made her smile. She liked being here. Even if the other son turned out to be like the boys in the alley, he would endure it without complaint.

His father made his way to the chariot and motioned for Jonathan to join him. Jonathan stepped up to the platform, clung fast to the bronze rail and planted his feet on the wide wooden planks. A servant passed his father the long leather ropes that would guide the horses.

His father grinned down at him. "Ready?"

More than he could say. Jonathan nodded, and his father snapped the leathers. The chariot rumbled forward and rocked Jonathan's balance. Even so, he clung to the rail with one hand and waved back at his mother with the other until she disappeared behind the stone wall. Rocking about was already making him dizzy, and he hoped he wouldn't vomit the best meal he'd ever had all over his father's chariot.

People on the street made way for them, several calling greetings to his father. One man with dark hair and a brilliant blue tunic beneath a milk-white toga stopped in the street and stared at them. His arms moved but instead of waving, he crossed them and his expression turned angry.

"Who is that?" As soon as the question left his mouth, he regretted it.

His father slowed the chariot, watching the man as they passed. "Soon you will know."

They passed the man, but when Jonathan looked back, he'd turned to watch them as the gap between them grew.

"Jonathan." His father's somber expression softened. "Let us vow to one another as men to leave all that concerns us here in the city for now. To consume this time as if it were the finest vintage and make of it a memory worthy of carrying to the afterlife. Agreed?"

As men. Jonathan's chest expanded. He didn't know how to set aside worrying about his mother, his father's other son, or the strange man. But he would not disappoint his father. "Agreed."

At the city gate, Jonathan learned he was wrong. He'd never been outside the city walls before. The rolling hills speckled with vineyards and the fields of waist-high grasses on either side of the stone highway were as overwhelming as the stream of ox-drawn carts and clusters of travelers streaming into the city.

"Today we make our own road," his father said, and turned the pair of black stallions sharply to the right. The grass made a distinct swish and crunch as the horses trampled it that mingled with the creaking of the wheels on either side of the chariot. "Hold fast."

Jonathan gripped the rail tighter and his father snapped the leather ropes. The horses snorted and surged forward. Jonathan's body jerked back as if a boy from the alley had grabbed him from behind. His arms locked as he clung to the rail, the wind blew in his face so much he could hardly keep his eyes open. For the span of a breath, he wanted to shout for his father to slow down. Until he glanced up and saw his father's face. *His* father.

He straightened as best he could and turned full into the wind. His knuckles ached from his grip on the bronze rail, now warm from his hold. The horses pounded across the expanse of grasses and trees, sweat gathering on Jonathan's back even as the wind drove it from his forehead. He wasn't aware when he lost his fear. Only that he had when a wheel hit something that jarred them both into the rail and each other. Instead of cringing and wanting to slow down, Jonathan felt a thrill run from his feet to his hands. The same one he saw in his father when he turned to him and smiled.

His father slowed the horses then, and when they came to a stop, Jonathan was breathing almost as hard as they were. His father looked down at him, his charcoal and ash hair rumpled like his toga. "You were afraid but you did not bend to your fear. You remained strong until the fear bent to you."

The respect in his father's voice was something Jonathan wanted to drink of for a lifetime. He didn't know what to say, or if he should say anything.

His father clasped his shoulder, grinned, and turned back to the horses. "Your mother will be furious."

Jonathan laughed because it was true, letting go of the rail with one hand to clutch the pinch in his side.

His father snapped the leather ropes and the horses raised their heads to walk forward. They settled into a steady pace that felt much like a crawl compared to their speed only moments ago. "Her happiness means much to me but preparing you for life as a Tarquinius means even more."

"She will understand."

His father laughed then and raised a brow as he tilted his chin toward Jonathan. He slapped the leather again to lift the horses into a jog. "I'm sure she would. But I don't plan to tell her we galloped over the countryside on your first chariot ride."

"Why not?"

"I'm not that brave."

Stunned, Jonathan cast a sideways glance at his father, keeping his expression neutral. Until his father winked at him and began to laugh again.

Back at the villa, no servant waited to greet them inside the gates. His father frowned and Jonathan followed his gaze. Another horse stood at the bottom of the steps leading up to the open front doors. The horse dripped with foamy sweat from its ears back to the empty saddle on its back. Dionysius emerged at a dead run and skidded to a stop halfway down the steps.

His father stopped the chariot, but didn't move. He stared at the servant and the servant stared back before the man on the steps turned to look straight at Jonathan. He'd seen enough pity on the faces of others to know it instantly—but for what?

And then he knew.

He jumped from the chariot and ran toward the open door. He climbed the steps and raced through the room with the fountain. A servant emerged from a doorway ahead and he flew toward it—toward the voices inside it. *God, please. I beg You.* He rounded the corner and skidded to a stop. People stood all around them but he couldn't take his eyes from his mother.

She lay on a couch with her eyes closed. He crept toward her. "Mother?"

She didn't move. No one did. He knelt beside her and took her hand. The chill of her skin was like a slap. No. Please no. He blinked the tears back as he squeezed her hand and watched her face. Nothing. She would never open her eyes again.

"I told you the gods would never allow this," a voice said.

Jonathan turned in the direction the voice had come and met the hard glare of the man from the street—with the blue tunic and white toga. It wasn't what he'd said that scared Jonathan. It was the man's ears. They stuck out too far—from a face that looked like his.

The man standing beside him cringed. "Please, my lord. The boy has just lost his mother."

Not lost. She was right here. Jonathan squeezed her cold hand and touched her cheek. This time he expected the cold but was still stabbed by it. She was gone. His mother was gone. His father entered the room and stopped at the end of his mother's couch.

A man approached him. "Apologies, old friend. Your servant summoned me as soon as she fell in the atrium. By the time I reached her, she'd passed into the afterlife."

Not the afterlife, eternal life with Jesus, but the words stuck in Jonathan's throat. God had ignored his pleas and taken her from him anyway. His father moved to kneel on her opposite side and took her other hand in his. Jonathan tried to force back the emotion still building inside.

The man in blue and white stepped forward. "Father, I—"

"All of you out."

Silence fell over the room as everyone stilled. "Master, shall I—"

"Everyone out except my son." His father's gaze held Jonathan's for a long moment. "Now."

One by one the people filed out, last of all the man in blue and white. His half-brother. Someone closed the door to the chamber. His father kissed the back of his mother's hand, and when he looked at Jonathan, his eyes were wet. When his father reached across his mother and put his hand on Jonathan's shoulder, the last of Jonathan's restraint shattered. He collapsed on his mother's chest and surrendered to the pain.

CHAPTER 3 – WORTHY

The warm garden with its fragrant blooms and tranquil fountain spray failed to soothe Jonathan as they normally did. Nothing would make this day better. He made his way to the bench he and his father shared the day they first met and sat down. The pair of crested larks he'd come to think of as pets weren't in their flowering bush beside the fountain. He scattered the bread crumbs he'd brought for them anyway.

Father believed Jonathan spent so much time in this garden because he preferred being outdoors. The truth was Jonathan preferred being anywhere his half-brother Manius was not. In the absence of their father, he'd proven himself capable of far worse than the boys in the alley.

"You look deep in thought, my son. What troubles you?"

Jonathan's gaze flew from his sandaled feet to his father. "Nothing."

His father frowned and sat beside him, shifting a roll of green cloth from under his arm to his lap. "I will respect your privacy, but you look just like your mother when you try to lie."

Jonathan touched the carved bone horse head resting between the fabric of his tunic and his chest. The day after his mother's death, he'd taken her most treasured possession, tied it with a leather cord, and hung it from his neck. It never left him, not to sleep or to bathe. "I was remembering her."

His father looked out over the statues. "I know what today is. Four years has not dulled my memory of her either. A thousand years could not. My only comfort is she lives on in you."

Jonathan's chest tightened. His father so rarely spoke of her. When he did his eyes always misted as they did now. "Thank you, Father."

The carving above his heart meant more now that Jonathan knew its origin. How his mother had been born a slave into his grandfather's house. How his father had carved it from the leg bone of an ox for her as a girl, and loved her when she'd become a young woman. His grandfather had sold her, his father unable to find her, until their reunion at a feast years later. His father hadn't recognized her, even in the intimacy given as a gift to him by her master. Why she never told him who she was until she'd brought Jonathan to him was a question that would forever linger for him and his father both.

"I brought you something for the feast tonight." His father unrolled the fabric in his lap and held up an emerald tunic trimmed in intricate patterns of gold thread. "When Dionysius told Deborah it was for you, she tried to refuse payment again. He left the coin and ran. She wishes you to visit."

Manius would be furious when he saw Jonathan clothed in this. He fought the frown with a swallow.

His father sighed and lowered the tunic to his lap. "I know you have the economy and modesty you were reared with. But you are also a Tarquinius, and the son of a senator. "

Jonathan took the tunic and let the fine nap of the wool slide between his fingers. "Forgive me, Father. I am grateful."

"I know. You always are. And you can show me by granting my next request."

"Name it and see it done."

"I wish you to meet the daughter of my colleague this evening."

Jonathan slew the frown before it reached his mouth. Not another one.

"I have long desired an alliance with that family to put to rest some tensions that have remained for two generations." His father grinned. "Try to like her, Jonathan. I've given you time to form a bond on your own and now must exercise my power for your own good. Your brother cannot marry until his service in the army is complete, and I cannot place the future of our line with him for reasons I suspect you already know."

Father had never spoken so honestly about Manius before. His half-brother's debauchery and exploits were whispered in hushed tones out of respect for their father. That he openly acknowledged them at last saddened Jonathan. He'd wanted so much to shield him from the worst of truths regarding his other son. "If he comes tonight…"

His father sighed and turned to face him. "Do your best to appear as if you do not loathe one another."

Father knew. Jonathan couldn't believe how thoroughly he'd failed to hide his true feelings. The crested larks swooped down into their bush, calling loudly. How he longed to fly away himself rather than face the disappointment in his father's gaze. "Father, I—"

"He is my son, as are you. Therefore I know he is more to blame than you for the distance between you both. As am I. In trying to right my many failings as a father with both of you, I only succeeded in making more."

Jonathan rose from the bench to stand before his father. He refused to tell him the truth about Manius, but he could speak the truth from his own heart. "I could have no better father than you. I am grateful for the life and the proud name you have given me. Manius seeks only to make certain I am worthy to be called a Tarquinius, Father—as do I."

His father rose, setting the tunic aside. "You already are, my son." His hands rose and he gripped Jonathan's shoulders tight enough to be uncomfortable as he stared into him. "If any royalty remains in the Tarquinius blood, it all resides in you. Only in you do I see the shadows of the Etruscan kings of our ancestors. Only in you does my hope for our future rest."

Jonathan could not bear his father's gaze and looked away. If Manius thought too little of his half-brother's worth, his father thought too much of it.

His father bent to retrieve the tunic and placed it in Jonathan's hands. "Please take this inside now. I should like to be alone for a while."

"Father." Jonathan dipped his chin in respect before departing, grateful to retreat to solitude himself. He'd accepted long ago that he would never again know the simplicity of a life with no expectations to fulfill or fall short of, nothing to be proven or disproven. For the love he bore his father, he couldn't allow himself to fail.

Chapter 4 – Rescue

Jonathan trudged through the street toward the forum, properly attired in his new tunic. Though it was early evening, a cold mist had settled over the city. He used a fold of his toga to wipe at the droplets gathered on his face. "This dark mist is a portent, Dionysius. We shouldn't be going."

Dionysius didn't respond, and when Jonathan looked left to see if he'd fallen behind, he saw her. A soiled tunic stretched taut over the swollen belly—leaning against the corner pillar of the temple of Saturn. Her eyes begged for the bread her mouth did not, and Jonathan's heart ached for her and the unborn child. If she or the little one survived the birth, both faced a future as bleak as this day—one he'd lived for twelve of his sixteen years.

A path opened to her on the stone-paved street, but Dionysius appeared in front of him with crossed arms. His gaze turned as hard as the steel he wore at his side. "I swore an oath to your father you would not be late."

"Father will understand." He would disapprove, but he would understand.

Nearing the woman, he found her older than he'd expected. When he stopped an arm's length from her, practiced seduction replaced the honest need in her eyes. The scents of street and sweat clung to her like the remnants of her garment, and her cold fingers slid up his arm. "The young girls inside don't yet know half of what I do. Let me prove it to you for a *denarius*."

He pulled his arm from her grasp and held her cold, damp hand in his. Rubbing the skin firmly would bring some heat, as he'd learned as a boy when there had been no coin to buy coal or wood for the brazier. She frowned and tried to tug her hand away, but he held on. Her eyes were the brown of young tree bark. Nothing like the green his mother's had been, but that didn't matter.

She carried a child. One he could save. "Why did you not rid yourself of the child?"

She blinked and withdrew her hand.

If she'd been a temple prostitute, as her sleeveless tunic and short hem suggested, or part of the brothels he'd never visited, her masters would have insisted on it. So she'd either fought to keep the child, as his mother had, or would leave the child to die once born. He searched her eyes, trying to pull the truth from them. He had to be certain. "Why?"

She turned away, and a rip in her tunic revealed dark scratches across the skin of her back—too shallow and narrow to have been a whip. She'd quickened her pace and would be lost in the crowd any moment.

He took a step to follow, but Dio moved between them again. "My lord, I beg you to let her go and—"

"I have a denarius," he yelled.

She turned to stare at him, along with several other men and women. Let them stare. He held a hand out to Dio but kept the woman in his line of sight. "I have a denarius."

Dio pressed the silver coin into Jonathan's palm. He held it out to her and waited. Finally she came to him, her gaze flicking from the coin to his face.

"What happened to your back?"

"A man with a denarius." Her throat rippled in a swallow. "I will do whatever I must for yours."

With his free hand, he reached forward to take hers. She allowed him to, her eyes wary, and he folded the coin into her palm. He let go and took a step back. "It's already yours."

She waited, but he stood still, reassuring her it was a gift. When she pulled the coin tight to her chest, the seed of a smile broke the corners of her thin lips. “May Jupiter favor you for your kindness, my lord.”

He may no longer embrace the God of his youth, but he hadn’t adopted the idols of his father either. “You can favor me. Tell me why you keep the child.”

Could the child inside her feel the hands she splayed over her belly? “I want someone to love. Someone to love me.” She stroked her belly again, still gripping the coin tight, and met his gaze. “Is that selfish?”

“No.” He held his hand out to Dio for another coin, blinking against the moisture in his eyes. It was the stench of the street, nothing more. Not the way she’d rent his heart with her words. “And I promise you this. No matter how much you love your child, he will always love you more.”

“Even when he’s cold and hungry?” Her eyes implored him, but she hadn’t even glanced at the new coin in his hand.

“Especially then.”

She took the coin and bowed her head toward her feet. They were as caked with filth as the cobblestones beneath them. “Thank you, my lord.”

Dio cleared his throat—a gentle reminder they needed to be on their way. Jonathan touched her chin and invited her to look at him again. She did, and the gratitude in her eyes was enough to make her beautiful in a way she hadn’t been before.

“If you know the insulae closest to the river near the Temple of Diana, go there. Ask after a woman named Deborah and when you find her, tell her Jonathan sent you.”

“Why?”

“It will be a place of refuge for you and the child you carry. But you must tell her Jonathan sent you. Will you remember?”

“Yes, my lord.” She blinked, but not before the sheen in her eyes became a teardrop that streaked her pale cheek.

Dionysius touched his elbow. “We must go.”

"Remember what I've told you. The insulae nearest the river, in the shadow of the Temple of Diana. Ask for Deborah. Tell her Jonathan has sent you."

"I will, my lord."

Jonathan turned from her toward the north part of the city and this feast he would rather not attend. Dio closed the distance between them until he all but prodded Jonathan along. He glanced back over his shoulder but couldn't see the woman. The streams of people were too thick. A loose pig scurried past with a rope around its neck. The squeals it made rivaled that of the young boy chasing it. If someone cut the animal off, cornered it without getting bit, then the boy could—

"The feast, my lord." Dio's tone matched his scowl as he marched on, shouldering Jonathan in the process.

Someone else would have to help the boy. "Remind me, which of us is the servant?"

Dio surprised him with a rare grin. They wove through the narrow street, between carts and booths peddling everything from a bowl of vegetable stew to amulets sworn to protect against any poison and across the forum, poisons sworn to never fail. The rattle of chain and throng of people gathered around a platform tightened his empty stomach. A slave market—where many a man, woman, or child would be sold to masters without his father's benevolent nature. Through the linen of his toga and tunic, he touched the horse head carving hanging from the leather cord around his neck. Always hidden but always with him, like the memory of his mother.

Dio noticed, and as sure as the sun and moon would never share the sky, he was about to say something to try to cheer him up. "If a thief were foolish enough to attack me for your money pouch, he'd be disappointed when he opened it."

This time Jonathan grinned. Dio could sense his moods the way cattle could a coming storm. Other than his father, there was no one he was closer to. "Any chance I could give you the rest and we go to the races instead?"

"Now who jests?"

True. Dio would never acquiesce unless Jonathan commanded him. If they missed the feast, Father would be disappointed in them both. No matter how much he'd rather take off the toga, climb to the upper tiers of the Circus Maximus with the peasants where he felt most at home and cheer for the blue chariot, he would never knowingly disappoint his father. Not when the man had risked so much in his political standing to publicly and legally claim Jonathan as a son.

"What must I do to make you look as if you're going to a feast and not a funeral?"

"Forgive me, Dio." He plastered his best fake smile in place.

From his frown, Dio wasn't fooled but seemed content to let it go. He moved right as they walked, opening a better path. After traveling a few more *pedes*, the stone walls and iron gate of the villa they sought appeared.

Dio stopped at the gate and turned toward Jonathan. "How long will you try to honor her memory at the expense of your own peace?"

The question rocked him to his core as his entire body went rigid.

"You can't rescue them all," Dio continued. "Even if you controlled the wealth of your father, you still could not. Your mother lived a hard life as a slave, a harder one once free, and the greatest gift she ever gave you and my master was to bring you home. You are allowed to enjoy the life of privilege the gods have given you. You deserve this life, and I pray to the gods I live long enough to see the day you believe that too."

He'd heard that so many times, dressed in different words, from his father. But never from Dio. "How long have you wanted to say that to me?"

"Since you ordered me to carry the lifeless infant you found abandoned on the bank of the river to Deborah."

"Four years?"

"Yes."

"The child lived."

"So can you."

Pounding feet announced the approach of a litter. The four slaves who bore the curtained platform stopped in unison and lowered the poles. Jonathan glanced back to Dio. His gaze was now trained on his feet, and his sword hand held his other wrist at his waist—a servant once again.

"You there. Who are you?" The newcomer stood still while one of his slaves straightened his toga to ensure the crimson trim showed above the folds at his elbow. Even without the trim, Jonathan couldn't have mistaken this man for anything other than a senator. With a girth that size, rings on every finger, and a wife as young as Jonathan, no one could. But which one was this? Decimus… something. No, that one had a mole the size of an olive pit on his cheek.

The senator turned to Dio. "Is he mute?"

"No, my lord."

If he were, he could tolerate these gatherings better, because no one would attempt to engage him in meaningless chatter. "Forgive me. I am Jonathan Tarquinius, younger son of Poetelius Tarquinius Cornelius."

"Jonathan, you say. I was beginning to think you were an invention of your father. Like his ideals for reform." The man chuckled, but would sober in an instant if he turned and saw the way his wife was eyeing Jonathan. Yet another reason he hated these gatherings.

"How is your father?"

"Well, and looking forward to seeing you I'm certain."

"You have no idea who I am, or you would know he is not looking forward to seeing me. No matter. I was young once and cared for nothing but wine and women."

And likely still did, like so many of his kind. While all around them, thousands of people suffered. "After you, Senator."

He followed the man in, with Dio three steps behind.

Dio was right. He couldn't save them all. He couldn't save himself from the betrothal he feared was coming. How was he supposed to celebrate surrounded by men of indifference who lived for their own wealth and pleasures at the expense of others?

The same way he always did—with a fake smile, counting the hours until it was over.

Chapter 5 – Taken

After enduring the gathering within long enough to please Father, Jonathan retreated to their host's garden. Moans came from a pair of prostrate bodies in the shadows of the shaped hedges. Even out here there was no escaping the lust and ambition tainting everything about the crowd inside. Picking up a stone and flinging it at them would be childish—and embarrass Father—but he ached to do just that. The water in the fountain chilled his fingers and then his face. He wiped the droplets gathering on his chin with the edge of his toga. The lingering mist would replace them soon.

"Your father summons you."

He spun and gravel scattered beneath his sandal. "Don't sneak up on me."

"Apologies, my lord." From the tight set of Dio's lips and crinkled cheeks, he'd meant to startle him. The man's grin was a month's journey from an apology in this one-sided game of his they'd played for four years.

As the closest thing Jonathan had to a true friend, he'd allow the insolence to pass—for the thousandth time. "What does father require?"

"You already know."

Jonathan rubbed the back of his neck and tipped his face to the moon. She would be as ruined by her wealthy upbringing as the ten young women before her.

"You have cared for none of them because you've set your mind against it. Try to make an effort and thank Jupiter your father considers your wishes at all. Such a thing is unheard of among the *patricians.*"

"So is adopting an illegitimate son birthed by a freed slave."

Dionysius glanced around them before locking his gaze with Jonathan. "That is your brother speaking. Not you."

"It doesn't make it untrue. Or that I came to be like this." He jerked his chin toward two pale bodies in the shadows. "Or that my mother spent more than half her life as a slave and I spent most of mine without a father."

"A father who is waiting for you, and longs to see you happy."

For the love of his father, he would make an effort.

"Stay vigilant." Dio fell into stride beside him. "Manius is here."

Were it not visible in both their faces, Jonathan would swear on his mother's urn it was impossible they shared a father. So would Manius.

Servants with pitchers of wine and trays of delicacies wove through the throng of bodies filling the great chamber. In the center, three slave women danced around a man costumed as Liber. Jonathan hated the seventeenth of Martius and this feast. He would spend a few marks of the water-clock with their host's daughter and leave before the *orgia* taking root out in the garden would wind its way inside and bloom.

Manius reclined beside their father, watching the dancers with unveiled eagerness for the very things Jonathan wished to flee.

"You sent for me, Father?"

"I feared you'd left without meeting Hadrianus' daughter."

Their host beckoned to someone in the crowd with raised fingers. "Daughter, come."

The crowd of people between them parted and there stood a girl. Fine linen the color of a sunrise hugged her body. Dark hair hung in ringlets beside a round face and stopped above the beginnings of breasts rising gently above a golden sash. Lips the color of a seashell twitched in a grin—but an innocent one, if her eyes spoke truth. Not the way other women smiled at him. She approached, stopped, then dipped her head and bent her knees in a small bow. "Welcome, my lord."

He opened his mouth, but a mangled breath more gasp than greeting filled his ear.

Her father chuckled somewhere behind him. "I told you when he beheld my Hadriana that Cupid's arrow would not be needed."

Manius shot to his feet and gripped his half-empty goblet like a weapon. His face flushed the color of the wine he spilled in his haste as he stormed toward the garden. The great room quieted as heads swung his direction.

Father frowned and turned to their host. "Excuse me a moment."

"Of course."

Father rose and followed after Manius while Dio assumed a place on the wall nearby. With his gaze and a raised brow, he reminded Jonathan of the importance of relations with the girl and her family.

Their host returned his attention to his daughter. "Hadriana, keep Cornelius' son entertained until his father returns."

"Yes, Father." She grasped Jonathan's hand and he followed. Her lavender scent and soft skin against his fingers sent a ripple of pleasure through him as they approached a cushioned couch against the wall. The horse-hair stuffed cushions in finely dyed purple linen were as luxurious as those in his father's villa. He sat down beside her, noting that quite a few people still observed them. She shifted to better face him and her thigh brushed his. Her expression lacked cunning, so it had either been an accident or she was wholly unaware of the effect that would have.

Her delicate brows arched above a perfectly shaped nose. "Your skin and speech are Roman, but your name is not."

The boldness in her question surprised him, though it was one he'd been asked before. "I'm named for the husband of a Judean woman who helped my mother raise me."

"Was she from Jerusalem, one of the cities that revolted?"

"Yes."

"I'm surprised your father allowed it."

"He didn't know." The words had slipped from his mouth, but as they hit his ears, he cursed himself for speaking them aloud.

She looked as if she considered this but left it alone. And he liked her a little more for it. A small scar marred her forehead, but asking its origins might embarrass her. She told him of her new kitten and the way her mother bemoaned the snags in her sash whenever she was allowed to play with him. Hadriana had named him Hercules, but her mother said it invited misfortune on them all to name an animal after a god. They called him Hannibal now, after the defeated Carthaginian general from some three hundred years before.

Not the least bit timid as he was, she did most of the talking while he checked the entrance to the garden often. Dio would meet his gaze and shake his head the smallest measure. Manius finally returned without their father and strode toward their host. They exchanged a few words he couldn't overhear, and then Manius found the slave girl he'd been watching earlier. He jerked her close and said something in her ear. A servant with a wine goblet blocked Jonathan's view and when the man moved, he'd lost Manius and the girl. He rose from the cushion in an instant, a boulder in his gut.

"Jonathan?"

Hadriana was, of course, confused. She was protected, while the girl Manius had hauled away was not. "Apologies. There is an urgent matter I must attend."

He skirted the edge of the chamber, but still didn't see them. Dio had moved and glanced toward a tapestry near his shoulder. From the fastenings at the top, it covered a passage of some type. Dio moved to pull open the edge and follow.

Jonathan had to do this alone. "Stay here."

"You know I cannot. Manius is in high temper."

"That was a command, not a request."

Hurt flashed in Dio's face, a pain Jonathan felt like a dagger to his belly. He would make amends later, but right now he needed to find Manius.

Plentiful wine had a way of kindling his half-brother's dark passions. Anger swelled them like wind to a fire.

Behind the fabric, enough light spilled into the corridor to make out a long passage. Wooden doors lined both sides, but only one had a trace of light beneath it. He checked that his dagger rested in easy reach at his waist and opened the door.

He'd been prepared for what he'd see, but his jaw still tightened.

Manius' head jerked toward him. "Go away."

"You know that is not what our host had in mind when he agreed."

The slave girl scrambled from beneath Manius but he yanked her back by her hair. Her muffled cry from beneath the sash tied at her mouth hardened Jonathan's resolve. "Let her go."

But Manius laughed. "Leave us. Go weep for your dead harlot of a mother."

Would that he could slit that sweaty throat wide open. "Let. Her. Go."

"Stay and watch if you like. It might make a man of you."

"Release her or Father learns the truth of Arvala's death."

Manius froze. His dark eyes nearly disappeared as his gaze narrowed. The young woman twisted upright, but Manius made no move to grab her. She fled, and he rose to his feet in a smooth motion. His hand came to rest on the jeweled handle of the dagger sheathed in his belt.

Backing down hadn't been an option from the moment Jonathan had ordered Dio to remain behind.

"Arvala killed herself."

"Your lusts killed her. I saw you heave her body over your chamber railing that night." The memory still made his insides burn. "I'm surprised you thought to put her tunic and sandals back on before you dumped her to shatter on the stone below."

For the first time in as long as he'd known him, Manius appeared afraid. Yet his voice dripped with bravado. "If you wove this tale why not speak of it then?"

"Because she was already dead and it would only wound Father."

"Those things are still true."

They were, and it was lawful for a master to kill a slave for any and every reason. Their father, however, led the handful of senators who thought this unjust and sought reform. Father would be furious at Manius and his punishment substantial. They both knew it.

Jonathan forced a confidence into his posture and expression he didn't truly feel. "You don't have to hurt them to enjoy them."

"How would you know?"

"Stop hurting them. If I learn you've done this again, I will go to Father."

Manius grinned, the wine on his breath strong enough to carry the arm's length between them. "Understood."

Jonathan stepped back into the hall, keeping his hand on his dagger until Manius departed. The weight of what he'd done at last made his knees tremble as he leaned against the wall.

A figure came toward him, silhouetted against the light from the main chamber. "Are you well?"

Dionysius. Jonathan breathed easier and pushed away from the wall. "Yes, but I want to go home."

Dio sighed and stiffened in the dim light. "Manius has already worn on the generosities of your father's colleague. If you rush away as well it will further offend him."

"Manius left?"

"Angry and in haste, embarrassing the master yet again."

Jonathan smoothed his hair and hoped the trembling in his fingers would stop before anyone noticed. "A little while longer then."

Hadriana watched him carefully while he returned to the cushion he'd left her on. "Are you well?"

"I am now. Forgive my rudeness, and tell me more about Hannibal."

She dipped her chin, and pink colored her cheeks. "If it pleases you."

It pleased him because Father was pleased, and in truth he did want to discover more about this beautiful and intelligent girl. But not tonight. Not with a raw spirit surrounded by those who wouldn't have raised voice or hand against Manius for his shameful pleasures.

Slaves departed and returned with more cushions. Time for him to leave, and he hoped Hadriana's father would keep her far from what was about to unfold. Father dismissed him, and their host bid him to return soon. Perhaps he would.

Mercifully, Dio was quiet as they walked. Street torches had already been lit and their flames gave the evening mist a luminescent sheen and distracted from the vermin darting between them.

In sight of the villa gate, a woman in a peasant tunic emerged from an alleyway. "Please, my lord, my child!" She turned and bolted back the way she'd come.

Dio grabbed his arm. "It's dark, my lord. We must—"

An infant's cry pierced the air and Jonathan jerked free. He plunged toward the sound, and slowed when shapes appeared in the shadows. Four men waited in front of a woman holding the screaming baby. He jerked to a stop, and Dio slammed into him from behind.

Dio's iron grip crushed his upper arm as he threw him backward. "Run."

He drew his dagger instead but a resounding pop filled the alley. Why hadn't the men moved? Why hadn't Dio? He glanced right and in the dim shadow saw the bolt of a crossbow protruding from Dio's chest as he sank to his knees.

Jonathan dropped the dagger and fell to his knees beside Dio. A baby was still crying but—

Strong arms shoved him to the street, flattening his body to the filth-covered stone. He fought against the weight on his back as more men surrounded him.

"Is it him?" a voice asked over the squalls of the child.

One of his captors pulled at the leather cord around his neck. "He's wearing the horse head. It's him."

"Don't tarry." The gruff voice was close, but not the man pinning him down. "Kill him."

"No." His captor twisted his arm behind his back. The searing pain in his shoulder rivaled the sight of Dio's lifeless body beside him.

"We kill him, or we don't get paid."

Manius.

"We'll get more for him as a slave."

Jonathan threw his weight hard to the side, but couldn't free himself. Pain exploded in his skull and everything disappeared.

Chapter 6 – Slave

Squeals pulled Jonathan awake. Ropes chafed at his wrists and wrapped tightly around his mouth. His eyes weren't bound, but there was no light, only heat and an oppressive weight holding him down. The harder he tried to free himself and draw a full breath, the deeper his panic became. Pigs. The squeals belonged to pigs. Why couldn't he smell them? The aroma surrounding him was earthy, but not foul. He breathed as deep as the thin air allowed. Grain. He shifted between the canvases pressing him on both sides. They'd put him between bags of grain in some type of cart.

Dio was dead. Dio was dead because of him. That pain overwhelmed the ache in his temple. Whoever attacked him had taken his tunic and sandals. He worked his hands to his chest and found his mother's carving. Relief poured through him they hadn't taken that too. He'd have to escape. The longer it took, the harder it would be to get home.

"I think he's awake," a voice called out.

The cart came to a stop, and he tensed.

"Get him out. We're far enough from the city." That voice was nearer. "Free his mouth and give him some water."

The grain was lifted and the sunlight clamped his eyes shut. He squinted, trying to see, while rough hands forced him to his knees. Grass covered hills, fields and vineyards stretched in every direction, dotted with trees, the stone highway looming in either direction. Armored men on horseback surrounded a caravan of wagons and people—most with their wrists bound—being herded like the pigs with them. His throat clenched, even after the man holding his arms removed the rope from around his mouth.

Another man with a gold key hanging from his neck watched from atop a horse. "I am your new master, Fabricius Clavis."

Master? "I am—" His voice barely rose above a whisper and he coughed, hoping to sound like his father. "I am Jonathan Tarquinius, a citizen of Rome and the son of Poetelius Tarquinius Cornelius, the praetor."

"And I'm Gaius Julius Caesar." The man laughed and gestured to his horse. "And this is Romulus."

Laughter rang out through the guards.

Jonathan drew up straighter, jerking his arm free from the man who held it. "I'm no slave. You appear Roman, so you know who my father is. He will reward you for your trouble, but you must release me at once."

The man's brows arched, and he edged his horse closer. "You don't give the commands here, slave." His expression changed, and his voice lowered. "I am the father of the man who attacked you. Therefore you know that even if I wished to release you, I cannot."

"I told you the price he would bring—" the man behind him began.

"I told you to be silent and never act without my approval again. Were it not for your mother I would turn you in myself. Now get him some water and chain him with the others."

The man pulled Jonathan from the wagon. His feet hit the ground, and he straightened. They weren't going to let him go. Trying to run would end badly, but he had to try.

A few strides gave him hope until he heard a horse galloping behind him. Something snared his ankle and he slammed into the stone highway face first. A knee to his back kept him there.

"We've got a runner." Someone laughed and strong hands forced Jonathan's ankles into thick metal bands. The chain rattled, chilling him as much as the cold metal. He wanted to scream in outrage, but couldn't draw the breath required. But he could still fight. He had to.

"Be still, slave." A hobnailed sandal crushed his throbbing head into the stone pavers of the highway. Grit ground into his skin as he struggled against the brass studs digging into the flesh of his cheek.

"Careful of his face," Fabricius yelled.

The guard above him chuckled but the foot left his face. They replaced the rope at his wrists with iron. A sword tip pressed between his shoulder blades convinced him to lie still.

They hauled him to his feet and yanked him toward the wagon. Jonathan thrashed at the man closest to him, trying to use the chain as a weapon, but stumbled. The guard passed the links through a ring at the rear of the oxcart while the ringing laughter of the others reminded him of the bullies in his childhood.

"Enough delay." Fabricius turned his horse toward the head of the procession. Guards assumed their posted positions, and the slaves leading the oxen urged them forward.

Jonathan didn't move, even when the oxcart drew the chain tight. The unforgiving irons jerked him to his knees, towing him like a boat anchor on a smooth river bottom. Only the stone wasn't smooth. Soon his knees trailed blood on the dirty gray stones. The shackles on his wrist were going to tear his arms off.

"Get up, or be dragged the whole way."

A whip cracked and the lash on his back forced a groan through his dry throat. After several tries he managed to bring his chained feet beneath him. He had to concentrate on keeping pace with the cart to avoid being dragged again. Smaller stones cut the tender soles of his feet, but he put one foot in front of the other—over and over—plotting escape and revenge with every step.

After three days, the whips no longer drew cries of pain. So to punish his continued escape attempts the guards took to using the wooden shafts of their spears as clubs. The physical punishment chiseled away at his resistance, leaving a hollow void.

Tonight his head rested between the wooden spokes of the oxcart they'd chained him to. The flies feasting on his shredded back irritated him more than the pain of a broken rib. Pain he could only avoid the rare moments sleep would overtake him. A cruel kindness, for in sleep visions of Dio's death returned.

He wasn't the only one still awake. The soft weeping of a child mingled with the crackle and snap of the guard's watch fire. The woman holding the little girl against her breast and stroking her hair carried the child most of the day. A mother, made more devoted from their shared oppression. And for the first time since his own mother died, Jonathan lifted the voice of his heart to his forgotten God.

But no deliverance came. God did not spare him now, as He hadn't spared his mother four years ago. Somewhere along the *Via Appia*, the last ember of Jonathan's faith turned to ash—snuffed by the lashes and blows that fell like rain, mile after mile.

At the slave market in Capua, Jonathan was stripped of his ragged loincloth and scrubbed with oil and hyssop. He was given a cloth to wrap around his waist, and his wrists were bound again, with rope this time. The guards led him to a platform in the street with the others. One by one Fabricius Clavis marked a price on a slate and hung it around their necks. When the man reached him, Clavis frowned and reached for his mother's carving.

Jonathan flinched and met the man's gaze. "Please," he whispered.

The slave trader's hand hung in the air like the indecision in his eyes. His mouth tightened and he raised the slate and hung it from Jonathan's neck, leaving the small pendant. The guard who'd beaten him after his last escape attempt shoved him toward the steps to the platform. Jonathan took an open place in the line of bodies and kept his gaze on his bare feet.

No insult Manius or the bullies in his childhood ever hurled brought the shame now pouring through him. Children sold first, led away by their new masters. The girl he'd watched on the road sobbed, reaching for her mother, who stood rooted beside him. He felt the child's pain, and her mother's, as keenly as his own wounds.

A few inquired about him, but none would pay the price written on his slate. He hadn't looked to read it, nor did he want to. Whatever the sum, Fabricius held firm to it, and Jonathan kept his eyes on his blistered feet for hours. Thirsty and exhausted, he raised his head when a flash of bold color touched the edge of his vision. A large litter passed near, carried by eight men wearing bronze slave collars. The sheerness of the partially drawn blue curtains revealed a woman lying within. As they passed, the angle changed, and he glimpsed her face.

She was Helen of Troy reborn—beautiful enough to cause a war. Too far to see the color, her eyes were no less striking, and they watched him as much as he watched her being carried away from him. Her hand moved the curtain edge so she could still see him as the litter moved through the crowds. Her lips moved, and the slaves halted in unison. When they lowered the litter to its rests, she stepped from the curtains without ever taking her gaze from him. Her regal bearing as she approached parted the people between them like the prow of a great ship cutting through calm water.

"Lady Valentina, what an unexpected pleasure." The slave trader bent low at the waist.

She ignored him and her perusal intensified. "Turn around, slave."

Jonathan presented his back to her, his legs unsteady after being still for so long.

"Did he refuse your advances, Fabricius?" Her voice was as captivating as her face.

"His manner needed refining, my lady."

"Did it?"

Her amused tone made Jonathan uneasy as he stared at the dirty stone wall in front of him.

"Turn and face me," she ordered. "And remove your cloth."

Every muscle tightened in protest.

"Obey the lady." The edge in the slave trader's voice held warning.

He still didn't move—except to tremble like a snared hare before a starving wolf. A guard approached and uncoiled the whip in his hand. They would have their way, with or without the pain. With his bound hands, he pulled the tuck of the linen at his waist free. He wished for death behind his closed eyelids and turned to face them.

"I'll take him."

Jonathan wouldn't look at her, even after he wrapped the cloth back around himself. Not an easy task still bound, but he managed. The guard put his whip away and removed the slate from Jonathan's neck.

Fabricius looked pleased. "As for payment—"

"I don't expect you to make a gift of him." The woman crossed her arms and though a head shorter than the slave trader, seemed to still look down at him. "His price will be taken from what you owe my husband."

Fabricius smiled, yet his lips were as tight as the fists at his sides. "Do give him my regards."

The guard tied a lead rope to Jonathan's wrists and pulled him from the platform. The woman's slave occupying the end position on the litter poles took the rope. The woman climbed back into her litter, her gaze on him until the curtain blocked her from sight. He'd been bought and sold like the cattle bound for the temples to be sacrificed. The way she'd looked at him gave him little hope his fate would be any better.

Chapter 7 – Lost

The villa Jonathan followed the slaves into rivaled his father's in Rome. Two armored men with spears in hand and swords at the hip flanked a pair of wide wooden doors. Between them a tall man in a fine tunic hurried down marble steps and stopped at the same time the slaves carrying the litter did.

Valentina stepped out of the litter and regarded Jonathan with a look he'd seen too many times to mistake. She took his rope and dismissed the litter bearers with a flick of her free hand. "Has the master returned from Pompeii?"

"Yes, Mistress, about midday," the new servant answered.

"Why he visits that dreadful place is beyond understanding. There's nothing left of it." She spoke to the servant, yet continued to watch Jonathan.

"I believe he meets with his overseer there, Mistress."

Valentina leveled a hard look at the man. "It was not a question, Brennus. If I wanted to know anything about my husband or his concerns, I would not ask a slave."

"Apologies."

Her gaze returned to Jonathan, absent the desire from a moment ago. "What's your name?"

Dare he tell her? The House of Tarquinius descended from the Etruscan kings who first ruled Rome. Would she think he mocked her?

"Answer the mistress," Brennus said.

"Jonathan."

She studied him and from the tight set of her face, something displeased her. Perhaps that would work in his favor.

"It doesn't suit you, but nothing better comes to mind I haven't already used. You may keep it." She passed the end of his rope to Brennus. "See Jonathan's back is tended and he begins his duties tomorrow."

"What are those to be, Mistress?"

"I will let you know when I've decided."

Jonathan followed them up the steps. The guards at the door exchanged amused grins the moment Valentina passed them. A reprimanding glare from Brennus smoothed their expressions. Jonathan's bare feet padded over a tiled mosaic floor depicting hunters pursuing a stag. Corinthian pottery lined the walls in rich hues between two large couches with cushions plump as a full grain sack. The first doorway in the passage to the left of the central garden revealed a chamber with an entire wall covered in shelves of scrolls, hundreds of wax tablets, and baskets on the floor filled with more scrolls. Valentina left them at the second doorway, entering another chamber. Hers? The deeper into the villa Brennus led him, the flooring turned from mosaic tile to bare stone. The furnishings became sparse and poorer quality.

It was like walking backwards through his life.

The scent of onion and burning wood strengthened as they approached what could only be a kitchen. Inside the room, a heavyset woman with grayed hair stood behind a table, pulling feathers from a dead goose. Beside her a younger woman sliced onions. Both stopped their work and stared at him.

"Who's this?" the older woman asked.

"Trouble." Brennus dropped the rope and crossed his arms. "From the looks of him he has an insolent tongue or clumsy hands."

"You don't know that." The younger woman approached and began to untie the rope binding Jonathan's wrists. She was about his age it would seem, from the smoothness of her face. Onion and… a pleasant scent he couldn't identify clung to her.

"Thank you," Jonathan whispered when she finished freeing his hands.

She gave him her gaze and the faintest of smiles before coiling the rope and handing it to Brennus. Jonathan would have thrown it into the hearth and let the blaze beneath the large bronze pot consume it.

"Cyra is right." The older woman glanced at Brennus. "You should show him the kindness you were so in need of when you first came."

Brennus' scowl became a frown. "You might as well be head servant, Frona. Prepare him some food. Cyra will see to his wounds while I fetch him a tunic and sandals." He turned toward Jonathan and the hardness in his features eased. "Count yourself favored of whatever god you worship. You could have ended up in worse places."

He didn't worship a god. Not anymore.

Frona resumed her feather plucking. "I make a salve that will heal those knees."

Brennus snorted. "It's not his knees that are cause for concern. It's his back." He turned to Jonathan. "Show them."

Jonathan turned, grateful he was allowed to keep the rest of himself covered this time.

A soft gasp made him turn again. Women shouldn't have to see such things.

"Was that deserved?" Frona asked.

How should he answer? This entire situation was unjust, but the beatings were punishment for attempting escape.

"If they were undeserved," she said, "you'll find here the master never raises a whip without cause. But if you bring trouble, we won't tolerate it and neither will the master." She chose that moment to flip the dead goose.

"I understand."

"Good then." Frona's smile returned as she yanked more feathers. "Cyra, take Jonathan to a storeroom and clean his wounds. Brennus will bring the salve."

"Yes, Mother." Cyra motioned for Jonathan to follow.

They entered a passage off the kitchen and then the first room to the left. Large *amphorae*, probably filled with wine or olive oil, stood like legionnaires against the far wall. Woven baskets of produce, sacks of grain and salt, and the familiar stink of *garum* filled the room. The flavored sauce made by taking fish entrails and salted water and letting it set for two months had been a favorite of Manius.

Jonathan hated it for no other reason than that.

Cyra turned an empty crate on its side. "You should sit here."

She filled a bowl with wine and moved behind him. Wet cloth touched his wounds and his back arched.

"I'm sorry." Her touch was gentle, like her voice.

She continued to clean the grime and dried blood away. Worse was coming. When he cut himself on a potshard in his father's garden, Dio had cleaned the wound with wine and packed it with salt to prevent fouling. It was the first time Jonathan had ever cursed. He had half expected Deborah to appear and swat his head, but she hadn't. He'd avoided her after his mother's death, preferring to send coin, which she tried to send back in the beginning. He'd always meant to visit her one day, to try to understand how their God had failed him. Now it was too late.

Because God had failed him again.

Cyra rubbed the salt into the first stripe. Even though he was prepared, every muscle went rigid and a sharp hiss passed through his teeth.

"I'm sorry."

The guilt woven into her tone bothered him. He turned to see her as well as he could over his shoulder. "Thank you."

She was younger than him, maybe a year or two, with light brown hair and eyes. Eyes that looked away as her cheeks turned the color of pomegranate.

Brennus appeared in the doorway. "Here's Frona's salve." He set it down on the floor near her. "Call out if you need anything, Cyra. Anything at all."

Did he think Jonathan meant to harm her?

"I will."

She waited for him to leave before continuing with the salt. Jonathan endured it by holding his lower lip between his teeth. Until a question came to him he thought she might answer. "Why does Brennus say I should be thankful to be here?"

"He has been with many houses and served in the grape fields of the last one. It must have been very bad, because he imagines this to be paradise."

Cyra took up the jar of rust-colored cream and began to apply it. The salve brought some relief, burning less than the salt. "I saw his back once, without a tunic. It looked worse than yours. The scars I mean."

Scars. He hadn't thought that far. She knelt at his feet to clean and tend his knees. From the color in her face, she shared his discomfort at her nearness. He remained still, with new thoughts of escape. From here that would be the simple task. Avoiding recapture and returning to Rome would be the difficulty.

Cyra stood and lifted his wrist to apply salve to the chaffed and bruised skin. The shackles had punished his every movement for days, but her gentle touch as she rubbed in the cream soothed more than his wrists. "Thank you."

Her forehead wrinkled as she looked him full in the face. "You say that often. Why?"

"My mother taught me if I feel it but say nothing, it's wasted. Does my gratitude bother you?"

"No, I'm just not accustomed to hearing it." She stared into his eyes for a long moment, before looking away as she rose. "We should return to the kitchen. I'm sure by now Frona has a meal for you." She gathered the salve and soiled cloths before Jonathan followed her out. In the empty kitchen there waited a plate of boiled carrots, roasted fish, and a large chunk of bread. Beside the meal lay a folded tunic and leather sandals.

"I should return to my duties." Cyra moved toward the passageway but turned back and smiled at him before disappearing beyond the plaster walls.

It pained him to pull the tunic over his head, but then the fabric fell in place and covered him. The sandals were tight, but a rubdown with olive oil would cure that later.

He savored the hot, hearty meal and relaxed for first time since waking up in a slave cart. At the moment he had food, clothes, and no one beating him.

He was picking the last of the fish from the bones when Brennus appeared in the doorway. "The master summons you."

Jonathan sprang to his feet to follow, but grabbed the last bite of bread and stuffed it in his mouth before jogging after Brennus.

"Be warned the master is in high temper. The mistress has reduced one of his accounts by three thousand *sesterces*."

Jonathan halted midstride. "Three thousand sesterces? That's seven hundred fifty denarii… that's… twenty-five *aureii* of solid gold."

"I can't count that high. Make haste." Brennus set off again with a lengthened stride. Jonathan moved to catch up, though he wanted to be going the opposite direction.

They reached a chamber at the end of the passage. Beside Valentina, her husband Gaius Florus sat straight as a Roman highway, with an expression as flat and hard as the stones that paved them. Jonathan had been right to fear. This chamber was small like the kitchen, but the far half of the floor rose up to elevate the master's long couch, ensuring that even seated he would look down on whoever entered. Potted palms on either side of the long couch looked like they should be holding spears instead of the pair of exotic birds Jonathan had never seen before.

Brennus stopped and bowed low. "Master."

Should he bow? Valentina looked scared and that made him happy. Unless he should be scared too, more than he already was.

Gaius Florus was gray enough to be his father but far from being frail, judging by the strong curves of the shoulders filling his tunic. The man's gaze traveled from the floor to Jonathan's face before turning to Valentina. "Three thousand sesterces?"

Her face paled, and Gaius turned back to him. "What are you called, slave?"

"Jonathan."

"My lord," Brennus corrected him. "His name is Jonathan, my lord."

Gaius sighed and crossed his arms. "What do you excel at?"

Surviving a beating. Trying to save women like his mother. Neither were answers he could give.

"Excellent." Gaius flashed a glare at his wife and turned to Brennus. "My wife has paid five months' profits for a simpleton. What do you think should be done with him?"

They could let him go.

"Gaius, please." Valentina grabbed his arm. "You weren't there. You didn't see the horrible way Fabricius was treating him. He was flogging him even as I passed."

Tears welled in her eyes. That she could lie with such emotion was both impressive and disconcerting. She reminded him more and more of Manius.

"Have him remove his tunic and view his back. I know it wasn't my place to spend such a sum without permission, but I couldn't leave him in the hands of that dreadful man. I couldn't."

"Stop crying." Gaius shoved her hands away and shifted on the couch to face her. "You and I both know, as will everyone in Capua, this young man isn't here because of his back. The poles of your litter can't possibly hold any more slaves better suited to a brothel than a merchant's villa. Therefore I will decide what becomes of him."

Her posture wilted. "Gaius, I—"

"Do not speak."

Jonathan could no longer enjoy her fear. Gaius appeared ready to strike her any moment. She didn't deserve that, no matter how much she'd humiliated him on the slave block.

Gaius massaged his forehead and released a long sigh. "Three thousand sesterces," he mumbled. His head finally came up. "What were your duties in your last master's house?"

He had no answer for that either. But he needed to think of something. Quickly.

But Gaius' patience was gone. His face turned crimson and he stood. "Answer me!"

Brennus stepped forward. "Jonathan knows mathematics, my lord."

Gaius' brow dipped as his chin drew back. "Do you?"

As well as he knew the constellations and the names and reigns of all the emperors back to Augustus Caesar, the first. This time he remembered the important part of the answer. "Yes, my lord."

"Do you read?"

"Yes, my lord."

"Can you scribe?"

"Yes."

"In Greek?" Gaius' anger must be cooling. His tone was softening, and his face returning to a normal color.

"And Latin, my lord." Perhaps they had young children the man wanted tutored as Dionysius had taught him. "I know much literature, philosophy, and astronomy as well."

"And how would you compare Roman philosophers to the Greeks?"

The man was clever. Very clever. "Forgive me, my lord, but as Cicero has been the only Roman philosopher of note, I think it unfair to compare him to the collective teachings of Socrates, Plato, and Aristotle."

A grin formed at the corner of Gaius' mouth. "What of Ovid?"

The man could test him all he wanted. "Roman to be certain, but a poet and not a philosopher, as I recall."

From the way Valentina had tensed at the mention of Ovid, she'd probably partaken of the poet's more erotic writings.

Gaius leaned forward and clasped his hands between his knees. "How is it you're educated?"

Should he tell him? Brennus' gaze implored him to answer as much as Gaius' commanded. He'd tell the truth, because he respected this man already in a way he never would his wife.

"I'm a Roman citizen, my lord. I was born free to a freed slave, the son of a patrician noble. When my father learned of me, he adopted me and raised me as a son until my brother attempted to have me killed eight days ago in Rome. The assassins sold me into slavery instead."

Gaius and Valentina, even Brennus, stared at him as if he'd claimed to be Caesar. After a long moment, Gaius spoke. "That does explain everything."

The tension in his body melted like fog in the sun. "You believe me."

"You have no reason to lie, and I'm an excellent judge of character." Gaius glanced beside him. "When not blinded by beauty."

He was going home. "My father will repay you what your wife spent to acquire me, and more I'm certain."

"I said I believe you, Jonathan, not that I planned to free you."

"I don't understand."

"Every slave was once free. Perhaps even a person of distinction in another life that no longer exists. Unless they were born one like Cyra. Even the head servant in my father's house was a prince in his homeland. It did not make him less of a slave in ours. What we were matters not. Only what we are in the present. And in the present I have great need of you."

Ache exploded in his chest. Not his battered ribs, but in the center, where his hope of returning home had been forced back into its grave. Gaius and his wife were more alike than he'd first believed. Greedy and without honor, like Manius, who would have taken a lampstand and bludgeoned everyone in this chamber by now and simply walked out.

Walk out. He'd been foolish not to think of it before. Bide his time, a few days perhaps, then leave under cover of darkness. By the time they missed him he'd be out of the city and would somehow make his way home.

"Brennus will show you to my library," Gaius continued. "Familiarize yourself with the location of my wax tablets and scrolls. Tomorrow, I'll begin showing you your duties with them and going over my various interests. Brennus can educate you on the rules of the house. There is but one I give personally."

Gaius turned to Valentina, who still hadn't stirred at his side. "Anyone who touches my wife forfeits their life. Am I understood?"

"Yes, my lord." Jonathan understood, but it seemed Valentina should be the one being threatened. Although the way Gaius continued to glare at her, perhaps she was. He could endure her for a few days if he had to.

"One more thing, Brennus," Gaius said.

"Yes, my lord?"

"I want a slave collar on Jonathan before sunset."

It was like getting cleaved in two. Gaius Florus might as well be chaining him to the wall. Field slaves, oarsmen on ships, and other slaves likely to flee were made to wear slave collars, or marks burned into their skin. If Jonathan ran and was caught in a slave collar, he would be returned to Gaius Florus within days.

He was never going to see his father or his home ever again.

CHAPTER 8 – STAND

After two and a half hours by the water clock, the figures recorded on the scroll still would not tally. Jonathan put his elbows on the master's writing table, closed his eyes, and rubbed his temples. What was he not seeing?

Everything, unless he opened his eyes and returned to his work. A low chuckle rumbled in his chest. He dropped his head back to stretch his neck and concentrate.

Finding the theft had been easier in the beginning. Master Gaius had dealt decisively with the thievery among his captains and representatives in their Greek and Egyptian ports. After four years, those that remained and those added to their numbers were either trustworthy or more skilled in their deceit. Jonathan would find the error or the missing goods. He always did.

He grabbed the horse head hanging from his neck and stroked the smooth bone. Cracked vessels or leaking corks? On every single amphora? Did they transfer it to new containers on a different ship while at sea? Wouldn't a passenger have reported it? Maybe not, if bribed.

"You're working too hard." Cyra stood in the doorway, leaning against the frame.

How long had she been there? "So are you."

She straightened and glanced behind her before approaching. The smile she wore said they were alone. He rose from the stool and met her on the other side of the table. He slipped his arms around her waist and pulled her against him. It had been so long. She tucked her head against his chest and embraced him in return. "Do you know what I like best about watching you?"

"No."

"The way even at rest I can see your strength. Like a catapult the moment before it fires."

He smiled against her hair. "Is that all?"

"No. I like how your hair reminds me of charred wood after a rain, it's so black. I like the way your emerald eyes see things others do not. In scrolls, in problems, and… in people." She shifted to meet his gaze. "It's hard to pretend I feel nothing for you when we're not alone."

This stolen moment was dangerous, yet he couldn't bring himself to let her go. Not when it could be months before he could feel her in his arms again. Brennus, Marcus and Titus, or any of the other slaves could appear any moment. He couldn't trust them not to report to Valentina. Behind their master's back, their mistress had made it clear if she could not have him, no one would.

He glanced at the doorway. Still vacant. He knew he shouldn't, but it had been so long.

Cyra's gaze was on his mouth. She wanted it too.

He never should have kissed her that first time. Or the second. Or allowed her the third. Because now they knew what they were denied in the long months between.

"Cyra?"

He jumped at Frona's voice, but not as much as Cyra, who put an arm's length between them in a single gasp. "Mother."

Frona's disapproving gaze traveled between them. "The mistress said to make haste. She's waiting. And you and I will discuss this later."

Cyra's look of shame angered him. "Frona, I can—"

"You're the head servant, Jonathan, but Cyra is still my daughter. I will do what I must to protect her. As would you, if you truly cared for her."

That stung. Deeply.

"The mistress is waiting for you. She shouldn't have had to send for you twice."

His gut twisted. No wonder Cyra had lingered in his arms. Even now there was an apology in her eyes. He wanted to cup her face, tell her everything would be all right, but the only thing he hated more than a serpent-tongued liar like Valentina was the thought of becoming one too.

Cyra hugged her arms to her chest and started toward Valentina's chamber. Neither of them met Frona's gaze as they passed her, and the house felt unnaturally quiet in the late evening. The calm before the storm. Which is exactly what this would be.

Entering Valentina's bedchamber always seemed to make Jonathan's slave collar tighten. From the white-knuckled grip on the bronze goblet and the way her eyelids blinked slower than they should, she'd already consumed enough wine to be dangerous.

"You sent for me, Mistress?"

She patted the small portion of couch with her free hand. "Come sit beside me."

So tonight she would skip the few menial tasks that ordinarily began this game of hers whenever the master was away. His jaw tightened as he approached. He sat on the edge of the cushion as far from her as possible, with both feet flat to the floor and his hands to his knees. The potted palms on the far wall sat in shadow, beyond the strength of the lamps. Enough light reached them he could still count the fronds.

One. Two. Three.

Valentina set her wine on the low table beside her.

Four. Five.

She writhed between his back and the wall.

Six.

Her hands squeezed his shoulders, through the thin linen of his tunic. "You're always so tense. A massage would soothe that."

Seven. Eight.

She ran her hands down his arms.

Nine.

Her fingers passed the ends of his sleeves and met his bare skin.

His restraint collapsed, and he rose and strode for the closed door.

"Jonathan, stop."

Years of conditioning to obey every command drew him to a halt.

"I did not dismiss you." Anger had risen through the slur in her voice.

He was about to tread on slippery ground. "What is it you require, Mistress?"

"For now, that you come sit back down."

Every step back to that couch put another stone in his stomach.

She slid her bare feet into his lap. "You may not relish a good massage but I do. Begin with my feet."

"If you desire a massage I will have Cyra heat stones—"

"I don't want Cyra, Jonathan. I want you to rub my feet. Now." Her lids drooped as she reclined deeper against the cushion at her back.

It might work. He took one of her feet and rubbed the arch in slow but firm circles of his thumbs. In time, the pitch of her breathing changed. She was falling asleep, as he'd hoped. He stilled, glancing to see if she reacted.

She did, shifting to pick her goblet back up. Her heel jabbed his thigh as she twisted for the cup. His swift intake of breath was all that kept him from cursing.

"Tell me more about yourself," she said.

I hate you. "There's little to tell, Mistress." He hated calling her that too.

"You don't say much."

The corners of his mouth lifted without permission. There were many things he wanted to say to Valentina, but any one of them would see him flogged. Her free foot maneuvered to caress his arm, from elbow to shoulder. He imagined breaking the foot he held in his hands. The toes first, one at a time, then a hard twist at the ankle. Then she would be one of the lame, begging in the streets while some other rich merchant's wife ignored her from within a litter carried by slaves. He couldn't suppress his grin then, even crushing his bottom lip between his teeth.

"I like you so much better when you smile." Her free foot left his elbow for his lap, but it did not come to rest there. Her caress invaded and he bolted upright. The sudden movement spun her off the couch and she fell to the floor, splashing the blood red wine everywhere. "How dare you."

He strode toward the door. *How dare he?*

"Stop."

But he would not.

A sharp pain hit between his shoulder blades. The heavy bronze goblet rolled at his feet, the metal rim on the stone echoing through the tension. He wanted to break her neck. Cut her lying tongue from her mouth. Crush those eyes that always stripped him bare as she had that first day.

She approached and the temptation to hurt her grew as the distance between them closed. "My husband may treat you like the son I have yet to give him, but you are still a slave. My slave."

The foulest name he knew almost left his mouth. Only the lessons learned under the whips on the long road from Rome kept him silent. The fury in her eyes blazed the worst he'd ever seen. She was going to have him beaten anyway, and that freed his tongue. "I may be a slave—but I still choose my friends."

Her palm tore across his cheek. As his head snapped sideways, the last of his restraint shattered. He raised his arm to slap her back. Her scream snapped him back and stayed his hand. She ran for her couch, screaming as she went, and grabbed one of the cushions.

He ducked and the silk pillow sailed past his head. Cyra burst through the door. His honor demanded he stay and protect her while his head screamed they were all safer the farther he was from Valentina.

He raced for the garden—the only place here that ever reminded him of home. Flames from the torches on the columns forming the perimeter lit the path to the fountain. The cool water eased the sting in his cheek but none of the anger flooding his veins. He splashed more water on his face, then his arms, trying to wash the memory of her touch away. A lizard appeared on the stone rim of the lowest tier of water. Its round, shiny eyes watched him, blinking every few seconds.

"I envy you."

The lizard cocked its angular head, as if truly listening.

"I envy you your freedom," he whispered. The green pointed head flicked toward the villa and then it scurried away.

"He went through here." Brennus' voice carried from within.

The ex-head servant carried a coil of rope and Titus and Marcus followed, each with a spear leveled right at his chest. Jonathan retreated as his heartbeat sped so fast he could hear the blood rushing in his ears. Another step back and his calf connected with the edge of the fountain.

"Don't fight, Jonathan." Brennus made a loop in the end of the rope. The smugness in his expression was unmistakable. He'd needed no persuading to mete out whatever punishment Valentina had decided upon.

Nothing ever changed. The selfishness of others would always control him.

No more.

He would escape or die trying.

Jonathan allowed his rage to burst forth in a shout as he charged. The thick wood of a spear shaft slammed below his knees. He smacked the stone so hard his next breath wouldn't come. He scrambled to grab the spear, to fight or fall on it, but Marcus kicked him. A sword hilt battered his skull above his left ear. The same place Manius' assassin had struck.

The same black oblivion pulled him under.

Cold water shocked Jonathan awake. He raised his head and coughed but the motion pulled at his arms. Rope at the wrists—they'd tied him between two of the *peristyle's* pillars. Brennus set the hammered bronze pail down beside Valentina. Marcus and Titus were with them, still clutching their spears beside the doorway into the villa. Where were Cyra and the others?

Valentina uncrossed her arms and stopped close enough that she stood in his shadow cast by the torches behind him. Her fingertips wiped at the water pooled at his chin and she frowned. "It pains me to see you like this."

He righted his feet to stand as straight as the bonds would allow. His sandals were still on, and his tunic. The chill of the wet linen against his skin was nothing like the eyes of the woman before him. "Then release me."

"I will. When you've been punished for your defiance, and I'm assured it won't happen again. Slaves are killed for far less transgressions, so I expect you to be appropriately grateful."

She took his head between her hands and her lips parted. He tried to turn away, but she gripped him tighter and pressed her mouth to his. Her body followed, pressing the weight of them both against his wrists. The pain at his shoulder pushed a groan through his throat, and she kissed him deeper. Helplessness fanned the flame of his hate until seething fury overcame the pain.

He bit her.

Valentina cried out and jerked back. Blood glistened on her lip. She touched her mouth and stared at her red fingertips, then at him. "Brennus, bring a whip."

His chest tightened. "The master will never stand for this. Not when he's told the truth."

"The truth is what I want it to be, Jonathan. You will see."

Jonathan pulled hard at the ropes at his wrists, straining as Sampson must have against the pillars of the Philistine temple. The fibers groaned and stretched, but held fast, as he knew they would.

Brennus returned with the master's leather chariot whip coiled in his hand. At the sight of it pride was forgotten. He would beg, plead forgiveness, anything.

"Ten lashes, Brennus."

It was the pleasure in her face, echoed in her voice when she said it, that returned his resolve. Beneath that flawless skin, rich linen, and jewels, lived darkness deeper than a cave on a moonless night. Brennus grabbed Jonathan's tunic sleeve and ripped it clear to his neck. When he tore the other side, the edges fell away and hung from the leather belt at Jonathan's waist. Jonathan pulled the edge of his bottom lip between his teeth and closed his eyes.

Stillness descended so complete he heard nothing but the gurgle of the fountain behind him for a long moment. Then leather whistled through the air and a hundred scorpions stung his back as the first lash fell. The second always hurt more because you'd been reminded what was coming. On the sixth, he lost the fight to keep his cries of agony silent. With the eighth, the burning in his eyes opened a deeper well of humiliation as tears wet his cheeks. The tenth he welcomed—because it marked the end.

She came to him again and raised his head with both her hands. Her expression had softened, and she brushed his damp hair back from his forehead. Her fingertips traced his cheek bone. A touch so gentle he barely felt it, unlike the blood trickling over the skin of his back. "Now then," she said softly. "Are you ready to be my friend?"

If he gave in, the pain in his body would end, but a deeper ache would replace it. The pain of knowing he'd sacrificed the remnant of his honor as a man—and as a Tarquinius. That was enough of an answer. "No."

Valentina's nostrils flared beneath her narrowed gaze. Behind her Brennus stood, watching and waiting, as did Marcus and Titus. Three men he'd commanded less than an hour ago.

She crossed her arms again, studying him as she had that first day on the slave block. "Brennus, summon Fabricius Clavis. Make certain he brings a cart with him."

"Now, mistress?"

"Yes. Tell him he'll be well compensated. Tell the other slaves Jonathan stole a thousand sesterces from the master and fled. Any of them saying differently will share his fate. Am I understood?"

Cyra.

"Yes, Mistress." Brennus disappeared into the villa. He would be headed to the stables for a mount and to issue Valentina's edict. Cyra would be so afraid. Frona's protective interference that had angered him earlier now gave him a small measure of reassurance. Frona would keep Cyra safe. That's what mothers did. But what would become of him?

"Guards."

Titus stepped forward. "Yes, Mistress?"

"Beat him."

Marcus crept forward and stopped behind Titus. They should all three be playing knucklebones in the kitchen over bread and figs as they did almost every night, taunting Marcus for his inability to grow a full beard.

"For how long?" Titus asked.

If she could hear the tremor in his voice, she didn't care. "Until I tell you to stop."

Conflict arm-wrestled in Titus' eyes as he swallowed. A former gladiator like Marcus, they'd been made to do things far worse before the master bought them as bodyguards.

Valentina stepped back, and Marcus took the place opposite Titus. He flipped his spear sideways, the tipped end behind him and watched Titus. So did Jonathan.

Titus took a deep breath and turned his spear as well. His face emptied of all emotion and the shred of hope Jonathan had left died with the first blow.

Chapter 9 – Sons

Fabricius Clavis would have sent a curse-filled reply back with anyone else's servant but Gaius and Valentina Florus. Traveling at night in the dark was dangerous, even with torchlight. The Florus servant had been silent the entire way and his servant was having a difficult time keeping the ox moving.

At the villa, Valentina herself came to meet them. She carried something in her hand—that jingled. "I need you to dispose of a slave. My husband will believe he's run away with the coin I'm about to pay you. Before you think about bribing me in the future to remain silent, consider I can hire an assassin as easily as I can hire you. So all we have to settle upon is price."

Were it not for her body, he would swear on Jupiter's throne that she was a man. "Shall you name a price, I counter it, you offer a figure somewhere in the middle and I do the same until one of us agrees?"

"No. You take this and do as I've instructed." She extended her arm and a leather pouch dangled from her fist—a small leather pouch.

"That doesn't look like much."

"They're aureii."

He smothered the surprise before it reached his face. "How many?"

"Ten."

A thousand sesterces, nearly a year's income in trade for him and two and a half times the amount a soldier collected a year. For keeping a secret and getting rid of a body?

She lowered her arm and came close. So close he almost took a step back. "Do you agree to my terms? Or need I find someone to bury you both?"

If he were Caesar, he would give her a legion and set her loose on any rebellious frontier. "I agree."

Valentina graced him with a smile and pressed the pouch into his hand. He opened it and counted the gold coins, making certain there was no silver or copper mixed in before tucking the pouch in his belt. Once content they'd closed their deal, she headed inside and her head servant turned his horse for the rear of the villa.

The ox pawed at the stone pavers and his servant tugged its rope to quiet it. Burning the body like the barbarians would be fastest but would draw attention. Digging a hole would take longer and this time of year the ground was hard. The *ludis* of Caius Pullus was several miles west, but he was always in the market for fresh bodies for the lions he kept. Fabricius could go there, sell the dead slave for a few denarii, and be home before midday.

Two formidable looking men in full armor with swords at their sides dragged the dead slave from the villa by his arms. The larger one lifted the man's body and laid him in the ox cart, arranging his arms and legs with reverence while Valentina watched from the doorway.

Fabricius nodded to them and climbed on the bench seat beside his servant. "To Caius Pullus' ludis."

After nearly an hour on the road, losing the road once when night clouds covered the moon, nature called. Fabricius stood relieving himself on the side of the roadway thinking if this were anyone but Valentina Florus, he'd dump the slave's body here and go home. But no one risked making an enemy of Gaius or Valentina Florus, so to the ludis of Caius Pullus he would go.

"Master," his slave called.

Fabricius swung around and uttered a curse as he wet his sandal. "What?"

"He opened his eyes."

He stomped back to the wagon, straightening his tunic. The man lay still as a fallen cedar under the dim light from the torch. "You're mistaken."

Fabricius raised the bronze torch pole through the rings securing it to the cart and brought it closer to the young man. Beneath the dried blood and bruises was a handsome face and well-built frame. He seemed familiar, almost like the young man his son had… by the gods, it was him. Fabricius' gut twisted as he thought of his son's foolishness that had made this young Roman noble a slave. He turned away and reached for the wagon bench, hesitating at the last moment.

This man was also someone's son.

He turned back and put two fingers to the slave's throat. The drumming of his life was faint, but still there. "He's still alive. We must make haste to the ludis."

Fabricius dropped the torch back into the holder and climbed to the bench seat. His servant goaded the ox on though, if possible, the creature seemed slower than before. All gladiator schools housed a *medicus*. Perhaps at the ludis they could save him. When they finally reached the great stone walls of the gladiator school, lather dripped from the ox and Fabricius' brow.

The sky was turning pink with the promise of sun and sounds of combat already filled the compound. A large iron gate opened and the sight of thirty or more men armed with weapons, even wooden ones, kept Fabricius on edge beside his servant.

Caius Pullus stood on a balcony, leaning on the top edge with both arms. "What do you bring me that would wake even you at this hour?"

"An opportunity. But you should hasten," Fabricius yelled up at the *lanista*.

Caius disappeared from the balcony, and Fabricius climbed down from the bench. The hard packed sand stirred very little beneath him, tread by hundreds of men training to fight and kill. The slave looked worse in the hint of daylight, but life still drummed in his throat.

The lanista was in a simple tunic and plain leather belt as he approached. Normally when Fabricius saw him in the city, he was more richly dressed. Caius reached them and looked inside the walls of the cart. He raised the young man's arm and then dropped it before turning toward him. "How long has he been dead?"

"He's still alive."

"I won't pay extra for that."

"I didn't bring him for the lions. I want you to save him, if you can."

"The ferryman has him by the leg and he smells dead already." Caius studied him, his thumb to his chin. "A shame though. I've traded in flesh more than half my life, and even crushed I can see he was well formed."

"He can fight."

Caius snorted. "What's left of him disagrees."

"No, you don't understand. I've traded him before. Four years ago in Rome. On the journey to Capua he ran at every opportunity. It took countless beatings for days to subdue him, and every time it took more men to regain control of him. He was learning to fight without knowing it."

"How did you come by him again?"

"It's better if you don't know."

"He's stolen?"

"No." Not from his last master anyway. "I give you my oath of honor."

Caius continued to examine the slave and, from his expression, he was wavering.

Fabricius would need to tread carefully. Caius Pullus was known for greed that rivaled his and a temper worse than Valentina possessed. "His face alone would be worth trying to save. You know the only thing women love more than a gladiator who can actually fight is a handsome gladiator that can fight."

It was a long moment, one the slave didn't have, while Caius decided. "Fifty sesterces."

"Done."

Caius grinned. "I would have paid a hundred."

"I would have given him to you."

The grin disappeared. "Let me get him to the medicus and I'll send your coin out."

"My gratitude." Fabricius had done what he could for the slave. The rest remained for the gods to decide.

Tender grass cushioned Jonathan's back where he lay sprawled in the shade of a great olive tree. The vast, unspoiled countryside with its clear, fast moving stream and wildflowers was so peaceful that after a time, he no longer cared he couldn't remember how he came to be here.

Nessa had worked beside Quintus for nine years, four of them in this ludis, and never seen a body so brutalized. "What do you think they used?"

"A pole of some kind." Quintus scrubbed at more of the dried blood on the slave's back. "Before or after they flogged him. They knew what they were doing."

"Killing him?"

"That's what I can't fathom. There is very little coloring of the skin here." Quintus pointed between the man's hip and lower ribs. "And here. Front or back. Instead of the prime area to inflict the most damage, they beat him everywhere else, where the largest bones would give him some protection."

She poured fresh water into the bowl for Quintus. That whoever had done this did so with an expert hand deepened her anger at them. Every shade of an evening sky striped his chest, back, thighs, and shoulders. It hurt her to look at him, especially his face and head.

Quintus would finish cleaning the stripes on the man's back and close the four deepest wounds with pinched metal thorns. Not as tight a seal as suturing them with horsehair, but much faster. He paused with the cloth and pressed his fingers below the man's jaw. "He's crossing the Styx."

She never argued Quintus' pagan beliefs, but knew he meant the man was crossing the river in Greek lore that separated the world of the living from the dead. They'd already closed the wound on the back of his head, and the man hadn't stirred. Not a whimper, a blink, or twitch. "Are you giving up?"

"Of course not." Quintus glanced up at her. "Not because Caius demands he live but because by everything I know, he should already be dead."

Nessa had felt it too, unease within when he'd been carried in and dumped belly-down on their table like a sack of grain. She and Quintus shared the same goal to alleviate suffering and preserve life. Strange in this place, but she'd felt something stronger than ever before that this man *must* survive. At the shelves, she brought down the jar of powdered ram's horn and the various ground herbs to mix the healing drink Quintus would want next.

God, place Your hand upon him. Bind up his wounds and deliver him from death.

Jonathan waded into the stream. The sharp coolness of the water was refreshing more than uncomfortable. Smooth rocks and firm mud made walking to the center easy. It made no sense that the current slowed the deeper he waded in, yet it did, as if inviting him to swim. He turned his face to the warmth of the sun and floated on his back, lost in the purest serenity he had ever known.

Nessa poured water and wine into a new bowl as she had hundreds of times, forming the base for the healing drink.

Quintus had closed the wounds but the man had lost so much blood, much of it under his skin and from his head. "As fast as the knock in his throat is, I should be able to see it in his neck, not have to press deep to find it. His *humours* are badly unbalanced."

Of course they were. He'd been allowed to bleed freely, and it was unlikely he'd been given water or wine for as long.

"Lay a sheet of new linen on the table there. We need to get him on his back now."

She'd just finished when Quintus returned with the two slaves who'd carried the man in.

"Put him on his back over here and be gentle with him, or Caius will hear of it."

The men did, taking greater care with the man's body this time, though he still didn't stir. Nessa waited until they left before taking another square of linen to drape over his waist. Quintus allowed her modesty when it didn't interfere with their work, and for that she was grateful. She returned to the bowls to complete mixing the solution Quintus would need soon. Two more measures of—

"Nessa." The urgency in Quintus' voice quickened her chest as she turned from the shelves. His fingers were pressed deep into the man's neck. "Entreat your God."

He always said that as a last remedy, though it was her first and she already had. She dropped the pestle into the bowl and rushed to place both her hands atop the slave's head, careful of the metal thorns pressed into his scalp. "May I do so aloud?"

They were alone but he still scanned the room, lingering on the doorway. "If it will help."

A faint voice penetrated the water covering Jonathan's ears. Had someone joined him in the stream? He pulled upright to listen and a dull ache passed across his back. The voice grew louder from somewhere beyond the mountains, or maybe the sky, but how could that be? He knew that voice. It belonged to his mother. Where was he?

The skin of his temples where Nessa's fingers rested was warming. That could be him taking her own heat instead of life returning from within, so she would keep her eyes closed and her petition before God until something happened.

"Lord, not a sparrow falls to the ground You do not see. Deliver this man in need of Your healing. Hear the prayer of Your servant. Reveal Your greatness by Your mighty hand and show Your power as in the days of the prophets and kings. Lord, breathe life into him again as in the beginning."

Jonathan craned his head, with the water still swirling past him. It was not his mother's voice, but it was her words. Words of prayer familiar from his youth, yet the tenor and pitch of the woman's voice speaking them were not. The louder the voice grew the sharper the discomfort in his back, spreading now to the rest of his body. The pain centered in his head like it was being crushed by a millstone, so strong he clutched it while his knees buckled. What was happening? He turned for the shore and stumbled. The water closed over him, taking the light, the voice, and the air he needed to breathe.

"Set Your angels around him. Within him. Lord, I beg You—"

The head between her fingers trembled and a faint choking sound broke into her prayer.

Quintus reacted immediately and grabbed the bowl holding the healing drink and a sponge. "Continue your prayers, but from his feet."

Nessa let go of him and scurried to the other end of the table. His feet were soft on the top and rougher on the bottom when she gripped them. Still much too cold, but Quintus hadn't told her to cover him with blankets or furs yet.

Quintus soaked the sponge with one hand and with the thumb of the other, pressed the man's mouth open. She tightened her hold on the man's feet and began to pray for Quintus as well. Unlike brutalizing a man, what he was about to do required true skill. Squeeze too slow and the liquid would trickle in the airways. Too fast and by the time the throat swallowed there would be too much to consume and choke him.

"Lord, please. Steady them both," she whispered.

The peak of the man's throat moved without a cough or gag. The rate of release was perfect.

"Well done, slave. Well done." Quintus refilled the sponge to try again. "Now stay with us."

Chapter 10 – The Ludis

The air smelled thickly of pungent herbs. Jonathan blinked, and the wooden beams above him lost their blur. Thick fur covered him, thick enough to be a bearskin. A slight flame somewhere to his left revealed only shapes in the deep shadows surrounding him. Where was he?

Turning his head toward the light extended the ache in his head down to his neck. A woman slept on a table beside him, fully dressed in a simple sleeved tunic and sash with both hands tucked beneath her head. By her clothing she was a servant, but whose?

His fingers curled when he asked them to. And his toes. But reaching for his neck required much more effort. The bronze slave collar was gone. He felt higher, then lower, his stomach clenching. Sweat dampened skin and nothing more. His mother's carving was gone.

Was it not enough to take her from me too soon? You've finally taken everything from me. Everything. He leaned to sit up. A mistake, and a groan broke the silence. It must have awakened the woman, because she stood. She reached for his face, and he shied from her touch.

Her hand stilled in midair. "It's all right. May I?"

She wasn't slender or beautiful the way Valentina had first appeared to him. But something in her face seemed to soothe his fear. Her eyes were dark and filled with a concern belying the joyful curve of her mouth. He gave her a small nod and willed himself to hold still.

The backs of her fingers touched his forehead and lingered there. Her smile grew when she removed her hand. "Your fever's broken."

"Where am I?" His voice emerged raspy and slight, and as unfamiliar to him as this place. She used the small lamp to light a larger one. An entire wall of ordered shelves and cupboards stood opposite him with pouches, jars, vials, and folded cloths of every size. A large table surrounded by four stools dominated the center of the room. Suddenly the odor of herbs made sense. A place of medicine. What didn't make sense was why he was in one. That beating had surely been meant to kill him.

"Where am I?" he asked again.

"The medicus chamber." She picked up a bowl and swirled it in her hand, carefully avoiding his gaze.

"Yes, but where?"

Something sad flickered through her expression when she met his gaze. "Please don't talk so much. You need to drink this and then rest."

That she ignored his question deepened his resolve to know. Jonathan pushed up with his elbows to try to sit up. Pain shot through his sides, across his back, so powerful it was like being beaten a second time. His eyes clamped shut as he fell back with a whimper in his throat.

"Don't." Her hand pressed his shoulder as if to hold him down. "You will reopen your wounds." She was upset. Her brow was furrowed and her mouth pulled flat. "We've had to keep you on your back so you could swallow."

But as she continued to stare at him her expression turned tender, almost sorrowful. The hand at his shoulder moved behind his neck, and she eased his head up. She tipped the edge of the bowl to his lip. The thick liquid tasted bitter, and he spit it back in the bowl.

"It's soured," he rasped.

"No, it will heal you. And you *can* drink it. You have been for three days."

Three days?

She raised his head again and returned the bowl to his chin. "Please try."

Jonathan managed three full swallows before his stomach threatened to retch. She removed the bowl from his mouth and set his head back down. "Well done. Now please try to sleep. You need rest to heal." She grasped the fur that had bunched at his waist and pulled it up to his shoulders.

"First." He swallowed. "Tell me." He breathed deep to steady his voice. "Where I am."

"I've already told you. A place of healing. Now please rest." She wouldn't meet his eyes and began to turn away.

He pulled his arm free of the fur and grabbed her by the wrist. The searing pain was intense but worked to strengthen his grip. "Don't play games." He fought the dizziness with clenched teeth. "Where—am—I?"

She hadn't tried to pull free. Her expression wasn't one of anger now, but one of sorrow. "The ludis of Caius Pullus."

A ludis.

He released her, and his arm dropped like a stone. He closed his eyes and struggled just to breathe. Better he had died. The only reason they would work to heal him now would be to kill him later—as a gladiator.

He felt her hand on his shoulder again. "Rest now. Please."

"Rest? You want me to rest?" Anger was overtaking the pain with every breath. It felt better. Much better. "How can I rest? I escape death to discover I'll be killed later for sport, surrounded by people cheering for my blood."

He would sooner die by his own hand. He'd wished for death, begged it to come while Marcus and Titus had struck him again and again and again. To escape the pain, yes, but in that moment, he'd seen death as its own kind of freedom. It had been within his grasp.

"Why would you help them do this?"

She had no answer for that either, but this time he hadn't the strength to compel her. She took hold of the arm hanging at his side and laid it across his chest. Her gentleness, after he'd been so rough with her, unsettled him more. The serenity in her expression opposed everything inside him.

"This life comes to an end for us all," she said. "Whether slaves, soldiers, or kings. It doesn't have to be something you fear."

His mother hadn't feared death. He could still remember the peace in her expression, as if she slept and would awaken any moment. He doubted he would look that way, lying crushed and bloody with a sword sticking up from his back. "You should have let me die."

"It was up to God, not me. You're immortal until His work for you is finished."

Jonathan's jaw tightened. She'd said God. Not Jupiter, Juno, Isis, or 'the gods' like most who didn't worship a particular one. She'd said God as in *the God*. The God of his mother and Deborah. The One he'd once been foolish enough to believe in as well. "I don't believe in God."

"Whether you do or do not does not change His will for you."

Her arrogant certainty aggravated him. *Deeply*. "You know nothing of what you speak."

"I know He returned you to this life for a reason."

"He did nothing."

That calmness about her remained as she watched him. A grin slowly formed on her mouth. An urge to knock it from her face tingled through his hand. Shame flooded him in an instant. He looked away and drew a deep breath that hurt his chest but helped clear his head. What was he becoming?

Shadow fell over him as she adjusted the fur, tucking it in around him. Her grin remained. While the abhorrent thought to hit her didn't return, his annoyance did. "Something amuses you?"

She straightened and stared down at him, smiling even wider now. "For someone who doesn't believe in God, you're very angry at Him." She turned and extinguished the larger lamp, leaving only the faint light from the smaller one again. "Now rest."

She returned to the table beside him, rested her head on her arm like a cushion, and closed her eyes. That smile remained a long time, until sleep eventually erased it from her lips.

Though exhausted, in pain, with a terrible fate looming before him, sleep wouldn't come. He lay there staring at the wooden beams, her words echoing in his mind.

What was all that banging? Jonathan opened his eyes. Daylight lit an unfamiliar ceiling. Where—everything flooded back as he eased his head up to look around. The slave girl from last night stood at a waist-high shelf pouring white powder into a bowl. She looked shorter in the daylight, and younger than he remembered. Her gaze met his, and her smile reassured him, though he didn't know why.

"You're awake." She poured water from a red clay pitcher into the bowl and carried it to him. "Drink this."

She slipped her hand beneath his neck to tilt his head up more and put the bowl to his lips. The drink overran the edges of his mouth and dripped down his neck. It wasn't as bitter as last time which helped, because it kept coming well after he would have stopped if given the choice. When the bowl emptied she took it from his mouth and lowered his head.

"Every time I wake you force more potions down my throat."

"Yes. It's why you keep waking."

Her brown eyes were full of light. She must be laughing at him inside. A sudden explosion of sound from beyond the wall drew her attention—a clamor like thunder, followed by what could only be a victory shout.

"Tao." The slave girl shook her head, still grinning. "He must have awakened in a bad mood." She turned to Jonathan and her smile fell. "As have you." Her hand came to rest on his arm through the thickness of the fur still covering him. Her touch was unassuming, unlike Valentina's had always been. Was she waiting for an explanation for his gloom?

He'd been fighting all his life. To survive. To understand who he was. Now they would put that in an arena, where thousands would pleasure in his suffering instead of a few. Even if he could give his despair words she wouldn't understand. She looked too innocent, and part of him didn't want to take that from her.

A man wearing a bone-colored tunic entered the room. He wore no belt, but it would have taken two to circle his middle. Black eyebrows were the only hair on his head. They looked like two giant caterpillars that threatened to roll down from their wall of pale skin any moment.

"Quintus, may I get you anything?" The slave girl looked happy to see him. Beside this man, she appeared much thinner than he'd thought her to be last night.

Quintus regarded him with eyes so dark they were almost as black as his eyebrows. "No, I'm fine. How is our, what is it you say, Lazareth?"

"Close. Lazarus."

Their reference to the man Jesus raised from the dead, according to Deborah, annoyed him. He could throw out some names of his own for what they were doing to him, starting with Judas Iscariot. Granted, Judas had betrayed Jesus to be killed, and these people had saved his life. He'd be grateful if he was any place other than a ludis.

Quintus pressed cold, plump fingers to Jonathan's neck. The woman's light touch on his arm tightened slightly. Her mouth had flattened as she stared at Quintus. "What do you think?"

"Stronger." Quintus pressed his fingers lower on Jonathan's neck. "His humours are still out of balance. We'll keep filling him up until he's flowing out again."

The slave girl blushed. A surprise. The reference had embarrassed her. In a place like this? The pink in her cheeks, however, was lovely. How had he thought her so plain last night?

"Perhaps he could have some honeyed wine now." She left his side for the counter on the far wall and returned with another bowl. This time instead of raising Jonathan's head, she handed the bowl to Quintus.

"Let's see how you do." Quintus put his hand behind Jonathan's head and tilted it forward. The wine tasted delicious on his tongue after so much bitter herbs and salt. Quintus let him drink until the bowl was empty. "Excellent. It seems Nessa's God favors you, slave."

Nessa. An unusual name. "So she says."

"Even so, you need to preserve your strength and allow your body to recover. Resist the urge to touch or scratch any wound. We have metal pins holding the deepest of them closed. Your cracked ribs should help keep you still, and those will take the longest to mend. Nessa will remain with you. I'll return this evening to clean and repack your wounds with herbs and salt. For that I can give you undiluted opium to help with the pain. We've been mixing some into your solution to help you sleep."

Why the effort and expense if they were just going to kill him later?

"Rest." Quintus turned to Nessa. "This afternoon he can have the barley porridge, but strain it so he won't have to chew anything. The less he moves the better, until his skin returns to its normal color."

She nodded and Quintus headed for the white cloth hanging from the top of the doorway. He brushed it aside but turned back, his face somber. "Should you feel well enough to try some ill-conceived plan of escape and your injuries don't kill you, the guards will."

Nessa blanched at Quintus' warning, but Jonathan didn't. That was good to know.

The medicus departed and Nessa's smile returned. It was nearly part of her face it seemed, like her nose. He'd only known two other people so perpetually joyful. Deborah and his mother. He reached for the carving at his throat and remembered it was gone. Gone forever like his mother—and his life.

"Rest," the girl said. "I'll be nearby if you need anything."

"Thank you." He hadn't meant to say it. Habit had done so, but he could tell it pleased her. She returned to the shelf across from them and settled on a stool. She took a fistful of leaves from a cloth pouch and tore them into tiny pieces, dropping them into the large clay jar beneath her hands. She hummed as she worked, and after a while, her gentle voice drowned out the sounds of combat beyond the wall. With his eyes closed and his body relaxed beneath the thick fur, she sang him to sleep.

The day passed slowly while he woke and slept in endless cycles like the sun and moon. Every time his eyes opened, Nessa was there with her bowl.

By late afternoon, he wanted to try holding it himself. When she finally relented, she helped him raise his head and tucked a thickly rolled cloth behind his neck. Holding the bowl steady and keeping his head upright exhausted him, and he spilled a fair amount. Even so, taking back some measure of independence had been worth the tremendous effort.

He appreciated her thoughtfulness when she left him the necessaries to tend his other needs while she went for more water from the fountain. Jonathan learned much about the ludis as he listened to the almost constant sound coming through the wall. It seemed the only time the sound of sparring ceased was for the midday meal. The porridge she gave him to drink had been hot and savory, and he'd managed to drink a second bowl.

Quintus returned that evening with a large bundle Nessa spent a lot of time sorting and putting away on the shelves. They helped him turn onto his stomach to redress the wounds on his back. Several times he almost blacked out, from the pain or the opium they'd given him, or both, he didn't know—or care. More painful than the salt Quintus applied to Jonathan's lashes was the knowledge he hadn't deserved a single one. It wasn't Nessa's voice that carried him to sleep this time, but a burning hatred for Valentina that reached all the way back for Manius as well. If he was ever going to put a sword straight through someone, it would be them.

CHAPTER 11 – SHARDS

The crack of wood on wood pulled Jonathan awake. He needed to relieve himself, badly, but neither Nessa nor the bowl for that purpose were anywhere in sight. The large chamber pot she emptied it into, however, was in the far corner of the room. Sitting up was its own kind of torture, but he managed. Turning to swing his legs down—even worse. The cold stone floor chilled his bare feet, and every part of him screamed in protest when he straightened, especially his left side. The fur he'd planned to wrap around him for the journey slipped to the floor. He bent to retrieve it, and the shards of pain slicing through his back changed his mind. Hopefully, Nessa wouldn't return anytime soon.

He shuffled along the wall to the chamber pot. Slow as a snail, but he succeeded at the task. Faint singing mingled with his heavy breathing. That could only be Nessa, and she was coming fast. Too fast for him to make it back to the bed.

The only thing in reach was the chamber pot. As exhausted as he already was, it might as well be a tree stump. She was coming through that sheet any moment. Think. *Think!*

He swore and pressed his back into the wall, trying to become part of it while covering himself with his hands. The plastered wall mauled his barely healing back, but he held silent and froze.

She came through the curtain carrying a pitcher. Her gaze went to the empty bed, and her song died in her throat. She spotted him and jerked back so fast she fumbled the pitcher. "Oh!"

Her smile returned, as crimson flooded her cheeks. The amusement in her face reminded him of Valentina. It infuriated him in an instant, so to spite her, he dropped his hands.

She dropped the pitcher.

The clay exploded, and water splashed every direction, drowning her gasp as she spun and put her back to him. "I'm sorry. I didn't think you would be up yet. Walking, I mean, not awake, but I didn't—I'm sorry."

Her nervous stammering salved his pride. A little. He reached the bed and managed to squat and retrieve the fur with a minimal increase in the pain all over. Working back into the bed and beneath the safety of the blanket—much more—but keeping his teeth clenched helped.

"May I turn around now?"

If he said no, how long would she stand there in the wet ruins staring at the wall? His conscience smote him. The woman had tended his wounds and shown him kindness. She didn't deserve that, even if she had meant to mock him with her smirk, which he began to doubt. "Yes."

She turned as Quintus came through the curtain carrying a large bundle wrapped in brown cloth. He surveyed the shards of pitcher and water stains on the floor, and then studied the two of them. "What happened?"

Nessa rubbed her empty hands together. "We're going to need a new pitcher… and a tunic for…" She met his gaze and the flush in her cheeks deepened. "I'm sorry. I still don't know your name."

"Nessa, you're bleeding." Quintus bent toward her feet.

A fine line of blood oozed from a cut above her sandal strap. She turned her heel out. "I'm sorry, I didn't feel it."

Quintus cast him a look of disapproval that made him want to dissolve into the floor like the spilled water. It was as if the man knew it had been his fault. "Come sit. I'll tend it and have a slave clean this up and get our patient a tunic."

Watching the doctor remove her sandal, clean and dress the cut, made him feel even worse. A slave came and took away the shards of the pitcher. He returned with another pitcher and a folded tunic. The shelf received the pitcher, and the tunic he set on the end of Jonathan's bed, giving him an appraising stare before departing. Nessa remained statue-like on the stool where Quintus had ordered her to remain.

The medicus emptied the bundle he'd carried in and put away herbs, vials, and a few things Jonathan didn't recognize. No one spoke while the incessant clashing of training filled the awkwardness. Quintus shelved the last glass vial and swore before turning to Nessa. "They didn't include my mint, and I paid for it. Will you be all right while I go back for it?"

"I'm fine."

Quintus glanced at Jonathan. "Are you sure?"

"Yes, I'm sure." She stood as if to prove it.

"If you need anything before I get back, call for one of the guards." Quintus gave Jonathan the same warning look Brennus had given him the first day at the Florus villa. This time he probably deserved it. He fully expected Nessa to flee the room as soon as Quintus left.

She watched him leave, and then turned her gaze on Jonathan. She smiled, again, the same warmth in it as before. His surprise tripled when she stood and brought the stool to the side of his bed and perched on it like she planned to be there a while. Her eyes were brown—a rich, warm brown like the fur covering him.

"I'm sorry about your foot."

"It's not your fault. It's already forgotten."

The pink that returned to her cheeks said otherwise, but he was content to let it go. As a servant of the medicus, how she wasn't accustomed to nakedness seemed as out of place as… as… well, as her. Anyone who used the public baths was. Of course it was one thing to walk through the baths from pool to pool, another to be stripped naked on a slave block, and something else entirely to assault a woman's sense of modesty.

"What's your name?" she asked. "It bothers me to keep referring to you as 'slave.'"

"It's what I am."

"It's the position you hold but it's not who you are."

A particularly loud crack of wood on wood drew her attention to the window opening. The sunlight fell on her dark brown hair and streaks of deep honey appeared in the strands. A tendril above her ear had escaped the simple knot at the base of her neck and shimmered like a new copper coin. How would it feel between his fingers? Soft like Cyra's?

Cyra. What had they told her? Was she well? She'd never truly been his, yet she'd been taken from him just the same.

He emerged from his dark thoughts to find Nessa watching him intently. She chuckled. "Don't worry. Wood on wood is good. It means the sparring is evenly paired. It's when the recruits are paired with the gladiators this room fills up."

"I thought everyone in this place is a gladiator."

The corners of her mouth and eyebrow rose together. "Even me?"

"You know what I mean."

Her face fell flat and she sighed. Too slow to be frustration. It was that sadness again. Something he understood.

"Only recruits who complete the training and pass the final test receive the mark and become gladiators. Until then they eat, sleep, and train together, alongside the gladiators but never with them. The recruits aren't considered worthy to cross swords with the gladiators until they prove themselves and receive the mark. That is how it is done in this ludis. I don't know if it is that way in all of them. Are you thirsty yet?"

Her moods changed as fast as the leader of a chariot race. "I'm fine."

She rose anyway and went to pour him a cup of what looked like plain wine. She carried the cup to the table beside him and resumed her seat on the stool. "In case you change your mind."

"You're stubborn, you know that?"

"I do know that, but I think I'm in good company, considering you still don't want to tell me your name."

"My name is Jonathan." *Jonathan Tarquinius.* He hadn't spoken his full name in four years, but he would never forget it either.

"A strong Jewish name. A great warrior and prince."

"Who fell in battle along with his father and brothers," Jonathan finished. "I know the story." He looked away as memories of Deborah and his mother came, reminding him of another time and life he would never know again.

"It's not a story, it's a history. Were you named for him?"

"It doesn't matter. It's just a name someone had once, I have now, and someday someone else will have it."

"Names are important, even more than great wealth. If you know the history of your name, how is it you do not know that?"

"I know the Proverbs of Solomon, Nessa. Parchments full of an old man's musings." His agitated tone should tell her to drop it. She was poking into a part of his past he didn't wish to revisit.

"How can you say that? Solomon was the wisest of kings. He not only gave us the Proverbs, but built the temple as well. Surely you know of the temple in Jerusalem."

Her dismayed, no, disappointed look, snapped the last of his self-control. "Yes, I was taught of Solomon's temple. The Babylonians destroyed it."

"We rebuilt it," Nessa answered, with a proud gleam in her eye.

"No, Herod the great finished it. Not that it matters," he snapped. "There's nothing left of it now. Titus and his legions destroyed it. You do mean that temple, yes? The temple that lies broken and burned in the wastelands of Judea? Its silver and gold plundered and used to build his father's great arena in Rome? Whose priests and worshipers were crucified to line the road for miles? The rest made slaves and scattered across the empire? Do you mean—*that*—temple?"

He'd spent his breath in his anger and his harsh panting hurt his side. He'd hurt her too, because her eyes grew wet and red. She wiped at them with a sniff, pouring rain on the fire of his misdirected rage.

"Nessa, I'm sorry."

"Please excuse me." She hurried from the room, tangling in the sheet door in her haste.

He closed his eyes and breathed deep, a new fear rising through the haze of pain. Had slavery finally destroyed who he truly was, or revealed it?

Chapter 12 – Histories

Nessa didn't return. Hours passed until Jonathan could no longer endure the guilt of having released his pent anger on her. He would seek her out and apologize. Perhaps learn more about this place while doing so. The simple task of pulling the tunic over his head sent waves of pain everywhere, but he deserved it after the way he'd behaved. Standing again required tremendous effort, but the fur remained on the bed this time. He'd made it halfway to the sheet door when the cloth swept open.

Quintus strode in and pulled to an abrupt stop when their gazes met. "Get back in bed right now." He glanced around the room. "Where is Nessa?"

"I don't know. She left a while ago and hasn't returned."

"Get back in bed before you bleed again."

He could argue, but truthfully, he was already winded and wouldn't make it much further anyway. Returning to a sitting position on the thin cushion-covered table had him panting and wishing for unconsciousness. His back itched, his head ached and—

A string of curses preceded the arrival of someone else. A man stomped in after ripping aside the sheet door. He wore a wide leather belt, loincloth, and sandals—no tunic. Jonathan couldn't see his face because the man held his nose with both hands. Blood streamed through his fingers and down his neck.

Quintus frowned as the man threw himself on a stool. "Again?"

"Don't start," the man growled through the hand covering his face.

"You and Festus need to settle your differences."

"We will. In the arena." Hostility dripped from the man's voice and vehemence shone in his eyes. He reminded Jonathan of Manius. For that alone, he already didn't care for the newcomer.

"Hold still. I'm going to set your nose." Quintus put his thumbs on the sides of the man's nose and pushed the cartilage back into place with a painful snap. The man didn't even flinch. "How did he provoke you today?"

"Tried to steal my bread again. Thinks he's above the rest of us because he *chose* to be here." He grabbed the towel out of Quintus' approaching hand and held it to his nose. "He still imagines himself a legionnaire. Determined to conquer in the barracks as he *thinks* he did on the frontier. He's not even a first pole. I will avenge my homeland when I take his head one day."

"Yes, yes I know. When all the Romans are dead and you have avenged your homeland, only then will you rest. Hold the cloth there until it stops bleeding." Quintus took his time washing his hands in a large bowl of water.

The man must have felt Jonathan's stare. He turned to glare and pulled the blood-soaked cloth from his face. "Why don't you have a statue carved of me?"

"Leave him be, Seppios, he means you no disrespect," Quintus said.

Jonathan wasn't about to give the man bleeding like a sacrificed pig the satisfaction of looking away. He held his gaze without blinking.

Seppios rose to the open challenge.

Quintus moved between them in an instant, his substantial presence breaking their line of sight. "Enough. Return to training."

Seppios shifted to the side to resume his glaring. When he started toward Jonathan, Quintus pushed him back.

"Now. Or next time I'll leave your nose crooked."

A long moment passed before Seppios moved toward the door, his gaze still fixed on Jonathan. Even when the sheet door fell back between them and the man was gone, Jonathan could feel that gaze locked with his own.

"Don't let him vex you." Quintus shook his bald head and scratched his ear. "He hates all Romans. Even those who mean him no harm."

"Why?"

"He's a Celt. A conquered people, though you would never know it by Seppios. That entire land could accept Roman rule and their lives would change very little and even then for the better. They would pay taxes to Caesar instead of their king and in return be given roads, trade, protection, and peace. Instead, they fight for something they can't hear, see, or touch. Most to the death, though I'll never understand why."

Jonathan understood. "The man he spoke of, what did he mean when he said he chose to be here?"

"Festus is a contract gladiator. A retired legionnaire. He's still a second pole, because he insists on fighting like a soldier and not a gladiator."

"There's a difference?"

Quintus scoffed. "As much as Chian wine and that pig swill sold for a copper at the baths. Although you've probably never had Chian wine from the Greek isles but yes, a vast difference."

Jonathan almost asked him to explain. But killing was killing, and Jonathan had seen enough of it in the arena alongside his father when he'd had to attend. For some unknown reason it was Quintus' assumption he'd never tasted Chian wine that bothered him. He'd enjoyed many fine wines daily at his father's table. "I've had Chian wine. I've also had Caecubum wine."

Quintus' massive brows rose. "You're too young to have had Caecubum wine. Caesar Nero destroyed the vineyard that produced it when he built his canal to Ostia. And if a master ever caught a slave sipping their Chian wine he'd have him killed."

Jonathan didn't argue. His past was something best forgotten anyway.

The sheet door moved, but instead of Nessa another stranger entered. A well-dressed stranger. The older man's eyes perused Jonathan without ever reaching his face. "How is his recovery?"

"He will live. The rest is up to you and Clovis."

The resignation in Quintus' tone made Jonathan uneasy. The visitor finally looked Jonathan in the face. The man's stare was more menacing than Seppios and Manius combined.

"I am Caius Pullus, the greatest lanista south of the seven hills. You have the good fortune to be under the care of my physician and not in an unmarked grave. You begin training with the new batch of recruits in eight days, so enjoy the last rest you'll ever have. We train every day in my ludis."

The doctor stiffened. "He shouldn't—"

"Nonsense." The lanista raised his hand. "You and your little Jewess have done a fine job with him. The fresh air and exercise will do him good. You'll see."

The man left as swiftly as he'd entered, without a backward glance.

Quintus stared at the doorway long after the curtain dropped. Then he moved to his shelves and began preparing something Jonathan would probably have to drink. The banging and pounding as he did so competed with the sounds of the training through the wall behind him.

The curtain door swept open and there she was, avoiding his gaze with her red-rimmed eyes. "Are you having trouble finding something?"

Quintus' anger seemed to dissipate the moment he saw her. Perhaps she had that effect on everyone. "No. Have you been crying? Is it your foot?"

"I'm fine. What can I do?"

"Ready or not in eight days the slave—"

"Jonathan," Nessa said, still not looking his direction.

If Quintus minded his servant interrupting him, it didn't show. "Caius calls for Jonathan to begin training in eight days."

"That's too soon."

"I know." Quintus sighed.

She finally looked at him. The pity in her eyes chaffed, though he preferred it to anger.

"To further complicate matters, I must depart for Tarracina. A messenger brings word my sister is ill. The thieving sorcerers they call physicians there have done all they can."

"But that's halfway to Rome. Who will tend Jonathan?"

"You. I need you to remain here. The only way I'm going to calm Caius with being away for more than a day is to leave you here and have Alexander on standby."

"You hate Alexander."

"I know, but if Seppios and Tao tangle and do any real damage to each other, send for him at once. I need to speak with Caius. He vexed me so much earlier I didn't have a chance. You'll be fine."

She forced a tight smile.

Quintus patted her on the shoulder as one would a daughter. "You'll be fine."

Now they were alone, Jonathan could say what he needed to. "I'm sorry for earlier."

"You were already forgiven." She took his cup from the table beside him to refill it, still without looking at him. She brought him the cup and finally met his gaze. "Seventy times seven." Her smile returned. "But don't try for more needlessly."

Deborah would have liked her.

Nessa tucked her hands into her lap, and her expression turned serious. "How does someone know so much about a God he doesn't believe in?"

No sense reopening that wound any worse. He'd rather know about her. "How do you know so much about God?"

"My father was a priest in the temple you spoke of earlier."

His throat tightened.

"My mother never could convince him Messiah had come in the time of their grandfathers. But she never gave up. Or left his side. Even when he fell in the battle for the temple."

You're a callous fool.

"She never spoke of the things she saw there when Jerusalem was taken. Or what happened afterward. I know she survived where many did not, and what remained of our people Titus spread throughout the empire in his return to Rome. She would speak often of my father though and all he had taught her. She learned of Messiah in Jerusalem, from the daughter of a woman Jesus saved."

"I thought Jesus came to save everyone." *You're doing it again.*

Her mouth tightened just before she spoke. "I find your sarcasm refreshing. Indifference would be worse."

He wasn't being insolent to agitate her. Rather, he feared the day the stories would fail her in her moment of greatest need and destroy everything she'd believed in. As it had for him.

She leaned toward him and her face relaxed again. "If you know so much you know that's not what I meant. The woman who taught my mother about Jesus was the daughter of a woman caught in the act of adultery. Under the law the penalty for such an act is death by stoning."

"Not Rome's law."

A hiss died in her mouth as her lips tightened like a bowstring.

Jonathan almost laughed. That made three, but he had a long way to go before he'd need to worry. Four hundred and ninety times was a lot of forgiveness.

"Not the laws of Rome, the laws of Moses, but that's not the point, Jonathan."

She put enough emphasis on his name that he knew he needed to interrupt less. Otherwise she might leave again.

"Men had caught her in adultery and gathered to stone her. Jesus spoke on her behalf, telling the men gathered that if any of them were without sin they could throw the first stone. No one did. Someone can't experience God's intervention like that and not want to share it."

"That's a nice story. It was not among the many my mother or the woman who helped raise me knew, but they're all just stories. Like soldiers' tales of battle. Begun in a scrap of truth once, but with every retelling becoming less what is true and more what we want to be true." He downed the wine in his cup. It certainly wasn't Chian, but it quenched well enough.

"How can you say that?" Her fallen look pricked his conscience.

He hardened himself against it, determined she learn the truth from him now and not in a crisis, as he had. "I just know."

"You're wrong." She let her words hang there, as if daring him to refute her.

He admired her refusal to yield, however mistaken her beliefs. After all, he'd believed it once. "Then we agree to disagree."

"We nothing. I agree you're wrong. I can assure you it was no *story* that kept you from dying when you were brought here barely breathing." She stood up and crossed her arms.

Doing so accented her breasts, and he had to concentrate to stare at her face and not her chest. "You and Quintus saved me."

"God saved you. Even Quintus says you shouldn't have survived."

No, he shouldn't have. To tell her they should have let him die would only rile her more, and he was too tired to try to explain why. Tired from sitting up. Tired from trying to reason with this headstrong woman. Most of all tired of being bent to the will of others. No amount of brute force would ever be strong enough to break him again.

Perhaps she sensed it, for her demeanor softened. She took the empty cup he had been holding like a weapon and set it on the table. "Lord Caius is always firm to purpose. If you're to begin training in eight days, you need to lay back and rest. Less talking."

Jonathan eased back flat on the cushion. It hurt his back but felt good to relax too. She put her palm to his forehead, the same way his mother would check for the heat of fever anytime he sneezed as a child. He closed his eyes. She didn't lift her hand, but instead swept his hair back toward the crown of his head. Over and over. He opened his eyes, and an indefinable expression covered her face. He blinked and it was gone, her usual warm smile in place.

"Less thinking, too. Just rest." She pulled the fur up to cover his chest and began singing that song again. Through the now familiar sounds of men learning how to kill and be killed, her touch and her soft voice lulled his exhausted mind and body to sleep.

CHAPTER 13 – CHOICES

The days passed and moving became less painful. Simple tasks like feeding himself required less effort. With Quintus gone, Nessa experimented with a paste she made. Heavy and cold like mud, it stank but took the pain away better than the opium she still sprinkled in his wine. She said it would close the wounds faster, and Quintus could take the pins out soon. Jonathan had to take her at her word. He still hadn't seen his back but wasn't sure he wanted to after seeing his face.

He'd asked for a polished metal, a good knife, and oil that he might shave. She'd handed him a gleaming bronze disc the size of a bowl, and he raised it to see himself. The visage staring back at him sent a shiver of fear through him. It wasn't the yellow and green of the fading bruises or the beard he'd never seen himself in before. Instead it was the hardness. The anger.

Manius stared back at him from the metal.

Jonathan closed his eyes and shook his head to try to clear it. Then he gazed into the metal again.

Still there.

He brought the metal closer, almost to his nose, where he could only see his eyes. Green, like his mother's.

I'm nothing like him.

Nessa held the metal for him while he shaved, humming that song he'd come to enjoy as much as the faint scent of honey that clung to her. He looked and felt more himself when he finished. Even with the hardness permanently etched in his eyes.

He saw one other gladiator in that time—a short, stocky man called Amadi. Nessa spent a long time massaging the thigh the man had injured in training and then spreading her paste on it. Jonathan didn't like seeing her laugh with him. Not at all. When the man finally left, Jonathan hoped he wouldn't come back.

But this morning, she was the one who hadn't come back. Not only was she missing, but so were the customary sounds of training. A servant he'd never seen before entered at midday meal but carried only a single plate.

"Where is Nessa?"

The man ignored him, so Jonathan tried again in Latin instead of Greek. "Where is Nessa?"

Still no answer. He was either deaf or indifferent. Jonathan rose and covered the short distance to the table where his plate had been left. He felt much stronger today. The previous day he'd spent stretching, taking short walks about the room, and receiving a long massage from another slave that had done marvels for his arms and legs. He had protested the massage but Nessa insisted. As she promised, it had taken the stiffness from his muscles and joints.

He ventured toward the doorway after selecting a pear. It was overripe, the flesh softer than it should be, but he'd never been selective about food. A trait learned in poverty he never lost, even in the bounty of his father's house. He pulled the sheet door back to find a guard posted outside, as expected. They'd been switching off at routine intervals for days.

"Back inside, slave," the man said gruffly.

Jonathan eyed the *gladius* slung at the man's waist and the spear he held like a staff and decided to comply. That fight was coming—but not yet.

He finished his pear and had a piece of bread almost in his mouth when a new slave came in carrying sandals, followed by the guard. "Put these on. Caius is ready for you."

He set the bread down to take the shoes. Anxiety battered his resolve as he laced them to his feet. He had hoped to see her one last time. He took one last look at the room before following the slave. The guard trailed him as they passed through a long corridor Jonathan didn't remember.

It ended in an open courtyard. Men in wide leather belts and loincloths lined one side, Amadi and Seppios among them. Near the group, but not part of it, stood a tall, muscular, blond man with a sword at his belt and a whip in his hand. His iron gaze fell upon Jonathan. That was hardness. A lifetime of it.

Chained to a wall behind him hung a man whose back had been laid open, probably by the whip in the blond man's hand. How had he not heard the man's screams? Probably because they beat him senseless before whipping him, by the purple marks all over the man's face and neck.

Never again.

The slave Jonathan followed veered off, and the guard behind him used his spear to point Jonathan toward a group in the center of the yard. Ten or twelve men stood gathered, wearing simple slave dress. A few wore chains. One in a tunic and fine toga stood out like a stallion in a herd of pigs. Jonathan moved toward the rear of the group but searched the people watching them for that round face full of light—one last glimpse of her before the end.

Beneath a balcony across from them a large wooden door opened. Caius Pullus emerged in a tunic and toga fit for an emperor. He strode toward Jonathan and his group before stopping beside the blond man with the whip.

"I am Caius Pullus, lanista to the gods themselves. If you are stronger than you know, you might one day be worthy to call yourself a gladiator."

The lanista paused to look each of them over in turn. "If you survive the training and pass the final test, you will be given my mark and join the gladiators. Those of you who do not will be sold. Slave or contract, I make no distinction. So for the freeman among you choosing this life for the next three years, do so with that knowledge. I am looking for one thing and one thing only. Champions. Anything less is a waste of coin."

Men like him were all the same—bent on greed. Jonathan spat at the ground at his feet.

"Clovis is my right hand." Caius gestured to the tall blond man who had the whip and sword at his belt. "Some of you will break under the weight of his instruction. Others will flourish. Learn all you can from him. My reputation as a lanista and your very lives depend upon it."

Clovis stepped forward. "You will now come two at a time, and swear the gladiator oath to our master, Lord Caius. In doing so, you take control of your own destiny. Some of you for the first time."

The man in the toga and another man stepped forward. Both sank to one knee with their fist to their chest and repeated Clovis' words. Two by two they went. Some eagerly, some reluctantly, five pairs in all. Jonathan and the trembling slave beside him remained. Clovis motioned them forward. Jonathan remained rooted, as did the slave beside him, who'd begun to weep.

"You receive the sword either way," Clovis said. "Give the oath and it's placed in your hand. Do not and it goes in your neck."

A guard stepped forward from the shadow of the balcony and drew his sword. The action emboldened Jonathan. It crippled the weeping man beside him, who dissolved into a heap of rattling chain.

Jonathan stared in defiance at Clovis, then Caius. The cords of the lanista's neck stood out while Jonathan channeled every rebellious thought he'd ever had into the gaze he kept leveled at the lanista. In the corner of his vision, he saw the guard move behind the slave and his sword rise. The man screamed as the sword flashed down. The courtyard fell silent and the shape of the guard disappeared behind him. He kept his gaze on Caius, a man so like Manius and Valentina he now embodied Jonathan's hatred for all three of them.

No more whips. No more chains. No more feeling like a caged animal instead of a man. He could go to his knee to make the killing thrust clean as the slave's had been. But he didn't. He would die on his feet. Not his knees.

Caius held a hand high to still the guard ready to execute him. "Quintus assured me you had the strongest will to survive of anyone he has ever seen. The ungratefulness you show by throwing your life away after I spent so much coin to save it is insulting."

"But I am grateful," Jonathan said. "I'm grateful you will not profit from my death and even more so I've cost you something already. I know Latin. The word lanista means butcher, and I will not be sacrificed on the sand for coin. In death I am at last my own master."

Caius' face flooded with crimson. Jonathan heard the guard behind him shift, readying to thrust the sword straight through him. He closed his eyes, tipping his face to the sun. His life would end here, but it would end his own.

"Wait," Caius yelled.

Jonathan opened his eyes.

A grim smile on the man's face rocked his resolve. The lanista waved off the guard and motioned for the trainer. "Clovis, bring Brutus to the arena. Then have this *master of his own fate* taken to meet him there."

Laughter rippled through the gladiators. Guards advanced all around him. They meant to make him fight anyway. Jonathan grabbed for a sword, a spear, anything so they would have to cut him down.

But it was the road from Rome all over again.

There were too many and they were too fast. He struggled but they still succeeded in chaining him. The pain in his body threatened to pull him under again as they dragged him kicking and cursing from the courtyard through a dark tunnel. The stone scouring his back turned to sand when they emerged in sunlight. The guards threw him facedown into the hot sand, pinning him to the ground. The cold metal shackles were taken from his wrists and the guards backed away. He needed to charge them again, but his back and sides had taken a beating and it hurt to breathe.

When he finally had the strength to climb to his feet, he was alone in a great expanse of sand. He didn't recognize it as the arena at first, because he'd never seen it from the center looking out. This arena wasn't round. The wall forming the long side gave it two distinct corners where it met the wall curving along the stands for spectators arched around it. He had no intention of fleeing this Brutus like a coward, but if he did, he'd be cornered either direction. The stands above him filled with gladiators, guards, recruits, and slaves. Still no Nessa, and for that he was glad.

The trainer approached the lower wall and tossed a short wooden pole into the sand a few paces from Jonathan. Instinct demanded he pick it up, but he fought it. His life would end his own.

Caius Pullus remained standing at the top, his arms crossed. "Slave," he yelled. "This is my answer."

A heavy set of hinges squealed behind him. He turned to see a gate sliding open. This was it. Gladiators were meant to make a show of killing, but Jonathan would not make a show of dying. He would have to fall on Brutus' sword quickly. One moment of courage and—

Over the groaning metal a new sound carried. The fearsome roar crushed his resolve.

From the shadows of the gate emerged the biggest lion he had ever seen.

Brutus.

Chapter 14 – The Lion

The lion trotted toward Jonathan, mouth open and gathering speed.

Not like this.

Jonathan dove for the stick near his feet.

The lion roared and the soft booms of paws slapping sand quickened.

He grabbed the stick and turned, wielding it like a spear. The stands erupted with cheers, but he trained every sense on the open mouth and roaring lion running straight at him. He couldn't hurl the short wooden shaft like a spear and risk missing. Not if he was to avoid a gruesome death. He bellowed a cry as loud as the lion and charged the beast as fast as his legs would move in the shifting sand. He dropped to his knee and slid low, missing the lion's massive paw as it swung where his head had been. The stick entered the gaping mouth between the fangs and he held on, their momentum driving it deep into the lion's throat. He clung tighter as his face slammed into the thick mane and the lion's chest crashed into him.

The strangled gagging was deafening and the crushing weight of the lion was going to kill him. Fur filled his mouth and nose as the animal writhed. Sunlight and air reached him and he threw himself to the side, scrambling in the sand to roll free. The lion collapsed on his leg, pinning him down again.

Blood poured from the lion's mouth in torrents, turning the sand to dark mud near Jonathan's head. He lay panting in the hot breath of the lion where the stick still impaling it jutted from its throat.

He'd done it. He'd refused to bend to the fear, as his father taught him. He'd chased a lion and lived. He turned his head toward the stands. Clovis ran toward them, his sword already drawn. Death would come now. A quick thrust of the sword and it would all be over. *My life ends my own.*

Metal pierced flesh, but he felt nothing, other than the fire in his leg spreading to his back. He opened his eyes.

Clovis' sword stood in the great cat's side. He pulled the blade free and stepped toward Jonathan.

"Stop," Caius shouted from the stands. "Don't kill him."

Clovis lowered the sword.

Guards came through the gate. Chains rattled between them.

It was never going to end.

Jonathan bellowed a scream of pure rage. Strength like he'd never known flooded his veins and he kicked and kicked at the carcass trapping his leg. The lion's body rocked enough that his foot almost slid free. He kicked harder, sweat and sand stinging his eyes. The sandal straps broke and his foot flew free like an arrow.

He leapt to his feet and rushed Clovis. The man slipped to the side and swung his sword in an arc. Jonathan didn't try to duck but Clovis flicked his wrist. The flat side of the blade struck Jonathan like a lightning bolt. He crumpled to the bloody sand. Nothing would move. Not his fingers or his head. Not even his tongue and the curses streaming from him wouldn't turn to sound.

The chains were close. The guards were surrounding him. Please. *Please.* His body woke up and he clawed for the trainer's leg. The man kicked him in the stomach. White spots flashed through his vision as Jonathan grabbed for the man's sandal and caught a fistful of straps.

"Enough." Clovis' sword swung again.

Clovis wiped his blade clean on the lion's fur. "Get him to a cell."

Now that the danger had passed, Caius jumped down from the stands as he had a moment ago. "I said not to kill him."

"He's subdued, not dead, unlike Brutus." Clovis sheathed his sword so forcefully he almost tore the leather casing free of his belt. Brutus' death was as much their fault as the slave's. Caius for not listening that this was too risky, and his for pitying the slave at the last moment and throwing him the *pugil* stick.

"Take him to the medicus chamber," Caius ordered the guards who were fastening the slave into shackles.

"Nessa isn't here. Quintus sent a messenger for her last night. Even if they both were, that slave belongs in a cell. Better yet, in the mines or the afterlife. Anywhere but this ludis."

"No. The courage required to mock me in my own ludis, then to chase a charging lion with a stick? That kind of courage can't be taught, Clovis. We must harness it. "

"And if we can't? His defiance will spread to the other men like plague."

"Find a way." The lanista's tone left no arguments. "Keep two guards on him at all times. See if you can patch him up until Quintus and his little Jewess return. If not, I'll send for Alexander."

The guards dragged the slave away by his wrists to the barracks.

That left but one body to contend with. "What of Brutus?"

"Have him skinned. Take the pelt to the priests at the temple of Mars for a votive offering from the House of Pullus. Feed the rest of him to the others and work with the beast master to train a new leader. The cats turn as much profit as the men, and they're better behaved."

Clovis loathed the entire process the first time. The idea of repeating it even more. "You know what that requires."

"I'll see if I can buy some old or sick slaves at a good price. You know what the editors of the games pay for a lion that won't cower by the doors and make the crowd angry. One that can show the others what to do."

"I have not been away from the arena so long that I don't remember."

"Good. Make me a new lead lion and a new gladiator. Find a way. He may not fear death, but he clearly has some preference as to the manner. Threaten crucifixion, castration, whatever it takes."

That was not the way, but Caius never listened. The dead lion at their feet was proof.

"Yes, my lord."

The splitting ache in Jonathan's head was almost an old friend. Sand covered his body and now his same bed in the medicus chamber. Back here meant they were going to patch him up again. He wanted to die. How much clearer could he be?

Two guards stood near the doorway—still no Nessa. He sat up slowly and pulled the edge of his tunic up to see what hurt the most. The lion had clawed his upper thigh. A long wound, but not deep. At least from what he could tell under the sand and drying blood. Not much damage for having survived a charging lion. Maybe he should have just let it eat him.

The trainer entered. He stopped an arm's length away and stared at him with those cold, hard eyes. An old scar ran from his ear to his jaw. Jonathan could imagine the man's face covered in the blue paint of the Druids as he and his countrymen charged the armies of Rome.

"I don't understand you, slave. You act eager to die but twice now have fought to live. Explain."

Jonathan refused to answer. He no longer took orders from anyone.

The trainer put his hands on his hips. "Try harder to speak."

"Try harder to understand."

One of the guards approached the bed and raised his arm to strike him.

The trainer raised an open hand and halted the guard. "I have seen many men in this place who embrace death but none quite like you. Make me understand why. If you can."

"Why did you kill the lion?"

"Its death was certain and it was suffering. It would have been cruel not to."

"Then you should understand me."

The trainer studied him for a long moment. "Your death is far from certain, and the life of a gladiator a far cry from suffering. Ask any one of them who survived the mines and quarries before taking up the sword in the arena."

"You know nothing of suffering."

"Enough of his mouth, Clovis." The guard who tried to strike him earlier reached for his sword.

"Leave us," Clovis said.

"Caius ordered him guarded at all times."

"Don't insult me. I will guard him. Leave us until I order you to return."

The man followed the other guard through the sheet door but gave Jonathan a glare as sharp as the weapon he'd tried to draw. Clovis set the whip in his hand on the table beside him and sat on Nessa's stool. He regarded him a long moment.

Jonathan wanted to look away but somehow couldn't.

"You don't really want to die," Clovis finally said.

"You know nothing of what I want."

"So there is something you want." Clovis crossed his arms and continued to stare at him.

Of course. Freedom. "It doesn't matter anymore. Nothing does." The claw wound in his leg throbbed, and he raised his knee to examine it.

"Jonathan."

He'd become so accustomed to 'slave' from anyone besides Nessa that hearing his given name snapped his head up.

Clovis leaned forward, his stare intense. "You don't really want to die. You just no longer know why you want to live."

The truth of that statement settled deep within. No one had ever put it into words before. "I'm not going to fight. Not for the bloodlust of a mob or a man who profits from it."

"No one has ordered you to fight yet."

"What was the lion?"

"A failed execution."

"My apologies." Jonathan laced his tone with mock sincerity.

"You are refusing a life you know nothing of, in favor of death. Something you also know nothing of. That is not fearless, or noble."

Noble. Jonathan almost laughed. If Clovis only knew.

"Train with the others. Learn something of the life you so hastily dismiss."

"To what purpose? Finding myself on the other end of a sword held by a man who will kill me or spare me on the whim of another? I won't live like that. Not another day. Not ever again."

Clovis studied him for a long moment. "Why do you assume you'll be the loser?"

The question stunned him. More so that he didn't have an answer. What if he were the victor? Was that better or worse, to have to kill for the same blood sport he refused to die for?

"Train under me. You may find there is more about yourself you don't know. You can choose to throw your sword away at any time, if you have the courage to pick it up first. You needn't decide now. I can clean up that scratch until Quintus and his slave girl return."

"Where is she?"

Clovis' blond brow lifted at the question. "Fond of the little one?"

He shouldn't have asked.

"Well, I'd prefer her to my battlefield medicine too." Clovis gathered water and a cloth and scrubbed the sand from the wound as Frona would scrub a floor. When he finished with the gash in Jonathan's leg he went to work cleaning his back. Jonathan bit his lip to stifle a curse when the trainer rinsed his handiwork in salted water rather than wine. He could have sworn the man enjoyed it. Clovis wrapped the wound on his leg so tight the lower half felt as if it might shrivel up and fall off.

"On your feet now. Follow me."

Jonathan rose from the bed and the pain in his leg vanished under the tightness of the dressing. They followed the perimeter of the courtyard to a row with many doors, all standing open. Some of the gladiators training in the courtyard paused their sparring to stare at Jonathan and Clovis as they passed.

"This one is yours." Clovis entered a small cell. A long, low wooden bed identical to his in the medicus chamber filled one side. A table with no stool held a clay pitcher and clay cup. In the opposite corner beside the door sat the clay chamber pot. Clean, since he'd seen it before he smelled it.

Clovis took a small, corked vial from his belt and set it on the table near the cup.

"What is that?"

"Hemlock."

Jonathan couldn't believe it. "A poison?"

"Men who truly want to die usually find a way. Some men take the oath to avoid a sword to the throat, not because they intend to honor their vow. We find them with cloth-stuffed throats or stabbed with a broken table leg they sharpened on the stone floor. I'm not going to waste my time on you if *this*"—he held up the vial—"is really all you want."

He returned it to the table and looked Jonathan squarely in the face. "It gets no easier than this. Drink it all with a full cup of water. You will fall asleep and never wake again. In this life at least."

Clovis sighed heavily and left, shutting the cell door behind him. The bolt clanked into place, and his footsteps retreated into the distance. Jonathan sat on the edge of the bed and rubbed his still aching head. He stared at the vial until a slave brought him a crust of bread and a pear.

The texture of the bread resembled sandal leather, hobnails and all, but it gave him something to do besides think about the poison. The juice of the pear ran down his chin, reminding him of the many times Nessa had held a cup to his lips. When the distraction of the food was gone, he listened to the gladiators through the small grate of metal bars in his door.

The one called Tao was cursed often. Sometimes even his mother. Those curses usually followed a particularly loud crack of wooden weapons or thump of a body hitting the ground. He recognized Seppios' angry voice, yelling for a new sword and after some time, a new partner. The second one must have fared better. The relentless cracking lasted longer at least.

A snap of a whip preceded a sudden quiet, followed by many footsteps and the sounds of doors being closed and locked all around him. Soon the square of sunlight on the shadowed wall faded completely. After a time, a faint torch glow replaced it.

Alone in the faint light, he stared at the vial that was now a malevolent presence filling the tiny room. *It gets no easier than this.* The man was brilliant. With a single glass bottle, he'd given him complete control of his fate. The power of the choice was exhilarating, and that was cause to reconsider over and over again.

Hours passed like minutes. Every memory Jonathan ever had played through his mind. But there was one memory that stood out from the others, that settled his indecision.

In it, he wore his newly acquired *toga virilis,* a gift for his fifteenth birthday. Now that he was officially a man, he would accompany his father to the games. His mother and Deborah had hated them, but the way Manius carried on about them, Jonathan had been curious.

The morning beast shows had been exciting, seeing various animals chained to each other in fights to the death. A bear had made a mess of a bull, but not before being gored so badly it had to be carted from the arena by a slew of slaves, a hundred arrows sticking up from its fur like some great sea urchin.

It had been the three elephants that made his stomach quiver. After being paraded around the arena, the *beastiarii's* arrows wouldn't pierce the animal's hide, so they turned to spears. The crowd went wild when the biggest elephant charged, trampling a few of the hunters before it too looked like a sea urchin. A baby elephant stood in the center of the arena, the hunters surrounding it with their spears while the mother elephant stood near her dead mate.

The hunters began to stab the baby over and over, its feeble cries enraging the mother, who shrieked and knocked hunters aside right and left with her trunk. She stood over the body of her dying child, covering him with her shadow as if to shield him from the pack of hunters.

Jonathan's throat had tightened, his eyes burning. The little trunk rose slowly, covered in blood and sand, and entwined with his mother's. He wanted to scream for them to leave her alone. One by one each *beastiarius* retrieved its spear from the fallen elephant and surrounded the mother guarding her dying calf. He rose from his seat as the spears were thrown. Blood poured from every wound covering her gray skin. Her legs buckled and her great ears twisted and flapped like loose sails before she fell, crushing her baby.

Jonathan had sunk slowly to his seat, unnoticed by the others.

"It's a shame about the little one," one of his father's colleagues said. "Someone could have had it for a pet."

"They don't stay small. I purchased a tiger cub last year for my wife. She adored it, but it kept killing too many of the slaves when it grew. I made a gift of it to the emperor for his December games. She raises those orange and white bearded fish now."

Slaves in the arena sank great metal hooks into the carcasses of the elephants, and teams of oxen hauled them away. He had to look away when they dragged the baby out by its trunk. Another group of slaves emerged and removed the bloody sand, raking it smooth for the midday executions. After the carnage of the beast hunts, he doubted his ability to endure the executions.

He excused himself to purchase refreshment for him and his father, taking his time about it. When the cheering of the crowd died down again, he returned to their seats with wineskins and a basket of cut fruit for the main event—the gladiator contests.

The first round wasn't as bad as the elephants. There were so many fighting *en masse* it made it difficult to tell what was really happening. No one was killed. The fallen were allowed to leave the arena through the gate of life.

It was the last match that had given him nightmares for days afterward. A long fight the crowd approved of, by their incessant cheering. The referee had separated the pair of men after a particularly solid blow. One of them stumbled and fell to his knees. He leaned forward and put his sword hand out to keep from falling on his face, and with the other, slowly raised two fingers.

The crowd began to wail their disapproval.

"What's happening?" Jonathan asked his father.

"The man gives the *missio*, conceding defeat and asking mercy of Domitian."

"They're not men, Cornelius, they're gladiators," said the man who had earlier bemoaned the dead elephant calf. "*Inferi*."

Jonathan had not heard that term before, even in his extensive studies with Dionysius. "What does inferi mean?" He whispered the question to his father, lest he embarrass him if it should be something he should already know.

"Lowest of the low."

"Oh."

The emperor rose from his seat in the *pulvis* overlooking the arena. He surveyed the fifty thousand people in the crowd. What was he looking for? Jonathan watched the man on his knees, still holding up his two fingers. His victorious opponent stood to the side, sword ready and head trained toward the emperor. Domitian extended his hand and slashed the air with his thumb.

"What's happening?"

The kneeling man slowly lowered his arm and the one standing raised his sword high. Before his father could answer, the sword fell and severed the fallen gladiator's head from his body. Screams of joy erupted everywhere and the men around Jonathan laughed. The victor walked to the helmet where it had rolled and picked it up. He shook it until the loser's head fell free and rolled at his feet. The crowd roared like a mighty beast with a single voice.

Jonathan froze.

The head on the sand had black hair. Like his. A moment ago it had been a man—with desires and fears and maybe a family.

"Cornelius," a voice nearby said. "Your son does not wilt like a woman at the sight of a severed head." The man clapped his father on the shoulder. "You should be proud, my friend. Your son is a true Roman."

A true Roman.

Jonathan uncorked the vial and poured it into the empty cup. He filled the cup with water from the pitcher until he felt it on the fingertip he had placed just inside the rim. Slowly, he raised it to his lips and drained the cup. "Forgive me," he said in a choked whisper, to the memory of his father—and the God he swore no longer existed.

Chapter 15 – Lied To

The metallic scrape of a door bolt roused Jonathan awake like cold water. Memories of yesterday flooded through him as he sat up—alive. The door swung open and sunlight silhouetted a hulking form. The man stepped into the shade of the small cell.

Clovis.

Jonathan swung his legs to the side and came to his feet, ignoring the smattering of aches and pains. "Why am I still alive?"

The trainer eyed the empty bottle of poison on the table and frowned before crossing his arms. "There are two ways to forge a gladiator. Neither is easy, but you have chosen the hardest." He picked up the empty bottle and cork and refastened them. "It was spiced nectar, not hemlock."

"Why?"

Clovis snapped his fingers and tucked the empty vial in his belt. A slave entered and handed him a small bundle of leather and cloth. "Now I know how committed you are to resisting, you should know that I will be as committed in my task of training you."

This couldn't be happening. Lies—more lies so people could still take from him with impunity. "Knowing I'd rather die?"

"You want to die, fine. Do it in the arena. I will teach you how." He dropped the sandals, belt, and loincloth at Jonathan's feet. "Should you attempt escape or provoke the guards, rest assured a quick, easy death will not be your fate. I will chain you to a wall, cut open your belly, and let the carrion birds feed on your guts while you die slowly, and painfully."

The lion would have been merciful compared to vultures fighting over his entrails, their claws digging into his flesh while they feasted. He stared at Clovis in disgust. "I'm sure I wouldn't be the first."

His cold blue eyes flashed. "You're right. My father was fortunate enough to die in battle against the Romans. My older brother was not. As for the fate my mother suffered, there aren't enough men in the ludis to kill you the way she died."

Jonathan's mouth went dry as terrible images filled his mind.

Clovis walked backward toward the door. "Dress quickly. The last man to the courtyard gets lashed."

So Clovis and his master wanted to continue to lie and play games. Jonathan would play along then, for now. He stripped off the dirty tunic and dressed in the loincloth, wide belt, and sandals. Clovis had said if he had the courage to pick up the sword, he could throw it down at any time. And Jonathan had the perfect time in mind.

He elicited a few open stares making his way to join the other recruits. The men had already paired into little groups, eager to keep their distance from him. The gladiators were in various stages of stretching and each already had a shield and practice weapon at his feet, except for those Jonathan recognized as *retiarii,* who had a net and trident instead of a shield and sword or spear. Clovis showed no expression when they made eye contact. Jonathan turned to the balcony above them, but Caius wasn't there looking down like the god he must imagine himself to be.

A sharp pain stung his back and he winced.

Clovis pulled the lash of his whip back toward him and coiled it. "Don't be last again."

Jonathan bit back the curse that almost came from his lips. Another bite of the whip wasn't worth it.

"Pick up a beam," Clovis snapped. "It's time to work." He barked orders all morning, snapping his whip when they weren't followed fast enough. Jonathan and the other recruits shouldered the heavy beams and were made to perform endless maneuvers with them. One by one the beams began to fall, along with the men who dropped them.

Jonathan lasted longer than he expected. When he couldn't take another step and collapsed, he lay panting beneath the beam. Clovis' whip hit him on the back. It must have been in a healing place, because it hurt so much. He rolled the beam off and came to his knees, then his feet, glaring at the trainer. Hoisting the beam took two attempts, but he finally shouldered it and fell in step with the others.

Blood seeped through the linen binding on his thigh. If Clovis saw the bright red stain coloring the dusty cloth, he ignored it. Jonathan tried to, though the ache became more intense every hour.

Finally Clovis called for the midday meal. Jonathan lined up last of the recruits, who would be served after the gladiators. A slave handed him a bowl with what looked like the same stew he'd eaten with Nessa. His hunger burned as much as his muscles, and he'd hasten down anything short of raw meat.

As in the courtyard, a dividing line existed between gladiators and recruits. There were no empty tables or benches and the few with room enough for him held men whose faces said he was unwelcome. Too hungry to care, he made his way to the corner and sat on the floor against the wall. His bowl was halfway to his lips when a familiar voice called out.

"Lion killer, are you too good to eat with the other maggots in training?"

Seppios. The Roman-hater with the bloody nose. A sudden quiet replaced the laughter, warning him a moment before Seppios appeared from between the rows of tables, stopping so close to him Jonathan had to look up to see him.

"Did you not hear me, maggot?"

Seppios kicked the bowl.

Hot broth splashed Jonathan's face. The wooden bowl clanged and rolled in a circle on the floor like a cart that had lost a wheel. Seppios laughed along with the other men.

Jonathan let him laugh. Long enough he wouldn't be watching for it. Then as fast as he could move his good leg, he kicked him in the groin. Seppios hunched over with a grunt and Jonathan sprang to his feet and put his knee in the man's face. As his head snapped up from the blow Jonathan slammed his elbow into the back of the man's neck. Seppios dropped to his hands and knees like a dog. Jonathan had received that series of blows so many times at the hands of Fabricius Clavis' guards, but never thought he could have given them.

For a single breath, no one moved.

Gladiators jumped to their feet. Benches flipped and curses flew. Seppios straightened with murder in his eyes. Jonathan was trapped in the corner with nowhere to go but through them. His quick death was coming after all.

The crack of a whip stilled his would-be attackers. "Enough," Clovis' voice boomed. "If you have time to brawl like infants you must be finished eating. Back to training."

Angry protests and groans rumbled until the whip snapped again. One by one the men filed out, with glares in Jonathan's direction. All except Tao, who stood calmly from his bench and drained his stew like wine before leaving. Jonathan shook the last chunks of food from his tunic and moved to join the others.

Clovis stepped in his path and jammed the butt of his whip hard into Jonathan's chest. "My men never kick an opponent in the groin. Am I understood?"

"He attacked me unprovoked. I—"

"I know he attacked you. I watched. You should have been on your feet long before he reached you. Even so, you defend an inferior position by forcing an equal disadvantage for your opponent. If you'd made that kick sweep from the inside and pulled a standing leg from under him, you would have brought him down to you. This is what you will learn in training. But first you must learn to stop being so reckless."

Clovis stepped aside for him to pass. Jonathan refused to rub at the tender spot the whip left on his chest and returned to his exercises with renewed purpose. There was nothing reckless about his plan. Nothing at all.

Completing the day's work required his remaining strength, and several times only the sheer will to prevail kept him moving. Eventually enough blood filled the cloth wrap it began to run down his knee. Clovis ordered a slave to bring him fresh linen and the trainer changed it in the middle of the training ground. The cut didn't look any worse than yesterday, but it didn't look better either. He wanted some news of Nessa and Quintus, but the way Clovis' brow arched when he asked after her yesterday had given him an uneasy feeling. He wouldn't do it again.

Some of the deepest cuts on his back must have reopened too under the strain of training. Sweat ran into them and burned the way Valentina's kiss had. There was no relief from that and Clovis repeated over and over between cracks of his whip that gladiators embrace pain.

Every so often, Clovis left the recruits and walked among the paired gladiators on the other side of some sacred line running through the middle of the training yard. He would break them into new pairs and send some to work on hitting wooden poles with their wooden training swords. Finally, Jonathan understood the one sound he'd never been able to figure out while recovering.

Seppios' glare as he hacked away at one of the poles left no question the man imagined Jonathan's head instead of the scarred wooden pole sunk deep into the ground.

When the day's training ended, Jonathan followed Clovis to a new cell. This one had no bed, no table, and a copper pot rather than clay. Once inside, Clovis ordered him to strip. He would get his garments and sandals back in the morning. Too tired to fight, Jonathan handed them over. Clovis locked him in and Jonathan settled gingerly on the stone floor. It was too dirty to lay on his back and too cold to lay on his front. He curled onto his side in the corner farthest from the door.

Firstly, he still controlled his fate more than they knew. They might have taken the table with its legs that could be sharpened into stakes, and the bed with its suffocating mattress. They might have taken his loincloth and belt, which when laced through the iron bars of the grate in the door would work splendidly. What Clovis didn't take was the long length of linen wrapped around his leg that would work even better.

But something besides fatigue kept Jonathan from strangling himself.

Hitting Seppios had felt good. Really good. He'd never willfully inflicted pain on another living thing in his life. Except for biting Valentina and punching the bully in his childhood. He'd thought about it often enough with Manius and more recently Caius Pullus, but imagining and experiencing were two very different things. He stretched out enough to pillow his head with his arm. If it had felt that good to hit Seppios over a spilled bowl of food, how much better would it feel to punish Manius for a stolen life? Valentina for sending him here? He envisioned their faces as they knelt before him, begging for their lives.

A vision of Nessa came. Humble and forgiving, of both his temper and the wound he'd caused her with the broken pitcher. The contrast jarred him, like breathing hot smoke instead of clean air. He remembered that too.

He'd been ten years old when fire engulfed the city. Pulled tight between his mother and Deborah like a blanket strung on a line to dry, they'd run hand in hand through the smoky darkness of the streets. Charred plaster and burning pieces of beam and cinders rained from above. Men, women, and children shouted and ran every direction. Dogs barked and yelped as buildings began to groan and collapse around them, silencing the screams until they returned worse than before. Those cries tore Jonathan apart while the hot smoke burned his eyes and throat. Harder days would follow, after the flames died.

He'd slept on the bare ground then too, much like now. He'd been strong for his mother, who would touch his hair and tell him not to fear. Deborah said God had a plan for them, to give them hope and a future. Jonathan didn't want hope and a future. He wanted bread and a bed, but had kept that to himself. Deborah had survived similar devastation during Titus' siege of Jerusalem, and her practical knowledge did more to get them through that time than their prayers.

Perhaps Deborah had known Nessa's mother. Had they shared a dipper of water, a beating, or worse, on the march from Jerusalem? Did Deborah still live? What of the women he'd sent to her over the years? Was his father still alive? Had he been searching for him and if not, what did he think happened? He'd known him only four years and had been parted from him for about that same span of time. He still missed him as he still missed his mother.

He reached for his chest, but remembered her carving was gone as soon as he touched his sweat-damp skin. She existed only in his memory now. The God she'd loved and served had ignored their prayers. God had plenty of chances to deliver her and him like the people in Deborah's stories. His favorite back then had been the prophet in the king's lion pit. God had sent an angel that shut the mouths of the lions and kept his faithful prophet from harm.

Jonathan felt a smile form on his lips—his first since waking up in this awful place.

He hadn't needed God to deliver him from any lion.

He'd killed it himself.

Clovis worked them hard sunrise to sunset. The other men still avoided Jonathan, but no one kicked his food anymore. He still ate on the floor in the corner like that first day, but in peace. He still slept on the floor of his bare cell but after three days he no longer woke with aches and pains. Clovis had pulled the metal thorns from his back and his scalp yesterday, cursing Quintus to Hades and back for not returning in time to take them out before the skin grew over them any worse. That had hurt, but not as much as the saltwater rinse afterward.

Caius watched them train twice a day from his balcony. The way he grinned at Jonathan whenever their gazes met said the man thought he'd won. When the right moment manifested, Jonathan would show him he had not.

This morning Clovis demonstrated a new exercise with the beam. Instead of carrying it on their shoulders and practicing footwork, the beam would rest on the ground and they would jump it side to side while holding their arms straight up. That was going to tax his wounded leg and his still tender ribs.

The hinges of the main gate groaned and he glanced up. Likely another visitor to join Caius on the balcony. But Quintus entered instead, carrying a large leather bag from his shoulder. Jonathan's breathing sped and he started toward the gate. Nessa entered, walking well and appearing unharmed, but her usual smile was gone. Her shoulders slumped beneath her tunic that was covered in a thick layer of dust. How far had Quintus made her walk?

Clovis' whip cracked. He looked from Nessa to Jonathan and shook his head.

Jonathan fell in sequence with the others. It would be enough for now that he'd seen her.

Alone in his cell that night, he tried to think up ways to see her, talk with her. Tell her about killing the lion. The easiest way would be an injury. But wouldn't she and Quintus want to see him anyway, to check his back and his leg? Why had they not already? Waiting would draw less attention—if he could stand it.

Sweat glistened on his arms in the morning sun. He could already feel it gathering between his shoulders and across his chest. Even so, the beam was getting lighter to lift and easier to carry. Caius took his place on the balcony but today he had guests. A man with silver hair wearing a fine white toga stood with a young woman.

Clovis snapped his whip and Jonathan looked away to avoid finding himself at the end of that whip when it snapped again. He threw himself into his maneuvers as did the others, but listened hard through the cracks of the sparring from the gladiator side.

"Behold the finest gladiators in the empire, Magistrate. You've made a wise investment."

"Vineyards and ships are an investment. Sponsoring games is an unfortunate tax of office."

Jonathan stole a glance to the trio. His gaze locked with that of the young woman. Had she been watching him?

"I would like a demonstration before I sign away 25,000 denarii."

"Then you shall have it, Magistrate." Caius leaned over the balcony. "Clovis, assemble the men."

Clovis crossed to the gladiator's side of the yard. "Formation."

The gladiators broke from their sparring pairs and formed a single line of men, their weapons and shields held at a proud attention that would rival a Roman legion.

"Tao, step forward," Caius called from above. "The champion of the House of Pullus, Magistrate."

Tao took a single step forward and nodded in respect. Something Jonathan would never do.

"Seppios, step forward," Caius ordered.

Seppios stepped forward but did not nod. Was it because Caius Pullus was Roman, or did Seppios simply hate the man as much as he did?

"Wait." The young woman raised a pointed finger between them. "I want to see him."

Caius blanched as he turned toward her father. "Apologies, Magistrate, but those are new recruits. They have yet to be trained with weapons."

He had a weapon. One their whips and chains would be powerless against.

The magistrate stiffened and raised his chin. "Even the newest army recruit knows how to hold a sword, Caius. I see no danger in it, unless, of course, you doubt the quality of your recruits."

An uneasy tension sparked the air. Caius turned toward him, his gaze narrowing. "Jonathan. Step forward."

Jonathan kept his expression empty while a slave brought him a wooden sword and shield. Seppios and the other gladiators' incredulous stares sang with contempt as he crossed the dividing line.

Clovis cocked his head to the side, and Seppios fell back in line. The cords on his neck threatened to tear his skin open. Tao didn't seem bothered, but he never did. The opponent didn't matter to him.

Jonathan couldn't agree more. He stopped a short distance away and waited for Tao to assume a fighting stance.

Tao faced him and dropped into a low crouch, with sword and shield raised.

Jonathan flung his wooden sword into the sand and a collective gasp echoed through the training ground. He turned to smile at Caius, who gripped the balcony edge as if it were his throat.

"Pick it up," Caius ordered.

There was enough space between Caius and his guests. Jonathan would have to be fast. Arrows would be flying for his chest from the guards on the wall as soon as they realized what he was about to do. He grabbed the round wooden shield by the edges, twisted, and flung it for Caius' head.

The girl screamed, her father cowered behind raised arms, and Caius ducked as the shield slapped the balcony edge and fell to the ground. Clovis' whip whistled through the air but Jonathan was ready for that too. He threw his arm up and intercepted the lash, letting the leather coil his wrist as he grabbed hold and jerked it toward him. The wooden handle was torn from Clovis' grip and bounced a puff of sand into the air when it hit the ground between them.

Clovis drew his sword and advanced toward him, his expression clear he intended to kill.

"Put him in his cell," Caius yelled from above them.

Jonathan couldn't look away. Clovis turned a darker shade of red as he stopped and looked up toward the balcony.

"Put him in his cell," Caius ordered again.

Four guards surrounded Jonathan. That he'd expected. Clovis sheathed his sword so hard his belt strained against his hip. They put shackles on his wrists and hauled him back to his cell, but he didn't resist. Whatever they did to him now, it had been worth it.

"You're supposed to be training him to fight, not humiliate me in front of the magistrate of Capua." Caius picked up his goblet of wine but instead of drinking it, he hurled it at the wall. The crash sent wine splattering floor to ceiling. "Train him!"

Clovis would take no responsibility for this. He would have killed the man the moment he'd refused to give the gladiator oath. "He has no regard for his life, which is different than not fearing death. He isn't trainable."

"Beat him until he is. Beat him until he yields!"

"As his last master did?"

Caius raked his fingers through his thin hair and paced the chamber. "Promises of freedom then? Isn't that what they all think they're fighting to win?"

"He's not going to fight unless it's against you. He only trained to await the opportunity to strike at you as he did today."

"So he likes revenge. That's something."

"And Quintus' slave girl, but that's useless. Quintus would never accept coin to offer her as a reward. From what I know of Jews, even if he did, I doubt she would go to his bed willingly."

"They are known for their purity." Caius continued to rub his chin for a long moment. "Did she and Quintus return yesterday?"

"Yes."

"Where are they now?"

"I would think the medicus chamber. Quintus' family member passed to the afterlife and it's left him a bit unsettled."

"Take Quintus to look over the new batch of slaves rumored to have come in from Germania. Within the hour."

"When I first told you of them you said—"

"The next person that refuses my command will have his tongue cut from his head. Even you."

"Yes, my lord." He would seek Quintus and take him on this useless task. Caius had never been one to make empty threats, and Clovis wanted to keep his tongue in his mouth where it belonged. It always came down to pain in the end. He'd learned. Every slave learned. So why couldn't Jonathan? Unless Jonathan was in so much pain already, nothing he or Caius could do would make it any worse. That would explain everything. Everything except why.

Maybe Clovis had put his sword in the wrong creature that day after all.

Caius watched Clovis and Quintus depart. He had some time to soothe his nerves before his task. From his balcony, he saw that Tao was in fine form, as usual. He sparred with Seppios, another fine first pole, with a temper as lethal as his sword. The rest of his gladiators knew how to make a reasonable show for the crowd, like Amadi.

Those slaves were the lifeblood of his financial empire, and Tao, his champion, was its beating heart. But champions never lasted. The emperor or governors freed them at whim. Caius still had to be recompensed for them the same as if the sponsor of the games had ordered them slain, but future earnings were lost either way. If no champion of equal standing and favor with the crowd stood ready to replace him, a lanista could be shut out of the games until there was.

This Jonathan had the face of Adonis. He'd slain Brutus with a pugil stick. That kind of fearlessness couldn't be trained, only honed. That was the problem. Clovis was right. Threatening to put him on a cross or throw him to a pack of wild dogs—without a stick—wasn't going to force him to yield. They were locked in a battle of wills and Caius had to gain the upper hand.

This… might.

Caius began his trek down the steps toward the barracks. Should it be required, he made certain his dagger rested in easy reach. He pushed aside the curtain and entered the medicus chamber.

She stood exactly where he expected. "Lord Caius. I'm sorry you've missed Quintus. He left with Clovis not long ago."

"I didn't come to see Quintus, Nessa. I came to see you."

Chapter 16 – Sacramentum Gladitorium

They came for Jonathan well after midday meal. Two guards remained outside while Clovis entered and threw a tunic and sandals at his feet. "Get dressed. Now."

Jonathan didn't move from the stone floor where his elbows rested on his knees. He didn't take orders anymore. "If you plan to beat me, I'll save you the trouble of stripping me when we're outside. If you're going to kill me, I'll leave this life how I came in."

Clovis kicked him on his back and drew his sword in the same instant. The steel at his throat kept him still while the hobnails on Clovis' sandal bit into his chest as the man's full weight bore down on his ribcage.

"Not—everything—is—about—you," Clovis growled between clenched teeth. "You made a game of your defiance without understanding who you were facing."

Jonathan lifted his head as far as he dared against the sword at his throat. "I know exactly who I'm facing. Caius is a man ruled by greed as were all my enemies before him. They stop at nothing to get what they want."

A muscle ticked in Clovis' jaw. "You've known that all along, and yet you persisted." He removed the sword from Jonathan's neck. "It's true

Caius underestimated you, but you underestimated him in turn. We both did."

Clovis backed away, his sword limp at his side. "Get dressed. Nessa awaits you in the medicus chamber." He hastened away and left the cell door open.

After the way he'd triumphed over them all earlier, he was sure they would kill him. Chain him to the wall and let the carrion birds eat his entrails and all that. Maybe they still would, but for now, he had a chance to see Nessa.

He dressed quickly and wrapped his loincloth tight to be sure he didn't repeat his earlier display and cause her to break anything else. He fought the grin trying to form, remembering her crimson cheeks and wide eyes. Clovis had already returned to training, and no one moved as he made his way to the medicus chamber. He entered the sheet door but she wasn't there. Neither was Quintus.

"Nessa?"

A faint sniff from the far corner of the room broke the silence.

"Nessa, is that you?" He passed the big wooden table and its stools, rounding the last bed before the wall, and found her.

She sat hugging her knees to her chest, as naked as he'd been moments ago. Her brown eyes were rimmed in red and her face awash in tears. She met his gaze and then dropped her head between her arms to hide her face. Her shoulders shook beneath the blanket of her unbound hair.

He sank to his knees and stretched forward to gather her discarded tunic lying on the floor near them. A single rip from the neck to the hem tightened his throat. He crawled toward her on his scarred knees as slow as he could to drape the garment over her. He tried not to touch her, but his palm brushed her knee as he covered her. She jerked tighter to the wall and a fresh stab of pain went straight through his chest.

Heavy footsteps signaled someone's approach. "Get away from her," Quintus' voice boomed.

Jonathan rose and stepped toward him, raising both his hands to show he was no threat. "You'll frighten her more," he whispered, stopping between them.

Quintus pushed past and stopped where Jonathan had knelt a moment ago. "Nessa, please tell me who did this. Let me help you." She didn't raise her head or move beneath what remained of her tunic. Quintus wrung his hands and turned to Jonathan. "Clovis and I found her like this when we returned, and she hasn't moved or said a word. What do we do?"

Jonathan's fingers curled to fists, and he had to work to keep his voice low. "You saw her like this and just left her?"

"To inform Caius. He assures me he'll feed the culprit to the beasts when Nessa names him, no matter who it is." Quintus turned and leaned toward her. "Nessa, please. Let me help you." He touched her elbow and she cringed with a broken sob.

Jonathan grabbed Quintus' sleeve and tugged him back. "Send for one of the slave girls," he said softly. Quintus frowned and opened his mouth, but before he could speak, comprehension washed through his face. He nodded and set off toward the doorway, hopefully to bring one of the women from the house.

The savage who'd committed this unspeakable atrocity better be praying to every god in every temple across the empire Caius found him before Jonathan did. He eased to the floor with his back to the wall so that she faced his side, and he the door. Away from her but still near. He leaned his head against the wall and tried for a soothing tone. "Quintus has gone for a slave girl. I thought you might feel better letting her help you. I'll leave when she comes and take Quintus with me. Would that be all right?"

"Yes." Her hoarse whisper was barely audible over the sounds of the training outside.

He fought the instinct to look her direction and focused on breathing in and out quietly. The rage inside and the memory of her vacant expression made it difficult. Quintus finally returned. An older woman followed him, wearing a slave tunic and a somber expression. He rose and went to meet them, but she strode past him toward Nessa. Quintus followed but Jonathan blocked his path. "She wants to be alone."

"She spoke?"

"Not exactly."

Quintus' eyes narrowed and again he tried to push past him.

Jonathan put his arm out and stood his ground. "Please. You must trust me. You saw how she reacted to both of us. Let the woman tend her while we find whoever is responsible for this."

Quintus relented and rubbed at his forehead. "Come with me."

He fought hard not to glance back as he followed Quintus through the sheet door.

A pair of guards approached them. "Lord Caius summons you, slave."

In the aftermath of finding Nessa, all memory of his victory over the lanista had been forgotten. It returned absent its former joy.

"We're going to see him now." Quintus motioned for them to move out of the way.

"Not you, medicus. Just him." The guard who'd spoken nodded toward Jonathan.

So be it. Jonathan took a step forward to follow them but Quintus grasped his elbow.

"Thank you," he whispered.

Jonathan nodded, wishing he could say more.

"Let's go, slave."

One guard led Jonathan while the other followed. He hated having someone at his back he didn't trust, but the guard in front of him must feel the same or they would have him between them. When they turned down a corridor he'd never entered, the reason for the unusual formation stood in front of him. The corridor ended in a narrow staircase.

They climbed until Jonathan paused at the large polished bronze hanging between two torches on the wall. The short beard had grown back and he still resembled Manius. The guard below shoved him with the heel of his hand and Jonathan continued on. He emerged in Caius' chamber.

Plush couches, Corinthian vases, and weapons and armor of every type filled the walls.

Caius stood near his balcony, watching. Jonathan surveyed the room again. A dream he'd not yet had was coming true. He stood, unchained, in a room full of weapons—with the lanista.

"That would be unwise." Caius' gaze flickered from Jonathan to the sword mounted on the wall near him. "Though I would have been disappointed had you not at least considered it. I've told Clovis there is a gladiator inside you."

"That may be but I will never fight for you." Jonathan shifted his weight from his injured leg, now throbbing from the effort of the stairs.

"How about kill for me then?"

"Not unless you're committing suicide. Then I could help you."

"A pity." Caius crossed his arms and took a few steps toward the far wall. "I'd hoped we might finally agree on something. Clovis told me you were quite fond of Quintus' slave girl, but I'll let one of the guards execute her attacker if you prefer."

"You have him?" The question sprang from his mouth before he made the conscious decision to ask it.

"He was foolish enough to brag to another servant." Caius' gaze shifted to one of the guards behind Jonathan. "Bring him."

The pair of men returned quickly, dragging a bound and gagged man between them. He struggled and muttered something unintelligible over and over. The guards threw him to his knees and he began to weep. Nessa's grief had stirred Jonathan to compassion, but this man's tears drained it from him until only the image of Nessa huddled in shame remained. Her vacant expression and lifeless gaze were forever branded into his mind.

On the fringe of his awareness, Caius must have handed him a sword. His hand closed on the cool metal grip and he placed the tip of the polished blade at the base of the man's throat between two rivulets of sweat. Or tears. Maybe they were Nessa's tears. He searched the eyes of the man who'd stolen the light from the face of the gentlest woman he'd ever known. He leaned into the sword but his grip wavered. Would she want this?

Caius' shadow fell over the man at his feet. "He boasted he smothered her cries to her God with more than his tongue."

An untapped well of rage opened and Jonathan forced the blade through the man's windpipe. He didn't pull the blade free until the man's eyes were as empty as Nessa's had been. When he did, the body crumpled to the floor.

Jonathan trembled as the guards dragged her rapist away. He'd just taken a life. Justified in every way but… the sword slipped from his hand and clanged to the floor. He turned to Caius and the lanista's smile chilled him to his bones.

"You see, not only will you fight for me, but you'll kill for me too."

"That was justice."

"Yes it was. But mine, not your slave girl's." The guards returned and flanked Caius, who crossed his arms and chuckled between them. "The slave never touched her. He never even saw her. You killed an innocent man."

Jonathan searched Caius' face, his eyes, anything for some sign of deceit. There was nothing there but that calculated grin. "You… lied?"

"Sending men to their deaths is easy for me. How difficult do you think lying is?"

Not only had he killed, he'd killed an innocent man. His stomach heaved, and he doubled over and vomited, with Caius' laughter ringing in his ears.

"You showed me your Achilles heel, Jonathan. You may care nothing for your own life, but you care a great deal for the slave girl who helped save it."

Jonathan wiped his mouth with the back of his hand and straightened.

Caius' sneer widened. "Now that I know you would kill for her, I'm going to let you."

He was right. Jonathan was going to kill again. He reached for the sword near his feet, and the guards drew theirs and closed rank on either side of Caius.

"Unwise." Caius held up a hand. "You have yet to hear my terms."

It didn't matter. Jonathan reached down for the sword again but a guard kicked it away. His blade fell flat and ready at Jonathan's chest.

"Don't make them kill you. If you die, she dies too."

Jonathan froze.

"Her life is now tied to yours. If you succeed in killing yourself, as Clovis insists you will, she dies. If you make an attempt on my life, or anyone other than your opponent in the arena, she dies. If you fall in the arena, and the editor of the games doesn't spare you, she dies. So I would advise you to take your training seriously, now that both your lives depend on it."

The horror of Caius' decree thundered through him. Then a sudden realization gave him hope. The laws of Rome applied even in a ludis. He should know. His father was a praetor. "She's not your slave. Nessa belongs to Quintus. Under Roman law, you can't touch her."

Caius tucked his thumbs in at the buckle of his leather belt and cocked his head. "That didn't stop me earlier."

Jonathan couldn't breathe. He thought he knew what it was to hate—until now. Every bone and drop of blood together screamed to attack as his fists clenched. If he failed to kill all three of them, he risked her life. That threat chained him in place better than any iron could have.

Clovis' words returned. *Not everything is about you.* Anger became agony in a single breath. He'd done this. To her. To the man he'd killed.

"Now that we finally understand each other," Caius said, "I will offer you the oath of the gladiator once more. I trust this time you won't throw it away." He took a step toward him. "But first, I owe you a little something for all the expense and aggravation you've caused me."

Caius pulled his fist back. Jonathan turned his head fast enough to avoid a broken nose but not the blow. The ring on Caius' finger sliced Jonathan's cheek like a hot knife on honeycomb and his knuckles pounded the bone beneath Jonathan's eye.

Jonathan staggered sideways and Caius advanced. He punched him in the stomach and then kicked his injured thigh. Jonathan collapsed to his knees but used his arms to keep his spinning head from crashing into the floor. He gasped for air through the overwhelming pain.

"Since you're already kneeling, you can give me the oath. From then on you will obey me without question or delay, or I swear to you on all the coin in Capua I will waste no time in extracting the price of defiance from your little friend. Do you understand?"

He opened his mouth to answer, but no sound came. He coughed, trying to answer but—

Caius kicked him again. His sandaled foot struck the side of Jonathan's head and sent him to the floor. Everything around him darkened, but he fought the blackness.

"Much too slow." Caius grabbed a fistful of his hair and yanked Jonathan's head up. "Do you understand?"

"I understand." Jonathan forced the words through the blood running from his nose and lips.

Caius jerked his head back again. "I understand, Master."

His neck was ready to snap from the severe angle and his scalp was on fire. It would take more strength to say those words than anything he'd ever done, even watch his mother die. "I understand... Master."

"I thought you might."

Caius released him and he sagged to the floor.

"Give me the gladiator oath. I will repeat it if you need me to."

They'd broken him. Nessa too, for his defiance. He would give the oath and pledge himself to a lifetime of suffering—to spare her from any more. The three men standing over him waited. He sat back on his heels and cleared blood from his mouth with the back of his hand. "I will endure to be burned... to be bound... to be beaten... and to be killed by the sword."

The *sacramentum gladitorium* was done.

Caius nodded and uncrossed his arms. "Let's not waste any more time. Return to training."

Jonathan held his stomach and struggled to his feet.

"By the way," Caius said. "You're bleeding." He started laughing, and didn't stop.

Jonathan turned toward the stairs and the guards followed. The stairway seemed darker and he paused at the polished metal on the wall. The gash near his eye still bled, as did his nose. Blood gathered in the scruff of beard at his chin and more smeared the tunic on his chest.

He continued down, and near the bottom he missed the edge of a step and almost fell the rest of the way.

Clovis awaited him at the foot of the stairs.

Jonathan searched the man's face. "Did you know?"

"Not until after."

The man before him was the same person who had helped create this living nightmare, but at the same time, Clovis was different. The hardness was gone.

"I need to return to training." Jonathan took another step down and missed that one too. He stumbled forward and Clovis caught him by the arm before he fell.

"Tomorrow." Clovis steadied him before releasing his hold.

"Now." Too much was at stake.

Clovis held his gaze. There was a compassion there he'd never seen before. "Tomorrow," Clovis said more firmly. "Come."

Jonathan followed him toward the barracks. The guards did not. The men paused in their training to stare. What did they see besides his bloody face and the slight limp in his gait? Could they see everything had changed?

Clovis passed the door to Jonathan's empty cell and continued down the row of barracks. Where was he taking him? He opened the door to the cell Jonathan had spent his first night in. When Clovis had given him the fake poison. If only it had been real. Clovis gestured to the bed. "Sit."

The order was absent the hardness that normally accompanied anything coming from the trainer's mouth. Jonathan shuffled to the bed and sat, his stomach muscles knotting from the effort. Clovis stood in the doorway and called to a slave. He ordered a bowl of clean water and towels, a new tunic, and food. When they arrived, he had everything placed on the table and ordered the slave away.

Jonathan remained silent as Clovis wet the cloth and cleared the blood from his face. Instead of scrubbing like before, he dabbed at the dried blood over and over. The water in the bowl turned the pink of an evening sky, and he finished with cleaning and rebinding the wound from the lion that Caius' kick had reopened.

This was not Clovis' battlefield medicine from before. In his silence, in his lack of gruffness, he seemed to share Jonathan's grief.

Clovis poured a cup of wine and set it on the table beside the new tunic. He slid the plate of bread and boiled eggs beside them and gathered the bowl of dirty water and cloths. At the door he stopped. "Tomorrow then?" His tone and his gaze asked a deeper question.

Caius wasn't bluffing. If Jonathan took his own life, he would be taking hers. "Tomorrow."

Clovis nodded once, and from his expression, he understood. No more games. No more lies. The door closed and its lock slid home. Jonathan sat there on the edge of the bed long after the daylight faded from his cell. The food and wine sat untouched on the table, and scabs formed on the new cuts on his face. When he finally moved, it was to lie face down on the straw mattress. He gathered the blanket to mute his anguished sobs. By the time the moon reached its peak, he'd flooded the cloth with tears.

Chapter 17 – Teach Me

Jonathan stood dressed and ready when Clovis opened his cell door in the morning. They exchanged nods and Jonathan had a beam to his shoulder before the last recruit scurried into the training area. The beam never fell from his shoulders, though twice exertion put him on his knees. Both times he willed himself back on his feet with the added weight and drained muscles opposing him. At midday meal he took his familiar spot on the floor and devoured his barley porridge. He'd need the added strength for what he planned to do next.

Gladiators and the other recruits returned to the central training area. Jonathan followed them across the packed sand to the sacred center line—and crossed it. He needed to learn to swing a sword, not heft a beam sunrise to sunset. Hot sun and stares beat down on him as he walked to the chest of practice weapons kept deep in gladiator territory. The wooden sword was lighter than he would have thought. The shield felt about right.

Seppios approached, swinging his wooden sword in a perfect loop at his side. "Go back to the slop side, lion killer, before you really get hurt."

Low laughter rumbled through the gladiators.

Let them laugh. He approached Tao, who stood with sword and shield ready to spar.

Seppios stepped in front and put the tip of his wooden sword into Jonathan's chest. "I mean it, dung beetle. You have no business on our side."

Jonathan craned his neck to make eye contact with Tao over Seppios' shoulder. "You are the champion of the House of Pullus, are you not?"

"He is. Now get back to your side." The point of Seppios' wooden sword jabbed Jonathan's chest so hard he had to take a backward step to keep his balance.

It hurt but he pretended it didn't. Clovis watched them closely, but didn't intervene. All Jonathan needed was the champion. He met Tao's gaze. "Teach me."

Seppios' blunted sword tip rammed the center of his chest again. "You are unworthy to cross swords with us."

Jonathan fought back a grimace from the single point of pressure trying to separate his ribs. He ignored the pain in his chest and the man putting it there, still looking past him to the champion. "Teach me."

The sword flashed from his chest and a painful crack to his wrist knocked his sword from his grip. The wooden weapon dropped to the sand, and the training ground turned silent as a tomb. Jonathan stooped and picked up the sword. He rose and tightened his grip on both the handle and his shield, finding Tao's gaze again. "Teach me."

Seppios' sword thrashed with frightening speed, battering Joanthan's sword and shield free in a single arc. Jonathan staggered back and grabbed his injured forearm. He squeezed hard and discovered his other arm was injured too but if he kept squeezing, the numbness should go away and his fingers and wrists work again.

Clovis still hadn't moved. No one had.

Jonathan deepened his breathing to mask the pain building between his elbows and fingertips. He retrieved the sword and the shield and turned to Tao. "Teach me."

When Seppios attacked again, Jonathan tried to engage him but didn't know how. Seppios swiftly disarmed him and smashed his shield into Jonathan's unprotected side. Agony flew along his ribcage and dropped him to his knees. Seppios swung low and delivered another crushing blow to his wrist. Pain throbbed there like a second heartbeat.

"Go back to your side. While you still can." Seppios laughed again, but this time no one joined him.

Jonathan pushed up from the ground. Slowly, but he made it to his feet. He found his wooden sword and reached for it. He saw the vicious blow coming but couldn't—

Seppios' sword pounded his skull, driving his face into the hot sand.

"Stay on the ground where you belong, maggot."

Get up. You must get up.

On the third try, Jonathan made it to his knees. He crawled toward his dropped sword, the laughter dying away as he reached it. With the sword to lean on, he climbed to his feet. He held his ribs with one arm, his sword with the other, and pulled his battered body erect. Firming his jaw hid the grimace. The metallic taste of blood filled his mouth, but he dare not spit it away as he made eye contact again with Tao and took an unsteady step toward him. "Teach me."

Seppios raised his sword for another attack.

Jonathan flinched, his eyes slamming shut and head jerking sideways.

A sharp crack thundered through his ears—but no pain.

He opened his eyes and Tao's sword held Seppios' back. Their swords remained crossed, upper arms bulging from opposing each other.

"Enough." For a man the size of the champion, his voice seemed small.

Seppios' surprised expression turned angry. "But he—"

"Enough."

It took Seppios a long time to withdraw his sword. When he finally did, it was with a venomous glare at Jonathan.

Jonathan didn't return it. This had never been about Seppios.

Tao looked to Clovis, standing at the edge of the barracks where he'd been the entire time. The trainer nodded and Tao released a heavy sigh.

What did that mean?

Clovis snapped his whip. "Return to training."

The champion faced him, his gaze sweeping from ears to ankles and back. The frown didn't bode well. "First, take your hand from your side. Showing me where the pain is invites more in the same place."

Jonathan released his hold on his side and two-fisted the sword.

Tao circled him, rolling his dark shoulders as he moved past the edge of Jonathan's vision. "Second, never let opponents have your back. Better to lie upon it than have it exposed."

Wood pounded Jonathan's ankle and jerked his injured leg from beneath him. The momentum put him on his back in the sand again, dropping his sword to shield his eyes from the blinding sun directly overhead. A shadow fell over him, and the tip of a wooden sword poked the base of his throat. There was no force behind it, only enough pressure to let him know it was there.

Silhouetted in the sun, Jonathan couldn't see Tao's face as the champion spoke in his broken Greek. "What changed?"

Everything. "It doesn't matter."

"Answer me, or I teach you nothing else."

Jonathan turned his head to spit the blood collecting at the back of his throat and secure a moment to think. The more who knew, the greater the danger she would learn the terrible truth. If he lied simply to get what he needed, he was no better than Caius. "If I don't fight, another will be injured."

"Who?"

"Someone who is innocent." Or had been. He shoved the anguish back down with a single breath. He couldn't look back, only forward. He must learn to fight, and win.

After a long moment, Tao's sword lifted. "Stand up."

Jonathan set his jaw and rolled forward, climbing to his feet without grabbing for his side or his wrists.

Tao handed him his own wooden shield and sword and then retrieved Jonathan's from the sand. "Watch me. Then do exactly as you see me do."

Jonathan had learned much from the champion of Caius Pullus when Clovis' whip signaled the end of the day's training. He could now block, thrust and parry, but the cost had been high. Purple and blue mottled his skin, rivaling his first days here. When he headed for his cell, Clovis waved him away and used his whip to point to the group of gladiators and recruits disappearing into the barracks.

Jonathan followed at the back, and felt the steam before he saw the baths. It seemed obedience, no matter how ill-begotten, had its rewards. Thankfully, other than pointed stares and whispered conversation, the others left him alone. Even Seppios. The hot water soothed his exhaustion and infused his battered body with relaxing warmth. He would have soaked all night, but eventually a slave brought word he needed to return to his cell.

Guards watched him from their posts in the corridor and on the walls once outside. In his cell he found Clovis on the stool beside his bed.

The trainer pulled a roll of linen from his lap and swung his chin toward the bed. "Come sit. I'll change that dressing."

"Do you plan to never send me to the medicus chamber again?"

"That depends. Are you going to tell her?"

"No."

"You don't know if I meant Caius threatens her life, that you fight to defend it, or that I was innocent of this when I took Quintus with me that day."

"I will tell her nothing, but you are not innocent. Nor am I."

Clovis removed the wet wrap in silence. The long scab on the claw mark had dissolved in the bath. The wound appeared narrower, with clean edges. Healing slowly, but healing. Clovis finished the new dressing and rose from the stool. "You will train with the other recruits before midday meal, afterwards with the other gladiators. I'll pair you as I see fit."

"Tao is the champion. I must learn from him."

"You're no challenge to him and I can't have him losing form while you gain it."

"Fine." Jonathan reached for his cup to pour himself some wine.

Clovis put his palm over Jonathan's cup until their gazes met. "It's not your place to consent or refuse. Don't forget that." He left and shut the cell door, the bolt grating as it slid into the lock. How did Clovis expect him to ever forget he had no choice about anything?

Not even to live.

Days became weeks filled with blows, bruises, and blood. Always Jonathan's, but he remained an apt pupil under Tao's instruction.

"If you think you've been wounded, check. If blood flows out, so will your strength. Your strategy must change."

The fee for that lesson was a bruise on his hip the size of a stew bowl.

"Watch my eyes, not my hands. They will tell you where the sword will swing."

Jonathan had been slow to acquire this skill, earning cracked ribs that made it difficult to raise his shield for days.

"Learn to fight even after you have fallen. Most men are seized with fear once flat on their back."

His bath that night had been most welcome, though he doubted he would ever get all the sand out of his hair and throat.

"Your mind is your most powerful weapon, not your sword."

That was hard to believe, since Tao's sword left a dozen marks on him that day. The champion had been holding back.

"If it distracts you, force it from mind. If it fuels your focus, use it."

The champion was relentless in punishing Jonathan every time a slave passed through his field of vision and shared his attention. That should have conditioned him to remain focused—but it didn't. Sometimes the slave was Nessa and the blow was worth it.

"Never become parted from your weapon."

Jonathan fought his way back up from the sand under a steady rain of well-placed blows. He nearly broke his arm that day, but never lost his sword. The next morning his swollen wrist wouldn't bend at all so Clovis kept him strength training with the recruits until it would flex again.

"If your opponent gives you an opening, charge it with purpose."

When Tao gave him one, he charged. The champion knocked him to the ground and nearly unconscious. Jonathan lay there in the sand while Tao's laughter bellowed to the clouds above and he kicked Jonathan's dropped sword toward him.

"Of course, sometimes, dropped guard is a trap."

Rain fell one of those days, but still they trained. Clovis paired him with Seppios. From the man's expression, he'd been waiting a long time. But covered in sweat, sand, and bruises, Jonathan was in no mood for the man's mouth. Seppios insulted his mother and Jonathan snapped. He lost his temper, then his shield, and finally his sword. He ignored the solid blows striking his frame to tackle the man like a raging bear.

It took both Tao and Clovis to separate them.

"Ignore a man's taunts. Answer them with skill, not blind rage."

Tao was intent on driving this lesson home. For three days he called Jonathan's mother every foul name that existed in Greek. And a few in Tao's native tongue Jonathan remained grateful he didn't know. Lying awake that night the insults trekked through his thoughts. They no longer made him see red or hasten to defend her memory. He was losing the last shreds of himself, his spirit hardening as much as his muscles under the training.

"Embrace pain."

He had to, simply to keep training. Day by day he learned to ignore the pain. Think through it. Not react to it. Until at long last, the unthinkable happened.

He'd been sparring with Amadi and gained the upper hand. The gladiator lost his footing and Jonathan's sword went to Amadi's chest in victory.

"To underestimate an opponent is to have already lost."

Jonathan thought Tao said that more for Amadi than him, and all the other gladiators who had fallen silent to watch. Jonathan knew that better than anyone. He'd underestimated Caius and Nessa suffered for it. He was still afraid to face her. To see the revulsion in her eyes if she knew the truth or the horror if she learned her life hung in the balance of Caius' making.

The few times Clovis suggested Jonathan visit the medicus chamber, after particularly fierce bouts of education, he refused. Unless a bone protruded or the bleeding refused to stop, he could endure it. After all, he was learning to embrace pain. The more pain he learned to stand in his body, the more he hoped one day to be able to stand the pain in his heart. The festering wound where the loss of his freedom and the pain of inflicting Caius' cruelty on Nessa remained.

By December, the biggest games of the year, Jonathan bore no resemblance to the slave Fabricius Clavis had carted to the ludis. Eight weeks of training had made iron of the muscle beneath skin burnished copper from the sun. The other recruits presented no real challenge for him, and he held his own against roughly half of the gladiators. He had yet to mount a real offense against Tao and Seppios, but could stay on his feet much longer when sparring with either of them.

The gladiators still did not accept him. Nor did the recruits, especially after Jonathan decided he'd eaten his last meal on the floor. He took the open place on the bench. Conversation paused, then resumed as if he weren't there. For one day, Jonathan thought he'd been accepted. The following day he returned to the table and found it empty. He glanced over at them, packed elbow to elbow at the table beside his now private one, and sat down to his bread and barley porridge alone. *Embrace the pain. Don't show them where you're wounded.* He forced the biggest smile he could, and slid to the center of the empty bench while they stared.

Chapter 18 – Yours

The morning of the final test, Jonathan stood with the others near a chest-high platform formed from lashed timbers. Ten recruits remained of the original sixteen. One had died in training, collapsed under a beam never to rise again. Another had cut his wrist open in the night with a shard of his broken cup. Another, the quiet one with the long black hair had been bought by one of Caius' balcony visitors—a woman that reminded him too much of Valentina. Two of the weakest remaining hadn't shown one morning and Clovis refused to answer why. Later that day, the roaring of the cats, mingled with desperate wails, was heard from the arena on the other side of the barracks.

Jonathan pitied them, and the one recruit who'd attempted to run away the next day. Caius had made an example of him, and Jonathan wasn't the only one to leave his porridge untouched that evening.

Today Caius stood observing them from his balcony with a look of superiority that all but shouted he considered himself a god. Above them all, looking down, deciding their fates on his whims and wishes. Perhaps he was. After all, the God he'd once believed hadn't been any different.

The gladiators watched from the other side of the platform. The test was simple, though not easy. Disarm the guard on the platform so he yields, or knock him to the pile of straw below.

Clovis called for Jonathan first. Jonathan tightened his grip on his wooden sword and shield, and stepped forward toward the short ladder.

For a man of few words and typically quiet even then, Tao's voice carried to all four walls of their ludis. "Do not fail, lion killer, or I will look weak."

A few gladiators laughed, and Jonathan grinned. He climbed the rungs to the platform, brimming with confidence. Confidence well earned, for he bested the guard in a short volley of blows, taking none anywhere but his shield. The guard lost his wooden sword and threw his arms out in surrender.

No one cheered. It was not the gladiator way. He received nods of approval from Clovis and Tao and a scowl from Seppios Jonathan took as further proof he'd done well. Three others passed, and together they received the double P tattoo on the back of the neck. He would wear the mark of a Pullus gladiator the rest of his life, like the scar on his cheek that put it there.

That evening, the gladiators assembled in the courtyard to watch the recruits who failed the final test leave the ludis in chains, bound for the slave block, the mines, or worse. Clovis must have seen the pity Jonathan felt for them. "They continue on their path, as you will on yours. You've done well, though it should not surprise you Caius orders you be kept from the pregame feast tonight."

"What feast?"

"There is always a feast given by the sponsor of the games. The gladiators mingle with their followers and more often than not, privately entertain their most avid admirers, depending on what the host and Caius permit. I'm afraid you will not be coming."

"I passed the test. I bear the mark. Am I not a gladiator?"

"Caius intends to give you none of the pleasures of gladiator life, only its yoke. It would not be my way, but he is the master."

No one knew that better than Jonathan. "Tell him I'm grateful to be excluded so I may spend the night better preparing for my match tomorrow."

"I will, but without your insidious tone." It was the first time Jonathan saw Clovis with anything resembling a grin. The trainer's seriousness returned. "You fight en masse tomorrow, with the newest of the gladiators. The first fight is always the most dangerous. Spend tonight preparing your mind. Should you be victorious, and perform well, you may be chosen to pair in the next games."

"I will be."

Clovis did not reply as Jonathan brushed by him to enter his cell. Clovis locked him in and Jonathan turned and watched him through the grate in the door. When he was a good distance to the gate, Jonathan yelled, "Have some roast peacock for me."

The faint chuckle that carried to him could have been Clovis, but he'd never heard the man laugh before so couldn't be sure. The possibility it was brought a smile all the same. He removed his sandals and unbuckled his belt. Dried sweat caked the inside of the wide leather. A good scrubbing and oil would not only preserve it, but keep it from chafing as much. Clovis would probably have a slave see to the task if Jonathan mentioned it, even though he'd rather do it himself. He set the belt on the table, rolling his neck to alleviate the residual discomfort of the tattoo.

This evening his pitcher held water, not wine, but at least it smelled clean. He poured himself a cup but over the low trickle, the door bolt scraped behind him. "Forget something?" he asked Clovis as he turned.

Nessa.

She stood smiling in the door, holding a basket against her hip. "No, but you have." She laughed and pointed to the water flowing from the tilted pitcher in his hand to the floor, nowhere near the cup in his other hand. He yanked the pitcher upright and lost his hold on the handle. The vessel shattered on the floor with a splash.

A guard poked his head in the doorway. "All well in there?"

"We're fine, Luca." Nessa pulled the door closed and turned her amused grin back to him. "They told me you'd passed the test, but I think your grip might need work." She laughed again and moved past him to set the basket down on the table and pick up the wet, broken pieces of clay.

Jonathan knelt down to help. "You surprised me."

Her brown eyes met his as she picked up a bigger piece of the broken pitcher and held it up to him. "At least I had my clothes *on.*" Her smile stretched to her ears and then into her eyes. He wanted so much to carve that image into his memory, to hold as a talisman against the visions of her and Caius that filled his nightmares, together with the face of the innocent man he'd murdered. "I suppose I'm just clumsy."

Her brow furrowed, likely wondering at his sudden gloom. After the broken pieces were piled on the table, she produced a loaf from the basket and settled on the stool as if she planned to stay a while. The bed opposite her was the only other place he could sit down. She tore a large chunk from the loaf and handed it to him. "What happened to your face?"

"Which part?"

She leaned forward to trace the scar on his cheek made by Caius' ring. "Here."

The concern in her eyes woke a longing for more of her touch. She took her hand from his face before his body could respond—thankfully. "Training." That was neither true, nor a lie.

"Tao or Seppios?"

Jonathan ignored the question with a bite of the bread. The tender morsel was soft and tasted faintly of honey. Nothing like the dry crusts given them with meals. "Did Quintus send you?" He suspected Caius, perhaps Clovis, but Quintus was the safest way to try to find out without bringing up the monster that had scarred them both.

"No, but he let me come. I think he's glad I finally wanted out of the medicus chamber and our quarters. I'd heard from one of the guards you would be remaining here, and I've missed you."

He nearly choked on the swallow of bread. "You missed me?"

The pink in her cheeks deepened, but she didn't look away. "Is that so hard to believe?"

It was, but he wouldn't say so. Knowing her, she'd ask why.

"The way you rage against a God you say you don't believe in fascinates me. And I wanted to see how you are." She pulled two peaches from her basket and extended one toward him. "Quintus brought me these today. I was hoping to share them with you, and God has answered both my prayers."

His fingers brushed hers together with the delicate skin of the fruit, sending a quiver through his stomach. "Both?"

"That we get to share them, and that you are well."

"I didn't say I was well."

Her gaze roamed his body before returning to his face. "Nothing is bruised or bleeding, which is about all I had a right to hope for, *gladiator*." She winked at him before taking a bite of her fruit. Somehow she could chew and smile at the same time.

He longed to ask how she seemed so herself after all he'd seen her endure. But asking would only remind her of memories he yearned to exile from his own mind. He bit into his peach to do something other than stare at her. The sweet flavor proved a pleasant break from the food meant to aid his conditioning.

Her posture relaxed and her hair fell forward over her shoulders. His fingers itched to touch the dark strands. Long hair was rare among women in Rome, especially slave women. Wigs were common among the wealthy, and Jonathan didn't need to be skilled in mathematics to understand how one equaled the other. Her long hair was yet another thing about her that didn't make sense. "Nessa, how did you come to be here?"

"Most of the guards here are as fond of me as Quintus. Sometimes we treat them or members of their family outside the ludis. They'll usually permit me most anything when Caius is no concern, especially Luca."

"No, I don't mean this evening. I mean how you came to be here in the ludis with Quintus."

"That's a long story." Her gaze fell to the fruit cradled in her lap.

"I'd like to hear it, but only if you want to tell me."

When her head finally came up, the confident expression he'd come to depend on had returned. "Get comfortable. I'm not an orator like in the forum, so I might bore you to sleep."

Impossible. He scooted closer to the wall and drew his knees up so his bare feet rested on the bed. "I'm ready."

"I've already told you my mother was one of the captives Titus marched from Jerusalem. On the march she discovered she carried a child. God had given her a remnant of my father, and she prayed day and night I would be born healthy and strong. She was put on a slave block in every city along the way, but the hand of the Lord saw her unsold until she reached Pompeii. A lanista there bought her, intending to use her to reward the men, as Caius will sometimes do with his slave women." She swallowed.

"The first time she was sent to a gladiator, she explained she was widowed and had only the baby she carried in secret. Raban had compassion on her and spoke to the lanista, insisting my mother be given other duties, which she was."

"A gladiator commanded the lanista?" The notion was inconceivable.

"Raban was the champion and had a talent for getting his way." She laughed softly. "I think perhaps I learned that from him."

"You were close to him?"

"I was close to all of them. While my mother served them at meal times, I toddled after her wherever she went. The men all knew me, and looking back, I think for many I was a long-lost daughter or sister in some way. They spoiled me terribly. So did our lanista, who had no wife or children of his own. I think he had a great affection for my mother, for he often gifted her with jewelry and fine clothes. I was too young to know much more than that, but I remember. I also remember her being upset when Raban gave me a little wooden sword he had carved for me."

She jerked on the stool like someone had thrown cold water on her. "Oh, that reminds me." She reached into the basket on the table and her hand emerged with a thin leather cord dangling from her closed fist. "This belongs to you."

Her fingers unfolded and his breath stuck in his chest. His mother's horse head carving. He took it from Nessa's palm and traced the rounded ears and eyes that had nearly worn away. His own burned with the threat of tears as he held the figure tight. "I thought I'd lost this."

"Quintus cut it away when you first arrived. I thought it might be important to you so I put it aside but then forgot it. Forgive me for not thinking of it sooner."

"Forgive you? I can't…" His voice rasped with emotion. He slipped the leather cord over his head and the small carving rested over his heart once more. The horse head not only connected him to his mother and father, but was the only thing that truly belonged to *him*. Words were not enough, but all he had. "Thank you."

She'd saved his necklace. She'd saved his life too, and he'd been angry instead of grateful. "For this and… for saving my life."

Her expression softened. "God saved you."

He wouldn't argue. She meant well. "Thank you."

She looked down, and picked at the skin of her fruit for a long moment. Finally she met his gaze. "I didn't want to tell you, but that first night, while your fever raged, you would reach for your chest and call for your mother."

Why didn't he recall that, and what else did he not remember?

"Does your mother live?" she asked.

"No."

"I'm sorry."

"So am I." Jonathan set the remaining half of his peach on the table. His hunger remained, but no longer for the food. He wanted to know more about this compassionate yet strong woman so much like Deborah. He settled back against the wall. "Tell me what happened next to the little girl with the wooden sword."

"She lost her mother too."

Jonathan sighed. Would he ever not say or do the wrong thing in her presence? "I'm sorry."

"I was playing in the courtyard with my sword when the ground began shaking. Raban and the others stopped to stare at the mountain. It was puffing a dark cloud high in the sky. The strange cloud kept getting taller and the earth still trembled. The lanista was away so many of the guards left, probably to check on their families. Without the guards, some of the gladiators left. I don't think they planned to return."

Jonathan had heard the story of the destruction of Pompeii from his father, but never from someone who had been there. To his knowledge, very few of the city's people had escaped.

"The dark cloud grew, swallowing up the other clouds and casting a great shadow over the city. I remember being scared because Raban looked scared, and he was never afraid of anything. He and my mother gathered in the barracks to pray with some of the others. It became like night, and pebbles started falling like rain, but they floated in the fountains."

"Floating stone?"

"Of all different sizes. We'd never seen anything like it, and I've never seen it since. Raban grabbed me and my mother and took us to the master's stable. With no guards remaining, no one stopped us. Raban put my mother and me on the only horse left and led us out of the ludis. The strange pebbles kept falling. It scared the horse—that and all the shouting people."

Nessa's eyes darkened. "Not all the pebbles falling from the sky floated. Some were large and heavy. I could hear them hitting the roofs. At the edge of the city, one struck my mother. She fell from the horse, me with her."

She paused there a long moment. He longed to comfort her, but didn't know how.

She took a deep breath and continued. "I didn't understand, then. Raban knew she was dead and we had to leave her, but I couldn't. I kicked and bit him, screaming the whole time. I'll never know how he managed to get me back on that horse in front of him. We fled south, along with a few others leaving the city. With a horse we were faster, and Raban ran the horse hard. He stopped only once, to tear cloth from his tunic and tie it around our faces because there was so much ash and dust in the air we could barely breathe.

"Eventually the stone rain stopped falling somewhere on the road to Stabiae. It had been nighttime for so long, I didn't know how much time passed. We reached Stabiae, but Raban continued south. He said God would tell him when to stop. When I first saw sunlight, I thought for sure we would rest, but he kept going. I was still grieving my mother, and exhausted like the horse. Raban had to lead it while I rode."

A tremor passed through her and she paused. "Then it happened." Her gaze went through him as if she were seeing her memories and not him. "The mountain behind me roared like a great beast. Another cloud spread from it and fell down the side of the mountain. I've never seen or heard anything like it to this day, and hope I never will again."

She paused, another tremor passing through her. "Then the robbers came."

Jonathan's heart clenched.

"Five men on foot. They told Raban to hand me and the horse over and they would let him keep his life." She hugged herself. "He drew his sword, told me to hold on, and slapped the horse so hard I felt it. The robbers grabbed for us but Raban fought them. The hand of God kept me from falling. I know that now. Then all I could do was clutch tight with my legs and hold on to the horse's hair whipping in my face.

"We didn't go as far as it felt at the time. Quintus and his father saw me as I crested a rise in the road. They were heading toward the fire mountain to see if they could help. I didn't want to stop, because I didn't know if they were bad men too, but the horse slowed, blowing and snorting, and refused to go anymore. I told them what happened. They put me in their cart and hurried to Raban."

She hugged herself tighter. "He'd killed four of them. The other one must have run. Raban was badly wounded but still alive. Quintus and his father brought us back to their villa. They tried, but by sunset Raban was gone."

"Nessa, I'm so sorry."

A bittersweet smile formed on her mouth. "Thank you. When I think of Raban and my mother, my comfort comes in knowing they are with the Lord and I will see them again one day."

The paradise Deborah and his mother had taught him of as a boy. If it comforted her to still believe that, he was glad. "You must hate the men that took him from you."

"It took me many years to forgive them, but I never hated them. God wouldn't want that, nor would Raban and my mother. It was the hardest thing I ever had to do. Forgive them." Darkness filled her eyes and she held her breath for a moment. "Well, second hardest."

The peach in his gut turned over. He knew what she was remembering.

"I didn't thank you... for your kindness that day you found me."

"Don't thank me."

Her brow creased at the hard edge in his tone.

He hadn't meant for it to be there. "I'm sorry." *For so much.* "I'm sorry for what happened."

"It was not your doing. We are only responsible for ourselves before God and each other. One day we will have to answer to God, and through the Messiah's blood you can know God's mercy. I can—"

"You and I are in need of justice, not mercy." This time he didn't mind the bitterness seasoning his words.

Nessa frowned and her gaze narrowed. "You can't have both."

"I don't need mercy. I need vengeance."

"We all need mercy, and vengeance belongs to God. Have you never sinned against God?"

He thought of the innocent man he'd slain weeks before. "It's not the same as what was done to you, or to me."

"But it is." She leaned forward and placed her hand on the top of his foot. "We are all guilty and in need of God's mercy and forgiveness. We have no right to take of that and not give it to others."

"You forgive Caius?"

Her eyes widened and she drew her hand back. "Why do you speak of Caius?"

Curse his carelessness. The set of her face demanded a response. "It doesn't matter. I shouldn't have brought him up."

"It does matter." She leaned forward, the uneaten core of her fruit rolling from her lap unheeded. She grasped his hand in both of hers. "It matters a great deal. You must tell no one. Please, Jonathan. You must give me your word you will never speak of it to anyone. Even me. Please."

He pulled his hand free. "I won't speak of it again."

The intensity of her gaze seemed to mine his soul for the conviction lacking in his tone.

It frightened him, and this time he replaced the guilt in his voice with purpose. "You have my word."

She placed her hand on the back of his. "Thank you."

Should he? No, and yet, he couldn't stop himself. He turned his hand, savoring the slide of her fingers across his skin, until he could wrap his fingers around her smaller ones. Her hands healed, his killed, but for a moment they fit together. Intertwined, as their lives were. He could not fail her. Ever.

"Nessa," a voice called from outside his cell. "It's time."

She withdrew her hand with a sheepish smile. "Thank you, Luca, I'll be right there."

Her brown eyes bored into his with the slightest tilt of her head. "Jonathan, who is it you cannot forgive?"

Their faces flashed in his mind, one at a time. "Someday I may tell you."

"You'll never heal until you forgive. Even then, it will take time for God's peace to overcome the memories, but it can, if you seek Him."

"God had his chance." Jonathan swallowed against his tightening throat and looked away to the stone wall of his cell. "If He's there, He abandoned me a long time ago."

Suddenly her hands were on his face, forcing him to look at her. "God does not abandon us. He does not leave us, or forsake us. We turn away, and He allows us, but His love will pursue us. A love so strong He gave His Son for you. That Son willingly endured crucifixion so that all who call upon His name and believe can live forever with Him. Don't turn your back on that love."

With his head between her hands, her pleading face a breath from his own, her words pierced his defenses. He felt a stirring in his heart and mind and raised his hands to hold her wrists lightly. Warmth he didn't understand filled him. Not the warmth of desire, but the long forgotten hunger of a much deeper yearning.

The cell door opened, shattering the moment as Nessa released him. She backed toward the door, as reluctant to go as he was for her to leave. "I'll pray for you, Jonathan."

The guard gave him a cursory glance before shutting and locking the door. He remained crouched on his bed, leaning into the wall long after she left, replaying every moment of his time with her. Eventually the flame of the oil lamp on the table sputtered and died. Maybe it was the darkness that made him feel safe enough to try. Maybe it was for her, but he closed his eyes and bowed his head between his raised knees.

"God?" A heavy sigh left him and he swallowed. How long had it been? Eight years, except for the desperate pleas on the road from Rome. Memories of the steady diet of abuse on the long road to the shame of the slave block returned. With them Valentina's seduction, destroying the life he'd rebuilt after Manius' betrayal. Surviving execution, twice, so Clovis could cheat him out of suicide. Murdering an innocent man, and now having to fight and eventually kill again to profit the most evil man he'd ever known.

Where was God's love through any of that? The love Nessa said would never stop pursuing him? If God existed, and truly loved him, He'd done a poor job of showing it.

Jonathan turned flat on the bed, not bothering to move beneath the blanket. He relived Nessa's touch as she'd traced the scar on his cheek from Caius' ring. Her hands when they held his face. The feel of her hand in his. He clutched his mother's carving she'd returned to him and rolled over to face the wall.

There was a love he wanted to pursue him, but it wasn't God's.

Chapter 19 – The Games

Jonathan was the only *thracian* among the newest gladiators from the House of Pullus. The three other recruits had trained as *murmillos* and a retiarius, a net and trident fighter. The murmillos were so heavily armored and carried such large shields, Jonathan wondered how he could possibly win if paired against one when the en masse fighting began. He would have to. Nessa's life depended on it.

He tightened the leather cords of the wrap sheathing his sword arm. He rechecked the fastening on his metal leg grieves. The protection they would offer his legs that his shield could not was worth the extra weight. His bronze helmet with its grass-colored plumes fit well, but the grates in the faceplate impaired his vision. It would have helped to have been allowed to practice in it, at least once. Clovis entered with several slaves who began handing out weapons. Jonathan grasped the handle of the curved sword that marked a thracian gladiator, surprised to find it of a similar weight to his wooden training sword.

Clovis moved through them, checking buckles and adjusting armor. "When you take the sand, all your training will be forgotten." He turned slowly, surveying each of the men he'd trained. "Do not fear this. Your muscle and bone will remember." He took a sword from a slave, turning it so the rays of sunlight coming through the gate of life glittered along the steel blade. He thrust the tip into the hard-packed earthen floor and the hilt swayed like a young olive tree in the wind.

"You fight to bring honor to the House of Pullus." Clovis picked up the retarius' net and handed it to the gladiator. "And to yourselves." He picked up Jonathan's helmet and extended it to him, meeting his gaze. "And for those you hold dear."

Jonathan took the helmet and pulled it on. It was all the reply he could give.

Clovis plucked the sword from the ground and raised it high. "Pullus!"

The men raised their weapons in salute, all but Jonathan. Two slaves approached the gate from within the arena. The morning animal hunts and midday executions were finished. The games could begin. Clovis stood like a general surveying his legion as Jonathan lined up with the other men to take the sand.

Stepping from the shadows, the bright sunlight overwhelmed him as much as the sudden screams of the crowd. A referee wearing a blood-splattered tunic pointed his pugil stick at a spot on the wall Jonathan was to occupy. A second group of gladiators emerged from the gate behind them, fighters from another school. The referee directed those men to their places. A murmillo approached him, and Jonathan's stomach dropped. The man's shield reached from his chin to his knees and curved around him. It was practically a wall.

The gladiator assumed opening position, as did Jonathan, holding his much smaller shield close and his shorter sword ready. From the corner of his vision, the referee raised the stick and held it between him and his opponent. The crowd fell silent in expectation.

"Violente!" The stick slashed toward the sky as the referee jumped back.

Jonathan took the murmillo's first blow on his shield as the screaming roar of the crowd erupted. Clovis had been right. You forget everything, but the body does not. The blows were not as well placed as Tao's, or as physical as Seppios', but they were fast, even under the weight of so much armor. And there were many. Jonathan could only defend, giving ground in circles while trying to avoid the other fights going on all around him. He backed too close to a retarius, and the weights at the end of the gladiator's throwing net slammed Jonathan's back.

The momentary distraction gave the murmillo an opening. Jonathan's leg erupted in pain from a solid hit above his grieve. He didn't need to check to know the murmillo had drawn blood. It stained the man's sword.

The murmillo swung his sword again, and Jonathan met it with his shield. This time he didn't resist the blow. He let the momentum push his shield against his body and carry him around his opponent. He spun tight, dropping the shield and swinging his sword through the turn, opening a long and deep gash on the murmillo's back.

Roars of approval from the crowd surrounding them washed over the sand. Grasping the sword with both hands, Jonathan focused his strength on holding his ground when the murmillo's blade fell against his own. His opponent's size and weight put Jonathan at a disadvantage in a contest of pure strength, but Jonathan pictured Nessa's face and his shaking arms held fast.

The murmillo backed away. Jonathan sucked a deep breath of warm air from the growing heat inside his helmet. But the murmillo charged, the retreat having been a trap. Before Jonathan could tuck and roll toward his discarded shield, his opponent's shield struck the center of his unprotected chest like a battering ram. He lost his footing in the churned sand and fell hard on his back.

Don't panic. He rolled sideways and missed the downward slice of his opponent's sword. He scanned the arena while getting to his feet. They were the only pair still fighting. The murmillo's sword caught him on his shield arm, the one not bound in padding. He saw and felt it, and it was deep. He'd lost focus for a mere second and now would have to attack hard and fast.

They both bled now, and he must wear down the murmillo first. Use the man's weighty armor and heavy shield against him.

Jonathan fought on, ignoring the searing pain when he moved his arm to block blows with only his sword. Blood from the gash on his leg soaked the padding between his leg and metal grieve. The sodden cloth slid down his skin to bunch between the straps holding them in place. His arm was failing, covered in red and beginning to shake, but he fought on.

The energy of the crowd as they cheered the battle intensified. Other gladiators from his house shouted his name from their places on the wall. Jonathan fed on their encouragement like a starving lion with a fresh kill, letting the praise and the pulse of the crowd renew his strength as he continued to fight.

The murmillo's blows came in slower intervals, still dangerous, but not as heavy as before. Jonathan had worked their fight near his shield, and recovered it from the sand. He threw his shoulder down and plowed into the murmillo's waiting shield. When the murmillo braced against him, Jonathan raised his smaller shield and slammed it into the side of the man's helmet with every bit of strength that remained. The boom thundered through the air and the murmillo swayed.

Jonathan thrust his curved sword into the man's shoulder and jumped back, still gripping his sword and shield. From the blood on the metal, he'd gone deep. The murmillo struggled to hold his heavy shield in place. Blood ran from the wound Jonathan had inflicted.

Now. He needed to attack the opening now. Knock the man down and force him to give the missio in surrender.

Jonathan surged forward, but his legs wouldn't obey. They shook with the effort to remain standing. He gasped inside his helmet but there was only hot, sweat-tainted air. He put his sword to the sand and leaned on it, waiting for the murmillo to charge him.

He'd failed her.

But the man stood wavering like a long stalk of wheat in a strong wind.

The crowd cheered louder than ever. The murmillo crumpled to his knees, sword and shield falling to the sand. He swayed forward, revealing the long gash Jonathan's sword had opened. A back scarred by whips, like his own. The man raised two fingers toward the pulvis, asking to be spared.

Jonathan struggled to keep on his feet, the inferno of his helmet worsening as he panted. Through the eyeholes, the magistrate he'd humiliated Caius in front of rose and surveyed the crowd. Jonathan's heart pounded so hard he could hear the blood rushing in his ears.

Please. Please spare him.

The magistrate extended his hand, and gave the sign for life. Missio granted. That was the last thing Jonathan saw before his world went black.

Clovis watched slaves rake Jonathan's blood beneath the sand, preparing the arena for the next fight. Amadi would fight a retarius from a rival ludis. He'd trained Amadi two years ago, though it seemed longer. It didn't matter. No good came of growing attached to any of them. Strangers buried easier than friends.

Caius' gaze lingered on the far side of the arena. "Victors aren't usually *carried* out the gate of life. What did you make of his fight?"

Through years of practice, Clovis kept his expression emotionless. "I think he fights as a man terrified of losing and not as one who seeks victory."

"The outcome is the same."

If Clovis could explain the difference, and there was one, Caius wouldn't relent. He'd found the fastest way to control Jonathan and would now waste him as he had so many others.

"I told you we'd make a gladiator of him, Clovis, and so we have. I must return to the pulvis with the magistrate and that dog Lucius. He made a bet with me halfway through the fighting his murmillo would beat my thracian." Caius laughed. "It's a good thing Jonathan won. I can't afford to lose anymore. We must do well today."

"Your gladiators will give their all for you, my lord, as always." Clovis bowed low to avoid saying anymore. Then he hastened to check on their men. Something Caius himself should do if he had any respect for them at all.

In the *saniarium*, slaves scurried about collecting armor and weapons. Quintus and the other school's medicus saw to their gladiators, resting on benches and tables filling one side of the chamber. Quintus sewed a puncture wound on Taven's arm. The young gladiator was the smallest in stature of their new gladiators, but had been the first to claim victory in the en masse fight. Clovis approached them, careful to stay out of Quintus' torch light. "How are they?"

"Nothing to worry me yet, except for Jonathan."

The young lion killer lay still on a table in the corner of the chamber. Nessa hovered over him, dabbing sand from his skin with a wet cloth. Quintus had already bound the wound on his arm and his leg.

"He hasn't awakened?"

"No." Quintus pulled the horsehair through again with his fishbone needle. "Was he struck in the helmet or in the head?"

"Not that I recall, but I couldn't watch all of them at once. It may be battle fatigue. His fight lasted much longer than expected, and he's not in peak form yet."

"The crowd sounded pleased. I thought the ceiling would collapse on us all for a moment," Quintus said.

Clovis held his tongue out of respect for Quintus, who was Roman by birth. With few exceptions, Quintus being one of them, all Romans were the same. The larger the crowd, the deeper their thirst ran for blood and pleasure.

Quintus wiped his hands with a towel and handed a cup of wine to Taven. "Nessa and I will be ready for the others. Hopefully we will greet the night with none to mourn."

Clovis watched Nessa with Jonathan. She'd never looked up since he entered, still working to remove every bit of dried blood and sand from Jonathan's skin. "Tend the other men yourself when they arrive, if you can. Make certain Nessa is with Jonathan when he wakes."

"Why?"

"Because I've asked it."

Whatever ailed their gladiator, seeing her face when he first opened his eyes would do more for him than any of Quintus' herbs and treatments.

Jonathan woke to the one person he most wanted to see. Smiling—alive and unharmed—standing over him in whatever this large chamber was.

"Greetings." Nessa placed her hand on his arm, above a linen binding.

He had another above his left knee where the murmillo had gotten past him. Ten fingers Ten toes. No aching skull for a change. Hopefully the man he'd defeated would recover as well. "I'm still in one piece."

"A miracle, I know."

Miracle? He'd killed a lion with a stick. He'd been trained by a champion. And he was about to tell her so when her face crinkled in mischief. She'd been teasing him.

"You jest?" he said.

"Of course. I knew you would win."

Her confidence swelled his pride. Hopefully Tao and Clovis were proud of him too. As for Caius, he could—

"Now that you're awake, drink this." She handed him a cup of herbed wine and helped him sit up. Ah. He hadn't come out of that as unscathed as he thought. Opposite him, Seppios sat on a table while Quintus tended a wound on his lower leg.

Seppios looked up and scowled. "You cost me ten sesterces, lion killer. I wagered against you."

"Nessa could have told you I was going to win." Jonathan grinned at her but she raised her hand, cupped but empty, toward her mouth. He obeyed and drank the mix she'd given him. The herbs in the wine were ground so smooth he could taste them, but no flakes stuck on his tongue or teeth.

"God told me you were going to win. I asked Him for a sign this morning."

Jonathan sighed. Everything always came back to God for Nessa. It had been this sign, not her confidence in him after all.

"What does your God tell you of my chances in the next games, Nessa?" Seppios asked.

"I would not tell you even if I knew. You would only use it to wager."

"Enough, all of you." Quintus finished the knot in Seppios' dressing. "You'll wake Amadi."

Jonathan turned to the table on his other side. Amadi lay asleep or unconscious, his upper thigh heavily bound with linen. He hoped that was Quintus' work.

"I'm not asleep." Amadi spoke but his eyes remained closed. "I'm resting up for tonight when Caius sends my reward."

Seppios laughed. "Speaking of rewards, did you see how furious Festus was when that retarius finally made him yield? I've never seen Festus raise two fingers. I'll not soon let him live that down." His laughter halted. "Filthy Roman," he added, almost as an afterthought.

If ever there had been a man born to be a gladiator, it was Seppios. He was either asleep, or craving a fight.

"Leave him alone," Amadi said from his table, still with his eyes closed. "It's bad enough he'll have to hear us enjoying our women through the cell walls while he sits alone."

Nessa frowned even as she blushed and fidgeted with the wrap on Jonathan's upper arm.

"What's wrong?" he whispered.

"You won your fight. You will be rewarded too." Her glance darted to his eyes, then away as the red in her cheeks deepened.

Did that bother her because of her beliefs, or because it would make her jealous?

Seppios slid down from the wooden table and stretched his arms over his head. There were bruises on the inside of his arm, where the leather straps of his armored sleeve would have been. "You wouldn't know what to do with a woman any better than you do a sword, Amadi."

"All right you two," Quintus said. "Since you're feeling so good, go back to the holding area. You might be in time for Tao to show you how to win without getting injured."

Amadi and Seppios grumbled at this, but Quintus whipped at them with a cloth like they were sheep until they left.

"As for you." Quintus approached him. "Give me your arm."

Jonathan extended it and Quintus felt the skin of his wrist. After a moment, the chubby hand released him. "You're well enough to join them if you want to see the last match. Tao is very impressive in the arena."

Not as impressive as feasting on Nessa's smile and having her gentle touch soothe him. "I've fought Tao before."

She and Quintus exchanged a look he didn't understand.

Quintus crossed his arms over the expanse of his middle and shook his head. "No, you have never *fought* Tao. You have sparred with Tao. You have trained with Tao. But you have never *fought* Tao."

Nessa's hand tightened on his arm. "I pray you never have to."

"Me too." Quintus frowned and rubbed the top of his bald head. "That would be a real bloodbath, and I've brought you back from the dead once already."

"God returned Jonathan to this life, Quintus, though He chose you as His instrument." Quintus frowned but didn't say anything. Jonathan wanted to laugh, because he knew exactly how she'd made him feel. Although she gave Quintus some credit for his skill, which is more than she'd given him.

A slave charged into the chamber, and two guards promptly rushed from the gate of life and grabbed him by the arms.

"I need the physician." The slave struggled as the guards jerked him toward the other opening.

"It's all right. He's not armed," Quintus said.

The guards let the young man go, and he straightened his tunic and bowed to Quintus.

"Who are you?"

"Jonathan, my lord, slave to Lucius Garus. Our physician begs your help to save one of our men."

"Tell Alexander I will come at once."

"Thank you, my lord." The slave ran off as fast as he had come.

"Come, Nessa. I'm certain Tao's defeated opponent will need Alexander and me both, and your prayers to your unseen God." Quintus moved to gather his leather bundle of instruments and Nessa turned to follow.

Jonathan grabbed the edge of her tunic sleeve. "That slave had my name."

"It's not uncommon among my people, though not as common as David." Nessa smiled at him and shouldered Quintus' bag of herbs and linen.

"Won't Caius be angry you're helping his rival?" Jonathan didn't mind if Quintus left, but time with Nessa was a precious rarity.

Quintus tucked his leather roll under his arm and drew up to his full height. "I took an oath to heal at the Asklepian temple when I became a physician. That is what I do." He started toward the passage, but Nessa lingered.

"He'll be angry when he finds out," she said, her voice low as her smile spread. "All the more reason I'm glad we're going."

She was the most baffling person he had ever known. "What about your forgiveness?"

"I forgave him. That doesn't mean I like him."

She hurried away, glancing back before disappearing down the corridor. That fire within her was incredible.

He leaned up on his elbows to examine his bound arm and thigh, then the bruises on his chest and legs. He'd endure much more, and continue to inflict in kind, to protect that fire.

Anything.

"It was a good day's work, Clovis." Caius removed his toga to sprawl back across his couch. "I was sorry to see the magistrate spare Festus and the two recruits who lost. I would have welcomed being recompensed for them."

Clovis bit his tongue to keep from cursing his master.

Caius snapped his fingers and one of his concubines brought him wine. "Maybe I've been wrong."

"About Jonathan?"

"No, my compensation for a slain gladiator. A higher price is more profitable, but I fear it makes the sponsor of the games more determined to let them live, even when the crowd wants death. I think the crowd had riot in their hearts today when the magistrate allowed Festus to live. Mercy," he scoffed. "The blight that remains in our Roman virtue."

Caius set the wine down to pull the slave woman across his lap. "But the magistrate was impressed with our Jonathan. He asked I bring him for his feast next week." He shook his head as he tangled his fingers in the slave girl's hair. "It took that stiff-necked thorn in my heel to get us invited back to the private parties."

"Forgive me, my lord, but his injuries are such I doubt he'll have returned to form for demonstration by then."

"It's not for demonstration, it's for contest. The magistrate wants to stage a match for the guests of his feast. The winds of fate are finally changing."

Clovis wanted to yank the woman off the man's lap and pull the wine from his hand. Their men deserved better than this. "They need time to recover from their wounds and return to form. Fighting them injured all but ensures they will lose."

"Tao and one or two of the others didn't sustain injury."

"But Jonathan did, and—"

"Jonathan is *my* concern and you will continue to do as I command." The muscles in Caius' jaw tightened, making the cords of his neck stand erect like tent poles. "Am I understood?"

"Yes, my lord."

"All but three of the men were victors today?"

"Yes, my lord. Festus and two of the new gladiators. A strong day for the House of Pullus."

"Yes, but a long night for the girls." Caius stroked the leg of the woman on his lap. "The more time that passes between their win and their reward, the less effective the conditioning. Take two of the kitchen slaves from the villa for the new gladiators. They won't know any different. My slaves will see to the others. Take an amphora of *mulsum* wine for yourself. You've earned it."

"Thank you, my lord. I shall share it with the men if you permit."

"It's yours, I care not." Caius flicked the air with his hand and shoved the woman away. "But none to Jonathan. He receives no wine and no women."

Clovis withheld the sigh. This was not the way to draw out the warrior he'd glimpsed the day Jonathan crawled through the sand to retrieve his wooden sword and stand again and again, insisting Tao teach him. He'd observed it again today in the final moments of Jonathan's battle against the murmillo. Few men possessed such a will, forged of iron, that would battle on long after the body and mind were spent.

But Clovis was a slave as much as Jonathan. "As you wish, my lord."

If a woman came into his cell, what exactly was he going to do? Kiss her? Would kissing a stranger be anything like kissing Cyra had been? Jonathan hadn't thought of her in a long time. Not since that day Caius scarred his face and Nessa became his life. Did all women kiss the same? A shudder passed through him as he thought of Valentina.

Memories of her kiss brought a moment of clarity, followed by a deep sense of shame. He doubted women here chose to pleasure the gladiators of their own free will. They were slaves, like him, performing as they must. He would never willingly benefit from that, for it made him no better than Caius.

Besides, it wasn't lack of opportunity that kept him pure since his mother's death. Brennus often boasted of the local brothel and before that, Jonathan's father gifted him with a beautiful servant girl. A servant Jonathan summarily ignored.

He would never risk fathering a child who would grow up as he had, in hardship, without a proper father or name, assuming the child was allowed to live at all. That conviction was something he never spoke of. Nor would he ever speak of it, especially here in the barracks of the ludis.

Hinges groaned on the cell door adjacent to his. A shadow blocked the torchlight through his grate. Then it was gone. Another door opened and the breath he'd been holding left him in a rush. The sounds of passion soon returned, this time through the opposite wall.

He turned toward the quieter wall, wincing as his wounded arm bore the weight of his body. A new pain worked its way through him. For the woman who'd made the shadow. Jonathan had crossed swords with every man here. They were not gentle or patient, and he had no reason to believe they would be now. Even if they were, was her suffering any less? Less than Nessa's had been? If Caius forced himself on her again, what could he do?

Kill him.

Better yet, kill him long before then. After all, protecting her was the only reason he still breathed. If Caius ever strayed too far from his guards, Jonathan wouldn't even need a weapon. They'd made him into one.

Chapter 20 – Misused

Without his armor, Jonathan's body bore no resemblance to the gladiator that ignited the crowd in any contest he entered. His skin resembled a peasant's tunic, ripped and repaired so many times the past four years it would sadden the hardest patrician noble. Nessa had prayed over and helped tend every wound, but right now, she wanted to inflict some of her own on the man responsible. Her eyes burned as she held Jonathan's hand, praying for those grass green eyes to open. "He can't continue like this."

Quintus rinsed his hands and didn't respond. He had to be tired, redoing the horsehair sutures he'd done yesterday after the battle. How they'd broken between then and today when he checked them she couldn't understand. Nor why Quintus continued to ignore her while he extinguished two of the four lamps hanging from their stand beside Jonathan's table. Quintus remained silent while he returned his instruments to their places in his leather bundle.

Someone was going to listen to her. "You must speak to Caius again. Make him understand."

"I've tried. Clovis has tried." He put the last bronze wound clamp away and then shelved the tools before coming to her side and putting his hand on her shoulder. "We're doing what we can for him."

Were they? Was it right to keep healing him so Caius could continue to exploit him this way? She could switch the opium with hemlock without

Quintus knowing but—God forgive her. How could she think such a thing? Especially knowing Jonathan still rejected his need for Jesus.

"Keep him warm. Give him as much undiluted wine as he'll drink when he wakes and try to keep him still. His ribs kept that wound from being deep, but if it reopens…"

"I know." He'd lose even more blood, and there would be even less good flesh to try to close it again. At least this contest had been in their own arena and Luca had Jonathan brought to them right away. Jonathan's opponent had been brought to the table beside him. She'd had to ignore her tangled emotions when that gladiator's medicus had been unable to save him.

"Are you all right?" Quintus asked.

She looked up and forced a smile. "I will be when he is."

"I'm going to the temples for ox blood. I'll be back as soon as I can."

"You know he hates that."

"He loses it faster than his body grows it. Keep him warm. Fire the brazier hotter if you need to, and I'll return soon."

"Hurry, Quintus, please."

He squeezed her shoulder. "I will."

He wouldn't return until he'd found an ox about to be sacrificed. So much blood. It still made her sick to her stomach that so many people believed a gladiator's blood to be the cure for any infirmity. She'd fled the room the occasions Caius would summon Tao and Jonathan to this very chamber so the men who'd paid for it could collect it themselves.

There was life and healing in only one blood, and Jesus the Messiah had already shed it. That was the blood Jonathan needed. The truth he needed to accept. Before his own spilled again and he died, lost and unredeemed.

She brought the back of his hand to her cheek and the tightness in her chest turned to tears. She beseeched God to change Caius' heart. To ease Jonathan's pain. To continue to preserve his life. She prayed for the families and loved ones left behind by Amadi, killed in the December games before last, and for Festus, who she and Quintus had been unable to save last month, and the three others who had been killed in between. She asked

God to remove the hate in her heart for Caius. She'd been able to forgive him defiling her body, but slowly destroying Jonathan's for his insatiable greed she could not forgive.

"Help me, Lord. Help me turn the hate in my heart to the love You showed us on the cross. Help Jonathan to see and know that love. Please."

The hand she held twitched in a weak squeeze. "Don't..." His green eyes watched her, half open as he wet his lips and swallowed. "Don't cry."

Jonathan hated the anguish in her voice as she'd prayed. He hated the tears on her face, even as that smile of hers he'd come to need formed when she met his gaze.

She wiped at her cheek with the knuckles of her free hand. "Tell the bird not to fly." The smile faded and she stroked his shoulder through the thick wool blanket covering him. "Are you warm enough?"

Not really, but he nodded anyway. He remembered very little of his last contest, except for the crippling fear of being certain he was going to lose. The arm Nessa held looked all right. His fingers and toes moved. Beneath the blanket tucked tight around him his left leg burned when he flexed that foot. "What happened?"

"A better gladiator," a deep voice answered. "You almost took that *hoplomachus'* spear straight through your middle."

Tao approached, the sheet door fluttering behind him. Sand covered his chest and forearms, clinging to the sweat. He stopped near Jonathan's feet, crossed his arms, and shook his head. "I've taught you better ways to disarm an opponent."

He hadn't been trying to disarm him. Had he? No. No, he'd left the hoplomachus an opening to draw the gladiator in and open a wound on his exposed side. And it had worked, except the man feinted withdrawal at the last second but still managed to drive that spear at him like he was skewering a trout. Jonathan had rolled his shoulder back and dropped low, felt the spear tip in his side. He'd missed the man's knee, but his exposed torso had loomed inches from his sword and he'd…

"He left you no choice," Tao said, his voice emotionless as always.

Jonathan met his mentor's gaze and saw no disdain there for delivering a mortal wound that hadn't been commanded. Only understanding.

Nessa shifted on the stool beside him. But she hadn't let go of his hand. "Are you injured?"

"No. I came to see how the lion killer does and urge him to heal quickly. He and Seppios are the only sparring partners I must be awake to fight."

"I'll do my best." Though the longer it took him to recover, the more time he spent with her. Perhaps that wasn't true.

"You always do." Tao's tone echoed respect. "I need you on your feet. New recruits arrive soon. Maybe one will be as mule-headed as you were and offer us some amusement."

"Seppios can only hope." Jonathan took a deeper breath to keep speaking. "How is he?"

"Furious. It has become known that the fee for time with him in the private chamber is less than half of mine."

Jonathan chuckled and pain lit up his tender side. In front of his mentor, he did his best to stifle the wince in his throat. Nessa's cheeks turned brilliant crimson, so Jonathan chose not to respond to his friend's humor. That blush was lovely. He was the only gladiator that was never summoned to the private chamber. No reward after a victory ever entered his cell. Even if Caius thought he was punishing him, Jonathan preferred it that way. Though it did stoke his pride to hear now and then rumors of the sums of coin Caius had been offered for him.

There was only one woman he wanted to spend time alone with. Her grip on his hand had grown uncomfortably tight and her pursed lips so unlike her.

"Tao, Jonathan needs rest if he is to heal."

The edge in her tone must have surprised Tao as much as him. The champion's brows dipped and he stiffened, but flashed Jonathan a glance before nodding at Nessa and departing without a word.

Her gruffness had been uncalled for. "Besides you and Quintus, he's my only friend."

"You need to rest. Tao understands that, or he would not have left." She sniffed, and released his hand to wipe at the edge of her nose, reminding him she'd been in tears when he'd awakened, and still looked it.

"You need to stop crying. You'll frighten Quintus." He'd meant to lighten her mood. Bring the smile back to her face he so needed to see.

But she looked away instead. "They're used to seeing me cry."

He tried to keep the panic from his voice. "Why?"

"It doesn't matter." She rose and turned from him.

He seized her wrist before she could take a step. Pain bloomed in his side, but nothing like the pain of her jerking free of his grip. She knocked the stool over in her retreat and glared at him from where she'd stopped—out of his reach.

He should have known better than to try to hold her against her will, no matter how much he wanted an answer.

Nessa huffed and marched back to him. She lifted his blanket and moved his arm, checking for blood on the linen covering his side. "Don't do that again."

"You have my word. But I want to know why they're used to seeing you cry."

She pulled her lower lip in and held it there the way she did when she was contemplating something.

"I can't rest until I know. If you want me to rest, tell me why." Making it about him was low, but it would work. She would answer rather than let him remain troubled.

Eventually her gaze met his, a mix of anger and sadness. "Because every time could be the last time. Perhaps like Amadi, Festus, and the others, one day you will not wake again. Not stand again. Not breathe again." She hugged herself tighter and drew a deep breath. "I live with that fear, wondering what I could have said or done differently for you to open your eyes to the truth that you are still in need of Jesus, no matter how much you pretend otherwise."

It always came back to God for her. "Nessa, I—"

"No. I won't hear it all again, Jonathan. How God abandoned you. How I believe in a dream that one day I must wake from." Her words came faster, shorter, and so did new tears. "You asked why I cry. I told you. That is enough."

Quintus entered through the sheet door, took one look at her face and crossed arms, and quickened his pace. "Why are you crying?"

She dropped her hands and growled like a lion cub. "Can the reason for my tears ever be *mine alone*?" She stormed through the sheet door and her normally light footsteps stomped down the corridor until he couldn't hear her anymore.

Quintus removed a small amphora from the pouch he carried and uncorked it. "What did you say to her?" He emptied the thick, red liquid into a clay cup and stirred in several pinches of herbs and powders.

Jonathan stomach knotted at the sight of the foul drink. "Why assume I'm to blame?"

"Because you always are." Quintus set the cup on the wooden table beside them. "Don't think I've forgotten those first days when you last sent her crying from this room. She's stronger than any of you on your best day. She only weeps over you or when someone dies. Now I'm going to sit you up and for the love of the gods, don't use your middle to help. Let me roll you up."

It still hurt. Quintus put cushions at his back and handed him the cup. Jonathan sniffed it and blanched.

"You know you have to drink it while it's still warm."

"I'd sooner be cold and lightheaded."

"Drink it."

It tasted worse than Frona's goose liver stew and went down about the same. He couldn't stop swallowing because he wouldn't be able to start again.

"You're always lightheaded," Quintus said. "I don't know if it's because you've had your skull bashed so many times, or you were born that way."

Jonathan swallowed the last of the foul drink, but before he could offer retort, the familiar gagging sensation made him want to retch. It happened every single time.

"Don't you dare." Quintus tilted his head back to open up his airway and held it there.

Jonathan sucked his tongue to try to clear away the aftertaste. After a long moment his roiling insides calmed. He drew a deep, steadying breath, and Quintus released his head.

"I think you insulted me just now."

Quintus grinned. "Proof I'm right. I clearly insulted you. How you missed it is beyond me. You're going to need to be clearheaded and well rested. Caius orders you ready to entertain in three days."

Jonathan gagged then. "Three days?"

"I can give you a strong dose of opium to dull the pain. That's the best we can do. I've told him if you reopen that wound, not even I will be able to save you."

Caius was trying his best to get him killed. He always sent Jonathan into a fight before they'd allowed him to fully recover, but three days was suicide. He could be shield to shield with a new recruit and still lose. A single bump, blow, or swing of his own sword would open his side. He'd bleed to death before the crowd had finished their first wineskin.

"Perhaps it's an exhibition. Your mere presence at a feast commands quite a bit of coin now it's rumored. For someone who loses as often as you do, you sure impress the crowd while doing it."

"Tao is the champion of this house, Quintus, not me. And he is allowed to dine and drink with the others, while I'm left shackled and not allowed to move from wherever I've been put on display." Those nights were the slave block all over again, except for being allowed to remain clothed.

Quintus took a blanket and wrapped it around Jonathan in place of a cloak. He added more coal to the brazier and stoked the fire in it, filling the room with more warmth and the strong sent of char. It reminded Jonathan of the fire, the smoke, and the screams of the dying in his memories. He pushed those thoughts away, because dwelling on them only led to the faces of the men he'd killed. Three days. He was going to have to find a way to protect her. Now.

Quintus took the stool usually occupied by Nessa and pulled a parchment scroll from the folds of his tunic.

"What's that?"

"More reason for Nessa to cry." Quintus unrolled the parchment. "I'll read it to you."

Jonathan would rather read it himself, but no one here knew that he *could* read. Although it had been so long since he'd had anything to read, he might struggle. Especially if the writings were Latin.

"To all… lanistii…yes, that's right. Lanistii located throughout the empire."

Quintus made a fine medicus. An orator he would never be.

"Certain emissarii from the… *Ludis Maximus* will be traveling throughout the territories on orders from Lord and God Titus Flavius Caesar Domitianus Augustus Germanicus," Quintus huffed. "Domitian insists on his full formal title now, even in public."

"Yes but what are Caesar's orders?" He should just take the scroll.

Quintus frowned and returned his gaze to the parchment. "Seeking troupes of gladiators for the upcoming *Ludi Romani.* Only primus palus will be considered, and the *doctores* of the Ludis Maximus will have discretion over rankings, contracts, and compensation. Those interested may leave word with the local *aedele*."

Why was that supposed to make Nessa cry? "Caesar seeks gladiators. Why is that of note?"

"The last time gladiators were summoned from throughout the empire it was by Domitian's brother Titus, to inaugurate their father's Flavian Amphitheater."

"I remember. A hundred straight days of games."

"The only reason Domitian would summon so many gladiators to Rome is because the games will be extended, or they will be *sine missione*, and not enough will remain alive for the *Ludi Plebeii* in November."

Sine Missione. Fights to the death. Jonathan had already survived two of those matches. But if his tired mind had understood the letter, and they came here, he had a chance to go to Rome. A chance to return home.

Quintus let the scroll reroll on its own and set it on the table. He strummed his fingers on the wood surface over and over. "It is rumored, only rumored, that Hulderic comes out of retirement for these games at the request of the emperor, and even now travels from his homeland in Brittania."

"Who is Hulderic?"

Quintus' bald head reared back, his eyebrows shoving the folds of skin above them straight up. "They have taught you nothing. Here, lie back down." He eased the cushions from behind Jonathan and lowered him to the mattress. "Hulderic is called the Final Shadow. By the time he earned the *rudius* from Domitian, he had over a hundred victories and thirty kills. Domitian had to free him because no one could defeat him. Several times he defied the emperor's granting the missio and killed his fallen opponent anyway."

Jonathan settled beneath the wool blanket Quintus pulled back up to his chin, hoping warmth would return soon—along with Nessa. "The emperor granted the missio and this Hulderic ignored it?"

"Correct."

"Why was he not killed for disobeying Caesar?"

"The first time he should have been. A colleague who attended those games told me when the barbarian saw the arena guards coming to dispatch him to the underworld, he picked up the sword of the fallen man and together with his own killed them one by one, throwing their severed heads into the crowd. Like any good Roman mob, they were so entertained they screamed *mitte* as more guards were sent to finish him. Domitian dared not defy the crowd, so he gave reprieve. Hulderic fought another three years before he'd become so hard to control and cost so many gladiators, even in training, Domitian gave him the rudius."

"He earned his freedom?"

"Yes, but without honor. He is the worst kind of gladiator, Jonathan. One that toys with his opponents long after they have fallen, ignoring the rules of proper contest. No clean thrust to the neck or blade to the jugular. Instead he carves them like roasted pheasant. It's utterly un-Roman."

Footsteps approached, but they were too heavy to belong to Nessa. The curtain swept back and Seppios entered, holding his arm. A thick splinter as long as a hand protruded from the flesh above his elbow and blood covered his forearm.

Quintus rose from the stool and retrieved cloth, wine, and salt from his supplies. "What happened?"

Seppios assumed his familiar place on a far stool. "It's not important. Just get it out."

Quintus' mouth tightened into a hard line that matched Seppios'. He gripped the wooden shard and gave it a firm twist before yanking it out. Seppios howled, and the corner of Quintus' fleshy lips turned skyward.

Nessa would be horrified. And Quintus wouldn't have done it in her presence.

Seppios' hand jerked to cover the wound. "I wasn't ready."

"It's not important. Just hold still while I finish." Quintus pressed a generous amount of salt into the wound, making Seppios stiffen straight as a beam.

That had been long overdue and he was proud of Quintus for it.

Every man eventually had his limit. Caius had pushed Jonathan past his. Throwing him back into the arena in only three days was condemning him, and Nessa, to death.

So be it. Jonathan wouldn't live to see Rome again, but neither would Caius.

Clovis would rather send Jonathan to fight a pair of murmillos. Changing tactics after their master had won the war was a mistake. "You've given him no women for the past three and a half years. Why now?"

"Someone made me an offer too generous to refuse." Caius held a heavy leather pouch of coins high and then dropped it beside him on the couch. "That and accepting brought more enjoyment than the pleasure I've found in depriving him."

"If you value at all what I know of these men, particularly this one, do not do this."

"You're not usually so against them entertaining in the bedchamber, unless of course it's too close to a fight for your comfort."

"It is not for my comfort." Restraining his anger felt like carrying ten beams at once. "It is for the good of the men, and in turn, this ludis. And Jonathan has never been treated like the others. You overtax him in combat, allow him to be paired with superior fighters without proper time to return to form between contests, and then deny him the spoils his blood and sweat should earn him."

Caius' hand froze midair over his bag of coin. "Take care when giving your opinion so freely." His calculating gaze narrowed. "You forget yourself."

It was Caius who had forgotten. Forgotten his own father and mother had been brutally killed in this very room by a gladiator when their slaves revolted. But he was still the master. "Forgive me, my lord."

"I've told Quintus he is allowed to rest until Friday. The woman visits at midday sun. Make sure he's bathed and attired properly. I will send the tunic I want him in when I summon him. You are to remind him he performs all that I require, in and out of the arena. The penalty for defiance has not changed. Do you understand?"

"Yes, my lord." Caius was the one that needed to understand. Giving Jonathan an hour of pleasure, assuming he wouldn't consider it offensive and he probably would, would deepen his bitterness the next time the slave girls passed his cell by. But like everything, the master would have to learn the hard way.

CHAPTER 21 – HOUR

Jonathan could ignore the pain in his side only because of the beautiful woman kneeling beside the stool he rested on. If only she would smile at him, like he needed her to. One last time. One last time to give him the strength to do what he must. "Are you still angry with me?"

Nessa finished applying her special paste to his wound before answering. "No." Her brown eyes flitted up to his gaze for the first time in days. "Frustrated, but not angry."

She smiled then, and sweet relief flooded his weary body like the final snap of Clovis' whip at the end of the day. "It's early for this, is it not?"

"Clovis told me to change it early, and to give you plenty of opium for pain." Her smile fell away. "If you have to fight today…"

The fear in her gaze was unbearable as it went to the wound in his side. Even she knew he wouldn't be able to overcome that in the arena. But he didn't need to. Not this time.

He'd never tried before because the risk of failing was too great. But today, when he took the sand, and Caius rose to begin the contest, Jonathan would launch his sword straight for Caius' chest with the strength of the condemned and hope his sword did the work of a spear.

It was her only chance.

She sighed and gathered a wide roll of linen. He was glad Quintus wasn't here and Nessa would have to bind him. She unrolled the cloth, sweeping her hand along the smooth surface. If she found any uneven weave that would chafe him, she would cut it away or choose another piece. She only did that for him.

"Can you hold your arms out for me?"

He raised them and bit his lip against the stab of pain in his torso. The opium must not have taken effect yet. Nessa moved close enough the end of her braid brushed his thigh as she wrapped his waist. He breathed deep to keep from closing his arms around her. The intoxicating scent of herbs and the oil she bathed in made his mind mush. He bit his lip harder, concentrating on a crack in the wall.

Could he try? He'd fought wounded before. Never this wounded but, could he? He'd lost before, but given such a good fight the crowd had thundered with praise when he finally raised two fingers. As long as the crowd and Caius' patron were pleased, that had been enough to satisfy Caius. If it were a slave with a sword and not another gladiator, he might be able to. He would know in the first few volleys. But by then it would be too late. He wouldn't be able to stop the fight and return to his plan. Assuming he wasn't bleeding to death first. If the wound in his side reopened during the fight, he would be.

"Almost done." Her breath hit his chest like the warmth of the sun when stepping from the shadows on a winter morning. He tilted his head straight back and closed his eyes. Caius had been clear when he'd scarred his face. He fails, she dies. Death was failure. Killing him wouldn't be the end, unless Quintus and Clovis would protect her if Caius did in fact have someone or more than someone who would avenge his death on her, as he'd vowed.

The sharp discomfort when she tied off the wrapping brought him back. He looked into her deep brown eyes, still ignorant of all of this. Should he tell her? Tell Quintus? Why did every strand of the web in his mind lead her into more danger and not less?

She rose from the floor and put her hand on his shoulder. "After you've won, I'll be here when you wake. And Quintus will have returned by then.

Caius won't let you fight until he's here. I'm sure of it." She forced a smile, but the growing sheen in her eyes gave her away.

She wasn't herself today. No teasing him he needed a bath or making shadow animals in the lamplight with her hands that looked nothing like they were supposed to, especially the owls. No sparring with him about her God. How he'd come to cherish those times alone with her. He took her hand from his shoulder and held it. So soft. So strong. "I need to tell you something."

Her brow creased as she tensed.

"If I don't come back—"

"Stop." Her fingers flew to his lips.

He pulled her hand away gently. "I need you to listen."

"I can't." She pulled free of his grasp and backed away. "Not to that."

Clovis entered, his gaze darting between them. "Can't what?"

"Nothing." Nessa turned her gaze to him. "I'll be here. When you come back." Then she hurried from the room, with Clovis watching her.

Clovis could suspect nothing. Jonathan needed every advantage. To put from his mind all the ways this could fail so that it would not. "Am I fighting here or somewhere else?"

"You're not fighting."

Not fighting? "An exhibition?"

"Similar. You'll be given instructions when they're needed. For now come to the baths."

He followed Clovis down the familiar corridors. Relief he might yet see the sunset tonight with Nessa unharmed made his feet unsteady. He could stand for a few hours in his bronze chains and be gawked at and discussed as if he were a statue.

At the baths six slaves waited. They used enough olive oil on him to light every lamp in the ludis, working around the linen wraps on his torso and the two on his arm. A slave trimmed his hair while another shaved him. A third rubbed him down with crushed hyssop leaves wrapped in steaming cloth. Clovis stood watch, looking grim as ever, holding a new tunic that looked more suited to Caius than Jonathan. Maybe they meant to show him at the governor's villa again.

When time came to pull his tunic over his head, the pain in his side wasn't as strong as before. Hopefully the opium would last long enough for him to swing a sword against a slave for a few minutes if he needed to. "Are we traveling on foot or by cart?"

"Your visitor comes here."

No one came to see him here unless he was performing in the arena. "To the ludis?"

"To the villa. Come."

Clovis led him through another corridor that became familiar when they reached the stairs. Jonathan paused at the same polished metal on the wall. If not for the scar on his cheek to prove it, he wouldn't have thought the bloodied and bruised face he'd once seen in it was the same one returning his stare.

"Come," Clovis ordered.

Jonathan continued up, summoning his restraint in case Caius was present. Mercifully, the balcony was empty. No guards, not even Caius' slave girls were there. The faint stain on the wood floor that could only be the blood of the innocent man he'd slain tugged at him as he passed over it.

They followed another corridor to a single door standing closed at the end. Clovis put his hand on the latch and turned to Jonathan. "Caius reminds you that you obey him without hesitation and in exchange he honors your agreement. Do you understand?"

Understanding crashed through him like thunder. Panic coursed through his veins and every dark emotion he possessed battled en masse in his head. Could he do this? He'd been summoned. Not to fight but to, to—with a stranger. Who was in that room?

"I will wait in Caius' chamber and come for you in one hour." Clovis pushed open the door. The chamber was lit with lamps in the corners of the room. A low, wide couch bigger than any he'd ever seen sat in the center of the room, behind a cloaked figure standing with their back to him.

"One hour." Clovis gestured for him to go inside.

Jonathan could feel the sweat warming him and his heartbeat quicken.

Clovis leaned close. "Pretend she's her," he whispered, and propelled him inside.

He took two steps toward the cloaked figure and heard the door close behind him.

The woman turned and pushed back the hood of her cloak. It couldn't be. But then she smiled with all the lust his scarred back remembered.

Chapter 22 – Old Friend

Valentina's gaze crawled from Jonathan's face to his feet before returning to his eyes. "I was angry to learn you were still alive. Until I saw how much gladiator life agrees with you."

Her satisfied sigh ripped through him like a sword.

"If it was your allegiance to my husband that kept you from me, you're no longer bound to it. You can give in now to the desire that lies within you." She rolled her shoulders, and the edges of her cloak fell behind them to reveal a blue silk tunic clinging to her body like a second skin.

"My desire?" His voice trembled as he raised his hand to her neck and gripped as tight as he dared. With his other hand he traced her cheekbone, the smooth perfection of her skin. "My desire is to kill you slowly."

Her eyes widened in a fear he relished. He allowed his grip on her neck to tighten, his thumb pressing hard into the jugular vein he'd been trained to sever. "To watch the life drain from your eyes while I crush your throat."

Jonathan. Nessa's voice whispered his name like a prayer, breaking through the storm of wrath. For her, he found the strength to let go. The fear passed from Valentina's eyes as she swallowed and rubbed her neck. For one beautiful moment, he had controlled her. But it couldn't last. Though no longer hers, he was still a slave. She knew that as well as he did.

She put her hand flat to his chest in a gesture of unearned familiarity. "Is that any way to greet an old friend?"

He grabbed her bared arms and shoved her back as roughly as he dared, curling his hands into fists to keep from striking her. "Keep your prostitute hands off me."

Valentina straightened where she'd caught herself on the edge of the bed. "Careful who you call a prostitute, slave. I paid for the pleasure of your company. Not the other way around."

"It makes no difference which direction the coin passes, though you'd like to believe it does."

She raised her hand and swung, but he was faster. He snatched her wrist and held on before her slap reached his face. Her other arm shot up, and he grabbed that one and held both even tighter. Her struggle to free herself pulled Jonathan with her toward the wall. The instant he released her she would attempt hitting him again, so he held on. He flattened her against the wall with the full press of his body, less she begin to kick at him too. If she managed to strike him, he knew he would hit her back—and not be able to stop.

The need to exact retribution cried out with every breath. Trapped between the crush of his body and the wall, the heat of her breath covered his face as her chest heaved against his own. She finally stilled, and her gaze went to his mouth.

Her lips met his, scorching like salt in a fresh wound.

He jerked back and flung her away.

She toppled the brass lamp stand in the corner of the chamber. The clanging metal mingled with her curse as they both fell to the floor. She struggled to untangle herself while calling him names that even Seppios didn't use. Mingled with her cursing, the scent of singed wool reached him. Her smoking cloak turned to a flame she must have seen the moment he did. Her scream filled the room as the flame spread through her cloak and ignited the oil spread around her.

"Help me! Please!"

No. Jonathan remained rooted in place, fighting his instinct to snatch the covering from the bed and smother the flames. As many scars as he carried because of her lies, she deserved some scars of her own.

The door slammed open. Two guards rushed in with Clovis in their midst.

Jonathan held still while Luca's sword halted inches from his throat. Clovis pulled a wailing Valentina from the prison of flame and ripped the burning cloak from her body. He threw it onto the burning oil and shoved the couch further from the flames. The other guard carried the sobbing woman from the room.

A slave ran in with a pail of water, but Clovis yelled for him to bring sand instead. Smoke and burning wool made breathing in the windowless room difficult. When the flames had finally been extinguished, they were all struggling to breathe. Clovis motioned for the guards with a jerk of his head and grabbed Jonathan by the arm, hauling him back into the main chamber. Jonathan thought about grabbing for a sword on the wall, but Luca turned and set up his blade again the moment Clovis released him.

His trainer gave him a seething glare. "Caius will not be pleased."

No one knew that better than Jonathan, and here, away from Valentina, that reality sank deep. "Take me to him. Now."

Luca's sword edged closer to Jonathan's throat. "You don't give the orders, slave."

"Leave us, Luca," Clovis said. "Make sure Quintus is tending the woman's burns and that she's brought a new cloak."

The thought of Valentina anywhere near Nessa made Jonathan cringe, but he needed to address a more potent threat—immediately. "Take me to Caius."

Clovis crossed his arms and sighed, surveying the room they were alone in. "You could have refused her without setting her on fire."

"That was not my intent, though I'm not sorry for it. I refused her four years ago and she had me beaten so badly they thought I was dead." Jonathan's voice broke as his fears for Nessa grew. How could he have let this happen?

"Death may come for you now when Caius learns of this. His anger will extend beyond you. You know that."

"Which is why you must take me to him. Now."

Before Clovis could respond, the lanista entered, flanked on either side by a pair of guards. The men quickly filled the room and surrounded Jonathan.

Caius regarded him with the same hatred that had overpowered Jonathan moments ago. "You just cost me a hundred aureii."

Jonathan winced at the amount. Ten thousand sesterces—as much as if he'd fallen in the arena. Gaius Florus must be dead for Valentina to have given Caius such a sum.

Caius unsheathed his dagger and held it between them. "You can't even imagine all the ways I'm going to make you pay for this. Some of which I might make you watch."

Don't react. He must believe you. "Go ahead."

Caius' brows dipped and the knife in his hand wavered.

That was the uncertainty Jonathan needed to see. "I swear on my sword I would sooner you kill Nessa and me both, as cruelly as you can invent, before I would ever bed Valentina Florus."

"Nessa?" One of the guards had spoken her name. One by one their questioning stares came to rest on Caius.

"Out. All of you." Caius gestured toward the door with his dagger. "Clovis, you remain."

The way Caius held his dagger, Jonathan could seize it and cut the man's throat in seconds. But if Clovis intervened, or Jonathan failed to hit the jugular vein…no, this was still the best way to protect her—the only way.

When the three of them were alone, Caius took a step closer. "I think you lie. Nessa is your greatest weakness. You've proven it before." He turned the dagger in his hand back toward Jonathan's face, staring down the edge of the blade at him.

"Valentina is my weakness. Nessa is what I prize."

"If that's true, why refuse her? She told me she'd sent you here for trying to have her against her will."

"She lied. Then, today, and always. I hate her, and I wish her dead far more than I want Nessa to live."

The silence that followed would have invited the most timid of creatures to emerge. Jonathan forced himself to keep breathing, not to so much as blink or twitch.

Caius slowly lowered the dagger, but not his stare. "You vex me, Jonathan, and you cost me a great deal of coin. Again. How shall you make it up to me? Assuming I don't make Nessa contribute, which I still might."

"Let me do what I do best."

"Vex me?"

"Bleed for you. You know how quickly I'll earn that back. I can't if I'm dead."

Caius pursed his lips and closed the distance between them. He turned his dagger to rest the flat of the cool metal blade beside the hollow at the base of Jonathan's throat. "I'm not going to kill you. But I can't allow this to go unpunished. You're no good to me if I must be wary you will defy me again."

Jonathan resisted leaning away from the stench of Caius' breath, or the blade resting against his throat. "I have done nothing but perform for you in and out of the arena since you put this scar on my face. But I will not perform for you in the bedchamber."

"Because you can't?"

"Because I won't. And before you threaten to harm Nessa, consider this. If you touch her, force me to see that fear and pain in her eyes again, I will have died already. And I will never pick up another sword as long as I live, except to fall on it."

There'd been no need to fake the sincerity in those words.

Caius studied him for a long moment. "For the first time since I have known you, you impress me." He lifted the dagger from Jonathan's neck. "You impress me indeed." He walked to the tall floor lamp burning opposite the balcony and placed the tip of the dagger above the point of the greatest flame.

Jonathan looked to Clovis, but the trainer watched their master as he slowly passed the metal blade back and forth over the flames of the lamp.

Long moments passed and Caius seemed to have forgotten them both, his attention wholly on his strange task.

Finally he spoke. "I agree to the new terms of our arrangement. No summoning you to pleasure patrons, and no taking my own in your little Jewess. You will perform in the arena and at feasts only, and as long as you continue to perform well, she will live."

He turned toward Jonathan, the metal blade now blackened and smoking. "But we seal the deal properly. Give me your hand."

Jonathan's stomach dropped.

Clovis moved toward them. "My lord, I—"

"Silence, Clovis. This is between me and Jonathan." Caius reached his empty hand toward Jonathan, still gripping the smoking knife in the other. "Give me your hand."

Jonathan took a deep breath and held it while raising his right hand. He refused to look away or tremble in fear as Caius took him by the wrist, turning his sword hand palm up. Caius pressed the blade to his palm and the searing metal scorched through the first layers of skin as the stench of his own burning flesh reached his nose. The nerve endings below burned away in the blink of an eye, a last act of mercy given in the violent pain of their dying. But not before letting Jonathan feel what he could smell and hear beneath the hot blade. Every muscle in his arm tensed. His fingers curled in an attempt to flee the source of the pain, but he refused to cry out. Nor did he look away from the eyes of the man who continued to smile at him while holding his wrist tight and pressing the knife to his palm.

When all heat had been sucked from the blade, Caius tore the knife away and relinquished his grip on Jonathan's wrist.

He wanted to see what remained of his palm and cradle the burnt hand to his chest, but Tao's words were there at once. *Showing me where you are in the most pain only invites more in the same place.* Instead he lowered his arm to his side and remained silent, blinking fast to keep the moisture stinging his eyes from gathering in the corners.

Caius sheathed his dagger without cleaning the char and burnt skin away. "You are the first to not scream and cry like a child who's lost his mother."

A different hurt flashed through him at the thought of the carving resting against his chest. "Gladiators embrace pain."

"Yes. And you better than any I have ever seen. One day you may be my champion."

"I am Nessa's champion, not yours."

"Watch your tongue, slave, or I'll burn that as well."

The thought of enduring the pain shooting up his arm on his tongue made him swallow involuntarily.

"Clovis, see Jonathan to his cell. He returns to training tomorrow."

"Even before you made him unable to grip a sword, he was still too injured to wield one." The disapproval in Clovis' voice matched his posture.

"You coddle him. You coddle all of them. Perhaps it's time to retire your whip and find you other duties. Perhaps something in the kitchens."

Clovis uncrossed his arms to rest his hand on the grip of his sword. His usually stoic expression became one of indignation. The open challenge gave Jonathan hope, and he skimmed the wall for the sword he could reach fastest.

"Careful, Clovis," Caius said. "If I didn't know you better, I'd think that was a threat. You know how I deal with threats." His gaze went to Jonathan. "Rest him another day if you must."

He retreated from the room and Jonathan raised his hand to see it.

Then wished he hadn't.

Clovis came to him and took his hand to examine the burn. "I will see you rested until he threatens me again. Maybe gain you an extra day or two."

"Don't put yourself at risk for me."

"I do not need a champion as Nessa does."

Jonathan chuckled but the ache in his hand was excruciating. Not only that, lesser pain gripped his ribs, beneath the tunic and tight linen wrap. He pressed his elbow into his side and the discomfort eased. The opium must be wearing off.

"How's the side?"

"Hurts."

"The hand?"

"Hurts worse."

"I never tended burns on the battlefield. I want Quintus to see to that, after I've made sure your old friend is gone from his chamber. Better yet, gone from the villa."

"Better yet, gone from this life."

Jonathan followed Clovis toward the stairs, then down them. Clovis stopped midway and turned back to him. "Did you mean it?"

"Mean what?"

"You would rather see Valentina dead then Nessa live?"

Jonathan hesitated a mere heartbeat. Better if Clovis also believed the lie. "Yes."

Clovis turned away to continue down the stairs. Jonathan felt the weight of the man's disappointment but would carry it as he did any other wound. They passed along the edge of the barracks where the men trained. They took turns leering as he passed. Seppios offered a crude remark about Jonathan needing to go to the medicus chamber after being summoned to the upper chamber. Tao hit him in the back with his wooden sword and away they went. Jonathan and Clovis entered the corridor and then made their way through the sheet door.

Jonathan tensed as he surveyed the room, seeing only Quintus. "Where is Nessa?"

"Right here." She emerged from behind his table holding a bundle of blankets. "What have you done now? Reopened that wound?"

Jonathan didn't answer. Despite the pain in his side and his hand, all he could do was stare at her. She was so beautiful, and her smile had returned. If Valentina had been here, her evil had not touched Nessa. For that he was grateful.

"It's his hand." Clovis gestured toward Jonathan's other side. "He burned it on a brazier."

"Really?" Quintus eyed both of them. "The same brazier that burned the woman who refused to let me treat her and left, demanding her servant take her to a real physician?"

"The same." Clovis' gaze dared Quintus to keep asking questions.

Jonathan took a seat on the stool near the center table. Quintus took his hand, looked at the elongated wound ending in a tapered point, and huffed. Nessa surveyed the damage beside him. Her face twisted up and she tilted her head to view a different angle. "It almost looks like…"

"Nessa," Quintus cut in. "Cut me more thin strips of linen, please."

While she prepared them, Clovis took his leave. Quintus cleaned the wound before padding it and wrapping it tight while Nessa observed over his shoulder.

Jonathan ignored the pain in his hand to drink in the sight of her, made all the more radiant on the heels of his reunion with Valentina. Confronting her had been nothing like his imaginings. Rare nights when sleep refused to come he often pictured himself face to face again with both her and Manius. In his visions of vengeance however, he'd always been armed with a sword. Fire had made a poor weapon. She would live, but with scars. That would have to be enough—for now.

When Quintus finished, Jonathan stood and allowed his thoughts to return to Nessa. Everything Valentina was not. They weren't alone. She might not welcome it, but he couldn't stop. For the first time since he'd known her, he took her arm and pulled her to him. Her breath caught and her back stiffened the moment he closed his arms around her. A single embrace, and while she didn't relax against him, she didn't pull away. She was safe—the painful burn trivial in comparison. He released her and stepped back, unable to look her or Quintus in the eyes. He turned and retreated toward his cell, hoping he hadn't made another in a long highway of mistakes.

CHAPTER 23 – TREMBLE

When Jonathan woke, the angle of the sunlight on his cell floor was wrong. He dressed, found his door unbolted and the sun hanging low on the wrong side of the sky. The other gladiators were sparring, recruits were strength training, and the guards were lazily watching from their posts. A normal day in the ludis, except he'd missed most of it.

Clovis ordered him back to his cell and because the balcony was empty, Jonathan returned. His side and his palm only hurt when he moved them, so rest would be welcome. A slave brought a cold bowl of barley stew, bread, and watered wine. Jonathan ate alone, listening to the others spar and wondering what Nessa was doing. How she felt about the moment he'd held her yesterday. When the day's training ended, Clovis entered and set a small vial down on Jonathan's table.

Jonathan recognized the familiar shape. "Poison?"

"No. More opium for your pain. It's undiluted, so don't tell Quintus."

"A gift most appreciated." Jonathan poured the fragrant liquid into his cup and added more watered wine. Clovis was now on Jonathan's side. Of that he was certain. The trainer kept him in opium, and insisted he rest the following day as well. When Clovis did allow him to return to training, he forbade Jonathan from sparring, which disappointed both Tao and Seppios. Jonathan worked the pole instead, like a new recruit. This angered Caius, who scowled while grasping the balcony edge like a reluctant lover.

Jonathan made sure his back was to Caius before smiling as he hacked away with his wooden sword.

The dressing on his hand made gripping anything difficult, but he worked through it. His side pained him less every day, even without the opium he'd stopped four days ago. Quintus often warned the effectiveness diminished if overused, and Jonathan had no desire to become a slave to it as some did. One cruel master was more than enough.

When Clovis entered his cell in the morning and set another vial on the table, Jonathan shook his head. "No more. I told you, I'm embracing the pain."

"Drink it. You fight today. The emissaries from Rome have arrived in Capua. They visit the ludis of Pullus first, which is an honor Caius owes Tao, and you." Clovis poured the numbing liquid into Jonathan's cup and filled it halfway with water.

His rest was at an end. Time once again to see Caius pleased with him. Jonathan rose and drained the cup.

Clovis pulled his dagger from his belt and extended the handle. "No wraps. It makes you appear weak."

Jonathan took the knife and cut away the linen circling his middle. The crusty scab over the gash brushed away, revealing a newly forming scar. He cut away the wrap on his sword hand.

Clovis took one look at his palm and cursed.

The center of the bright pink flesh was painful to the touch. Jonathan pressed with his thumb and had to stifle a hiss. He reached for the empty cup on the table and tightened his grip until his knuckles whitened. Though painful, he could sustain the pressure. He set the cup down and flexed his hand. "The juice of that dagger-leafed plant must be working."

"Aloe is a great healer, if it can be found in the market."

Jonathan chuckled and flexed his hand again. "Quintus does bemoan the cost when Nessa slathers it on like oil."

Clovis stared at Jonathan, a faraway look in his eyes. "I once knew such devotion." He blinked, and the mask of hardness returned. "Make her proud today."

Jonathan and Tao would fight in the training area, where they could be observed more closely from the balcony than from the stands of the arena. The pair of officials from Rome wore tunics, not togas. They had the hardened look of Clovis rather than the pampered appearance of the magistrate and other Romans who frequented the ludis.

With trained eyes, the men on the balcony, including Caius, could likely tell Tao was holding back. The crushing force Jonathan normally encountered in Tao's blows wasn't there, though their speed and form remained the same. The match was still a struggle, but he felt the moment his second strength surged. His mind shut out all pain and any thought but victory. He rushed Tao, and the hilt of his sword struck a glancing blow off the champion's brow.

Blood flowed from the gash. Tao ran the back of his sword hand over his forehead and stared at the blood staining it. His gaze lifted and narrowed so much his dark eyes disappeared.

Jonathan was about to die. He almost turned and fled. The years of conditioning, coupled with his second strength, allowed him to maintain his honor as Tao came at him with the fury of a summer storm. Quintus' words from years ago returned—You've never fought Tao.

He fought him now. His wooden sword splintered and then cracked in half as Tao struck it again with his own. Jonathan dropped the broken stump and clutched his shield in both hands. He needed to close the distance between them before Tao took his head off. He pushed in with his shield under the steady rain of blows. Suddenly Tao thrust back with his own shield and threw his sword away.

The sight of Tao parted from his sword froze Jonathan in place. Tao's fist struck him in the face. He felt his head snapping him off his feet and the hard-packed sand slamming into his back where he fell. Blood poured into his throat, likely from a broken nose, choking him as he squinted against the sun above.

Applause rang out from the balcony. "Well done, Tao!"

Leaning forward to rise with dignity was out of the question. He rolled on his side and pushed up onto all fours, rising the shameful way, like a dog. He felt warmth at his side and looked down. The new scar had opened.

Tao still wiped at his brow and Clovis ordered them both to Quintus. Jonathan held his bleeding side with his good hand and his bloody nose with the burned one as they left the training area together. Tao's eye was closed against the blood sheeting from the wound above his brow to edge at his chin like a swollen stream. They entered and found Quintus and Nessa discussing some black herb on cloth resting on the table between them.

Quintus looked up and all but growled. He kicked his stool aside and made his way toward Jonathan. "That was almost healed."

Tao grabbed a cloth from the folded stack on the table near him and held it to his face. "You better set the lion killer's nose before no woman will have him."

Nessa shot Tao a dark look as she made her way to assist Quintus. Jonathan smiled though it increased the pain in his nose. Nessa cleaned Tao's face and applied a salve to it before he left without saying another word. Still a man of little speech.

Jonathan thought nothing could ever be more painful than having an arm put back in joint, until Quintus set his nose. He had a new appreciation for how often Seppios endured having it done.

Maybe it was the opium, or Nessa's nearness, or the concern in her clear brown eyes while she helped Quintus clean and dress the spear wound again, but Jonathan ached to touch her. Quintus sat at his back, so Jonathan let the fingertips of his burned hand come to rest on the smooth skin of her elbow. She trembled, and he almost drew back, until he saw her eyes.

There was no fear in them.

Like a whetstone caresses the edge of a blade it sharpens, he traced the silk of her skin to her wrist. Once there, he allowed his fingertips to play in circles on the back of her hand while he watched her face. The blush he loved appeared with a vengeance, and when her mouth parted, he wanted nothing more than to taste it.

"Nessa," Quintus called.

She jumped like a startled deer and caught herself on Jonathan's thigh before he could steady her. She looked at her hands gripping his leg so near his loincloth and jerked away from him, putting her palms to her cheeks in alarm.

He bit the inside of his lower lip to keep from grinning. Her innocence had been taken from her body, but not from her spirit. She was so beautiful.

"Nessa, are you all right?" Quintus asked from behind him.

"Yes." She straightened and kept her eyes averted from his face. She took the end of the linen with trembling hands and passed it around to Quintus.

"Are you sure?"

"Yes, I'm sure."

She was anything but all right from the flush staining her cheeks and the way her chest rose and fell as rapidly as his did before battle. Her response to his touch gave him a foreign sense of power but on the tail of that, regret. She wasn't a plaything for his amusement. She meant too much to him to treat her with anything less than the respect and honor she deserved. No matter how much he wanted to make her tremble again.

Quintus rose and came to stand in front of him. "All done. See if you can stand easily. If not, I'll tighten the wrap."

Nessa backed away, her gaze still avoiding him.

He stood and raised his arm on his wounded side to his shoulder. The movement was uncomfortable but bearable. "Thank you. Both of you."

Her head came up, and he thought she might meet his gaze, but she looked toward the door. Jonathan turned and found Clovis holding the sheet back. "We travel to Rome a month from tomorrow. Well done, Jonathan."

"Rome!" Quintus clapped his hands and shook like an excited child about to devour a sweet cake.

Nessa's round face beamed with excitement.

He was going home—to the city of his birth, the city of his father, his dead mother, and the man who shared his blood and betrayal. If Jonathan set eyes upon Manius, there would be no whip long enough, no chains heavy enough, and no cell strong enough to keep him from his vengeance.

Chapter 24 – Going Home

By tonight, Jonathan and the small caravan traveling under praetorian escort would reach Rome. Caesar had sent his own soldiers to see them safely to the Ludis Maximus. The nightmare of the attack that had killed Dio and made him a slave had returned the first night camped along the *Via Appia*, and continued unabated every time he slept. He would wake bathed in sweat between Tao and Seppios sleeping soundly beside him on their woven mats.

A single chain joined the three of them since leaving the ludis. The links lay piled between their feet on the wood floor of the oxcart as it rolled along behind Caius and Clovis, who traveled on horseback like their guards. As often as Jonathan found an excuse, he looked back to glimpse Nessa. She would be adjusting Quintus' sun shade in their cart, or pouring water for the guards. Two from the ludis including Luca, and eight from the emperor, all armored and armed. Something she said to Luca yesterday had made him laugh, and he tipped his helmet to her before fanning back into formation.

Jonathan didn't like that.

Tao's voice startled him. "She is the innocent."

Fear churned inside, but Jonathan didn't let it reach his face as he turned toward Tao.

The dark eyes of the champion studied him. "She is what changed you."

It wasn't a question. Jonathan glanced at Seppios, who appeared to be ignoring everyone, as was his custom. It seemed Tao already knew, so Jonathan gave him a short nod. Tao dipped his chin in that way of his that said they would never speak of it again unless Jonathan did. And he wouldn't. Nor would he risk watching her anymore.

The next few hours passed in silence except for the occasional snort of a guard's horse and the constant rattle of cart wheels on the cobblestone road. He told himself he wouldn't look for it. But he did. The grove of olive trees beyond a large boulder, nearly fifty cubits from the highway. He could recall everything about that day. Meeting his father for the first time. His first chariot ride as they raced through the countryside to that very grove. Life had been so full of promise then. Before God took his mother from him and Manius stole what was left of the life he'd rebuilt without her.

Tao's voice startled him. "I see trees. You look as if you see death."

The man was more observant than an astronomer.

Seppios chose that moment to stretch his arms high over his head, rattling the chain between them. His yawn of indifference offered Jonathan a diversion. "We bore Seppios."

"You do not bore me, Roman." He shot Jonathan a petulant glare. "Or should I say, the back of your head does not."

Tao laughed, and Jonathan swore silently. He might as well have stood up and called out to Nessa the last four days.

"Besides." Seppios stretched again and arched his back. "I dream of crossing blades with Hulderic."

The gladiator Quintus had warned of. The one the guards from Rome told stories of over their cooking fire. "What do you know of him?"

"He's my wooden sword. Caius is too greedy to ever free any of us. But the emperor—" The wheel of the cart hit a deep break in the stone highway, rattling their chain and jarring Seppios, who swore vehemently.

"The emperor what?"

"The emperor can. He would award the rudius to the gladiator who defeats the legend. The people would demand it."

Jonathan doubted they would ever find out. "Hulderic is legend for a reason. How will you defeat someone they say has no weakness?"

"Every man has a weakness," Tao broke in, casting a knowing look at Jonathan.

Seppios crossed his arms and leaned back against the side of the cart. "He has been away from the arena too long and returns only for coin. My plan is simple." He paused with a shrug of his shoulders. "I want it more."

Seeping the determination in Seppios' face, the hard jaw and flat eyes, Jonathan could almost believe desire was enough. But he knew it wasn't. If wanting to win more than anything would be enough to claim victory, he would be the one undefeated.

Their cell door slammed closed for the night, plunging the tiny cell into darkness. Jonathan collapsed onto his bunk, as did Tao and Seppios. They all were feeling the effects of the demanding regimen of the trainers of the Ludis Maximus. The three-level gladiator training barracks complete with its own arena was almost half the size of the Flavian amphitheater. It seemed Emperor Domitian had no intention of being the weak link in his family dynasty. He'd commissioned the project soon after being named Caesar. The barracks not only complemented the family legacy, but more importantly, provided Rome with a central and steady supply of gladiators.

The massive structure inspired awe in Jonathan as much as Tao and Seppios when they first arrived. Jonathan estimated there were nearly a thousand men in the barracks, quartered four to a cell roughly the same size as his own back in Capua.

Seppios stirred in his rack beneath Jonathan's. "I'm exhausted. I haven't trained this hard since our spies told my people the Romans were coming."

"Then rest. With your mouth," Tao said in the darkness

"Clovis was taking it easy on us."

Seppios ignoring Tao's command made Jonathan grin, but thoughts of their trainer stole the moment of levity. It was true. The past two weeks had shown them that the walls of this place and the men who ran it were the embodiment of all that was Rome. Like the war machine that had rolled over kingdoms and nations to form the empire, the training here rolled over them like a millstone on wheat until all chaff was gone.

Jonathan thrived under it, renewed with the hope born in him the day Seppios spoke of the wooden sword and freedom. Even the training here felt like true contest, which Jonathan was conditioned to win at all costs. So many spectators filled the seats of the practice arena that every day felt like an en masse match.

He'd searched the many faces as often as he could for one that matched his own. Getting word to his father could not be done through the guards, or haphazardly, lest the message be intercepted by Manius first. In addition to that risk, Jonathan had nothing to offer as a bribe to see a message delivered.

"Are you still alive, Roman?" Seppios asked.

Tao breathed a frustrated sigh in the darkness.

"Yes." *The most I've been in a long time.* "Does this disappoint you?"

"Yes."

Even Tao laughed then.

Jonathan lay awake long after the others slept. Two weeks had passed without a trace of Nessa and Quintus. He'd seen Caius three times, always observing with what could only be other lanistii. He knew with absolute conviction that if he were to fail, Caius would make good on his threat to kill Nessa—if for no other reason than to spite him, even in the grave.

He would train even harder tomorrow.

The fourth of September, the eve of the two-week long Ludi Romani. The Capitoline Trio—Jupiter, Minerva, and Juno—the heads of Rome's pantheon, would be honored. Jonathan had once considered them idols, their worshipers pagans. Now they were nothing but an excuse for games. And these games were to be sin missione, fights to the death. He would have to add another face to those that haunted his sleep.

He stood with Tao and Seppios among the other gladiators in the barracks as the trainers read aloud the schedule and pairings. Jonathan would fight a retiarius named Jelani. Jonathan knew him to be a good net fighter, though he had not been trained or matched with him yet. Jonathan had never lost to a retiarius, and that bolstered his confidence. They would fight tomorrow, the last match of opening day.

Seppios would wait another three days before taking the sand against the champion of a house from Ariminum in the North. Names continued to be read, men grumbling they had not been chosen to fight Hulderic. While secretly being relieved they were not, as he'd been.

Jonathan's gut tightened as contests dwindled until only Hulderic's remained, the final match on the final day of the games.

They called Tao's name.

Tao remained stoic, as was his custom. Seppios met his gaze, and Jonathan saw his same fears reflected there. But Tao said nothing as they trained, ate evening meal, or when he and Seppios left with the others for Caesar's feast. Jonathan remained alone in their cell, exempted from the feasting as always. So Caius maintained control even here.

Nessa did not come.

He longed for her there in the dark. The laughter in her brown eyes. The sweep of her hair when she moved. Most of all, the way her presence renewed something within him he couldn't put into words.

Would he die tomorrow? Would his father be among those watching? Would he recognize him when they called his name? Would Manius?

He'd feared for Nessa's life so long, thoughts of his own fate beyond death had remained a distant fog. What if he was wrong? What if like Deborah and his mother had taught him, hell awaited him, like all those who rejected God and the redemption of His Son Jesus? A faith he had once believed and then abandoned. Flashes of memories fed the turmoil within—the road from Rome, Valentina, the beating that nearly killed him. But strongest was the memory of his mother.

Still and pale in death as Jonathan had fallen on her body to weep. He clung to that memory like a shield against his fear. If he died tomorrow, and found there was a God waiting for him, at least they would be even. God had abandoned him first.

Jonathan waited for the guards to come take him from their cell to the arena. Tao clapped Jonathan's shoulder, his hand as heavy as the mood on what might be Jonathan's final morning.

Seppios broke the silence. "If you face another Roman, lion killer, I'd rather you win."

That was the closest Seppios had ever come to revealing he held Jonathan in any esteem. He grinned and they exchanged nods. Their cell door opened, and Jonathan let a farewell die in his throat. He would return. He had to.

The tunnel leading from the Ludis Maximus resembled a catacomb. Torches smelled of fresh pitch and made the air in the damp tunnel thin. He recognized a few faces among the group of thirty gladiators escorted by praetorian guards on either end of their procession. He didn't know who among them Jelani was. Nor did he want to. By this afternoon, the retiarius would be dead.

When they reached the pits below the arena floor, every sense came under assault. The rank smell of blood and animal dung hit first, followed by the stifling heat. Clanging armor, weapons being sharpened, and the growls and roars of caged animals across the staging area mingled at a deafening pitch.

The gladiators were directed to two large cells with benches. Jonathan found an unoccupied corner and sat. Others milled about, a few starting private conversations in various tongues, most of them Greek. He purposed not to think about Nessa, only his training. For his effort, she became all he could think about, except when the sounds of the games forced her from his thoughts.

The morning beast hunts made Jonathan's stomach turn with the memories of the slain elephants at his first games. Pulleys and chains rattled as slaves worked the gates, ramps, and platforms in perfect unison below the arena floor, sending the animals to meet their death above them. Soon the roar of the crowd beat like a slow, erratic pulse in time with the gates.

The executions came next. Though for the first time Jonathan could only hear and not see them, the burden remained the same. The deaths plagued his soul. Not for the arsonists and murderers, but the innocent Jonathan knew swelled their ranks—their only crime believing in the same lie he had as a child.

Slaves brought water and a midday meal Jonathan gave away. He never ate before contest. Even if that were not so, the heat and the carnage above him destroyed any appetite. A few others passed on their meal, but most ate undaunted. For half of the men here, it would be their last meal.

More slaves brought capes and armor, under the watchful eyes of guards. These were distributed among the gladiators, guards pointing out who was to receive which pieces. Jonathan was given a pair of knee-high leg grieves and the padded leather arm sleeve of his style, the *thraex*. The helmet was bigger than he was accustomed to but fit well enough when he tried it on. He was given a brilliant red cape. The cloak reminded him of the Spartans, the legendary warriors Dionysius had taught him about.

"Thraex," a stranger called from across the cell. "It's just for the opening ceremony. You won't have to fight in it."

A few of the men laughed, but Jonathan wasn't amused. The gladiator mocking him couldn't be more than sixteen or seventeen years old—too young to be here.

The young man slid on his shoulder guard. "Enjoy the opening ceremony." Then he grinned. "It's going to be your last."

Jonathan's empty stomach dropped. "Jelani?"

The young man finished buckling his shoulder guard. "The same."

He turned away from the young man he would try his best to kill in a few hours. But the face remained, burned into his memory along with those of the others whose lives he'd taken. They danced in an unforgiving mosaic he could never purge his mind of, even in sleep.

Guards ushered the gladiators into a double column near a ramp that took them up to the arena floor. Jonathan pulled his helmet on before they emerged. The visor shielded his eyes from the sudden burst of natural light, and more importantly, his face from anyone who might recognize him.

The crowd erupted into the loudest cheer of the day so far, making the wooden deck beneath their feet vibrate under the sand. Seeing the amphitheater from the arena floor for the first time, it was easy to understand why most of the beasts were terrified of it. The roar of the crowd was like a physical force buffeting from every direction—fifty thousand people. The lower two-thirds of seats were filled with white togas and dotted throughout with the slaves that served them. The upper rows held peasants, plebeians, and women. Jonathan circled the arena with the other gladiators, though he did not preen and strut like most who saluted their *amoratae*. He scanned the crowd instead for a face that matched his own.

Emperor Domitian was difficult to miss, clad in a purple toga and gold laurel leaf crown in the pulvis. The gladiators waited while Caesar, surrounded by his praetorians, came to the arena floor for the *probatio armorum*. This was not for show. It truly was an inspection of the weapons. All blades must be equally sharp so the contests would be decided on skill and endurance, not faulty equipment.

When Caesar was satisfied, he and his guards returned to the pulvis and the gladiators to their holding area. Jonathan removed his cape and helmet to lean against the wall. The rough stone adhered to the sweat on his bare back while he waited for his match to be called. Jelani eyed him from across the cell as he made practice swings with an invisible net. In a matter of hours, one of them would be dead. It had to be Jelani. For the first time, Jonathan purposefully recalled memories of Nessa's lifeless eyes and naked body huddled in shame to remind him why it had to be so.

The men were summoned in pairs, at intervals that held no rhythm or reason, much like the cheers of the crowd above. Some matches ended quicker than others, until only eight men remained. A guard reappeared, pointed to Jelani, marked the wax tablet in his hand, and pointed to Jonathan.

It was time.

He gathered his helmet and rose. In a ritual he'd performed a hundred times, he pulled the helmet on. The metal did far more than protect his skull. It silenced his mind, bound his conscience, and removed every thought but battle so that only the warrior within remained.

Jelani knelt before Jonathan on the sand, raising two fingers in a plea for mercy. Jonathan gripped his sword tight and held it ready while blood ran from his upper thigh, the only wound Jelani had been able to inflict with his trident. The emperor acknowledged the missio Jelani asked for with a sign of his own. Kill.

The young man accepted in the true tradition of the gladiator. He forced a leg up to kneel on one knee and raised his head without meeting Jonathan's eyes. This was a kindness only another gladiator would understand.

Jonathan inverted his sword and poised the tip above Jelani's exposed spine. He took a deep breath, held it, and willed the sword to fall. But instead of delivering the killing blow, his arms buckled and held. The battle Jonathan so viciously fought on the sand had moved inside his head.

The crowd that had cheered him for nearly half an hour turned on him, impatient for Jelani's death. Guards advanced from the gate, two with bows and nocked arrows pointed right at Jonathan's chest. The rest carried whips.

"Do not hesitate, thraex. They will kill us both," Jelani rasped from the sand.

A loose crescent of guards formed around them. "Gladiator, the emperor demands the *coup de grace*. You will obey or you both die."

If those arrows went through his chest, Nessa might as well be standing behind him. He had killed men before. An innocent slave and other gladiators in combat, most so grievously injured it was merciful to do so. But this was an execution. One without merit, for Jelani had fought extremely well. Jonathan had prepared for this moment for days, yet his arms refused to plunge that blade in. *Do it. Do it now.*

"Your choice." The guard pulled the string of his bow tighter and straightened his aim.

A guttural cry rose from the man at his feet as Jelani sprung up and impaled himself on Jonathan's sword, tearing it from his hands. It was too shallow to be a clean death stroke, and Jelani wavered on his feet, the way a wheat shaft cleaved at the ground will do the moment before it falls. An arrow protruded from his chest and another from his neck.

Arrows meant for Jonathan.

Jelani crumpled to the sand. Jonathan ripped his helmet off and dropped to his knees beside him. "Why?"

Blood ran from Jelani's mouth. He coughed, spraying Jonathan's chest in a fine, red mist. "Jesus said… love… our enemies." Jelani's dark eyes bored into his own. "No greater love… than this."

His eyes lost focus, and the groan of death tumbled from his throat before his body stilled.

Jonathan fought to keep from screaming. It was Deborah's voice that finished somewhere in Jonathan's heart. *To lay down your life for a friend.* Deborah's words, his mother's words, Nessa's words. The words of Christ.

CHAPTER 25 – LIFE

Jonathan propelled himself through the gate of life on stiff legs. His thigh wound still bled, but the numbness flowing from deep inside kept any pain away. At the *spoilarium*, he surrendered his armor and sword, flinching at the sight of Jelani's blood clinging to it. Had he pulled it from the young man's back? Had a guard, before handing it to him?

A slave gave him a wineskin, which he emptied in a single raise. Jonathan followed him to another chamber where a gladiator lay on a table, surrounded by blood. Quintus and another physician worked over him while Nessa stood at the end of the table, holding the man's bare foot and from the tilt of her head, praying to her God.

As if sensing his gaze, her brown eyes met his. The look in her eyes reached through his numbness. She came to him without speaking, never taking her eyes from his face. Her arms surrounded him and her head came to rest against his chest, still splattered with blood. The sigh that came from her as she tightened her embrace echoed his own as he closed his arms around her. He held her, but the peace that normally flooded him in her presence didn't come.

"Jonathan," Quintus said softly. "Let me tend that leg."

Nessa released him, and Jonathan caught a glimpse of her face before she turned away. No tears. He watched her from where he sat on a stool while she and Quintus tended his leg, but she deliberately avoided his gaze, and then his touch.

"What's wrong?"

"Nothing."

She turned away and he grabbed the rolled sleeve of her tunic to stop her. Her violent shudder slapped him as surely as any hand would have. "Forgive me," he whispered.

The glare in her eyes and the way she stiffened told him he'd made it worse.

"Nessa?" Quintus glanced up at her from below his bushy brows.

She dipped her chin and stood statue still while Quintus finished binding his thigh.

Was it the knowledge that because Jonathan lived, another had died? A gladiator hardly more than a boy. Did she see death when she looked at him? She must, for as soon as Quintus tied the last knot and returned to the gladiator on the table, Nessa followed.

Jonathan remained alone on the stool, watching her while she worked, which included avoiding his gaze. Even when the guards came to lead him away, she refused to look at him. He went to her, his world shaking more than it ever had. "Are you angry that I live?"

Moisture pooled in her eyes, which turned on him now, full of anger and pain. "If you think that you know nothing of me."

"Then why?"

"Because you do not live. Not in the way that matters. I pray and I plead with God, and with you, that you return to your faith in Him, and you do not yield. God does not intervene."

"Come, slave." The guard put a firm hand on Jonathan's shoulder.

She closed her eyes, crossing her arms as she turned away.

"Nessa, please." He reached for her, but the guard grabbed his arm while another put his hand to the hilt of his sword. He wanted to tell her what Jelani had done, how his words were burned on Jonathan's heart, but she kept her back to him. The hand on his arm grew more insistent, but Jonathan didn't fight it. He didn't have the strength or the will to fight anyone anymore. That realization filled him with fear as the guards tugged him along toward the long tunnel. He would have to find a way, or Nessa's face would join Jelani's in the nightmares he was certain would follow him to the grave.

Jonathan rested in his empty cell, absorbing the quiet of the barracks beyond the wooden door. Most of the surviving gladiators had already departed Rome with their masters. Only Jonathan and a few other survivors belonging to the imperial ludis remained. When Tao left that morning to take the sand against Hulderic, Jonathan embraced him as a brother. If he did not return, as Seppios had not, Jonathan hoped it would be because Caesar granted Tao his freedom for defeating Hulderic. Either way, he would miss his friend and mentor.

Tao was more a brother to him than Manius had ever been. So was Seppios. Jonathan had wept for him in the dark that first night. If Tao had also, he didn't know. Neither could bring themselves to speak of him. Gladiators die. Like lions and leaves. Jonathan's sole comfort was Seppios had not died by Jonathan's own sword.

Two weeks of solid rest were the most Jonathan ever had since becoming Caius' marionette with a sword. He flexed his leg, noting the trident wound in its three parts was nearly healed. It amazed him how quick his body could recover when allowed to do nothing else.

His mind was another matter. Nothing could force Jelani's death from his thoughts. The young man had taken the arrows meant for him. A sacrifice made more profound because Jelani gained nothing by it—except a more gruesome death. *Like Christ.* Now even without Nessa's presence, Jonathan couldn't escape thoughts of God.

Rapid footfalls sounded outside his cell door. They grew louder and then stopped. His cell door flung open. A trio of guards stood there, winded and breathing hard. "Make haste, slave. You've been summoned."

Jonathan slid from the upper bunk to the cool stone floor. "By who?"

"We'll explain on the way."

The guard moved away from the door, and Jonathan reached for his sandals. "Way to where?"

The guard strode purposefully toward him and seized his upper arm. "Now."

Jonathan began to protest until the other two other guards outside drew their swords. He allowed the guard to tug him outside his cell, and then the man shoved him toward the far side of the ludis. Another guard began to run ahead of them.

He followed at a jog, the wound in his thigh pinching, until a sharp point prodded him in the back.

"I mean run, slave. The mob threatens to riot even now."

So Jonathan ran, with two guards ready to kill him at his back and one who led the way. He knew better than to slow down, but his mind was racing as fast as his bare feet into the tunnel that led to the arena. Why was he being summoned? His thigh began to throb, but he gritted his teeth and pushed on. From the other end of the tunnel, silhouetted figures ran toward them. The torches on the walls were too far apart to make out who they were at this distance.

"Wait!" The shout filled the stone corridor.

That voice. "Nessa." Jonathan came to a stop, as she did.

Quintus lagged far behind her.

She grabbed his face in both hands, her eyes filled with tears. "Tao is taken ill. Caius sends you in his place."

In his place.

A guard grabbed Jonathan's arm. "We have to get moving. You hear them."

In *his* place. They were sending him to Hulderic.

"Jonathan, please." Nessa held his jaw tighter between her hands. "Repent and return to your faith in the Lord. Please."

Another guard seized her arm and yanked her back so hard she cried out as her hands were torn from his face. Jonathan slammed his fist into the guard's throat, dropping him like a stone. Swords pulled free of their scabbards and Jonathan spun and pushed Nessa behind him toward the wall. He shielded her with his body and watched the guards' eyes for who would take him down first.

"Stop!" Quintus reached them at last, out of breath and clutching at his chest. "In the name of Jupiter, stop. Give them a moment."

"We have orders. The mob—"

"A few moments more will not have them tearing apart the city, you fool," Quintus bellowed.

The guards lowered their weapons. Jonathan turned and took Nessa's tearstained face between his hands. He stored a vision of her deep brown eyes, even in tears, and his mouth descended on hers. She clung to him, returning the kiss that was everything he'd believed it would be the past four years.

Except for knowing he was about to die.

And if Caius were the man Jonathan believed him to be, so was she.

His anguish melted into his kiss, and he tasted Nessa's own through the salt of her tears.

The hands were on him again, silent but insistent.

He released her, lest they take her from him again by force. She dissolved into sobs, and Quintus put his arm around her shoulders and cradled her to his side.

His gaze found Jonathan's. "If I ever have a son I will pray to Jupiter he has your strength and honor."

A guard prodded him with a sword, and Jonathan began backing toward the arena. There was no time. "You must protect her from Caius. Demand the truth from Clovis. Swear to me, Quintus. Swear you will protect her with your life from Caius."

Quintus' thick brow furrowed. "From Caius?"

"Enough, slave. We go now."

Jonathan's last vision of the woman he loved would be her anguished sobs in the arms of another man. One Jonathan hoped would learn the truth and protect her. They jabbed him again. He could stand his ground.

Make them cut him down here in the corridor. Tell Quintus everything while he died and never set eyes on Hulderic.

Coward. He was still a Tarquinius. If he lost that, even in death, his enemies had truly won. He turned and picked up his pace. If he pushed harder, he could better warm up, and soon passed the guard in front of him. The ground shook under his feet as they neared the end of the tunnel. The mob was giving full vent to their impatience. Shouts and angry cries flowed down the tunnel like waves. Even the torches rattled in their wall brackets from the tremors above. Near the arena end of the tunnel, more guards waited, along with an army of slaves.

"What took so long?" a praetorian with a plume-crested helmet demanded.

"Apologies, Commander. We encountered a delay in the tunnel."

"Get him up to the arena at once or I'll make lamps from your skulls."

Slaves surrounded him, each with a piece of his armor. The way they rushed to prepare him reminded him of being readied for Valentina. Then as now, he would be made to suffer—always for the selfish pleasure of others. And Nessa with him if Quintus failed. It was too much rage all at once. It poured through his veins, his lungs, and his mind.

Tao's words came to him, unbidden. *If it distracts you, clear your mind of it. If it fuels your focus, use it.* Could he harness the rage and let it feed, not cloud, the warrior that would emerge when he took the sand? Would he have a chance that way?

He looked down.

He didn't even have sandals.

The leg grieves were strapped securely to his legs. The heavy leather strap securing his chainmail shoulder sleeve was pulled across his chest and buckled behind his back. When a slave approached with a helmet, Jonathan took it from him. This he would do himself. The metal muffled the light and sound around him as it settled on the top of his head and he fastened the chin strap. His breathing slowed. His raging emotions yielded to the warrior summoned to the surface.

They handed him a sword, then his shield. The ramp to the gate of life shook like the boarding plank of a ship in rough tide as he climbed it. Fifty thousand people screamed for the match to begin under a cloudless sky. The sand burned beneath his feet as the trumpets blasted, but the familiar flow of battle-readiness coursed through him—until he saw Hulderic.

The man was a giant. He wore no armor and carried no shield, only a sword in each hand. There was no nod of respect for an opponent. Instead, he laughed.

If he'd come to play, so be it. Jonathan didn't wait for ceremony or the referee. He charged, bellowing his best war cry as he churned up sand. Hulderic didn't even raise his swords. Jonathan's shield hit him square in the gut, and his sword was knocked harmlessly away by Hulderic's in a sweeping move so fast Jonathan barely saw it through the eyeholes of his helmet. The crush of the impact stunned him. He bounced off Hulderic without moving the man even a pace.

Hulderic advanced, swinging both swords in rhythmic arcs.

Jonathan gave ground while the crowd jeered his retreat. He wracked his brain for a way to defend, much less attack.

Hulderic's huge strides carried him ever closer, faster than Jonathan could back away.

Turn and run, or dig in?

Dig in.

Jonathan made his stand, shield high and close, sword at the ready.

Hulderic spread his swords like wings and swung them in toward Jonathan's neck in the blink of an eye.

Jonathan dropped into a low crouch fast enough to avoid having his head severed, but not fast enough to miss the blow. The heavy swords struck with opposing force on both sides of his helmet. The vibration against Jonathan's skull rattled him worse than the deafening sound. He shifted a bare foot to keep from going down.

Through the grated eye holes, Hulderic vanished.

For an instant Jonathan thought he'd been rendered blind from the blow, but a face, completely out of place, filled his vision. The gray hair pulled back in a simple braid. The weathered skin, the knowing eyes of Deborah.

'How did Nehemiah and the captives rebuild Jerusalem, Jonathan? With a weapon in one hand and a tool in the other. One stone at a time, my boy.'

Jonathan blinked and she was gone.

Hulderic stood waiting, smiling bigger than before, and twirling his swords for show to the roaring approval of the crowd surrounding them. He had not seized the opportunity to take Jonathan down. Overconfident. Like Goliath.

One stone at a time then. Jonathan had to rid him of one of those swords if he stood a chance. He charged again but led with his sword this time rather than his shield.

Hulderic answered with crossed blades that snared Jonathan's between them as he pivoted to let Jonathan blow past.

Jonathan felt his sword tangle, which had been his intent, but it was being torn from his grip instead of stripping Hulderic of one of his. If Jonathan lost his sword, he was already dead. He dropped the shield and held on with both hands as his momentum carried him around. The tangle of blades broke free and Jonathan tumbled to the sand and rolled away. He spun and regained a fighting stance, only to see he was holding half a sword.

Hulderic's were still intact. One in each hand.

It was all over.

True to Quintus' word, Hulderic was no gladiator. Jonathan could see it in the man's eyes as he advanced. He would toy with Jonathan to the screaming approval of the crowd until they tired of it. Only then would Hulderic kill him.

Jonathan labored through the one-sided fight as long as he could. Blood oozed from the many wounds Hulderic's blades inflicted on his chest, shoulders, and arms. None of them were deep enough to be fatal, likely by design. He'd lost his helmet long ago, but strangely, this spared him any more blows to the head. This blow, which he saw coming but didn't have the strength to duck away from, knocked him backward with the force of a battering ram. He fell onto the bowl of his fallen shield and pain rocked through his spine. He lay splayed on his back, broken and exhausted as the sky above him dimmed, and then brightened again.

"Up." Hulderic's command came in an accent as thick as his body. A shadow passed over Jonathan and a foot kicked his bleeding side. "Up."

Both grieves were still in place on his legs, but now they weren't protection as much as weight to have to contend with when trying to find the strength to rise again.

And this time he couldn't.

He couldn't even raise his head to try. Jonathan closed his eyes. *God, if you're really there... protect her.* A strong kick low on his side flung him over onto his stomach. Sand filled his mouth and nose, but he hadn't the strength to lift his head. *She serves you with all that she is. Prove you're there. Deliver her as you never did me.*

Another kick knocked him onto his back again, flinging his arm wide. The back of his hand collided with something too hard to be packed sand.

I am Jehovah.

Almost of its own accord, his hand dug into the hot sand. His fingers curled around the tip end of his broken sword. He opened his eyes to the blinding sky above him and saw what he must do. He could feel strength returning to his broken body, even as the blade in his hand cut into his own fingers as he gripped it tight. It was effortless to roll and pop up between Hulderic's knees. He plunged the broken blade high in the man's inner thigh.

Fifty thousand people fell silent.

Hulderic staggered back and stared down at the broken metal jutting from his leg. He swayed and dropped a sword to pull the shard from his body. A waterfall of blood sprung forth. He would be dead in moments and they both knew it. He stumbled forward, dropping to his knees to face Jonathan, kneeling in the sand turning to bloody mud beneath them.

Jonathan saw it coming, but had nowhere to go. The weight of his leg grieves held him in place as Hulderic plunged the broken sword tip into Jonathan's chest. It entered somewhere between his shoulder and collarbone, catching on the leather strap of his sleeve guard. The blue eyes of his opponent held no triumph. They held no expression at all. The man was dead. His body fell into Jonathan, pushing the broken blade deeper as he buried Jonathan beneath him.

Jonathan couldn't breathe. He couldn't feel, see or hear. Except one voice that was not a voice, speaking to him as it had moments ago.

Call to me and I will answer you, and show you great and mighty things.

The words of God spoken by the prophet Jeremiah, the God Jonathan had denied half his life. *Forgive me, Lord.*

Again I will build you, and you shall be rebuilt.

Darkness was coming, the familiar blackness sweeping him under, but this time Jonathan didn't fear it.

Chapter 26 – For That

Cool fingers stroked Jonathan's forehead, raking through his hair in a soft sweep over and over. A psalm of the shepherd king David surrounded him, the words of the song as soothing as Nessa's voice. He began to hum along with her and the fingers in his hair stilled.

"Jonathan?"

The pillow beneath his head shifted, and he opened his eyes. Even upside down in dim lamplight, she'd never been more beautiful. He concentrated on learning again the planes of her face and the color of her eyes.

"How are you feeling?"

He raised a hand to touch her cheek. White hot pain burst through his shoulder, stealing his breath and clamping his eyes shut. Two deep breaths embraced the pain and he ventured a glance down. Linen wraps covered his stomach, chest, arms, and his right hand where he had gripped the broken blade. He resembled one of the Egyptian dead.

"Seventeen." Nessa's voice rippled with pain, as if the wounds she numbered had been inflicted on her. "Most on your arms and chest, though mercifully only one deep enough to worry us." She shifted so his head rested at a more comfortable angle in her lap, and resumed stroking his hair. "Rest. All is well."

The compassion in her eyes echoed in her touch stole over him. So different from her anger that day after his match with Jelani—anger that she had every right to feel. He feared for her life every time he entered an arena. How much greater her fear must have been, carrying the burden for his soul all these years. He'd added to her suffering instead of sparing her more. "Give me your hand."

Her fingers met the palm of his un-injured hand and he closed his own around them. "Nessa, God delivered me from Hulderic. He spoke to me as clearly as I speak to you now."

A soft gasp passed through her lips.

He swallowed and began stroking her hand with his thumb. "When my mother died, in my pain and anger, I hardened my heart against God and His truth. But His love pursued me. Through all my years of bitterness and denial. Through you. With your voice." His own threatened to crack at every other word, but there was so much he needed to tell her. Too much time had already been wasted.

"You spoke His truth over me again and again, lived out Christ's love to me, and still I turned away, content in my own strength. Until it failed. I was a sword thrust from losing everything that mattered, the least of which was my life."

Mist gathered in the corners of her brown eyes. "Jonathan—"

"Let me finish. Please." He squeezed her hand again, savoring the feel of her fingers he intertwined with his. "You were right. I was alive, but not in the way that mattered. God wouldn't give up on me, like you wouldn't." He swallowed and watched her eyes. "And I love you for that."

She tore her hand from his and covered her face.

Had he misread her heart there in the tunnel? Misunderstood the way she returned his kiss? "Forgive me. If I've upset you—"

Her hand moved swiftly from her face to press firmly against his lips. She tilted her face to the ceiling for several long breaths. When she looked down at him, the intensity in her gaze caused something within him to shift. "I have known Christ since I was a little girl. I have seen miracles and tasted of the goodness of God in the darkest of places. But I have never, until this moment, known a joy as all-consuming as this."

There could be no mistaking the depth of feeling there in her eyes, the radiance in them unlike anything he'd ever seen.

"To hear you claim Christ, speak of God and His great love for you, it reassures me God always heard my prayers for you. In your repentance, you strengthen my own faith." The fingers at his lips lifted and came to rest on his linen-bound chest, her palm pressed flat above the steady beat of his heart. "I love you for that."

She sighed and placed her other hand on the crown of his head. Her smile returned, as beautiful as her answer. "I've loved you for so long."

He moved his hand to cover hers, for once easily able to ignore the screaming pain of his abused body. "I don't know how, or when, but I promise you this. With God's help, one day we will be free of Caius. I will earn our freedom and make you my wife. I swear it on my life."

Her smile turned bittersweet. "We are free of Caius. Not the way I'd prayed for, but I'm still grateful to God."

Jonathan suddenly became aware of more than her. The room, now that he looked about it, was one he had never seen before. "Where are we?"

"An inn near the amphitheater."

"Where is Caius? Quintus and Tao?"

"Quintus is here. Well, not at the moment, but he will return. Caius and Tao returned to Capua yesterday with the guards."

"Caius would never leave me behind. Something's wrong." He tried to sit up and almost succeeded before the pain in his chest knocked him back down.

"Please don't move. I'll tell you everything, but I promise you we are safe." She reached for something near her on the bed and soon a wineskin was at his lips. Her hand supported the back of his neck, and he had no choice but to drink. The wine refreshed him, though he remained wary of what would possibly motivate Caius to leave them in Rome.

When he finished drinking, his head rested again in the cradle of her lap. Nessa angled away from him to replace the cork in the wineskin and her inner forearm came into view. Rows of deep purple, fringed in green and yellow, marred her skin. His injured hand formed a fist even as panic swept through him. "What happened to your arm?"

She followed his gaze and shook the sleeve of her tunic so it covered the bruising. "Nothing."

"Nothing doesn't leave marks like that." When she wouldn't meet his eyes, his fear grew. "Did Caius—"

"No." She laid her hand against his chest again and with the other returned to sweeping his hair back slowly. "I was on my knees praying, interceding for you as you faced Hulderic. When the slaves brought you in I was so deep in prayer I didn't hear Quintus calling for me."

"And he grabbed you? Hard enough to mark you?"

"Don't be angry. You were bleeding everywhere, and still impaled with part of a broken sword. Thank God the arena attendants didn't pull it out before carrying you in. Please rest. I promise you we are safe."

He would have a word with Quintus when the physician returned. Only one thing would compel Caius to leave him behind, though it wouldn't explain Nessa's presence. Unless God had performed another miracle for him he did not deserve. Jonathan set his face like flint, every bit the man of twenty-four who had survived countless times in the gladiator arena. But inside, where only he and God could see and hear, Jonathan was a boy again, afraid of the answers to questions he must ask before the uncertainty destroyed him. He closed his eyes. "Did Caesar free me?"

He held his breath there in the darkness, hope bleeding through him with every breath.

Nessa's hand in his hair stilled. "No."

Jonathan exhaled, refusing to allow his disappointment to turn to weakness. He opened his eyes and drew strength from the love in Nessa's.

She smiled and resumed tenderly stroking his hair. "But you're alive. You've returned to your faith. There is much we have to be grateful for."

A door opened, spilling natural light and the soft sounds of distant revelry into the room. The wide figure silhouetted in the doorway could only be Quintus. "Is he awake?"

"Yes. He's had a half skin of wine."

"Good."

Quintus turned back to them after shutting the door, and Jonathan did a double take. Below the bald head and bushy brows was a stunning black eye. "What happened to your face?"

He glanced at Nessa. "You didn't tell him?"

"I hadn't reached that part yet."

"Tell me what?"

Quintus grunted and came to the bed. He felt Jonathan's forehead, then his wrist, all while grinning. "Caius lost you in a bet. He showed up with your new owner, Torren Gallego, in the middle of Nessa and me trying to keep you on this side of the Styx. Caius claimed my services were not part of the barter and ordered me to step away, which I had no intention of doing."

Jonathan felt the anger return, swirling among the revelation he now belonged to someone else. "Caius hit you?"

Quintus chuckled as he went to the table and poured something too thick to be wine into a cup. Bitter anticipation filled Jonathan's mouth.

"This is not from Caius. I told him I swore an oath I would uphold and didn't give a potshard whether you were his slave or not and kept stitching. He grabbed my arm and Nessa here flew into a rage unlike anything the gods themselves have ever seen. I got this from the back of her head trying to restrain her before she got herself killed."

Jonathan glanced up to admonish her, angry she'd put herself directly in the path of Caius' temper. But the affection in her eyes said she would do it again and lacked even a hint of regret. She stood ready to fight for him as he had her, and the corner of his mouth lifted. "You gave Quintus the black eye?"

The blush he loved crept up her cheeks. "It was an accident."

"The scratches she left on Caius' face were not," Quintus said. "I thought she was going to claw his eyes out. If Gallego hadn't grabbed Caius from behind, things would have gotten worse. By then soldiers had shown up. The good news is you live, and like always, though I don't understand it, you'll mend. The bad news is I'm out of a position. Gallego is paying for the inn and your care, but once you're well enough to travel to his ludis, Nessa and I are going to have to find work."

Nessa and I. She would be parted from him. Something he couldn't conceive.

Quintus brought him the dreaded cup. "Drink this."

Nessa's eyes apologized as she tilted his head up. Quintus placed the cup of animal blood and herbs to his lips. The familiar metallic taste was not as galling as knowing his time with her was short. Maybe days.

"Almost done," Quintus encouraged.

He managed three more swallows before the cup and then his throat emptied. Quintus wiped his mouth with a cloth and Nessa kept his head tipped back. Nausea swirled in his stomach, this time from more than the blood. Nessa's thumb tenderly stroked the skin below his ear. He'd never taken her touch for granted but he couldn't fathom being without it. Without her.

"Still all right?" Quintus asked.

Jonathan knew what he meant, so he nodded.

A knock sang out and Quintus eyed them both warily before approaching the doorway. "Who is it?"

"Quintus, may I enter?" The voice was deep, even muffled through the planks of the wooden door.

Quintus relaxed and opened the door. "Gallego, please come in. I'll see if I can find a stool for you."

"No, I won't stay long. I came to see how Jonathan fares."

The man stood shorter than his voice made him sound. He wore a modest tunic and belt. His face appeared too youthful for his dark brown hair to have flecks of silver at the temples. It was the air of assurance that clung to him like a cloak that struck Jonathan most.

The stranger tipped his chin in Nessa's direction. "Lady." His gaze met Jonathan's. "I don't know what impresses me more. Your stamina or the skill of your medicus."

Jonathan cleared his throat to make his voice strong, not an easy thing on the heels of his last drink. "Quintus is without equal in the healing arts. You should secure him at once for your ludis."

"I don't doubt it, but I have a competent physician who has earned my loyalty. I cannot afford both of them."

Nessa's fingers intertwined with Jonathan's. Gallego must have noticed, because his expression softened. "Would that I could."

Quintus settled on a stool and rubbed the top of his head. "We'll be fine. Something will come along."

Gallego turned to Quintus, the lamplight brightening a pale, jagged scar that ran above his right elbow. "I mentioned our introduction and the hardship it brought you to an acquaintance of mine. He informed me the Eighth Augusta's general, Marcus Cassius, is seeking a physician. The pay would be considerable. If you like, I can arrange introductions."

Quintus considered this, and Jonathan's heart sank further in his chest.

"Hippocrates did say war is the only proper school of the surgeon." Quintus' gaze turned to Nessa. "Germania will be cold. Colder than anything you've ever known."

"I go where you go, Quintus."

Jealousy singed through Jonathan at her ready answer and he tightened his grip on her.

Gallego noted the exchange before turning his attention back to Quintus. "I can send a messenger tomorrow for your answer when I rotate the guards."

"You guard me?" Jonathan hoped the edge in his voice matched the glare he pinned on Gallego.

"Of course." The man's casual smile returned but the creases in the corners told Jonathan it took effort. Their gazes locked like swords. Gallego was taking the full measure of Jonathan as he was doing the lanista. Jonathan fixed his eyes, determined not to blink first.

Gallego appeared equally determined, even when he spoke. "Quintus, would you give Jonathan and me a moment alone?"

"Of course. Come, Nessa."

She extracted herself from beneath Jonathan carefully. Her hair swung so close to his eyelids, they closed despite his concentration. He swallowed the moan threatening to escape as he grabbed the edge of the bed and raised himself to a sitting position. Dizziness nearly toppled his head into his knees, but he locked his elbows to brace himself upright. Nessa gave him a lingering look before Quintus ushered her out the door and closed it behind them.

Gallego approached and Jonathan had no choice but to look up at him. That was probably the man's intent. "Your former master bet a great sum on green at the Circus Maximus, but the red won. He owed me ten thousand sestertii and couldn't pay."

Jonathan let his anger at both men color his tone. "Interesting you can bet that kind of coin on a chariot race and not hire the best physician in the empire."

Gallego grinned and crossed his arms. "I don't typically discuss my finances with my gladiators, but for your knowledge, I did not bet against him. In addition to being a lanista, I find usury a very profitable side business."

"If you send your gladiators to collect, then for your knowledge, you should know I won't do that."

Gallego laughed, but there was no mockery or contempt in the sound. "No, I do not. In time you will find I do a number of things very differently from others in my profession."

"Which profession?"

"Both."

The pain in Jonathan's body grew steadily, but he embraced it to remain sitting up though his arms begged for respite. "So Caius used me to settle his debt?"

"In a manner of speaking. I watched you fight in Capua three years ago. From the way you entered the arena, favoring your right leg and not able to tuck and roll, I could tell Caius was fighting you injured. Even so, you made impressive work of the *secutor* you faced. I knew then I wanted you and offered Caius a fair sum. He said you weren't for sale at any price.

Then a few weeks ago, when you won the match against one of my best gladiators, I offered Caius fifty thousand for you and he again said no."

A shiver passed through Jonathan unrelated to the pain in his arms and chest. "Jelani belonged to your ludis?"

"He did." Sorrow passed through Torren Gallego's eyes. "You can imagine my surprise then, when on the last day of the games, Caius approaches me during the afternoon matches and agrees to my earlier offer. As soon as I signed the scroll, the rat told me you would be fighting Hulderic in moments."

That sounded like Caius. Exactly like Caius.

The lanista paused, his amused grin growing more annoying by the moment. "But the fates punished him, because you won. I paid the forty thousand with a smile on my face, because the gladiator that defeated Hulderic is worth five times that much. I know, because I've been turning down offers for two days."

Jonathan stared at Gallego with the growing sense that the man mocked him with his vast fortune. "Then I ask again, why can you not employ Quintus?"

Gallego's expression sobered and the arms he held across his chest tightened. "Let us be straight with one another. It's not Quintus you want to keep with you. It's the servant girl. I witnessed her attack on Caius when he interfered with treating your wounds. For a slave, that's certain death, so she regards your life above her own. You must feel the same, or you wouldn't be trying so hard to have me yield. And in truth, I could afford to, but it wouldn't be prudent. I already have a physician whom I trust. Quintus would tire of having so little to do in my ludis, since my gladiator troupe is small by design. He would have to leave on his own eventually, to maintain and improve his skill. Apologies my friend, but believe me, it's for the best."

"I'm not your friend."

Gallego's posture stiffened. "It's not a requirement that you are, though I hope in time you feel differently."

"Caius must not have told you how he compelled me to fight all these years."

A flicker of uncertainty passed through Gallego's gaze.

"He threatened to kill her if I didn't. And assured me he would if I were to fall in the arena or take my own life."

Gallego frowned, his head slanting in question even before he spoke. "Are you suggesting I do the same? Buy her from Quintus, assuming he would part with her, and then threaten her safety so you will keep fighting? Is that what you really want?"

Hearing it put back to him so clearly filled Jonathan with shame. He dropped his head and closed his eyes as the weight of his hypocrisy crushed him.

"I have a better plan."

Jonathan raised his head but this time didn't have to look up at Gallego. The lanista had closed the distance between them and squatted so they were now eye to eye.

"Fight for me because you want to. Discover what it means to truly be a gladiator, not a man dangling over a cliff by chains of fear for the life of the woman he cares for. In time you will earn your freedom, and then you can pursue hers, or whatever you want most."

Jonathan huffed, locking his elbows to remain upright. "All lanistas speak of freedom. The way husbands speak of marriage to their mistresses."

"My gladiators will tell you I honor my word. Two earned their freedom last year."

"And Jelani?"

"Jelani and Daxus chose to fight in these games. You have nothing but my word on that for now, but when Daxus recovers you can ask him yourself. Either way, you are part of my *familia gladitoria* now. I prefer you embrace the opportunity and we see what you are capable of with proper motivation, rest, and better care. But if you know you will not, tell me now. You will never be as attractive to potential buyers as you are at this moment. Expectations for your return to the arena are running high all over Rome. I can take the next offer that comes without the risks of fighting you again and finding out you were lucky against Hulderic. I profit either way, but the choice is yours."

Jonathan weighed what he already knew of Gallego against the uncertainty of being sold to someone like Caius. Gallego waited silently beside him, still crouched on the floor, with no sign of impatience. Jonathan's respect for him grew once again. Breathing deep, he drew himself up to his full height in the bed through the pain that reverberated through every cut. He met Gallego's dark eyes, and then dropped his gaze and his chin, in submission and respect.

"*Dominus.*" The Latin word for master from his own lips felt strange. A title he'd never bestowed on Caius.

"Torren. My men address me as Torren, Jonathan, not Dominus. Or master."

Jonathan glanced up to see Torren's grin had returned as he stood.

"Do you think you're fit enough to be brought by litter to the ludis? I'd like you under better security as soon as possible."

"Where is the danger? Should Nessa not be here?"

"You still don't realize what you've done." Torren locked gazes with him, his grin turning rueful. "You slew Hulderic. He was an undefeated champion. His fame rivaled that of the greats. Spartacus. Priscus. Verus. You have a public now. *Amoratii* would swarm this inn and bring it down around us for a chance to touch their idol up close, which is why I've been bribing the innkeeper into silence."

"Then we leave tomorrow. I don't want Nessa in unnecessary danger."

"Done." The lanista stood and moved toward the door.

"Torren?"

He paused midstride and turned back. "Yes?"

"Thank you."

Torren gave him a silent nod before leaving.

Jonathan tried to lower himself back onto the bed but collapsed instead. The jar to his battle-scarred body filled him with fresh pain, but not as much as knowing this would be his last night with Nessa.

Chapter 27 – In Remembrance

Jonathan roused from sleep to Nessa's touch on his arm. She sat beside him on the edge of the bed and held the dreaded cup in her other hand. Oxen? Goat? Quitus insisted they were all the same, but he knew better. Pig was the worst.

"Relax," Nessa said. "It's only warmed wine with a pinch of powdered ram's horn."

"Thank God for that."

She raised his head and placed the cup to his lips. "I do. Even more to hear you say it."

He emptied the cup, grateful to be spared choking down any more blood tonight. That thought spun another, until he knew what he needed to do next. "Do we have any bread?"

"Yes." She left the edge of the bed and retrieved a loaf heel from the small table. "I'll help you sit up so you can eat."

"Thank you." With her help, Jonathan pulled himself upright, teeth gritted against the pain it caused. "Can I have more wine, please?"

Nessa gave him the bread first, then refilled his cup and handed it to him. He wasn't sure how to ask her for a moment alone that wouldn't feel like he was dismissing her or sending her away.

"I need to check something with the innkeeper," she said. "It may take a little while. Is that all right?"

He nodded and watched her leave. He couldn't remember back to the moment he realized Nessa could sense his every need and then meet it. Only that she had. There were many things he'd failed to remember, and hardened his heart against those things he did. It was long past time to repent. Without death looming over him.

Lord, when the path became difficult, I turned and fled like Simon Peter. I embraced my hate, and lived only for revenge, thinking I did so to protect Nessa. All along, You spoke Your truth to me over and over through her words, her hands. You healed this broken body in Your mercy again and again.

He ripped a bite of the bread and chewed while pain covered him. Not in his body, but in his spirit, as he thought of the Messiah partaking of the last supper with the twelve, including the very one who would betray Him. Jesus shared the bread He declared His body, and the wine that would be His blood, given as the new covenant and poured out in payment for the sin of mankind for all eternity.

A darker image followed. Jesus, beaten as even Jonathan had never been, and crucified as a criminal under the laws of Rome to fulfill the law of God. Christ's plea to the Father as He hung on the cross, "Father, forgive them, for they know not what they do."

Maybe those men hadn't.

But Jonathan had.

Forgive me, Lord. Forgive me. His hand trembled, rippling the wine in his cup. "I betrayed Your sacrifice in my denial. Though I'm unworthy to have received that salvation and to drink this to remember it, forgive me."

He drank the wine, feeling the weight of his failures and guilt drowning in the mercy and grace of Christ's atoning blood. A peace flooded through him, deeper than anything he'd ever known.

Torren Gallego's two guards fascinated Nessa. She watched them play knucklebones for nearly an hour, amazed at how the two men blended in with the travelers and dinner guests at the inn. They sat at the table closest to Jonathan's room, tossing the five shaped bones over and over. A room she and Jonathan would be alone in tonight.

Gallego had insisted Quintus accompany him to meet the general. When Quintus hesitated, Gallego looked directly at her and said, "I'm sure Nessa can take care of him for one night." The implication offended her, but not enough to speak up and defend her virtue. What remained of it.

Truthfully, she looked forward to the time alone with Jonathan. If the meeting between Quintus and the general went well this evening, they would be leaving for Germania within days. She would treasure this night, made sweeter in the knowledge Jonathan had asked for the elements of the Lord's last supper, presumably to take them in remembrance of Christ's sacrifice. Something Nessa hadn't done herself in far too long.

One of the guards dropped a bone from the table to the ground and bent to retrieve it. As he did, his gaze scanned the room from corner to corner without turning his head.

Nessa grinned when their stares met. She rose and went to them. "At first I thought you the worst guards I had ever seen, playing knucklebones instead of standing watch. But now I see it is part of how you do so unnoticed."

Pink climbed the tanned cheeks of one guard as he leaned back on his stool to balance it on two legs. "Any robber can tell you, the bigger the guard detail, the heavier the coin they protect. We find the best way to avoid a mob, even one that begins with a few curious onlookers, is not to tell them there's something there in the first place by standing on either side of the door."

"Well, I'll leave you to your work."

Nessa reached Jonathan's door and rapped gently.

No answer. He might be sleeping. She knocked harder, casting a sideways glance at the guards who'd stopped their game.

The door opened, and Nessa stifled a gasp.

Not only was Jonathan on his feet, but he'd removed most of his wraps and put on a tunic. "Come in."

She entered the room, checking him over for bleeding. "Why are you out of bed? And why did you take off your wraps? You need rest, and—"

He silenced her with two fingers to her lips as he nudged the door closed with his knee. "Nessa, I'm not a child."

The rough texture of his skin against her mouth startled her, but not as much as his eyes. They were different. Still the green of fresh laurel leaves she knew so well, but lacking something—something not to be missed. Even though the tight set of his mouth and the pinched outer corners of his eyelids signaled pain, he looked… strong.

He pulled his fingers from her lips, and her trapped breath released in a soft giggle. "You know, the missio is also two raised fingers. If I didn't know any better, I'd think you were pleading for mercy."

Jonathan laughed and Nessa drank the sound into her very being. "Maybe I am. I found the basket with clothes and medicine, but I don't know which vial is the opium."

"I'll get it." She found the proper amphora and mixed it with a fresh cup of wine. He waited patiently near her and as he drank the mixture, she stared at him in awe. Much more than his eyes had changed.

He set the empty cup down and flexed his good shoulder. "Where's Quintus?"

"With Torren Gallego. They return tomorrow."

The question in his eyes was unmistakable. "Tomorrow?"

"Yes." She wanted to look away, but couldn't. "Since you've taken most of your linens off, I'm going to make paste for your wounds."

He extended an arm and rolled his elbow toward the ceiling. "Most of these aren't that bad. The air is good for them. This one—" He looked down at his chest and covered the place the sword had pierced him. "This one hurts."

"I'd suggest you rest, but I'm afraid to." She meant it in jest, but he frowned and stepped closer, taking her by the wrist.

"I don't ever want you to be afraid again." His other hand cradled her cheek, the fingers slipping beneath her hair to rest against her neck. "And you will *never* have reason to fear me." He stood so close the heat of his wine-scented breath warmed the tip of her nose. His gaze moved from her mouth to her eyes as he leaned closer. Inviting, not expecting.

She arched her chin toward him in answer. Her eyelids drifted closed as his lips met hers. This kiss was nothing like in the tunnel, when she thought he would die. This was effortless and natural, like breathing, as the gentle brush of his lips explored hers. He released her wrist and his warm palms pressed her jaw between them, but she felt sheltered, not trapped. An unknown feeling began to grow from somewhere in her middle, and she raised her arms to draw him even closer. Her hands touched his back through the thin wool of his tunic and he went rigid in her embrace, his swift intake of breath breaking their kiss.

She'd been so lost in passion she forgot his wounds. She yanked her hands back to her sides and frowned. "I'm sorry."

His smile returned, and he didn't release her face. "Don't be."

She thought he might kiss her again, but a knock at the door intruded. Jonathan's grin disappeared. He motioned for her to wait and went to the door.

A servant stood outside with a large amphora and a pail. "Lamps, my lord."

Jonathan muttered something Nessa couldn't make out and admitted the small man. She poured more wine for them while the servant worked. He refilled the lamps with olive oil and trimmed their wicks much faster than the previous two days. The poor servant probably sensed Jonathan's annoyance from where he stood with his arms crossed in the middle of the room. She sipped her wine while avoiding the gazes of both men until the servant left, shutting the door behind him.

Jonathan sat on the bed, in the center of the thin mattress, while watching her.

Surely he didn't think… but he must, because his hand reached out toward her. Her heart took off like a rabbit running from an eagle. "Jonathan, I'm—"

"I only want to hold you. Please."

For years she'd wondered, sometimes even imagined, relaxing into his embrace, sharing a bed with him. But in her dreaming they were wed.

He withdrew his outstretched hand. "Forgive me for not thinking." The look of pain returned to his face. "And forgive me if I reminded you of him."

Him? Her brow dipped, and she almost asked who when it hit her. Caius. *No, oh no.* She rushed to him, knelt beside him on the bed, and took his hand. "You could never remind me of him." She squeezed his hand. "I trust you."

By the set of his face, he remained unconvinced. Heat rose in her cheeks while she debated continuing. She looked down at their hands. "It's what your touch—and your kiss— make me feel that I don't trust."

She risked a glance at his face. His mischievous expression confused her.

He pulled his hand free and leaned back against the wall carefully. "Maybe you shouldn't come any closer. I'm in no condition to defend myself if you attack me."

His effort at being stern, despite the boyish arrogance all over his face, failed miserably. Tears sprang to her eyes, from laughter for once, at the irony of such a statement. "Stop that. I can hardly breathe now."

He watched her, the smile fading from his face. "I'm going to miss you. Your smile and your laugh."

The words sobered her like a bucket of water to the face. "Is it wrong that makes me glad? I don't want you to forget me."

"Surely you know I'd never forget you, or I've failed far worse than I thought."

Nessa shifted to lean against the wall beside him. "I do know. And you never failed me. But whenever we're alone I always end up talking about me. I want to know about you and your life before you came to us barely breathing."

She wanted as many memories of him to carry with her as her heart could store. But his heavy sigh made her regret asking. She slipped a hand to his scarred palm. "Forgive me. You don't have to tell me."

"No, I think it's time I speak of it. I think I need to." Jonathan ran his other hand through his hair and sighed again before relaxing to meet her gaze. "I was six the first time I was made to feel ashamed for not having a father, or knowing who he was. I was twelve when I met him for the first time. The same day my mother died."

Her heart broke for him, and this was only the beginning—his brother's betrayal, the shame of the slave block, the cruel seductress and her treachery that sent him to Caius Pullus. His fear when the lion charged him. His anger at finding her violated. The horror of discovering he'd executed an innocent man. Nothing prepared her for what he would say next, through the tears glossing his green eyes.

"The things I've done, and the men I've killed…" He swallowed and the water in his eyes fell. "Caius threatened to hurt you again if I refused to fight. If I took my life, if I lost it in the arena, I would forfeit yours. And I couldn't let that happen, Nessa. I couldn't."

She touched the tears on his face, seeing beyond the shame and anguish there. He had fought for her. Bled for her. Protected her through his suffering. He'd loved her like Christ, without knowing it, and the flames of her love for him became an inferno.

Careful of his wounds, she embraced him. The cloth of his tunic warmed her cheek and the steady beat of his heart filled her ear for the first time. Countless times she'd felt it beneath her fingers, praying it wouldn't stop. The beat of his heart was the most beautiful sound she'd ever heard. *Thank you, Lord. Thank you.*

Jonathan cradled her to him, resting his head atop hers. His good arm tightened around her and all the fear and pain he had carried alone for years came forth while she held him.

Nessa awoke in Jonathan's arms, his warmth better than any blanket. The lamps still burned, but she had no idea how long she'd been asleep.

From the ache in her neck, it must have been hours. She listened, trying to make out Jonathan's voice above her, so quiet it could scarcely be more than a whisper. She tilted her head so her ear was free of his chest and the steady beat of his heart.

He paused, tightening his arm around her. She remained still, and after a moment, he continued. This time Nessa could make out the words.

A tear slid from her eye as she listened.

He was praying for her.

Chapter 28 – Respect

Torren wanted out of Rome. Were it not for the games, he would avoid the city altogether, with its politicians, praetorians, and poor. He wanted Jonathan safe within the ludis walls, and he needed to see Caelina. He missed her, which compounded his guilt as he waited for Jonathan to bid his woman farewell. "I think my newest gladiator is in love with your servant."

"He is," Quintus said. "The marvel is she loves him in return. I've known for some time."

Torren wanted to give them privacy, even outside the inn where people passed now and then on the narrow street, but the litter bearers and his guards already waited. He'd ordered his guards to lay linen over the cushions of the rented litter before their departure. The cost of the cloth would be small in comparison to replacing the cushions if any of Jonathan's numerous injuries bled on the way.

Jonathan removed a medallion or charm from around his neck. He placed it around the woman's neck before embracing her. Torren turned to Quintus, more to escape the sight of the lovers than anything else. "Would you ever free her?"

"She's been like a younger sister to me and knows nearly as much of medicine as I do."

"That's not an answer." The retort emerged sharper than Torren intended.

"Who would protect her and care for her if I did? You? Jonathan cannot."

A strong offer formed in Torren's head. One he wanted to voice, but couldn't. He loathed separating her from his new gladiator. But the quickest way to turn his men against each other was bringing a woman who belonged to only one of them to the ludis. He would never make that mistake again. "I was merely curious."

Jonathan approached them, the servant girl trailing in his wake. "Quintus, please send word to Gallego often and let me know you are both well."

"I will. Try not to give Gallego's physician as many sleepless nights as you gave Nessa and me."

Jonathan clasped the physician's shoulder. "I will trust God to watch over you both. For the sake of the legionnaires and the men they face in battle, I hope you often find yourself bored."

That remark was aimed at Torren more than the physician, but responding would gain nothing. Jonathan ignored him and climbed into the waiting litter. The tension inside the curtains would be as thick as the cushion they would soon share. Torren couldn't bring himself to speak to the woman or meet her gaze, knowing it would be red-rimmed, and he the cause. He nodded to Quintus and joined Jonathan.

"My servant will meet us at the east gate with a cart to bring us to the ludis. I have opium if the jarring becomes too great."

Jonathan didn't acknowledge him. He continued staring out the opening on his side of the curtained tent. Torren would tolerate the mute treatment, for now. Separating them was a necessary wickedness and his gladiator deserved the time to sulk. Meanwhile he would work.

Torren removed the ledger from his leather bag to review his accounts. After the cost of Jonathan's acquisition, his care and keep, the bribes that always associated a visit to the city, the bonus to Quintus, and two accounts he'd been unable to collect on again, the stay in Rome had still been profitable. He would reserve enough to call on Caelina several times and transfer the bulk to his shipping and usury interests. A few adjustments to the numerals in the wax coating of the bound wooden slats, and then he exchanged his ledger for his new parchments. A scribed copy of Ovid's Sorrows, a collection of poems he wrote after being exiled by Caesar Augustus.

Concentrating while traveling through crowded and noisy streets that reminded him why he hated the city became too great an effort after a few miles. Though the writings were evocative and it was as if the poet had given words to things Torren had only ever thought in secret. He put the parchments away and studied his newest gladiator. If the man reclined any closer to the edge of the litter platform, any stumble by the slaves at the poles would tip him out into the street.

"How long will you hate me for not bringing her?"

"I don't hate you." Jonathan met Torren's gaze, his green eyes overflowing with the anger he denied. "It would only disappoint her."

Torren guarded his expression. The first days with any new gladiator were precarious. Several in the past made the mistake of thinking him weak because of his relaxed manner. "So you enjoy crossing swords outside the arena as well?"

Jonathan's gaze returned to the opening. "It depends who it is."

He'd been dismissed, but he wouldn't push. Though he'd witnessed the long and bloody fight, it was hard to accept that the man resting an arm's length from him slew Hulderic. Torren would never have allowed any of his men to face the legend, even if he'd possessed one with enough skill to be chosen. Until these games, he'd never allowed his gladiators in contests promised to be fights to the death. Only the tremendous coin offered finally swayed him, and he let the men volunteer. But with Jelani dead and Daxus already back at the ludis with a busted sword arm that might never mend, he regretted giving in.

But if he hadn't, he wouldn't own Jonathan. Would he have knowingly traded Jelani's life for the most valuable gladiator in Rome? He wanted to say no. Though the offers he'd turned down for Jonathan recorded in the wax tablet in his bag, the highest a half-million sesterces—kept him honest.

The pain in Jonathan's chest worsened with every mile. He shifted repeatedly and thought of Nessa. The feel of her in his arms, the soft, almost purring noise she made in sleep, and the love in her eyes when he placed his mother's carving around her neck.

"Jonathan, I can't take this."

"You must. I swear I will come for you one day. Until then keep it close to your heart, as you are to mine."

It was Gallego's fault. Though without him, Jonathan would still belong to Caius and Nessa would still be vulnerable to his threats. Was one volatile madman better or worse than a harsh climate on a disputed frontier? It was too much pain to embrace this time—in his body and his heart. He'd sacrifice his pride. Whatever disparaging comment or mocking look Gallego gave him would be worth the relief. "Could I have that opium now?"

Gallego reached into his leather bag and leaned far forward with the vial. Jonathan took it, and Gallego's attention returned to his curtain opening with no comment or smug look of triumph. The sharp taste of the undiluted opium burned Jonathan's throat and set him coughing. He lay back, hating to display so much weakness.

He'd been up all night praying over Nessa and with the opium, the steady sway of the litter made his eyelids heavy. More weakness in front of the lanista. Yet the unusual man didn't seem the kind to hold it against him. Or attack it mercilessly as Caius had. Gallego appeared straightforward and a shrewd man of business, though not unjust, at least as far as he could tell. Other than being years younger and looking nothing alike, Torren Gallego reminded Jonathan of his father.

Torren loathed having to wake his sleeping gladiator. Assuming he even could, with the heavy dose of straight opium Jonathan had taken. But Jonathan woke on his own when the litter bearers set the litter on its supports at their stop. He climbed out stiffly, and the linen cover showed spots in a few places. He'd bled some on the way, but not as much as Torren feared. Quintus did good work.

The grass beneath Torren's sandaled feet felt as good as stretching his legs. His head servant Rufus waited with the wagon and a wineskin. Both were a welcome sight. He paid the litter carriers a little extra for a relatively smooth ride and approached his waiting wagon.

Jonathan stood at the rear, holding his right arm against his chest, unsure of what to do. After a full detail last night, Torren's guards were not as attentive as they should be from the backs of their mounts. He would make an allowance for them, but his head servant should have recognized the problem immediately. Climbing into a cart required two good arms.

"Rufus, we need a step."

"Yes, my lord." Rufus jumped to the ground, took a sturdy crate from beneath the bench seat, and hastened to position it on the ground at the wagon rear.

Jonathan still waited.

Torren gestured for him to climb into the cart first. He knew the man's pride demanded he do this unaided, so he didn't offer to assist. When they were both settled in the straw, he observed him from the corner of his vision. The tight set of his mouth and the way he clutched his arm to his side still made Torren wish he'd had his medicus Otho brought with the wagon. A full *quartarius* of straight opium should have worked better than this.

Rufus replaced the crate while Torren uncorked the wineskin and offered it to Jonathan first. The gladiator's forehead creased a moment before he took it with his good arm. With Caius Pullus for a master,

Jonathan was probably suspicious of anything resembling respect. That would take time to bring to rights, like his injuries, but Torren had time.

The December games were already contracted, and Jonathan and Daxus wouldn't be in them. Perhaps by the spring games, one or both might be ready. If Jonathan's form was even remotely in question, Torren would keep him from those games too. The gladiator must win his next match to secure his fame going forward. Torren wouldn't allow him back into the arena unless he was healthy and in peak condition. Waiting too long however, he risked all manner of censure from Jonathan's public and the organizers of the games.

The editors of the games could be handled with diplomacy and a few well-placed bribes, as long as Caesar didn't become involved. Torren was ready to be rid of Lord and God Titus Flavius Domitianus Augustus Germanicus.

From the secret gathering he'd been invited to attend while in Rome, he wasn't the only one.

CHAPTER 29 – WHAT HE HAD

From the size of the outer wall, Torren Gallego's villa was as large as Jonathan's father's. Inside the gate however, it looked like a ludis. A vast yard of sunken poles, hanging poles, a raised fighting platform, and a few beams lying strewn about spanned wall to wall. Only the gladiators were missing.

"Saturday is free day." Torren regarded him as the cart rolled toward the entry to the barracks. "The other six we train. Hard."

The man was a puzzle. He'd shared his wine, from the same skin no less, and ridden in the box of the wagon with him rather than the seat beside the servant or on one of the guard's horses. He behaved nothing like a master.

A young man emerged from open doors, running to meet them. Torren's son?

"Welcome back, my lord." A servant. The young man looked a year or two younger than Jelani. Had they been friends?

Torren nodded to him and handed the crate over the side of the cart to Rufus. Jonathan fought back a groan and made it to the ground without stumbling or embarrassing himself. The house, while massive, was only one level. Where would Torren observe the training from without a balcony? The lanista handed his bag to Rufus and motioned Jonathan forward.

"Come, I want you to meet the others."

Inside the house, furnishings and adornments were sparse compared to Caius' lavish style. The peristyle could be a second training yard for its size, but it lacked shrubs, flowers, and statues that a normal peristyle would have. A solitary olive tree shaded a servant at its roots, fashioning something from red clay.

The man noticed them, and Torren waved him down. "No need to rise. I'm showing our new gladiator around the villa and introducing him to his brothers. Jonathan, this is Cambyses, who we call Cam, the most spectacular murmillo the arena has ever seen. Cam, this is Jonathan."

Cam's eyes swept over him while he continued to mold his clay. "I didn't believe it when Torren told us a thracian from some obscure house in Capua slew Hulderic." The man's gaze rolled over him again. "And now I believe it even less. You look like he sharpened his swords on you."

Another Seppios. Rather than rise to the insult, Jonathan remained silent. After all, God had delivered him from Hulderic.

A grin formed on Cam's face as he laughed. "We'll teach you what the shield is for when your arms heal. Welcome, brother."

Torren knelt to examine the shaped clay in front of Cam's folded legs. "What are you making this week? Another bowl?"

"A carrion bird feasting on Anzo's severed head."

The vehemence in the man's tone was a sudden switch.

"Where is Anzo?" Torren asked.

"Medicus chamber with Dax."

"You two should settle your differences."

"We will. In the arena."

Those had been the first words Jonathan ever heard Seppios speak. The resemblance bothered him. He missed the big, Roman-hating Celt, and would mourn his loss in a new way now that his own faith had been restored. Not once had he ever shared the truth of Christ with Seppios, Tao, Clovis, or any of the others. He'd been consumed with denying it himself while struggling to survive. Now it was too late. For Seppios most of all.

Torren led him down a hall toward... cheering? Rufus stood beside a closed door with a large amphora of wine. Torren took it from him and nodded toward the door. "How are they?"

"In high spirits, my lord. Ramses has not yet returned. Cam is working his clay in the peristyle. Anzo visits with Dax."

"Good. Let me know when Ramses returns."

Rufus opened the door, and Jonathan felt very small. Seven men, who could only be gladiators by their massive builds, filled the room. Two arm-wrestled on benches while the others cheered them on. Each wore a black leather wrist guard on the right arm.

Torren appeared unaffected that none of the men acknowledged his presence. He approached the table and set the amphora of wine on it. "Keep at it, Styx. One day you may beat him."

The one wearing beads of sweat with the cords of his neck bulging must be Styx. His opponent wore a look of intense effort, but not strain. The man grinned and put Styx's arm hard to the table with a solid thump. "Not today."

The men around them laughed, including Torren—all but Styx and Jonathan.

The victor rose from the bench and surveyed Jonathan as Cam had. "So this is him?"

"This is him. I'm taking him to see Otho but wanted to introduce him to his brothers."

"Welcome to the House of Gallego, Jonathan. I'm Rooster, reigning champion of this house for the past two years, and this weak-armed wretch here is Styx. This is Julius, Wolf, Prito, Marius, and Sanballat."

"Did a lion get you?" Styx asked.

Jonathan followed their gaze to the long thin scabs on his arms. "Not this time."

Rooster's brow arched as he rubbed his hands together. "You must tell us of the other time when you are rested from your journey. And heal quickly. I'm anxious to cross swords with you."

Torren subtly inserted himself between them. "Patience. When Jonathan is healed and *I'm* ready, then we'll rank." He clapped Styx on the back, still brooding on the bench across from Rooster. "Keep at him, Styx."

Styx slammed his elbow back onto the table. "Again, Roo."

Rooster dropped to his bench and they clasped hands. The rest of them men resumed their encouragement and Jonathan and Torren were forgotten. They all looked—happy.

That should encourage Jonathan, yet it made him feel even more an outsider.

Torren nudged him toward the doorway. "Let's get you to the medicus chamber before that opium wears off."

The next hallway held far more doors than made sense. "Are these storerooms?" It seemed odd they would be so far removed from the kitchen.

"Bedchambers. Yours won't be ready for a few days yet, but Otho will want to keep an eye on you in the medicus chamber so that shouldn't be a problem."

Jonathan stopped and looked again at the doors. No locks. "You don't have cells?"

Torren turned toward him, the hint of a frown on his face. "Cells are for animals and criminals. My men are neither."

"You don't fear escape?"

"Should I?"

An honest question deserved an honest answer. "No."

Torren's posture relaxed and his grin returned. "Good. Come along then."

A few more paces down the long hall, and Jonathan remembered his question from earlier. "What does it mean to rank?"

"Ranking the men is proper contest to determine level of skill and who is champion. Surely you know this."

"I did not."

Torren swore and his mouth flattened. "Caius Pullus has the gall to call himself a lanista."

At the end of the hall, Torren opened the last door. The room inside was already crowded. The medicus, judging by the jar in his hand, did the same head to foot appraisal the others had. "You weren't jesting."

"No, I wasn't," Torren said. "But they tell me he heals fast."

The medicus gestured to the only open bed. "Put him over there."

Jonathan reached into his belt and freed the small scroll tucked inside. "This is instruction on the preparation of a paste to speed healing and reduce scarring."

The medicus reached to take it and Torren's eyes met Jonathan's. "Nessa?"

The sound of her name pried at the lid of his longing, but he didn't show it. "Yes."

"Few servants read and write. Most that do are scribes. Did Quintus write it down?"

"No, I did."

Torren's brow lifted. "You write?"

The surprise in Torren's tone annoyed him. Jonathan had been well educated in his father's house and knew a great many things besides how to swing a sword. "Yes, in both Greek and Latin."

"With which hand?"

Why did that matter? "My left."

Torren's eyes widened and he stepped closer. "Show me how you hold your spoon."

An odd request. As strange as everything and everyone in this place so far.

"Go on, show me," Torren commanded.

So Jonathan did, feeling rather foolish to be holding in imaginary spoon in the air.

Torren picked up a vial from the shelf closest to him and tossed it to him.

Jonathan caught it, but the quick movement sent a hiss of pain through his gritted teeth.

Torren swore again and then uttered a short laugh. "Caius Pullus had no idea what he possessed."

Jonathan handed the corked vial back to Torren. "I don't understand."

"You're left-handed."

The man on the stool, who must be Anzo, spoke first. "Did you even know?"

"Know what?"

Anzo scoffed and turned to Torren. "Will you train him to the proper side?"

Torren rubbed his chin and frowned. "I don't know. He did defeat Hulderic right-handed."

"And Jelani." The injured gladiator lying on the other bed spat the words with such contempt, he must be Dax. A thick metal splint surrounded his arm from wrist to shoulder.

Torren moved between them as he'd done with Rooster. "Jelani will not be forgotten, but you will treat Jonathan as he would have. Jonathan is a brother now, a part of this familia gladitoria."

A glance around the lanista revealed a glare on Dax's face.

"He's right," Anzo said, and Dax turned the glare on him.

"Enough." Torren crossed his arms and seemed to grow a hand-breadth taller. "You know our code of honor. Wolf and Julius were here when I last enforced it. You know me to be a man of my word. For the love of the gods, do not test me. I will enforce it."

Both men eyed each other without blinking a long moment. Dax finally relaxed the glare but didn't drop his gaze. "Understood."

"Good." Torren's easy grin returned, and he clapped Dax on the shoulder. "Get them both healthy, Otho. If you require anything for that paste, Rufus will pick it up when he goes for supplies tomorrow."

Torren left, and Otho had Jonathan strip to his cloth. He managed it without too much grimacing. A sour-smelling yellow salve burned like a branding iron in every one of his wounds. He'd rather it be Nessa's paste, and her touch that delivered it. Anzo seemed friendly enough. Dax couldn't be faulted for the animosity that lingered in his expression. If Jonathan were in the same room with the gladiator who'd slain Seppios, he'd react the same way.

Their meal was a stew as good as any he'd had in his father's house. Otho asked a great many questions about Nessa's paste. Half of which he didn't know the answer to. Anzo left first, and then Otho, after extinguishing the lamps.

Jonathan lay awake on the bed, fighting to remain awake. He'd rather sleep in the sand outside than fall asleep beside a man who probably wanted to slit his throat. In the dark, Nessa's face came to him easily. Her brown eyes and dark hair, and her smile that always drove the shadows from his mood.

Lord, protect her and Quintus. She told me I'm immortal until Your work for me is finished. Prove her right. Help me know how to help Dax so that we may grieve Jelani together. Help me to live worthy of his sacrifice—and Yours.

CHAPTER 30 – CHAMPION

Jonathan began the new day as he had every other for the past six months—on his knees. "Lead me in Your truth, Lord. Keep Quintus and Nessa safe. Remind her of my great love for her and surround her with warrior angels that will protect her from all harm. Give me strength and wisdom to honor you with the gift of this day, and shine your truth to those around me."

He rose from the cool stone floor of his room and donned his belt and sandals. The leather wrist guard with the mark of his house never left his arm, even when he bathed. Outside, Ramses and Julius already worked the poles in the training ground. They nodded in greeting as their wooden swords banged in time with each other against the scarred wood rising from the ground like limbless trees. Warmer air than yesterday hinted at spring. Perhaps the change in weather meant the heavens knew this was no ordinary day. One opponent remained in the rankings. Jonathan had bested all the others. Some easy, some not, but all while fighting right-handed. Today Jonathan would face Rooster for first position—that of champion.

He chose his preferred wooden sword and shield the others knew to leave for him and joined them. "You're looking well this morning, Ramses."

"I've decided I'd still rather have spent the three nights with my wife and children instead of better preparing to fight you. That is the only reason I lost."

Julius chuckled and gave the pole a particularly solid blow. "If only you possessed as much strategy as you do excuses."

The Egyptian grinned at them and spun his wooden sword in the air. "It doesn't matter. Roo will win. He always wins. You might as well concede defeat now before he puts bruises on top of all those scars."

"Will you fight him left or right-handed?" Julius asked.

"I don't know."

It was the truth, but Ramses must have thought it cunning by the way he laughed. "I think Jonathan plans to keep Roo guessing to the last possible moment and ensure we don't ruin his advantage."

Trying to correct him would be futile. When Ramses set his mind about something, nothing swayed him. This caused a tense moment on rest day a few weeks ago when Ramses accused Marius of cheating him at knucklebones. A servant summoned Torren, while Jonathan and Rooster fought to prevent a shouting match from becoming a physical altercation. Torren stormed the common room, his hair askew, wearing only a tunic—inside out—and threatened to cancel rest day till the December games if he was called away from his visitor ever again to settle a childish dispute.

So instead of arguing with Ramses, Jonathan resumed his pole work. With each successive blow of the wooden sword to the battered pole, the corded muscles of his arms warmed and stretched.

"Left hand," Torren yelled as he approached. "You won't improve if you don't practice."

Jonathan swapped his sword and shield. Fighting left-handed provided him a distinct advantage. For his opponent, everything would be backwards of what it should be. The difficulty was if Jonathan's concentration slipped at all in the pitch of sparring, everything felt backwards for him also.

Torren picked up a sword and shield. After six weeks recovering from Hulderic's blades, Jonathan had begun training to the shock that Torren was his own trainer—and a considerable opponent.

Torren assumed the beginning stance and beckoned Jonathan closer with his shield. “Left side. With me. And do not hold back today. Rooster will not, nor will I.”

He’d suspected Torren of holding back when sparring with him after watching him fight Roo to an impasse one day last November. If Jonathan weren’t also holding back when sparring with Torren, he would have known sooner. Something in his mind wouldn’t allow him to strike his best blows into the body of a man he respected as deeply as he did his Dominus.

Torren grinned and shifted his weight over his front foot. “Stop holding back. Fight me as if Nessa were the prize.”

He remembered her name. That shock ripped through him like a spear. Jonathan never spoke of her here, except alone in prayer. That Torren remembered her name after all this time made his respect for him swell and his sword arm falter.

Torren charged.

The impact sword to sword and shield to shield thundered through the training ground. Cheers erupted around them as Torren’s wooden blade slammed Jonathan’s elbow. The crushing blow knocked him sideways a full step and he spun to recover.

Torren crouched lower and raised his sword higher. “I told you I’m not holding back today.”

“Level him, Torren!”

“Show him who’s master!”

Jonathan lost his shield several parries deeper into the fight. In frustration he put his sword back in his right hand and attacked again. Sweat breached his brows and stung his eyes but he fought on. Without the shield he could move fast enough to counter every thrust of Torren’s sword, always mindful of that shield and the man’s feet while watching his eyes.

It was like fighting Tao again. Torren swung but reversed and spun at the last moment, slamming the flat of his sword into Jonathan’s right arm. Pain licked down to the bone and he bit his lip to keep from cursing.

“If I break that arm you might finally learn to use your left.”

Jonathan allowed the pain in and feigned injury, letting the sword tip fall and clutching at his upper arm. Torren hesitated, no longer the trainer but the lanista again, and Jonathan landed a stunning jab to his rib cage with his aching but very un-broken arm.

Torren's hip rolled back in the instinctive recoil that always accompanied that hit. Jonathan swept his foot between the man's legs and yanked the unsteady foot from under him. Torren landed on his back and Jonathan's sword pinned his chest before the sand settled.

Groans and cheers from the men swirled around them. Instead of making Torren give the missio, Jonathan offered him his hand.

"You've been holding back too." Torren took hold and pulled himself to his feet. His stare hardened and he brushed sand from his arms. "I'd stop. Roo will not."

"Roo is not my lanista."

"True, but anyone who crosses blades with you is an opponent. No more, no less. Lanista, brother, even Caesar."

Their circle of spectators parted as Rooster approached, sword and shield in hand. "Don't tire the lion killer before our contest. He'll cry foul, like Ramses."

Torren picked up his shield and sword from the sand and tossed them to Rufus. "Don't be anxious. I left plenty of fight in him for you."

The circle closed around them and Rooster rolled his head shoulder to shoulder and shook out his legs one at a time.

"Aren't you going to warm up first? I've got an amphora of Falernian wine on this."

Jonathan didn't have to look to know Wolf had spoken. Wolf bet on everything.

Rooster scoffed and assumed opening position. "Beating Jonathan is my warm-up."

Overconfidence was good. It would make it easier to lay the trap for the champion. Doing so was going to subject his own body to plenty of physical punishment, but the six months under Torren had him in peak condition. He could take it. Groans came from a few men when he picked up his fallen sword with his left hand and his shield with the right. Probably those with bets both for and against him. If he didn't think about it feeling backwards, it wouldn't.

Torren nodded in approval and held the pugil stick between them. "Places."

Jonathan crouched behind his shield, sword extended and ready. He dipped his chin and took a deep breath, summoning his focus. Somewhere in the stables a horse whinnied, breaking the hush that had fallen over the training ground. The soft whip of shifting sand said Rooster adjusted his stance. The stick flashed through Jonathan and Rooster's locked stares.

Jonathan sprang forward with a shield thrust. Rooster's eyes flashed wide when their shields met in a solid boom and propelled him back a step. Jonathan wasn't as fast or as strong attacking left-handed, but like most every gladiator in the empire, Rooster was unaccustomed to defending against it.

It wasn't an advantage Jonathan could hold for long, because a sword didn't block like a shield. Rooster was putting the pain to him on the left side with blows from his heavy wooden shield. Jonathan dug in and concentrated on defending. Not too much, just enough to keep his feet and keep drawing Rooster into the trap. All around them the other gladiators shouted encouragement.

His left arm was numbing from the numerous blows he'd suffered on that side. Most he could have blocked but did not. Rooster kept them coming, growing less and less careful with each blow as their sparring wore on. When the corner of Rooster's mouth lifted slightly after a solid blow to Jonathan's leg, it was time to spring the trap. Rooster's next swing hit Jonathan's shield and he let go of the grip, the force of the blow carrying the shield far to the side of them.

Rooster seized the opening and leveled a vicious swing toward Jonathan's now exposed ribcage, as Jonathan hoped. He ducked beneath the swing, moving his sword to his right hand and flipping it as he did so the tip of the sword lay flat against his elbow. In the blink of an eye, the wooden sword now protected Jonathan's forearm, and he slammed it full force into the side of Roo's head as the champion fought the momentum of his failed swing.

Rooster dropped face down into the sand.

Jonathan flipped the sword in his grip again and thrust the blunted tip between Rooster's shoulder blades. Cheers erupted from the circle of men around them. Jonathan found Torren among them, anxious to see if he'd pleased his lanista.

But Torren was rushing toward them. He dropped to his knees besides Rooster and turned him on his back. "Rooster?"

No response. His eyes were closed and his head limp.

"Fetch Otho!" Torren slapped Rooster lightly on the jaw as the brothers closed around them. "Wake up, Roo."

Jonathan cast his sword aside and crouched beside them. A hand to Roo's chest confirmed he was still breathing.

Torren shook Rooster's shoulder so hard his head rattled in the sand. "Come on, Roo, wake up. Wine and women wait in plenty. Wake up."

Still nothing.

Jonathan put both hands on Rooster's arm, bowed his head and closed his eyes. "God, I ask You to awaken Rooster. Clear his mind and open his eyes. Restore him in the name of Jesus Christ."

"Praying to Jelani's God for a miracle?"

Jonathan met Torren's stare. "Jelani's God is my God, the only God, Torren. He is God Most High, and still performs miracles as in the ancient writings. I know because I'm one of them."

"The miracle," Rooster rasped, "is Jonathan beat me."

Torren's eyes went wide as Rooster opened his and looked right at Jonathan. "You can let go of me now. I yield."

"Thank you, God," Jonathan whispered as he let go of Rooster's arm and sat back on his heels.

Rooster sat up and shook his head like a wet dog, flinging sand everywhere. He rubbed the side of his head above his ear. "I want to know one thing. Where did you learn that?"

Torren laughed and put a hand on Rooster's shoulder. "Have him teach it to you. Jonathan is the champion of the House of Gallego now."

Disappointment fell like a shadow over Rooster's expression. Even without that, Jonathan wouldn't have reveled in his victory. He rose and offered his hand to Rooster. The former champion grasped it after a long moment, and Jonathan pulled him to his feet.

Otho emerged from the villa at a dead run, and then skidded to a halt, his brow furrowing when he surveyed Rooster. "They said it was urgent."

Torren shrugged. "You're too late. Jonathan entreated his God and healed Rooster."

An image of Nessa flashed in Jonathan's mind as her words formed on his lips. "It's God that heals, though sometimes he uses people to do it." He ached for her, imagining how proud she would be for him at this moment.

Rooster removed a bronze and silver medallion from around his neck. "Here. This is yours." He placed the symbol of the champion of the House of Gallego in Jonathan's hand. "For now," he added, his grin returning.

Jonathan looped the medallion over his head. The sword-bearing griffin rested against his chest. Tao and Quintus would be proud of him too. He was champion.

Torren rubbed his hands together, anticipation clear on his face. "You're ready."

Chapter 31 – A Different Game

Torren caressed the beautiful woman beside him. "Wed me."

She stirred on the silk-covered feather pillow he'd bought for her five summers ago. Her skilled fingers stroked his chin. "I can't, *Amore*. You know that."

It never escaped him that as many times as they'd been together, Caelina never used his name. He was *amore*, like the others who could afford the thousand sesterces for the pleasure of her company. She kissed him lightly on the mouth and slipped from the bed like a shadow retreating from the sun.

Torren sat up on his elbows, wishing he possessed enough coin to keep her with him, only him, every day. "Dine with me before you go."

She pulled her silk tunic over her head, making even that look graceful. "I thought you dined with your gladiators in the evenings."

He suppressed a sigh. "No, I dine with each of the men in turn every Monday. You've said before how generous that is of me. Remember?"

She sat on the end of the bed to lace on her sandals. "I need to return home."

"This could be your home."

"I love Rome too much." She turned and presented him a sultry twist of her lips. "You know I only leave the city to see you."

Torren rose and found his tunic. Her visits to the ludis were not a privilege he'd earned. She didn't want it known her patrons included a lanista, though she could never afford to admit it. He buckled his belt, an idea forming to take her pride down a few rungs and test his theory about his champion.

"Did you know most lanistas reward their men with women after victories? I've always found it easier to give them a share of their winnings and let them do as they please with it."

"Do the *perditi hominess* even know what to do with coin?"

His teeth clenched through a sharp intake of breath. He spun to face her, surprised at how deeply her words had wounded him. "It's one thing for the matrons in the temples to refer to me and my men that way. But to hear it from *you?*"

"I didn't—"

"You call them lowest of the low. The rich men I share you with mock us, call us animals, barbarians, inferi. The same men who recount my men's battles in the baths, collect their armor for their villas, and hire their swords to defend their very lives. So tell me, who are the greater men? Who are the *true Romans*?"

He crossed to the window, unable to stand the sight of her.

"Do not be angry with me, *Amore*."

She sounded sincere, but when he turned to face her, her sky-blue eyes told the truth. This was business. No more. No less.

It would be for him too. "I'll let you make it up to me."

Seduction oozed in her smile. "What do you have in mind?"

"My champion performed exceptionally in all three spring games. Spend tonight with him."

Her smile vanished. "You said you didn't do that."

"I'm making an exception for Jonathan. He saves all his earnings. Never visits the brothels with the others. He won't bet even a copper on knucklebones."

"Then he wouldn't spend a thousand sesterces on me, even if he has it."

"I'm feeling generous."

A long silence followed as she worked her jaw back and forth and stared at the wall. Torren might not have the rank or reputation of her other clients, but his coin spent the same. Too much of which he spent on her and she knew it.

Finally her gaze, and that smile that lightened coin pouches, returned. "Five thousand sesterces and the standard arrangement. You tell no one."

Torren flinched at the price. But knowing who he could trust in the coming months would mean life or death. "Done. Provided you remain with him till dawn and *earn* the coin. No ordering him to the floor or insulting him as you did me a moment ago."

"He'll be well satisfied."

Her smug grin as she left cut him like a knife, providing images he forced from his mind. It was too late to call her back. Sending her to Jonathan was an inspired way to test how much Jonathan could be trusted to tell him the truth. He'd remind himself of that when he wanted to curse himself a fool for adding another lover to her collection.

He'd entered into a war, and war always meant sacrifices.

A gladiator was a slave. Even more beneath her reputation than a lanista. But, five thousand sesterces was a lot of coin. And all the talk in the baths, the forum, even the bedchambers of her other patrons about this gladiator had Caelina curious. Her two guards, Lucius and Octavius, didn't like this either. Because they'd be up all night or because she'd lowered herself to pleasuring slaves now she couldn't tell.

It didn't matter. They'd follow her into the deserts of Egypt if she asked them too.

For tonight they would wait at the end of the hall. At the last closed door, Torren's servant Rufus raised his hand to knock. She grabbed his wrist, careful not to spill the oil in the small clay lamp she carried. "Don't announce me. Make certain my guards are comfortable and we're undisturbed till morning."

"Yes, my lady."

My lady. Only servants called her that still. She unlatched the door, and it made no sound as it opened. Well maintained—like everything in Torren Gallego's villa. She crept in, the faint glow from the lamp revealing Torren's gladiator already asleep in his bed. Thank Juno for that blessing. She had no intention of waking him. Not until just before dawn if she could help it. Tiptoeing across the tiled floor, she felt ten years old again, trying to sneak from her bedchamber before *he* would come. She placed the lamp on the table and settled on the only stool in the room.

He slept naked on top of his blankets, and the skin of his back sent a shiver down her own. Welts covered it, some long and dark, most thin and white, like those on his arm. Above a thin chain on the back of his neck a strange symbol had been inked into his skin. His dark hair glistened in the lamplight. Damp from a bath? It couldn't be sweat, for none covered his skin and he smelled rather clean—another surprise.

His face was stunning, even marred by a small scar near his eye. Except for his back, he looked nothing like a slave. If she focused on that exquisite face when he woke, she could put from her mind she was being intimate with a slave again. At least this time she was a woman—and it would be her choice.

To pass the time, she counted his scars. After losing count where they crossed each other for the fifth time, she gave up. He shifted in sleep, adjusting the arm beneath his head and bending the leg closest to her. His hip bone popped, the way an old man's does, but he slept through it. Another hour or two and she would be fighting sleep. That would prove a problem, especially if he woke first.

But the fates weren't going to be so generous. Torren's gladiator shifted again and this time he opened his eyes. He shot up and yanked the blanket over his lap. "Who are you?"

"Calm yourself. If I were an assassin, you'd already be dead."

"Then who are you?"

His voice was deep, and as strong as his chest appeared. Scars covered it also, but they looked different. Made by weapons, not whips.

"A friend of Torren."

His expression remained stern as his gaze moved over the rest of her. This part she knew well. His breathing deepened and he swallowed, his gaze caught on her fullest curves.

She was in her element now. "He sent me in congratulations of your performance in the spring games."

"Did he?" His mouth pulled into a frown and rocked her confidence. "Please tell him I'm grateful for the gesture, but it's not one I can accept."

Caelina stiffened, nearly tipping backward on the wooden stool. "You're refusing me?"

"I mean no offense by it, but yes."

She'd never been refused. Not once, and this, this, slave stared at her as if he were serious. "Do you prefer men?"

"No."

What other reason could there be? "Then why?"

"I have reasons."

Injury? Religion? "What are they?"

"My own."

It didn't matter what his secret reasons were. She wouldn't be denied five thousand sesterces because of them. "I'm not leaving until dawn."

"Yes, you are." He pulled the blanket more securely around his waist and stood. In only two steps he turned for the door.

She leaped from the stool and reached the door first, barring it with her body. He continued to advance, the blanket trailing behind him. Out of time, all she could offer was the truth. "I can't leave before dawn or he won't pay me."

The gladiator stopped and inclined his head. "How much?"

"Five thousand sesterces."

His mouth parted as he stood there frozen.

That's more like it. "That's right, gladiator. I'm not some tired kitchen slave. I'm the highest-priced pleasure in all of Rome."

He suddenly grinned. Maybe she was making progress.

"Actually, I am. Torren earns five times that much for me when I appear in the arena."

His insolence was as overwhelming as his perfectly-muscled body. Didn't he know who she was?

He closed the distance between them and stopped in front of her. "Please make way."

"What do you intend?"

"To tell Torren I'd rather have the coin."

Rather have—

She slapped him.

His head snapped sideways and her palm burned from the impact. The fury in his eyes told her to scream. But he grabbed her by the throat before she could. His grip squeezed her neck as his gaze filled with wrath. She grasped at the wrist choking her, trying to call for help, beg him to stop, but no voice came. No way to call for help. It was happening again. She met his glare to try to plead with her eyes but there was no mercy to be had in his.

And then he blinked. The killer vanished and the prison of his hand released her.

Air never felt so good, but the cough that followed hurt, and still wouldn't let her scream for her guards.

He'd backed away from her, his eyes wide and his mouth parted, as if surprised he'd nearly killed her. "Forgive me."

Absolutely not. She rubbed at her neck, and the coughing stopped. She heaved several deep breaths and put her hand on the latch of the door behind her. Torren would have him executed for this. She'd make sure he did. But the man hugging his blanket to his waist was not the one who'd choked her. He wouldn't raise his head, and she could feel the remorse rolling off him in waves. The ridiculous urge to comfort *him* overcame her.

His head finally came up, though the regret was still in his eyes. "Forgive me. You reminded me of someone I once knew."

"Then I pity her."

"She doesn't deserve it. Nor did you deserve that." He raked his fingers through his black hair. "I'd rather you never slap me again, but I'll try to remember to turn the other cheek if you do."

He was mad. Mad like Nero. Maybe even Caligula. But Lucius and Octavius were still near. If she left now, she forfeited the coin and this would have been for nothing. Then there would be explaining to Torren, including the part where he refused her. She hadn't made the reputation that kept her in silk and pearls by admitting defeat. Surely a gladiator would understand that.

"I won't come near you, but I am staying till morning. I doubt Torren will ask, but if he does, tell him you enjoyed yourself."

He just stood there. Like a statue. A blanket-wrapped mute with sorrow in his gaze.

She sighed and crossed her arms. "Please."

The word tasted foreign on her tongue. She was used to hearing it, not saying it.

"Is the coin that important to you?"

"Yes." Her reputation more so, but he didn't need to know that. "Considering you almost crushed my throat, it's the least you can allow me."

He frowned and ran his fingers through his hair again.

Caelina wouldn't give him an opportunity to change his mind. She lay across the doorway, the cold tile chilling her through her silk garment. With her arm she made a pillow as the gladiator had done earlier and curled her knees in.

"You can't sleep on the floor."

"I can do whatever I like, and this way you can't sneak out without waking me."

"You have my word. I won't leave. Please take the bed."

"Not unless you put it in front of the door."

She'd uttered it in jest, but he turned to the wall and retrieved a brown tunic from a peg. He pulled it on with one hand while the other held his blanket in place. His sense of propriety was amusing. A laugh built in her chest, until he placed the blanket on the bed and began to pull the wooden frame toward her.

Caelina scooted out of the way and he slid the bed long-ways against the door. He didn't linger, simply walked back to where it had been in the corner of the small chamber and lowered himself to the floor. He faced the wall instead of her, stretched out on his side with his head resting on his arm. He'd left the lamp burning, and she could see him shiver on the cold of the stone floor.

She sat on his bed, guilt covering her along with his blanket as she lay on the thick cushion. An earthy, rich scent lingered on the fabric, like a newly plowed field, as complex as the man who'd made it. She'd seen the wrath in his eyes and felt the fury in the hand at her throat. Neither fit with the way he'd then given up his bed and, more intriguing, why he wasn't in it with her. She'd seen the way his body responded and recognized it in his eyes when he first looked at her. But he hadn't acted on it.

Why? She studied him in the lamplight. He'd nearly crushed her throat. It still hurt. Yet she felt safe with him. Safer than she had in a long time.

CHAPTER 32 – SILVER

Jonathan missed a block with his shield, and Styx's wooden sword thumped him hard against his ribs. He needed to spend more nights on the floor if one made him this stiff.

Styx frowned, the morning light of the courtyard shining off the sweat of his brow. "You're slow today."

"Don't get accustomed to it."

"And tender about it. What happened to you last night?"

"Nothing I wish to discuss." Jonathan stepped toward him and continued their sparring.

"By the gods, it's true then?" Styx swore and his grin widened. "I owe Wolf ten sesterces."

"Told you," Wolf yelled from where he sparred with Cam.

A sinking feeling told Jonathan he already knew the reason as he took another solid hit. With his shield this time. "Why?"

"I didn't believe he'd seen Caelina enter your chamber last night. Torren is mad about her. Half of Rome is."

A quick thrust to the knees should silence him. But Styx blocked it, still grinning.

"Well? How was it?"

Jonathan forced Styx to engage him sword to sword.

"Nothing— " *Crack.* "I wish—" *Crack.* "To discuss."

The grin on Styx's face widened. "You're cruel—" *Crack.* "Not to share." *Crack.*

A growl of frustration tore from Jonathan's throat and poured into his attack. Their sparring intensified, until Rufus approached them. "Jonathan, the master summons you."

Eleven pairs of eyes were on him at once. He dropped his training sword and shield in the basket and followed Rufus to Torren's library. His empty stomach churned with every step. In the library, Rufus closed the doors behind him.

Torren reclined on a couch, turning an unbitten apple over and over in his raised hand.

"Do you always tell the truth?"

"What?" Jonathan needed to choose his answers carefully to keep his word to Caelina without dishonoring God or himself.

"It's a simple question. Do you always tell the truth?"

"I don't lie."

"Ah, but that's not the same thing, is it?"

Jonathan's anger rose even as he tried to remain calm. "Am I accused of some transgression?"

"Not yet. Come sit."

Jonathan refused to look away from the penetrating gaze, or show signs of discomfort as he took the seat opposite his master. He'd done nothing wrong. Except for grabbing Caelina by the throat when she slapped him. For that he'd already asked her forgiveness, and God's.

Silence stretched between them until finally Torren spoke. "Did she please you?"

"She did all that I asked of her."

Torren's knuckles whitened on the apple that stilled in his hand. "Did she?"

"Yes." He'd asked her to take the bed and she had, and she didn't slap him again. "I appreciate the gesture, but bringing honor to the House of Gallego and the share of my winnings you allow me to keep are reward enough for me. You needn't send her again."

Torren set the apple down. From between the cushions of his couch he raised a hefty sack of coin and lobbed it toward him.

"What's this?"

"A hundred *aureii.* It's yours."

Jonathan couldn't breathe. Ten thousand sesterces. Not nearly enough for his freedom, but with the three thousand four hundred and sixty three he already had, perhaps enough for Nessa's.

"It's yours *if* you tell me the truth, not deliver clever answers designed to avoid deception." Torren sat up and leaned forward, interlacing his fingers and placing his elbows on his knees. "Did you join with her or not?"

The leather bag in his hands might as well be thirty pieces of silver. If he gave up Caelina, told the truth, the coin would be his. Torren had always proven himself a man of his word. But so was he, and he'd already given it in haste last night. He swallowed. *Forgive me, Nessa.* He extended the coins to Torren, his arms trembling under their weight.

"If you want details, you must ask Caelina. I cannot in honor say any more."

"Of course you can. She's a prostitute."

Jonathan met Torren's cutting stare over the bag of gold still between them. "I'm not."

Torren gave Jonathan time to change his mind. A long moment passed, and he didn't.

He was the one. A small fortune, but well spent to find out Jonathan couldn't be bribed. Their lives, and those of the others, were going to depend on it.

"I can see that you are not. For that you may keep it. Though I'm sure you'll want me to add it to your accounting."

Confusion filled his champion's face. "I don't understand."

He took the bag of coin and set it beside him. “It was a test. You passed.”

“A test?”

“It only took an extra thousand sesterces to get the truth out of Caelina.”

A storm formed in Jonathan’s features.

“Don’t be angry at her. She’s driven by coin. Besides, thanks to her, I know you can’t be bought. That’s worth all the coin I had to give both of you to find out.”

“Of course I can be bought. I’m a slave.”

Torren picked up his apple and took a bite. “You know what I meant.”

“Why is it that important to you, to know if I can be bribed or not?”

Torren feigned indifference while chewing the crisp fruit. Assassinating Caesar wasn’t a plan to involve others in sooner than required. “If and when the time comes, you’ll know. Until then concentrate on training. I sense the July games will be bigger and bloodier than even last year’s Ludi Romani. Now that Emperor Domitian has executed the consul and banished the man’s widow, Rome is restless.”

“Caesar banished his own niece?”

“It’s rumored she’s a Christian and wouldn’t worship her uncle’s deity. I think it more likely she was sent away and Clemens killed because they possessed sons that might one day challenge Domitian’s power.”

“Do the sons live?”

“For now.”

“I will pray for them.”

“Pray to your God for all of us. Domitian will court the people even closer now. That means bigger and better games. I need you to fight well and win. Much depends on it. Focus on that and nothing else. Agreed?”

Jonathan released a long sigh before standing. “Agreed, but I ask one thing.”

“What?”

“Don’t send me any more women. Unless they’re Nessa.”

Torren couldn’t help but grin. “Agreed.”

Chapter 33 – Defiance

Ludi Apollinares, Rome
July 13, 95 AD

Jonathan's breath heaved the hot, damp air trapped in his helmet, sand clinging to his sweat-covered skin. The gladiator lying prone at his feet raised two fingers in surrender. Fifty thousand people stacked to the sky all around him cheered to mark the moment. Proficient with his sword in either hand, and able to switch at will, Jonathan stood without equal in the arena.

Yet his opponent had fought valiantly, and Jonathan allowed the match to continue as long as he could to show it. The crowd battled for a unified verdict but neither opinion emerged a victor. Some of them likely recognized that Jonathan had purposefully drawn the fight out, and demanded death for the defeated. The others had been fooled by it or were simply in a merciful mood.

Jonathan waited with his sword poised between the man's shoulder and neck, at the edge of the man's helmet. The emperor would grant the man life on a mixed verdict. Ceaser's thumb was the one that mattered most.

But Caesar paid them no heed. The emperor sat engaged in animated conversation, surrounded by guards and guests in the imperial box. The crowd that had been screaming Jonathan's name for the last half hour was less patient. Angry at being kept waiting, the tenor of their cries changed. That finally captured Caesar's attention. After a brief glance at Jonathan, Domitian threw an indifferent slash with his thumb and returned to his conversation.

Jonathan couldn't believe it. Neither could the portion of the crowd who realized like he did what just happened and increased their cries of protest. Caesar had mistaken their impatience for a decision as death for the loser. The hoplomachus bleeding at his feet didn't beg. He closed his eyes within his helmet where he lay face-up in the warm sand and awaited the killing stroke with honor—a true gladiator.

Anger seethed within Jonathan as he tightened his grip on his sword. This was wrong. Caesar was throwing this man's life away as if he were the bone from a roasted pheasant leg. The man had fought well. Extremely well, considering he never had a chance against Jonathan left-handed. The crowd wanted him to live. Their white cloths and cries for missio still permeated the air. But Caesar had ordered death.

Jonathan breathed deep and pulled his elbow back and up, raising the sword for a fast, clean thrust. He had to obey.

Didn't he?

No.

Nessa's life was no longer at stake. She would be proud of him, when she learned how he'd died. And maybe, somewhere, Jelani would be too.

Jonathan set his shield down and grabbed the arm of his conquered opponent. "Get up." He hauled him to his feet, retrieved the longest piece of the man's spear, and put it in the man's hand. "If Caesar wants you dead, he can come kill you himself."

A fierce expression stole over the hoplomachus' face, and peace settled over Jonathan. God's work for him must be finished. He'd lose his life before he ever took another one without cause, and the indifference of a man, even Caesar, wasn't good enough.

The collective approval of the mob rocked the sand beneath their feet as guards began to flow into the arena. Jonathan picked up his shield, put his back to the hoplomachus, and let the guards fan out around them. "No killing."

"Them or us?"

"Them. They blindly obey. Spare them if you can." Jonathan cast one last look at Caesar. The emperor was on his feet, screaming something lost in the roar of the mob while praetorians and guests in the emperor's box scattered in every direction.

An arrow pierced Jonathan's shoulder. No warning this time. His focus honed in on the archers among the guards he faced. He charged, with a shout that echoed over the cries of fifty thousand more.

Torren sat statue still on his stone seat with his hand over his mouth. Jonathan was throwing his life away, a fortune in future earnings with it, and though he had no way of knowing so, months of planning.

Senator Nerva leaned closer, the abhorrently strong scent of sweat clinging to him. "Your champion defies Caesar. I hope that's not something I should expect from either of you in the future."

Nerva had no way of knowing that by sunset today he should have been made the new Caesar. He'd wanted to be kept from the *details* as he called them. Those details—the bribes, the maneuverings, the assassination—they were in ruins now. Because of *his* gladiator.

Domitian screamed orders and both prefects were sent to deal with the problem in the arena. Without the prefects in place, men the alliance had bought, the plan would be instantly aborted. No assassination today. At least not of Caesar.

Torren held his chin so hard his jaw ached, determined to speak with a calm he did not feel. "Don't worry, Senator. My champion won't survive defying Caesar. Few do, as you know."

The reminder they were in this together, even after success, could go to work on the senator. The emperor still stood, surrounded by servants and a few guests that remained. The prefects had left the box, and it appeared the others knew to abort. The alliance was safe, for now. For now, he'd have to resign himself to watching his best gladiator die.

But Jonathan wasn't dying. Guards dropped all around his sword like ripe fruit from tree limbs in a high wind. The hoplomachus defended Jonathan's back, and even with half a spear, defended it well. His gladiator still held his ground against the praetorians closing in among a field of fallen arena guards. A broken arrow shaft protruded from his shoulder, a long slash across his ribs bled, and blood flowed from somewhere on his thigh. Yet the two dozen or so challengers hung back, as the braver among them would move forward to challenge.

Jonathan's sword danced like a hummingbird moth in his left hand. His shield moved equally as fast in his right, both blocking and delivering blows. The pure union of strength, skill, and solid form holding firm in a hopeless fight took Torren's breath away. It was beautiful to watch. The way Torren's father had been—one with his sword.

But there were too many. Jonathan's swings were slowing, his shield missing more and more hits, and the hoplomachus looked nearly spent. The circle of praetorians closed in on his champion from all sides now, like a pack of wolves on a tired stag. The violence from the sand bled into the tiers of seats, all the way to the upper rows. The din of the people became as crushing as the circle of praetorians about to take down their idol.

Nerva coughed and pulled his crimson-trimmed toga tighter around himself. "You see, Gallego? Even the common people have had enough of this emperor."

Torren couldn't think about Caesar or the many reasons they needed to free Rome from his tyrannical rule right now. That was Jonathan standing in the center of that circle of death. For the first time, this was no acceptable loss measured in coin and steeped in tradition. He tore his gaze away, unable to watch his gladiator—and friend—be struck down.

The shouts surrounding them erupted with fresh intensity.

Torren thought he might be sick.

Nerva grabbed his arm. "Look."

Not wanting to appear weak in front of the soon-to-be emperor, Torren returned his gaze to the arena floor. Men from the first rows of seats had jumped the retaining wall and were running toward Jonathan, *who still stood!* They advanced on the guards, shaking fists in the air that made the folds of their togas whip like sails in a storm. Several of them picked up the weapons of the fallen guards.

Rome was rioting.

Nerva's grip on his arm tightened. "We must go. Now."

Pure fear filled the older man's face. Fear echoed in the faces of the nobility around them, those that hadn't already begun to pour into the arena. Rivulets of darker-clothed peasants ran down from the upper sections to mix with the white of the patricians as men continued to pour into the arena.

Water trumpets blasted from the pulvis, loud and long.

Domitian frantically waved the sign for life, his golden laurel leaf crown askew. The voice of the mob ebbed, its pack mentality fractured. For the space of two heartbeats, no one moved.

Sweat invaded Jonathan's eyes but he dared not blink, surrounded by a wall of praetorians. He watched the eyes and weapons of those still standing for who would attack next. The man at his back bumped against him. "Still with me?" he yelled.

A grunt answered him.

The hoplomachus still stood. That was a blessing.

Over the horizon of helmets a mounted prefect galloped toward them. The soldier yanked the reins of his horse hard, and the animal reared and pawed the air. "*Cohort*, stand down! Stand down all of you!"

Stand down? If they were taken alive, they'd be tortured before being crucified or fed to the lions. Jonathan stepped forward and swung his sword at the guard nearest him. The sound of their steel clashing set other swords against each other, and the fighting all around them resumed.

In the corner of his vision, the prefect's horse barreled toward them. "I said stand down! The gladiators will live. Stand down you fools, all of you."

Reluctantly the praetorian Jonathan fought withdrew, holding his shield high.

Jonathan glanced to the pulvis, where Caesar waved the sign for life over and over. "God spares us for the moment, my friend."

"Which god?"

"There is only one God." Jonathan remained battle ready, watching everyone around him in turn. A few of the praetorians he'd wounded might ignore the command, judging by their murderous glares. Now that the pitch of the battle had ebbed, he felt the ache of his wounds. Felt his insides grabbing for air not tainted by the heat and sweat of his helmet. Felt the trembling of his muscles as he maintained a defensive form.

Spectators who'd spilled onto the arena floor rushed to clamber back over the wall. Caesar's clemency had little chance of including his impromptu defenders. Slaves and citizens alike pulled them up. Several of the praetorians began to grab for the slower among them.

The prefect raced his mount in a tight circle around Jonathan and the hoplomachus, between them and the guards. "Cohort, stand down. Stand down or be flogged, the lot of you. Let them go."

When the last spectator made it back over the wall, the prefect dismounted. Jonathan tightened his grip on his sword, beginning to feel the exhaustion deeper as his battle rage continued to recede.

The prefect approached, without drawing his sword. "Surrender your weapon."

"No."

"Surrender the weapon." The man extended his hand. Close enough Jonathan could sever it in one strong swing. "None formed against you will prosper."

The words of the prophet Isaiah in Deborah's stories. From the lips of a praetorian? The prefect himself? Jonathan's sword tip faltered toward the ground. The man drew nearer, and closed his hand on the flat of Jonathan's blade, his eyes imploring.

"Tell your master Torren to do nothing until I send word. You must tell him. Now release the sword."

Jonathan's every instinct railed against him, but he finally let go.

The prefect tossed the sword to another guard. "Let them pass."

He dropped the shield and cradled his arm against his chest, careful of the arrow shaft sticking out a hand's width from his shoulder. The gate of life opened, never more beautiful than in this moment.

Thank You, Lord. Thank You.

The other gladiator tried to keep pace beside him. From the wounds on his arms and chest, he'd suffered bitter punishment in the fight, as had Jonathan. But they were still standing.

"You must tell me of this God of yours. A God who makes even Caesar yield to a slave."

Jonathan pulled his helmet off and grinned at the man as they limped their way toward the open gate. "There is only one God, my friend. And it seems His work for me is not yet finished."

CHAPTER 34 – AFTERMATH

Cedars along the stone highway stretched their long shadows in Torren's path as his horse ambled along. He remembered these trees when they were no taller than his knees. When his wooden sword was half the size of his father's, and his desire to please him knew no end. What would his father think of this?

Torren glanced at the ox-drawn cart rolling along beside him. Underneath that blanket and the watchful eyes of his medicus, lay what was left of Jonathan. Caesar had ordered him scourged—a generous punishment, merciful in the extreme, considering he'd openly defied him.

Torren had the people to thank for that.

"How is he?"

Otho raised the blanket and grimaced. "Keeping him in delirium is all I can do until we reach the ludis."

The scourging Jonathan endured had quelled Torren's fury at him for ruining everything. Months of planning, hours of covert meetings, all wasted. He'd had to return his full payment for these games—a hundred thousand sesterces—in apology. Feigning sincerity to Caesar while apologizing for his gladiator's defiance required every bit of Torren's will.

Domitian was supposed to be dead and Nerva the new Caesar. Torren had been close enough when he'd knelt at the emperor's feet, to rush Domitian and snap his neck. He would have been killed by the guards without the prefects there to control them, but his reward in the afterlife would have been taking the tyrant Caesar with him. He would have done it if he'd been certain all in the alliance were still committed.

"He's strong. He'll pull through," Rooster said.

Torren glanced over at Rooster. He must have hopped from the other cart, but how long had he been walking between them?

"He will," Rooster reassured him, before falling back.

"I hope you're right." Torren cast a hopeful glance at Otho, but the man frowned.

"He'll live. Whether he fights again or not I can't say. His shoulders—"

"I know." Torren kicked his horse into a trot and let him pull well ahead. He couldn't think about that right now. The earnings could be won back, even without Jonathan, and another attempt on Caesar planned. The increased danger lay in the time it would take. Caesar could replace the two prefects suddenly, like he did last year when their first attempt failed. The prefects led the praetorians, Caesar's private army.

Without Norbanus and Secundus, the alliance would crumble. Given this failure, the price of the praetorians' allegiance would be higher. The others in the alliance would blame Torren. They would want him to pay the difference alone, which Torren wouldn't, even if he could. They were in this together or not at all. The longer they tarried, the greater the risk of discovery or Emperor Domitian accusing any one or all of them of treason. Of course they *were* plotting treason, unlike the many lives Domitian had ordered taken the past five years—men whose only crime was their wealth. Wealth Caesar would claim after their executions.

Torren turned and looked back at the men following him. Apart from Otho, Rufus, and the two guards traveling with them, each of his twelve gladiators was a proven crowd favorite. They were known by name, though none as well as Jonathan. Alone they were valuable, together worth a fortune, and he would free every last one of them, even Rufus, before Caesar would have them.

But it wouldn't come to that. That's why he'd entered the alliance in the first place.

Before enduring Caesar's wrath, Jonathan delivered a message from Norbanus that made it sound like the prefect remained committed. Nerva would distance himself, but he'd don the purple when the time came. The three other senators who were the true power in their alliance, particularly Senator Tarquinius, would want to know what went wrong, to relay to their buried followers in the senate. All the while, some errant word spoken by a dimwitted slave into the wrong ears could send them all to crosses. Or the arena. That would be an ironic end for a lanista. Be sentenced *ad gladitorium*, death by gladiator.

His horse chose that moment to stumble. Torren nearly fell from the saddle. A bad omen to be sure. Eventually the walls of his villa broke the horizon. His horse whinnied and picked up his pace. Torren reined him in, and patted his neck.

"I know, old boy. Me too."

He reined in even more to allow the carts to catch up with him. Otho still wore a frown. He could frown all he wanted, so long as he made sure Jonathan recovered. He rode first through the gate, and nearly fell from the saddle again.

Caelina stood waiting for him in the shade of the roof edge.

"What are you doing here? I didn't send for you."

She wore new silk—probably bought with his coin. Her lips blossomed into that sultry pout he knew so well. "Is that any way to greet a woman you propose to at every opportunity?"

"That refuses me repeatedly." Her charms wouldn't work, not today. Knowing he wouldn't be able to afford her company for months chafed as much as her unannounced visit. "Why are you here?"

She held a scroll out to him as he dismounted. "This came for you."

Torren took the rolled parchment, but the wax seal of an unknown emblem was already split. His heart kicked in his chest. "You opened it?"

"Don't be angry. You should have been back before today. None of the servants knew why you delayed, and I thought it might contain important news."

The scroll was from Quintus. Inside it was a smaller one addressed to Jonathan. He shoved both in his belt. Thank the gods it wasn't from Norbanus, or another of the alliance. Torren shuddered at the thought of what he would have had to do if it had been. "I am angry with you."

If she heard him, she didn't care. She peered inside the cart where Jonathan lay. "Why does your champion not wake?"

"He's sedated."

Otho peeled away the thin blanket that kept the road dust and flies from Jonathan's wounds, and Torren nearly retched.

Caelina gasped and clutched the wooden side of the cart. "What happened?"

The horror in her eyes hurt. When he'd injured himself in one of their more amorous romps, her concern had been late, and forced. They were a matched pair, she and him. Always wanting most whatever they'd been denied. "He disobeyed Caesar."

She stepped back in the hard-packed sand as Styx and Rooster carried Jonathan between them. Otho struggled to support Jonathan's head and shoulder his bag of supplies. Caelina rushed forward and took hold of Jonathan, not the bag. Seeing her fingers buried in Jonathan's hair twisted his gut. As he wrestled his jealousy under control, Ramses jumped in his path.

"Torren, would you permit me to—"

"Go. Be back in a week."

His gladiator's eyes widened. "A week?"

"You fought exceptionally well. I want to see more of that. Rufus will issue you your coin before you leave." Unlike Jonathan, Ramses never put aside any of his winnings. Every sesterce went to his wife and children as soon as it was earned.

"I don't know what to say."

"Say nothing. Be back in a week, ready to train for the September games."

"Thank you."

Torren watched the man scurry off and noticed Caelina's guards, Lucius and Octavius, sparring with *his* wooden training weapons. "Rufus, meet me in the library. We must discuss how Caelina has made herself the lady of my villa in my absence."

"Y-yes, my lord." The fear in the man's eyes needed to be there. Torren could not risk anyone coming and going at his villa or through his property unguarded—even Caelina. Not if they were to save Rome. And their lives.

Jonathan saw the soldiers coming for him. A swarm of arrows rushing toward him. The sand churning beneath him as he tried to fight. Swords and shouts from hundreds of faces. Some were the men he'd slain. Other faces he'd seen many times. Broken bread with them, but their names wouldn't come.

Only hers. Only her name, when her face would shimmer before him among the others. *Nessa.* He tried to reach for her, but she would fade too soon. The other faces swirled before him again, this time with voices.

"Is it safe to keep him under this long?"

"You're the gladiator, Ramses. I'm the medicus. Go away before you rouse him."

Ramses. A pharaoh's name. It seemed more familiar than that, but why? The faces disappeared but left a great shadow he couldn't see beyond. He couldn't be sleeping. He could feel himself breathing, but his eyes wouldn't open. His fingers wouldn't move. Nothing would work, except to swallow. Fear tightened his chest like the straps of his armor, but he couldn't be dead. He could still hear. Still taste, though he wished he couldn't. He swallowed again to clear the bitter foulness from his mouth but it remained. It almost tasted like… opium? No. Too much. Too strong. He had to tell them. Tell them to stop. No more. But the words wouldn't come—only a soft moan.

They must have heard, because they poured more down his throat.

Chapter 35 – Healing Arts

Caelina had finally come to him first. Torren watched as she dressed, feeling more of a man than he had in months. He was tempted to propose to her again. Petition she remain with him here at the villa for a while at least. He held his tongue however and purposed to be grateful she'd come to him—with no mention of coin.

She slid her foot into her leather sandal and her gaze to him as she tied the straps. "How does your champion fare?"

It wasn't her question so much as the tremor in her voice when she asked that gave her away. Torren kept the hurt in his chest and off his face while he buckled his belt. At least she'd waited until they were dressed to ask. "Otho says the skin is closing."

He received a report from Rufus twice a day. If his father were still alive, he'd curse Torren's weakness for being unable to bear the sight of his shredded champion. He could stomach blood and slaughter, and like a good Roman, did not fear death. What he feared was what men could do before they killed you. Jonathan's beating was a small taste of what Torren would suffer if Caesar learned of the conspiracy.

"Torren?"

He put his back to her to put his own sandals on, and so he could try to hold on to his hope things between them had changed. "Yes?"

"May I see him?"

He tried to keep his voice indifferent. "Why?"

"I've an interest in the healing arts."

More lies. Like her claim she'd missed him. He'd been a fool to hope. To keep from striking her, he crossed his arms and turned to face her. "You didn't come for me. You came to see Jonathan, didn't you?"

She looked away, her silence a resounding yes.

Curse her. Curse her to the depths of the underworld. He stalked toward her, his grip on his own arms painfully tight, and stopped an arm's length away to look down on her. "You can see him."

Her sky-blue gaze met his, slicing his heart.

"But in payment. And do not ever pretend you genuinely care for me again. I'm not one of your old senators or young noblemen to be made a fool of."

She didn't move, or speak, but he knew she was listening. Good. He wanted her to hurt as much as he did.

"Consider it a bargain. I charge five times your fee for my champion to appear, but you need sleep with me but *once*."

Her chin dipped as if he'd struck her, and something he'd never seen before flickered in her gaze. She returned his stare for a long moment, one in which he wanted to take back his cruelty. She rose and walked to the closed door.

Torren almost reached for her. "Caelina, wait."

Her hand stilled on the latch but she would not look at him.

"He loves another." *As I love you.*

She looked back at him then, her eyes twin ponds of sadness. "I know. I read the letter." She sniffed and straightened to her full height, her gaze narrowing to a knife-point. "I wouldn't want you to feel cheated, Torren. You may send for me four more times."

She opened the door and left at a pace bordering on a run.

Go after her. Beg her forgiveness. He took a step forward, but Rufus appeared in the doorway with a small scroll.

"Apologies, my lord, but the messenger said it was urgent."

Torren broke the seal and squinted to read the tiny script of the short message. Senator Aurelius would speak for Vibianus and Nerva. Senator Tarquinius would attend if able to do so without arousing suspicion. Both prefects would be absent, and Norbanus would be sending a trusted servant in his stead. In hours. "When did this arrive?"

"About two hours ago. I would have—"

"I know. Ready my horse and a mount for Rooster at once."

"Yes, my lord."

Curse his standing instructions. He would need to ride hard to make the meeting place at the appointed time. This was dangerous, assembling almost the entire alliance in one place. And why would Tarquinius call such a meeting if he weren't certain to attend? Torren still didn't trust the man.

Trust or no trust, he would have to go. Torren grabbed his cloak from its hook on the wall and tucked his dagger into his belt. If this were a trap, he'd kill himself before they took him alive. The memory of Jonathan's back would ensure it. Torren wouldn't raise two fingers to any man, especially Caesar.

Caelina pushed open the door to the medicus chamber. Floor lamps burned bright, flooding the room with light. In the corner, Torren's medicus poured a dark liquid into Jonathan's mouth while a slave held his head back to help him swallow. From the bed they had him laid on, Jonathan's fingers clawed at the air while his wrist jerked at his side. His head twitched as if he'd been stung by a honeybee, spilling some of the liquid.

"What are you giving him?" she demanded.

"More opium."

"*Still?*" It had been over two weeks since her last visit. The slave she first thought supported Jonathan's head was instead holding it down.

Otho grabbed Jonathan's jaw and pried it open. "He thrashes about without it and reopens the wounds."

Jonathan's fingertips straightened toward her, though he couldn't see her. He must have heard her voice, because his fingers curled in, grasping for her—grasping for help. His weak moan called to her as if he'd shouted her name.

She rushed forward and shoved Otho's vial-filled hand away from Jonathan's mouth. "You idiot!"

The small bottle shattered on the floor, releasing the pungent scent of the drug. The servant stepped back, sparing her from knocking him aside as well. She leaned over Jonathan, her heart breaking as the vial had. The idiots had him on his back. His back! The sparkling eyes she remembered as the color of a new leaf were gone. Dull green stone replaced them amid vein-filled white as they darted everywhere but her face.

"It's all right. It's all right now." She placed the backs of her fingers against his cheek, below that scar near his eye. Beneath the damp sheen of sweat his skin felt like a gold necklace left in the sun all day. She looked to the slave trembling in the corner. "Get me cool, fresh water. Fill the vessel so that it chills, then pour it out and refill it. Bring it to me at once and summon both my guards."

The slave glanced to Otho without moving, and she almost reached up to slap him. "Do as you're told."

The servant hastened for the doorway, and Otho grabbed her elbow. "Torren instructed me—"

"Torren knows nothing of healing, which is the only reason you're still here." Caelina jerked free of his grasp. Her guards would be here in moments, and Otho wouldn't dare harm her. "I don't pretend to be a medicus, but I am an expert in opium. You've poisoned his champion with so much of it his body will now demand it. Jonathan knows that and is trying to fight it. Leave us."

When he hesitated, Caelina turned her look of absolute authority on him that never failed her. When he left, she extinguished all the lamps save one in a far corner of the room. Fresh folds of linen lined a shelf on the wall, and she stacked several on the table near Jonathan's bed. In a matter of hours this sheen of sweat would swell to drench his bed. Tremors would seize him between bouts of retching and nightmares, if he even slept at all. From the potent scent of that single vial, Otho had used prime liquefied poppy—the purest opium that existed. The kind she'd given control of her life to for two and a half years. The memories sent a shudder down her spine as she brought a stool beside Jonathan's bed.

His hand shivered in hers. His eyes continued to skitter beneath closed lids. He was about to spend three days in the underworld, but she would pass through with him, as her dearest friend had for her. She placed her other hand on his forehead, the skin aflame beneath her palm. "You'll endure this. You will. But you have to keep fighting. Be strong now."

She recalled the night he'd given her his bed and slept on the floor. How many times since then had she wished they'd shared it? She searched the table for a cup and saw the scroll addressed to him she'd read on her last visit. Her eyes grew damp, but she blinked the wetness away and leaned to whisper in his ear. "Be strong for her."

Nessa rolled in her cot until she could stare at the canvas roof of the tent she shared with Quintus. Sleep would not come, but tonight she couldn't blame Quintus' snoring or the frigid wind whipping the tent walls.

Jonathan was in peril.

When she'd prayed for him tonight, and said his name aloud, a heavy sense of foreboding had filled her. She remembered it well, though she hadn't felt it in ten months. How could she forget? She'd lived it every time he entered an arena. He'd surely been in games since they parted, so why now? Why tonight?

"What is it, Jonathan?" she whispered. But her restlessness grew. Finally she shrugged from beneath her furs and pulled on her leather boots. They were cold, but not as cold as it would be beyond the tent. Her cloak would be warm. The soldiers had taught her to sleep with it at her feet. She untied the straps of their flap door, trying not to let any wind in that would wake Quintus. By the time she re-tied the last strap, her fingers were numb. She breathed on them before pulling them in the folds of her thick wool cloak.

The torches at the ends of their corridor burned bright. She would be able to find her way even without them. Every legionary camp throughout the Empire, anywhere and anytime, would be organized this same way. They'd told her that because of that, the soldiers, officers, and slaves could move themselves, supplies, and messages swiftly, especially if attacked.

Nessa walked toward the perimeter of their camp, needing the solitude of the forest. No new snow had fallen the past few days, so it only took a few minutes on the packed paths.

"Where are you going, soldier?" a deep voice called behind her.

She turned and pulled the hood of her cloak back.

The man's hand left the hilt of his sword. "Forgive me, Nessa. I thought you a deserter."

His face was familiar. The disjointed shoulder from four days ago, but she couldn't remember his name. "How is your shoulder?"

"Mended. My gratitude to you and Quintus again, but why are you outside your tent?"

"I need to go for a walk."

"At this hour? In the cold?"

"I need to."

The soldier frowned, his forehead wrinkling his brow beneath the line of his helmet. He walked to her and handed her his torch. "Take this. Don't move beyond where the watchmen can see it, or I'll rouse some friends and come looking for you. The raiders prefer the dark."

"I'll be careful, and I won't go far beyond the camp, you have my word." She took the torch, surprised at how heavy it was. The soldiers carried them with such ease.

At the gate of the wall of timbers forming the boundary of their camp, the snow deepened. Trudging through it was exhausting, but she reached the boulder she'd aimed for. Sticking the torch into the snow at her feet, she swept the caked snow from the rock before sitting on it. An owl screeched from a tree near her and she almost fell. She didn't cry out, thankfully, or the guards would sound the alert. The entire legion would be armored and in formation long before she could find a commander and explain.

She dried her hands on her cloak before reaching inside the thick wool and wrapping her fingers around the carving near her heart. The restlessness in her spirit wasn't a false alarm. Jonathan was in trouble. He was hurt, or in danger, or wavering in his faith. She brought his mother's necklace to her lips and kissed the nose of the little horse. In the knots of the leather cord, she inhaled the remnant scent of his sweat though the cold air burned her nose.

Nessa pulled her hood back over her head and drew her cloak tighter around her, still clutching his carving. She might not be able to hold him, reassure him, help heal him, but God knew exactly where he was, and how and why he was in danger.

"God, the scrolls tell us not a sparrow falls to the ground You do not see. Wherever Jonathan is, protect him. Heal him. Show him Your power as in the days of the prophets. Hear the prayer of Your servant, Lord. Please. Keep our Jonathan safe..."

CHAPTER 36 – SCARS

In Jonathan's darkness, ants still crawled all over him, although he'd given up trying to make them stop. But through the itching, he felt a soothing stroke on his upper arm.

"Nessa?" Was that his voice? It had refused to respond for so long, he couldn't tell. Why wouldn't his eyes open?

A slight weight lifted from his face and he blinked, squinting against the dimness as if it were full summer sun. Caelina stood above him, holding a cloth dripping water. Dark circles framed her eyes, and her unkempt hair surprised him. Even so, she was still the most beautiful woman he'd ever seen. A face even Valentina would envy. He remembered it in pieces. A woman's voice piercing the darkness, breaking into the nightmares, calling for help before men would come hold him down.

"There's the green eyes I remember." She smiled and dabbed his brow with the damp cloth.

"You tended—" A cough cut off a voice that sounded nothing like his own.

"Shhh." She set the cloth beside him and stroked his forehead. "The worst is past, but it is far from over."

"Where's Torren?" he rasped.

"In the city. Called away on some urgent matter and has yet to return." A frown graced her full lips as she straightened. "That concerns me more than I want to admit." She flinched, as if she hadn't meant to speak her thought aloud. "Don't tell him I said that." She retrieved the cloth and wrung it into a bowl beside her. "I'll have to mind what I say now that you're coherent."

"How long?" he whispered.

"Four days to purge you of the opium. You were in its grip much longer."

"What day is it?"

"The twenty-ninth of *Iulius*."

Jonathan counted back, willing his mind to compute the numbers. "Seventeen days?"

"Nineteen. Though with as much opium as that idiot medicus gave you, it might as well have been months."

"Where is he?"

"I don't know. Nor do I wish to, though I'm certain he awaits an opportunity to cry to Torren somewhere." A knock on the door, painfully loud, stole her gaze. "Come in."

A man entered, wearing a tunic but no armor, and carrying a bowl and pitcher. Caelina seemed to know him. "Set it there, and then have a slave bring me some blackberries and honeyed wine."

"Yes, my lady." He departed, closing the door behind him.

"Your servant?"

"One of my bodyguards." She rose from the stool and took up another bowl from the table beside her while casting him a sideways glance. "You bloodied the other's nose the day before yesterday."

Did she jest, or he not remember?

"Can you turn on your side for me?"

Jonathan managed it with only a single wince and lay facing the wall. Caelina rubbed something on the wounds of his back. The coolness of the healing balm and the peculiar scent he breathed as Caelina worked, so different from Otho's remedies, turned his heart in his chest. "You made Nessa's paste?"

"I found instructions on a scroll while looking for salt. It seemed promising, though I've never seen so intricate a combination before. I sent a servant to the city for the onion and aloe leaves. The scourge marks are nearly healed. The puncture on your shoulder and the gash on your thigh are taking their time. This paste quieted the fouling in them."

Jonathan lay there staring at the sand-colored plaster wall. Several times while drugged senseless, he'd been able to form a prayer begging God for help. He'd sent deliverance, this time through Caelina. In silent prayer he thanked God first. Then he turned his head to glance behind him as much as his neck would allow. "Thank you."

A long moment passed in silence as she continued to rub the paste over his back. "Don't thank me. Forgive me for—" She breathed a long sigh. "For last time."

She could mean slapping him, trying to force him to lie, selling the truth afterward, or all three. It didn't matter. Jonathan grinned, seeing Nessa's round face in his mind. *Seventy times seven.* "I'd already forgiven you."

"How? I hadn't asked yet."

Jonathan waited. The answer for that couldn't be spoken toward the wall.

She tugged his shoulder toward her. "I'm finished."

Lying back did not pain him as much as knowing that even hundreds of miles away, Nessa still cared for him through her paste. *Father, protect her and Quintus. Guard her with warrior angels and a wall of fire Lord, and if it be Your will, please reunite us soon. Give me the words I need now to serve You.*

Caelina poured a cup of water and helped him drink most of it, though a good portion ended up on his bare chest because of the tremors passing through his hands. When he'd settled beneath his blanket and she on the stool again, he began.

"I'd already forgiven you because forgiveness doesn't depend upon a request or a confession of wrong. I have received it and must return it to those around me." His voice grew stronger with every word. *Thank you, God.*

"That doesn't make sense."

He would have to show her the way Deborah had taught him as a boy—with a story. "Let me try to explain. There was a servant who owed his king ten thousand talents."

Her head dipped and her lips curled. "What kind of king trusts a slave with ten thousand talents?"

"I don't know but regardless, one day the king commanded the servant be sold along with everything he owned, even his wife and children, to pay the debt."

"Why had the king not done that before?"

"It doesn't matter." God help him, was this a taste of what he'd put Nessa through all those years?

She blanched at his tone, and he breathed deep to cover the sigh. "Apologies."

A rueful grin formed at the corner of her mouth. "I know. I'm always interrupting. Most men never seem to mind, at least not until after ..." Her smile vanished and shame filled her eyes.

All the more reason Jonathan needed to answer her well.

Her mask of confidence returned as she stiffened. "What happened to your servant and his family?"

"He prostrated himself before his master, begging more time and promising to pay the debt in full. The king was moved, and forgave the debt."

She opened her mouth, and then quickly reclosed it.

Jonathan fought a grin and continued. "This same servant was owed a single denarius by a fellow servant. He sought the man out and demanded payment, and that servant too begged more time and promised to repay. But instead of forgiving this small debt, the man had his fellow servant thrown into prison. The king was told, and called for his servant, demanding to know why he did not forgive the debt as the king had forgiven him. Then the king delivered the wicked servant to be tortured, until all he owed was repaid."

She seemed to contemplate this, and Jonathan prayed while he waited, flexing his toes to try to stop the twitch in his foot beneath the wool blanket.

"I understand your story, even if it's absurd, but not what it has to do with you or me."

"Because I don't want to be the wicked servant. I have been forgiven much, Caelina. Much more than I could ever repay."

"By Nessa?"

"Her also. But I was speaking of God."

"Which god?"

"There is only one God. The true God of all creation."

"What has this god forgiven you, Jonathan?"

Murder. Pride. Rebellion. He was silent for a long moment. "Many things."

Her brow arched and her stare gained strength. "And Nessa?"

He'd said Nessa's name earlier, but the way Caelina asked, and stared at him now, implied she knew more. "How do you know of Nessa?"

A knock interrupted and her servant entered with a wooden bowl and a large clay cup.

Caelina took them and set them on the table beside them. "These are grapes."

"There are no more blackberries, my lady."

"Has Torren returned?"

"No, my lady."

"You and Octavius may retire for the evening."

"Yes, my lady."

The man departed, but not before taking a long glance at Jonathan.

Caelina returned to the stool beside him. "You should try to eat something."

Jonathan took the small cluster of grapes she handed him and worked one free of the stem and into his mouth. He crushed it between his teeth and the spray of juice tasted wonderful, but didn't distract him fully from the unease of a moment ago. "How do you know of Nessa?"

Her mouth tightened and she turned to reach for something among the bowls and towels cluttering the table near them. "I read this."

She wouldn't meet his eyes as Jonathan took the small roll of parchment in his hand. He uncurled the stiff papyrus, and even with the fine tremor in his hand could read the script. The name at the bottom quickened his pulse. Quintus Blasius.

Jonathan,

Germania is a rugged place, but Nessa and I have settled into army life quite well. She has befriended several of the local village families, and when her duties here allow, she spends time with the children. The legion does not advance, but the patrols are attacked on occasion, and we had a small skirmish with a large group of raiders three days ago. Many were wounded, but not a single soldier was lost. The general was pleased. I learned he would be sending dispatch to Rome and hope this message reaches you. Nessa has worked beside me without sleep or complaint for two days, so excuse both of us if this is difficult to read or I do not copy her words to you exactly. I will try, and hope you are well.

Beloved, God renews my strength daily as we are parted. This is a beautiful place, and in the trees and mountains I see so clearly the work of our Creator. The children here bring me so much joy, and several of them have become followers of our God. I pray their faith grows stronger and spreads to others. I asked the Lord for a sign you are well, and the following morning a beautiful rainbow filled the sky. I will trust Him and His mighty right hand that in His time I shall see you again.

She blushed so red here I could see it by the light of the lamp. She wants to say I love you but I have known her since she was ten years old, and she's embarrassed to ask me to include it. She loves you, Jonathan. I hope you are able to earn your freedom and join us. Rome could use your sword.

Quintus Blasius

Jonathan read her words to him over a second and third time before allowing the scroll to reroll in his hand. He clutched it to his chest and stared at the ceiling as he thanked God for her safety and for the letter.

"You must truly love her."

He turned toward Caelina with a twinge of guilt at having forgotten her presence. "I do."

She leaned toward him, resting her crossed arms on the edge of his bed. "Enough to wait for her?"

"Enough to die for her." He willed his eyes not to drop below her chin as her posture begged. "I almost did. Several times."

"How?"

"My lanista before Torren threatened to kill her if I ever failed in the arena. The only reason I pledged my life as a gladiator was to protect hers."

She stared at him a long moment, searching his steady gaze. Abruptly she straightened, putting distance between them. "I would give anything to know that kind of devotion." Her lower lip trembled and she looked away. "To have the love of a man so powerful he would give his life for mine."

She rose from the stool but before she could turn away, Jonathan reached for her arm. His touch stopped her and brought her gaze back to his. "You already do."

"Torren loves only his coin and you—" Her gaze turned hard and unflinching. "You love another woman. A *slave no less.*"

Why did it matter to her that he loved Nessa unless… understanding flooded through him, and he released her arm. He'd been a fool not to see it before, and that only made him long to comfort her all the more. "Not the love of men, Caelina. Not Torren or me, but Jesus the Messiah. He loves you, and He did die for you."

"I do not know this man of whom you speak. And he does not know me."

"But He does know you, and you *can* know Him in return. Do you remember the story I told you about the servants?"

"Yes."

"God is the king. We are born owing a debt we can't pay on our own, that we increase the longer we live in darkness and embrace our own way."

"I don't understand."

"When God created the world, and the first man and woman, He set them in paradise, but they chose to believe a lie. They chose their own way over God's, and God had to send them from His presence, because they were no longer holy. Every man and woman born since has carried that mistake that separated us from God, and will for all time."

Her pale brows furrowed as she frowned. "That hardly seems fair."

"Perhaps, but I have lived long enough, known enough of men and women, both good and bad, to know any one of us would make the same mistake they did. We still make it generations later, choosing our own way over God's."

"What does it matter? Your God sent us away in the first place."

Her expression told him he'd only confused her. How could he help her understand the most important of truths when all she knew was coin and buying and selling? Including herself?

And like manna from Heaven, there was the answer. "Your two bodyguards, you provide for them, do you not?"

"Of course. They serve me."

"And they answer to you and you only?"

"Yes."

"What if one day you discovered they'd stolen all your jewelry? Every last strand of pearls and all the gold and emeralds you possess."

"They'd never do such a thing. If they need anything, I give them coin for it."

"All the more reason you'd be angry. Maybe someone lied to them, and told them you'd been cheating them. Or maybe you didn't know them as well as you thought. What would you do?"

"I'd have them flogged and demand it back."

"What if they couldn't give it back? What if they'd lost it all and hid from you?"

She swallowed. "I'd send Torren after them, to demand they make it right."

Thank you, Lord. He studied her in the lamplight as he continued. "Say you did and they killed Torren because they didn't want to hear him, even though they knew they were guilty. So you sent others, trusted servants or friends, and they beat and killed them too. What would you do then?"

She shifted to lean her hip against his bed. "I don't know."

"They could never make that right again, could they? Even if they brought you all the riches in the Empire, which they couldn't, is there anything they could ever do to make that right again?"

"No."

"And if they had children, and their children had children, would those childrens' inheritance include that unpaid debt to you along with the lands or riches of their father?"

"Yes."

"But even if your guards were found remorseful, if they returned what they'd stolen and begged your forgiveness, swearing to never betray you again, they'd still be deserving of death by then, wouldn't they?"

"Yes." Her gaze darkened. "A slow, painful one."

Jonathan had been anything but Christ-like the last ten years of his life, but he prayed God would understand and grant him grace as he continued. "But what if I offered you my life in exchange for theirs? The highest priced gladiator in all of Rome, yours to send to fight, or to sell, whatever you wished, as long as you pardoned them in exchange."

She scowled and shifted again, this time to face him more fully. "You would pledge your life for two murderous, thieving guards as you did for Nessa?"

"If I did, they would be foolish not to take such an exchange, wouldn't they?"

"As would I," she added, her gaze turning pensive.

"Do you understand now that all of us—Torren, me, you, even Nessa—that we were born the thieving guards? On our own we could never do enough to pay God back for what the first man and woman did in turning away, or what we add to that every time we ignore Him and choose our own way and worship gods of wood and stone—or coin—instead of the One true God that created us and everything our eyes can behold?"

"Then what does your God want from us, if not coin, or bulls and goats like the others? Especially if He can never be appeased?"

"He wants us to believe in Him, and in His son Jesus, who gave His life for ours. Only His life was still without fault before God, and only His sacrifice, trading His life for ours, restores us to God when we accept it and call on the name of Jesus as Lord."

"This Jesus you speak of, was He not the Nazarene executed in the Judean province of the empire two generations ago for inciting rebellion against Rome?"

"Yes." And here was the difficult part. "But He rose from the dead."

She pursed her lips for just a moment. "If you believe that, Jonathan, the opium has done more damage to you than I thought."

Her insult meant she'd at least heard him and considered his words enough to frame a reply. He stifled a grin as he formed a reply of his own. "Who was the first emperor?"

"Augustus Caesar. Everyone knows that."

"Are you sure?"

"Of course I'm sure."

"How do you know?"

She frowned and stepped closer to him, then touched his forehead with her hand. He took hold of her wrist, tightening his grip through the tremors in his fingers. "Answer me. How do you know?"

"Because." She pulled free and took a small step back. "The historians wrote about it. He has statues and monuments that remain today, and the people still talk about all he did while he reigned."

"So from stories and writings handed down from the people who saw for themselves?"

"Yes."

"That's exactly how I know of God, Caelina. And of His son, who did come to earth as a man, who performed many miracles before dying in our place and rising from the dead. He offers us life eternal with Him if we will but call on His name and follow Him. Repent and be baptized."

"And if I don't?"

Jonathan swallowed, knowing he must tell her the rest, no matter how difficult. "Then when you die, you'll spend eternity in a place of torment forever separated from God."

"I don't believe in the afterlife."

"That won't matter once you're in it."

Her eyes widened, and she stood silent a long moment, staring at him. Jonathan prayed fervently she would understand and come to repentance. She opened her mouth to speak but then bit her lip and sighed. The questions were there in her eyes, but the sound of heavy footsteps drew her attention to the hall beyond the chamber. The wooden door flung open. Torren stomped in, a blood-soaked wrap high on his arm. More splattered his ripped and soiled tunic.

Caelina rushed toward him. "What happened?"

"Get out of my villa. Do not return unless I send for you." When she didn't move, Torren's blood-stained fingers bit into her upper arm as he yanked her toward the door. "I want you out of here, now."

"Torren, stop." She resisted and stumbled across the stone floor.

Jonathan's entire body tightened as he tried to sit up. "Stop it. You're hurting her."

Torren threw him a glare so full of venom that for the first time, Jonathan feared him. "Be silent. You and I will speak later." Torren pulled Caelina through the doorway and down the hall. She continued to protest, her angry voice carrying back to him.

He tried to sit up again, intent on following. A wave of nausea stronger than he was pushed him back on the bed. He might not be able to move, but God certainly could.

Father, protect Caelina as You protect Nessa. Let Your truth take root in her heart and bring her to repentance quickly. Strengthen and guide me through these storms. The one that remains in my body and the one I fear is coming.

Chapter 37 – Assassins

Torren washed the dried blood from his dagger, the image of Caelina screaming "I never want to see you again" burned indelibly in his mind. Even if there had been time, he wouldn't have been able to explain without placing her in more danger. The safest place for her was as far from him as possible, and that knowledge hurt as much as the wound on his arm.

Rufus approached with his hand out. "My lord, let me clean that."

"No. I want you to put Styx, Ramses, Dax, and Cam on watch tonight with Wolf and Prito. No switching off. They guard sunup to sundown. Unlock the weapons chest and see they all carry steel. If they see any riders approaching, they're to alert and arm the others."

His head servant's normally stoic demeanor faltered. "My lord?"

"Relay my order, Rufus. No more questions."

"Yes, my lord."

Torren sheathed the dagger and strode for the medicus chamber. If the six men who ambushed him and Rooster outside the city were assassins sent by Caesar, Domitian knew by now Torren had escaped.

Otho stood in the hall, waiting for him there as he had at the gate when Torren first arrived. "My lord, I wanted to—"

"Caelina orders every man about as if he's a slave, and while Rufus is, you are not. I return to find she has made herself not only master of my villa again, but this time my medicus as well."

Otho's gaze narrowed. "You bend to her every whim, yet we are expected to stand against her?"

Torren's fists clenched so tight his nails dug into his palms. "You have one hour to collect your belongings and be on the other side of my walls."

Otho's mouth parted and he raised his hands palms up. "All the years I served your family count for nothing against the whining of that prostitute?"

"This isn't about Caelina. This is about my *champion*. You said you were sedating him for pain. Pain, Otho!" Torren was in plenty himself right now, spurring his anger. "She told me you gave him enough opium to nearly kill him instead of closing his wounds properly."

"Stitching them all would have taken a full day. You don't know how many there were."

"Oh yes I do. I had to watch them given from the first to the last. If you value your life, you will leave now without another word."

"You owe me for the month of *Iulius*."

"Take an ox and cart. That's worth far more than you deserve."

Torren didn't wait for a reply, if the man would be foolish enough to give one. He brushed past him to the chamber and slammed the door behind him.

Jonathan sat in bed eating grapes from a bowl as if it were rest day. If he'd killed his opponent that day as commanded, none of this would be happening. His frown when their gazes met, as if he were the one with a right to disapprove, grated on Torren. He was about to tell him so when Jonathan spoke first.

"You needn't have been so rough with Caelina."

Without truly deciding to, Torren lurched forward and backhanded him across the face.

Jonathan's head rocked on his shoulders and banged the plastered wall beside him. The bowl of grapes fell, the clatter of wood on stone as it rolled echoed all around while Torren stared at it in disbelief.

He'd just broken the foremost rule of his ludis. How many times had he told the others? Never strike another in anger, outside of training and combat. And he'd just done that very thing. Unease whirled through his empty stomach and his chest heaved. But regret would serve no purpose. It was done. So why couldn't he bring himself to meet Jonathan's gaze?

"There's a paste in that bowl there." His champion's voice held no malice. "It will ease the pain of your wound and speed healing, but you'll have to have Otho apply it and wrap your arm. I don't think my hands would be steady that long."

Torren stared at the grapes on the floor at his feet. Torren would rather Jonathan had tried to strike him back. "I sent Otho away."

"Why?"

"You need ask?" Torren met Jonathan's stare then.

The sight of the new cut on Jonathan's brow pained him more than his own wound, which he set about tending. Jonathan watched him but remained silent. Torren preferred that for now. The strange smelling, rust-colored paste did take the sting from the gash as promised. After tying off a new wrap with his other hand and his teeth, no more reasons remained to ignore Jonathan.

"Do you need something for your eye?" he asked him.

Jonathan touched the small wound with his fingertips. The thin line of blood must have dried, because none came away on his fingertips. "No. I'm fine."

Torren sighed and collapsed on the stool beside the bed. No one in this villa was fine. Not while Emperor Domitian still lived. "Rooster's dead."

Saying it out loud was as difficult as it was for Jonathan to hear, judging by his champion's expression.

"We may all be dead by morning. That's why I had to send Caelina away."

"Then I need a tunic and a sword." Jonathan shifted under the blanket, but Torren put a firm hand to his shoulder.

"No. You need to heal. You're the best sword I have, the best I've ever seen, but if the men that attacked us were sent by Caesar, not even you can save us."

A long moment passed before Jonathan spoke. "This is my doing."

"Yes, it is." Torren regretted the terseness, but it was the truth.

Jonathan leaned to rest his head against the wall and clutched the blanket at his waist tighter. "I didn't intend to bring danger to you or my brothers."

"It is your fault, but not for the reason you believe." Torren drew a deep breath and held it. Rooster was dead, and if they survived the night, Jonathan would need to take his place. It was time to tell him. Everything. The spent air in his lungs left him in a rush. "I'm part of an alliance to assassinate the emperor."

Jonathan didn't react, but that made Torren more nervous. He waited, unsure if he should continue.

Finally Jonathan spoke. "I've no affection for anyone who claims to be a god, but Domitian is no Nero."

"He's smarter than Nero. He appears less a tyrant by choosing targets carefully under the guise of treason trials. Since crushing Saturninus' rebellion in Germania, he's made sure every general in every legion is loyal to him. The senators in the alliance supported Saturninus in secret, but they chose the wrong replacement, the wrong method, and ignored the praetorian element. Jupiter himself could descend from the heavens and name a new Caesar, but if the praetorians don't support him, he's dead already. That's why I'm the emissary between the senators involved and the praetorian cohort. Only together will we succeed."

Jonathan eyed him warily. "Why are you telling me all this?"

A muffled sound came from outside the door. Torren raised his finger to his lips and drew his dagger. He crept to the door, standing well to the side, and reached for the latch with his heart hammering his ribs. He flung the door open and nearly stabbed Rufus, who jumped back faster than Torren had seen the older man move in years.

"Rufus. I thought—" Torren sheathed his dagger and tried to breathe deeper to slow his racing heart. "What is it?"

"Forgive the intrusion, my lord, but Otho says you have dismissed him and given him an ox and cart. In his haste I feared he might be stealing them."

"He's not stealing them. I gave him an hour to be on the other side of my walls. Are the men armed?"

"Yes, my lord. They asked many questions. They want to know where Rooster is."

Of course they did. What could he tell them? "Tell them I'll be there soon, and to keep a sharp eye toward the city."

"Yes, my lord."

Torren closed the door and turned back to Jonathan.

"Are the praetorians coming?"

"I don't know. The prefects are part of the alliance, but if they're compromised…" Torren shuddered at the thought. Feeling out their allegiance had taken months, followed by weeks of negotiations and committing them to the cause. They were running out of time. Domitian had declared two more wealthy nobles traitors to Rome last week. No one subjected to a treason trial was ever found innocent. Not a single person in six years. As wealthy as Torren was, especially with Jonathan, he couldn't be far behind.

"You said earlier I was responsible. How?"

"The last day of the Ludi Appolinares, after the final match you were in, Prefect Norbanus was going to slay Domitian there in the pulvis. He and Secundus, with the allegiance of the unit commanders, were going to name the new Caesar. We were going to quickly sway the mob right there, who is no lover of Domitian either. The plan was perfect."

"What happened?"

"You." Torren crossed his arms over his chest. "When you didn't give the coupe de grace, Caesar sent the prefects after you before Norbanus received the signal all was ready. Without him in place, everything collapsed."

"I didn't know."

"It doesn't matter now. What does is that failure weakened the resolve of the senators outside the alliance, and I have no way of knowing if the men who attacked Rooster and me were assassins sent by Caesar."

"How many?"

"Six. They wore plain clothing but each carried a gladius and knew how to use it. We killed four of them before Rooster fell. I made it back to my horse and outran the last two on the way back to the villa. They must have given up or turned back."

Jonathan's eyes became slits, and his jaw tensed. "You sent Caelina directly into their path."

"Only two attackers remained, and their mounts are already spent. If there is a confrontation, her guards can handle them, and Caelina is very adept at taking care of herself. Besides, you know as well as I that if the full cohort marches on us, no one within these walls will be spared."

Torren seized a cup that looked like it held wine and downed it. Wiping the back of his mouth, he set the cup back down on the table. "If the Fates favor Rome, and us, those men were nothing more than thieves who chose the wrong victims. We should know by morning."

"I want to stand with you."

"No. You've been twitching since I walked in. You can't grip a sword, much less swing it where it needs to go."

"I will not lie here while you and my brothers are slaughtered. I won't. I can't."

Torren pulled his sheathed dagger from his belt and set it on the mattress next to Jonathan. "I do not ask. I order you as your Dominus. If they come, do not let them take you alive. If we live there is much I will require of you, but for now pray to your God that He might spare us and we may yet set Rome free."

Jonathan held Torren's dagger in his hands. Torren asking him to pray God would spare them while he plotted the murder of the emperor felt wrong. In fairness, when the guards stripped Jonathan and hung him from a beam overhead, he'd wished Caesar dead too. Torren hadn't intervened as they prepared to give Jonathan the scourging Caesar ordered—twenty-one strokes.

He'd been right to fear the *flagrum* each of the *lictors* held ready. The strands of the whip resembled unraveled rope. With one look at them, his hatred for his half-brother returned full force. Jonathan was a Roman citizen, exempt from scourging as a form of punishment. Not only was he a citizen, but a Tarquinius, a noble in blood and name.

But it hadn't mattered, because he couldn't prove it.

The first lictor struck him, and the intensity of the pain overwhelmed his mind. When the second lictor's lash fell, he cried out, in spite of having purposed not to. The lictors traded blows on his back with rhythmic precision while he prayed to lose consciousness. He lost count when his mind retreated after the second blow and didn't return until the beating ended.

In the days that followed, while Otho doused him with opium and filled his wounds with pure salt, only thoughts of Jesus kept him together. Jesus had gone from his scourging to a cross. Jonathan had gone home.

He'd known he would survive somehow. Even in the midst of the nightmares—Nessa trapped beneath Caius, the faces of the men whose lives he'd taken—he'd known even then that God held him.

Torren wanted his help to kill Caesar, provided the praetorians didn't slaughter them all first. Jonathan picked up Torren's dagger from his blanket and held the bone handle against his chest. He needed to pray for protection for all of them, but most of all for wisdom and direction. If God's work for him included assassinating Caesar Domitianus Augustus, God would have to write it on the wall.

CHAPTER 38 – SACRIFICE

The praetorians never came, though Torren kept the men on alert for days. Jonathan recovered after weeks of bed rest and careful training Torren oversaw personally. His champion's physical strength returned, but not the stamina. Jonathan could no longer battle rings around his opponent as he could before. If the fight wore on, his attacking blows faded to hasty blocking and his breathing labored between coughs. The only reason Jonathan never ended up in the sand with two fingers to the sky is because he could switch to that lethal left-handed fighting style at will.

That had saved him in the arena the two times he'd fought for Caesar since the opium ordeal. In an effort to save face and show a merciful side, Caesar had invited Torren and his gladiators back to the games. But it was too little, too late. As long as Torren breathed, Caesar's breaths were numbered.

During that time, Torren discovered Rufus was a decent medicus in a bind. What he lacked in expertise he made up for in obedience, unlike Otho. That should have Torren in a better mood, but it didn't. Because Caelina was still making good on her vow to never see him again.

He'd sent scroll after scroll to her for nearly a year, apologizing for throwing her out of the villa and explaining it had been for her own protection. All returned unopened. The last one she'd taken the trouble to burn first, and Rufus carried the ashes back along with a message.

"The lady wishes the fabled plagues of Egypt upon you, my lord."

So much for diplomacy.

He should go to her himself and see if that would change her answer. Whenever he visited Rome, however, managing both the alliance and Jonathan required his full attention. Jonathan's increased fame meant he could no longer attend the pre-game feasts safely without packing the hosting villa full of extra guards. His champion had nearly been ripped apart this spring when his amoratii broke through the perimeter of guards. Bruised and scratched back at the Ludis Maximus, the men teased Jonathan that they might as well be praetorians and he Caesar.

Neither he nor Jonathan shared the men's humor.

The new date had been set. Two months to the day, September 18th, the last day of the Ludi Romani. Emperor Domitian's stranglehold on Rome would end.

If the plan failed again, the alliance would collapse, and even with Jonathan protecting him, the reason he'd involved his champions in the first place, they would all likely end up dead. All the more reason he needed to see Caelina one last time.

Torren pulled a scroll from the pile on his desk. He'd stopped writing new ones after she'd rejected the tenth. No sense wasting parchment. "Rufus?"

His head servant emerged from the hall. "My lord."

"Take this to Caelina's villa. Take whatever coin you need and buy her the biggest pearl necklace the merchant on the *Sacra Via* has. You know the one, near the Arch of Titus, where I bought her the emerald earrings two years ago."

Rufus frowned. "My lord, with your permission, I shall send Ica in my stead. He's trustworthy and will carry out your wishes as if he were me."

Torren studied his servant's downcast eyes. The man had never refused a command before. "Why don't you want to go?"

Rufus pursed his lips and refused to look up from the floor.

"Answer me."

"Forgive me, my lord. Last time she sent me away she threatened to turn her dogs loose if I returned. I've seen them, master. They're as big as boars, and I believe she meant it. I don't think she would recognize Ica, or harm him, otherwise I wouldn't suggest it."

Curse her insufferable pride. He sends her from the villa in haste to protect her, and she shuns him. Jonathan spurns her and she salivates for him. The comparison spawned an idea—brilliant but devious.

"Send Ica. But he is to tell Caelina that Jonathan wishes to see her."

"My lord?"

"You heard me."

"Yes, my lord."

She'd be furious, but at least she'd be here and furious. An audience with her at last. "Before you summon Ica, tell Jonathan he's to accompany me to retrieve Ramses. Have horses readied for both of us."

"Yes, my lord."

"No one is to know I send for her in Jonathan's name. I'll explain when she arrives."

"And if she refuses again, my lord?"

Torren was certain, though that was its own secret wound. "She'll come."

When they mounted up, Torren said it would be a two-hour ride to Ramses' cottage. He'd remained silent since then, but Jonathan didn't mind. Though Torren's horse, with the gaping hollow in the side of the animal's head where its eye should be, always made Jonathan uneasy.

The quiet ride through the countryside reminded him of the chariot ride with his father the day they met. The olive and pine trees and occasional flocks of sheep or goats with their shepherds soothed him. Even though the animals would taint the breeze, it felt good to be outside, without a wall or boundary in sight.

Except that Torren swayed in the saddle too much, as if he'd all but given up holding himself erect.

Jonathan nudged his horse to close the gap between them. "You're deep in thought or nearly asleep. Which is it?"

Torren continued to stare straight ahead. "I contemplate."

Sometimes the best way to treat a festered wound was to cut it open. "Caelina?"

Torren straightened in his saddle without meeting his gaze. "No. What I'm going to do if Ramses is delayed of his own will." He kicked his horse into a run, leaving Jonathan behind.

Jonathan squeezed with his knees and picked up his pace as well, but left distance between them. He'd tried. Torren remained at a gallop until they reached a turnoff from the road to a small path. When a small cottage finally came into view, Jonathan's stomach twisted.

Ramses stood in the doorway with a rusted gladius in the ready position.

Torren dismounted, his hand moving to rest on the hilt of his sword. "Let's discuss this without weapons."

The faces of two children and a frightened woman peered out from the only window opening in the small dwelling. The boy's gaze locked with Jonathan's, and every remembered pain of his fatherless years swept through him. He slid from the saddle and moved toward Torren.

As did Ramses. "There's nothing to talk about. My wife is sick and our only slave has run away."

"And you want to share in his fate as a fugitive slave?"

Ramses edged forward, still leading with his sword. "I will not abandon my family to starve or freeze."

Torren's grip tightened on the handle of his own weapon. He held up his other hand, palm out to halt Ramses' advance. "If you force me to draw this sword, Jonathan and I will win. You already know that, and that I will sell you at the first opportunity since I can no longer trust you."

To stand with Torren meant a son and daughter witnessing their father cut down before their very eyes. Jonathan couldn't do it. Nor could he allow it. *Lord, help me stop this.*

No greater gift.

Jonathan's heart sped. *Lord?*

No greater gift.

He would die for either of these men already. That was the agony in the choice before him.

No greater gift.

What else did he have, besides his life? And then Jonathan knew. *I can't, Lord. Please. I can't!*

Torren drew his sword.

Ramses raised his rusted blade and dropped into opening position. The little girl flew from the hut and clung to his leg.

"Go inside, child!" Ramses tried to shove her to safety without giving Torren an opening.

Jonathan threw himself between their blades, an empty hand outstretched to each of them. "Stop!"

"Move. Now," Torren ordered, his voice slow and deep.

Jonathan turned to face Torren, keeping Ramses and his daughter behind him. "How much for his freedom?"

"More than he has." Torren's anger at the added betrayal flared in his dark eyes.

"More than I have?"

Torren's blade faltered and his stare tightened. "Yes."

Not enough. Never enough. How many friends would he have to lose? Seppios, Tao, Rooster, and now—wait—"What about Rooster?"

"Rooster's dead."

"He had no family to receive his saved earnings. Together with mine, is that enough?"

Torren frowned and Jonathan knew his master's thoughts at once. "He gave his life defending yours, Torren. If you profit from that, you're no better than Caesar."

"Jonathan, don't." Ramses spoke from behind him. Jonathan glanced over his shoulder to beseech him to be silent. Ramses' daughter, in her ragged dress and tangled curls, remained tight around her father's leg. The son had joined them, and held a spade like a club. There was so much of himself in that young boy's eyes.

The sound of a sword being sheathed snapped his attention back to Torren. The lanista stood tall and grim-faced. "Make no mistake, Jonathan. I will take your twenty thousand sesterces. You will begin again with nothing."

"I understand."

Torren stared at him a long moment, before turning away. He made swift strides to his horse and swung into the saddle to gaze down at them across the distance like a Roman general. "Ramses, come for your scroll tomorrow and return the horse of mine you have. And I swear by every god in every temple in the empire, if you ever threaten me again, I will speed you to your ancestors."

Torren's hard stare turned to Jonathan. "As for you—if you *ever* stand against me again—with or without a weapon, not even Nessa will know you when I'm through. Do you understand?"

He understood. He understood exactly what he'd just done and gave a solemn nod.

Torren yanked his horse around and kicked the animal into a swift gallop toward the road. Ramses' wife hobbled out of the hut. With tear-filled eyes she came toward him, arms out. Jonathan stepped away so she could go to her husband but she came to him and clung to him like a barrel on the open sea. Jonathan embraced her frail frame, thoughts of his mother intruding as he prayed for God to heal this woman. He hugged her and whispered in her ear, "May the Lord be with you."

Ramses handed his sword to his son and approached, holding his daughter's hand. "I have no words, brother."

"I don't want words. I want you to protect and care for your family and teach them all I've taught you about the one, true God."

"I will."

Ramses embraced him. The faces of his wife and children beside them became a fresco in Jonathan's mind. He would draw strength from this image against the regret he knew would come. It already fought its way in, and he needed to get going. He released Ramses and turned away. A light tug on his tunic stopped him.

Ramses' little girl held a frayed rag doll up to him that looked suspiciously like a gladiator. "You keep."

"No, little one. That's yours."

She pushed it toward him again. "Papa stay now. You keep."

He tousled her hair and tucked the little doll securely into his belt. His horse stood quietly while he mounted and took one last look at Ramses and his family before turning away. Away from the family he'd never had as a boy and the hope of his own with Nessa he'd just sold. He gave his horse a sharp jerk of the reins and kicked the animal harder than he should have.

The sight of Torren in the road ahead threw anger into Jonathan's storm. The lanista rode at a jog, but Jonathan didn't trust himself to be within striking distance of his master. Not when everything inside of him screamed that Torren's greed was no different than that of his half-brother or Caius and made his sword arm tingle. He urged his horse even faster and gave Torren a wide berth as they blew past.

Mile after mile they ran, passing a flock of sheep whose shepherds probably thought Jonathan was a messenger, as fast as he rode. When his horse began to labor, Jonathan finally slowed their pace. The animal's sides heaved against Jonathan's knees and white foam dripped from the glossy, wet neck. Jonathan dropped to the ground and led the horse beside him. Every time her nostrils flared, heat blasted his arm like a furnace, and several times she nearly stumbled. Remorse found room in his heart among the regret and anger. He led her at a turtle's pace a good distance, until he glimpsed a stream beyond a bend in the road.

He brought her to the bank and let her wade in to drink her fill. The sound of the water cascading further upstream soothed him, and he lay back on the grass while the sunshine warmed his face and arms.

This place reminded him of his vision when he'd almost died. The day Nessa entered his life. She'd become his life. She'd saved it, in every way. And he'd just lost her. Again.

His spirit begged the release of tears, but he held them in. Not yet. He mounted back up and pressed for the ludis, more mindful of the horse this time.

Rufus met him near the doors of the villa. "Where's the master?"

"Not far behind." He could hear the tremor in his voice. Not yet. *Make it to your room.*

"And Ramses?"

"Ask Torren." Jonathan slid from the horse and nearly stumbled when he landed.

Rufus took the horse's reins from where they now dangled on the ground. "Are you ill?"

"I'm fine." Jonathan ignored a greeting from Styx in the hall, then the questioning look that followed for having done so. *Hold it together. Almost there.* He opened the door to his chamber and shut it behind him, ready to collapse onto his bed with his grief.

But Caelina reclined in it, wearing a red tunic that matched her lips and twirling a lock of flaxen hair around her finger. "I'd hoped something passed between us those days we spent together. You're the only gladiator I would ever allow to send for me."

"I did not send for you." He could hear the husky catch in his own voice and breathed deeper to quell it.

Her sultry smile disappeared. "Yes you did."

"I swear on my sword I did not." He moved toward his table to pour himself a cup of wine and leave her a clear path to the door. "I need you to leave. Now."

She rose from his bed, but moved toward him instead of the door. "What game do you play with me?"

Games. Coin and greed. Stealing everything from him again and again. He poured the wine, but his muscles trembled from the wealth of emotion he struggled to restrain. So much so, more wine landed on the table than in the cup. "Leave now. Please."

"Not until you explain yourself."

An anguished cry roared from his throat and he flung the pitcher at the stone wall. The crack of the clay shattering only amplified his helpless rage. Wine ran down the wall, and broken sobs from a rent heart stripped the last of his dignity as he sank to his knees and dropped his head in his hands to weep.

Lord, I'm but a man. How long? How long must I wait for her?

Caelina came and knelt beside him. He looked up at her to beg her to leave him, but those weren't the words that came. "I've lost her again."

She put her hand to his shoulder, smoothing the thin wool of his tunic. "You don't have to always be strong."

"But I do, don't you understand that?"

From her expression, she didn't.

How could she? No one understood him—except Nessa. He buried his face in the sanctuary of his hands and spoke from behind them. "Please go."

The sound of rustling cloth signaled her movement, but no footsteps followed. Instead he felt a hand on his back and an arm loop around his body at the top edge of his belt. The weight of her head came to rest against the curve of his neck. She held him, and he let her. No more strength remained in him to fight.

In minutes, the heat of her breath became the heat of his skin where life pulsed in the cord of his throat. She turned and kissed him there, her lips soft and warm. He raised his head toward her. Her lashes swept down an instant before she touched her lips to his. The tide of sensation swept away the last of his reason and its torment of emotions with it. His eyes closed as he cupped her face in his hands and laid siege to her mouth.

The intensity of her response to his unrestrained desire stoked the flames of his passion, cauterizing everything in him but physical need—until she whispered his name. The voice in his ears didn't belong to the woman his shattered heart had conjured a vision of the second he closed his eyes. It belonged to the woman between his hands.

He pulled away, tipping his head back and breathing deep in an effort to clear his head. But even that failed, because her perfume swam in his lungs as much as the taste of her lingered in his mouth. *Jesus, help me.*

Her fingertips slid along his jaw. "What's wrong?"

He opened his eyes to meet her gaze. "Me."

She studied him for a long moment, and then her hands fell away. "I'm not her."

"Caelina…" He rubbed the back of his neck. What could he say that wouldn't wound her more than he just had?

She slid away from him and curled her knees to her chest. "You don't have to say anymore." Her head came to rest on her knees and her mouth formed an uneven smile. "I think I understand at last what I've made Torren feel."

"He cares for you a great deal."

Her head snapped up. "Don't defend him. If you did not send for me, he must have in your name."

"If that's true, he'll have more reason to be wounded by it than you."

"Why?"

Right now he didn't know who to pity more, Torren or Caelina. He hoped it didn't show in his eyes as he answered her. "Because you came."

"Of course I did. I thought you…" Her gaze moved to the floor. "Oh."

She rose and stared down at him. "Well, treachery or not, he will have his way. I'll see him, though not the way I imagine he's hoping." Her brow wrinkled and her mouth twisted, like she'd tasted bitter herbs. "What's that in your belt?"

Jonathan followed her gaze to the arm of the doll poking out of the wide leather at his waist. He stood and pulled the doll free, remembering the faces of Ramses' wife and children. "A gift from a friend."

Caelina reached for the doll, practically yanking it from his fingers. "You are the most peculiar man I have ever known." She turned it over and over several times in her hands, admiring the thin leather cords that formed the joints, the tiny wooden sword twined in one hand, and the charcoal face that had been drawn on its rounded head. Her eyes grew misty, and she shoved the doll back in his hands.

She couldn't hide the pain in her eyes. Stark and raw, the wounds behind them ran far deeper than unrequited affection.

"If I could see your heart, Caelina, would it look like my back?"

Her eyes widened and she swallowed.

A yes. "There is healing and comfort in God. Days like today, He's the only way I survive. I pray you accept the gift of Christ I spoke of that day and find peace."

The hunger for truth flared in her eyes. But in the next breath, it vanished and she retreated within herself again. The sultry smile returned, but it didn't fill her face. "I'll pray too. That you forget Nessa and one day love me instead."

He could sooner pull the sun from the sky, but he wouldn't tell her. He'd hurt her enough already. "God knows the man meant for you. With you as a wife at his side, such a man will be richer than Caesar."

She blushed, which he'd never seen her do before. She leaned forward and kissed his cheek. "As is Nessa," she whispered in his ear. Her embrace closed around him, her perfume washing over him again. She drew back, her face once again a beautiful mask of perfect poise, despite her red-rimmed eyes. "Goodbye, Jonathan."

He watched her leave, and closed the door to lean his forehead against the smooth wooden planks. He remained there a long moment, making certain he'd regained control over his emotions. Eventually he made his way to his table, trading the doll in his hand for the half-full cup of wine. He wished for more, but the rest was now a drying stain on the walls and floor among the broken pieces of clay that had held it. He bent and picked up a shard, remembering another broken pitcher.

"Nessa, I *will* come for you." He set the piece of clay on the table. "If it's the last thing I do in this life, I *will* come for you."

"The master summons you," the voice said again, something shaking his foot.

Jonathan opened his eyes to find Ica holding a lamp at the foot of his bed. He sat up and rubbed at his eyes. "What?"

"The master summons you."

From the disarray of Ica's hair and slave tunic, he'd been awakened as well. "How long since sunset?"

"A few hours. The master is waiting for you in the yard."

Jonathan pulled on his tunic and sandals, praying for restraint. It didn't take an oracle to know this was about Caelina, Ramses, or both. He padded down the dark hall toward the training area. The outer doors of the villa stood open, and Jonathan stepped through the doorway into the light of a full moon. Ica didn't follow.

Torren stood statue still in the moonlight, sword in hand. From this distance, Jonathan couldn't tell if the weapon was wood or steel. He wore only a tunic. No belt or sandals. Jonathan crept forward, his unease growing with every step. Another sword lay on the ground between them. Torren pointed his blade at the one in the sand. "Pick it up."

Jonathan reached down to collect the wooden training sword without dropping his gaze. "It's late for sparring, isn't it?"

Torren swung his sword in smooth arcs above his head. "You know the first rule of my ludis. Never strike another man in anger, outside of contest or training. In my entire life, all thirty-four years, I've broken it one time." He stilled the sword midair and dropped low in the moonlight—into opening position. "To keep from breaking it again, I'm arming you first. Now tell me, did you kiss her?"

Jonathan's entire body tensed, tightening his grip on the wooden sword. "Torren, I—"

"Is it true?"

"Yes, but—"

Torren charged. The sharp crack of wood on wood echoed in the courtyard, frightening away birds roosted in the eaves of the villa. The sudden whoosh of hundreds of wings surrounded them. Their wooden blades locked together at the hilt and became a contest of strength as Jonathan pressed.

"Traitor," Torren snapped as they pushed against each other.

Jonathan broke first, giving way and stepping back. "You're angry at *me*?"

Torren answered with another charge.

The sparring grew so intense Jonathan broke into a heavy sweat in spite of the cool night air. Several times he could have taken the upper hand, but this wasn't about which of them was the better gladiator.

And it only made Torren angrier. "Fight me!"

"No." Jonathan blocked another blow and continued to parry and swing, but only to defend. "I can't give you what you want."

"You know nothing of what I want!"

Jonathan shifted his weight as Torren's sword struck his, inches from his head. "I can't make her love you."

A guttural cry came from Torren that would wake the entire villa. His blows became so vicious Jonathan had to attack to avoid being battered to a pulp. It was like fighting Tao again, so he faked a stumble. When Torren charged it, Jonathan recovered at the last second and flipped his sword along his arm. Fast as a cobra strike, he drove it hard into the side of Torren's head. Torren went down face first in the sand—and didn't move. Jonathan dropped his sword and crouched beside him. "Torren?"

Torren rolled over and landed a solid punch to Jonathan's jaw. The blow knocked him back onto the sand and pain lit his face before Torren pounced. They fought barehanded on the ground, sand clinging to both of them as they wrestled with fists and knees tangling.

At last, Jonathan worked his forearm over Torren's throat and pressed him back into the sand. "Yield!"

Torren slammed his forehead into Jonathan's. The bone-on-bone collision sparked stars in Jonathan's vision as bright as those in the sky. The hiss of a dagger slipping its sheath screamed a warning before he was flung onto his back. A cold, steel blade bit the base of his throat, but Jonathan fought the instinct to freeze. He threw his weight to the side and struck Torren's wrist as hard as he could with the heel of his hand while smashing his elbow hard into Torren's ear.

Mercifully, it worked. The dagger cut his shoulder and not his neck. Jonathan snatched the weapon from the sand and put it to Torren's throat as he pinned him down in the sand.

His master panted beneath his own blade. "Are you going to kill me?"

"No." Jonathan pulled the dagger from Torren's throat and stabbed it into the sand beside them.

Torren's gaze flitted to the handle sticking up beside his head. "Why not?"

"Because you are not my enemy. And in spite of what you feel tonight, I am not yours." Jonathan took his weight from Torren and stood. The pain in his bleeding shoulder sieved through now the battle was over. He extended his other arm to Torren, who took hold and pulled himself to his feet.

Jonathan turned and saw they were no longer alone. Torren's shout had indeed awakened the entire villa. His brothers and the slaves were gathered near the doors in various stages of dress. Jonathan leaned toward Torren, speaking low to be certain none of the onlookers overheard. "You're going to have to trust me if we are to do what we must. We can't let Ramses or Caelina change that."

Torren retrieved his dagger from the ground and sheathed it at his belt. "Did you really kiss her?"

He'd failed God, Nessa, and Caelina in a moment of weakness and would make no excuses. He met Torren's gaze. "Yes."

"If she wasn't lying about that, then she probably wasn't lying when she said she hates me, called me a liar, and broke my favorite vase on her way out after she slapped me."

"For what it's worth, it was a mistake, and I wish I hadn't."

"It won't do any good. I wish I'd never met her and now that she hates me, I find I love her more than ever."

Torren only felt that way because he couldn't have her. Though for different reasons, Jonathan knew that pain.

Torren frowned. "Apologies for the shoulder."

Jonathan followed his gaze to the blood trailing down his chest to mix with the sweat and sand clinging to his skin and tunic. The hand-breadth cut wasn't anything some salt, wine, and Rufus couldn't patch up. "It's a scratch. Apologies for beating you in front of the others."

Torren laughed while they walked through the group of men who stared at them as if they were both mad. "I let you win."

"Of course you did, *Dominus.*" Jonathan grinned.

"Don't mock me in my own ludis. I'll have the ear of the emperor soon."

The reminder of their mission stole the moment of levity from both of them. Torren would have the ear of the emperor soon, once they put Senator Nerva into power as Caesar. That ear, and the favors it implied, would only be worth something if they survived Domitian's assassination and Nerva's ascent to power.

Jonathan feared Nerva wouldn't leave loose ends, especially ends capable of assassinating a Caesar. If Torren shared that fear, he never said. Jonathan could only pray God's work for both of them wouldn't be finished for a long, long time.

CHAPTER 39 – RECKONING

Jonathan pulled his cloak tighter against the cool night air. He and Torren were in a part of the city Jonathan had rarely traveled since returning to Rome. Torren's gaze moved to a doorway where the light of the street torches didn't reach. A man stumbled from the darkness of the entryway into the moonlight, and Jonathan drew his dagger from beneath his cloak and moved between the stranger and his master.

"Have you seen my sandal?"

The slurred speech was as strong as the smell of the vagrant, but the man wasn't missing a sandal. Jonathan scanned the area around them with sharp eyes, wary this was a diversion for other assailants. The man stumbled, and then collapsed into a heap on the dung-covered street.

Torren sheathed his dagger within the folds of his cloak. "He's a drunkard. Come, or we'll be late."

They walked in silence for some time, the dank air thick in the narrow streets between buildings almost as tall as the city walls.

Torren glanced at Jonathan as they passed beneath a street torch, and his pace slowed. "There's something I need to tell you."

Jonathan glanced about, but the street was vacant except for them. "About the plan?"

"No." Torren rubbed the back of his head as he walked. He only did that when he was uncomfortable with something—a rare occurrence.

"Then tell me tomorrow when it's finished." Whatever Torren wished to tell him shouldn't be driven into the open by the fear one or both of them could be dead by sunset tomorrow. His master frowned, but remained silent as they continued toward the senator's villa.

They turned a corner, and Jonathan recognized a street he hadn't traveled on in fourteen years.

"Do you see something?"

Jonathan pulled his hood over his head, fighting a chill not born of the night air. "No."

He needed to focus. Not on his past, but on the mission to deliver Torren safely to the meeting place and return him to the Ludis Maximus when it was over.

But the further they walked, the more familiar the route became. He glimpsed pale marble columns supporting a heavy bronze gate, and his steps faltered. Burning torches set on either side of the gateposts illuminated a crowned lion set atop a raised fist.

The House of Tarquinius.

Jonathan's heart hammered in his chest as he stopped close enough to feel the heat from the torches. "The meeting is here?"

"Yes." Torren nodded to the two armored men occupying the center of the stone paved entry, and continued toward the villa.

Jonathan forced his feet to hold a steady pace beside Torren. Father. Of course. Few men had commanded the respect and following among the senate Poetelius Tarquinius Cornelius did. Would Manius be here? What would he say for himself?

A servant he didn't recognize met them at the entry doors. He and Torren made eye contact, but no words or greeting were exchanged. The atrium was unchanged. He'd stood beside this very fountain with his mother, a boy of twelve, waiting to meet the man who'd begun his life and would change it forever. The gleaming white stone floor was gone. In its place a mosaic of gladiators in battle surrounded the fountain.

Torren removed the hood of his cloak when they were deeper into the villa, but Jonathan did not. He wanted to find and recognize Father first, especially if Manius was here. A servant met them in the corridor and motioned them to follow. On the floor against the wall, a small wooden sword and a stuffed linen rabbit lay forgotten. Signs of children, but whose?

The servant opened the door to his father's study, and Torren slipped in. Jonathan followed, but stopped near the wall when the door closed behind them. Among the small crowd of men in the room, there could be no mistaking Manius, even after ten years. He wore no sword, and the dagger at his waist would be useless against Jonathan. He'd imagined this moment for years and now it was here, he was unsure. Of many things. Except Manius would answer for what he'd done—with his life, the truth, or both. Jonathan was still deciding.

Prefect Norbanus was recognizable even without his uniform. Jonathan had a strong memory of him that day he'd survived defying Caesar. The stranger with him must be Stephanus, who wore a wound dressing on one arm from wrist to elbow. Norbanus passed a scroll to Torren. "We need to hurry. I must return to the palace before the change of guard."

"Yes, but first I want to meet the gladiator we're trusting with our lives." Manius even sounded like their father. "Among my colleagues in the senate, your name is spoken together with those of Priscus, Varus, even the gods themselves. 'The merciful champion,' they call you. Had I not witnessed it with my own eyes, I would never believe you slew the mighty Hulderic."

Jonathan's hand went to the handle of his dagger within his cloak. In slow, deliberate motion, he pulled his hood away with his free hand. "I'm very good at not dying."

The man who'd stolen everything from him stared, squinted, and then his eyes sprung wide.

He knows. Jonathan opened his mouth to demand where their father was, but Norbanus spoke first.

"I know you're an admirer, Senator, as are we all, but we must hurry. I must return to the palace before the change of guard. Those are the names." Norbanus nodded at the scroll in Torren's hand. "Do you have all the coin?"

"Two hundred thousand sesterces, in a chest at the inn," Torren answered.

Jonathan heard them, but kept his gaze locked with Manius, who had yet to move, speak, or look away. What was churning in his mind? Excuses? Escape?

"Tarquinius?" Norbanus asked.

For three breaths, no one moved or made a sound. Manius blinked, turning his head toward Norbanus but keeping his eyes on Jonathan. "What did you ask?"

Torren huffed. "He asked if you had the coin ready."

"Yes." Manius swallowed and took a deep breath. "Five hundred thousand of my own coin and a hundred thousand each from Aurelius and Vibianus, all here at the villa. Nerva is to deliver his hundred thousand when he is named the new Caesar and the senate has accepted him."

Manius took his hand from his dagger handle and wiped at the pebbles of sweat that had emerged on his brow.

"And the others?" Stephanus said.

"I've made it known among the leaders in the senate that anything less than accepting Nerva as Caesar would be fatal."

The slight lilt at the end of Manius' phrases still remained, along with the way he spoke of taking life as if it were a cluster of grapes to be plucked from a vine. Jonathan's grip tightened on his dagger so hard the carved bone handle cut into this fingers.

"Are you sure a million sestercii is enough to turn the entire praetorian?" Torren asked Norbanus.

"I'm confident in all but two of my cohort commanders. I believe they will turn with the others rather than stand against them. Neither of their cohorts will be on duty tomorrow at the palace. If they do not ally with us and swear allegiance to the new Caesar, I will allow them to leave the praetorian. I'm confident their men will remain under a new *pilus*."

"We should kill them," Stephanus said.

"No." Norbanus' tone held vehemence, as would Jonathan's in a moment. What was Manius going to do, and where was their father?

"Allegiance to Caesar should not be a death sentence," Norbanus continued. "If we kill them because they oppose us, we're no better than the man we're removing from power."

"Agreed," Torren said. "But this is all fruitless unless we're successful in our assassination. Tell me how that is occurring."

"The best way to hide is in plain sight." Stephanus gestured to the linen coiled around his forearm. "I've feigned injury and been able to conceal my dagger in the wraps here on my arm. Domitian will be watching and wary of everything. He believes he's going to die tomorrow and is determined not to."

"Someone has betrayed us." Torren's hand flashed to the sword at his side.

"No." Norbanus held a hand out in appeal. "Domitian believes the goddess Diana appeared to him in a dream and foretold his death tomorrow, down to the fifth hour. His court astrologer confirmed it in accordance with the signs of his birth. But we're using that against him. Tell him, Stephanus."

"Domitian will spend tomorrow in his chamber. He's had the walls covered in polished metal to see even behind him and will remain in there until the fifth hour has passed. It shouldn't be difficult to make him believe it is later than the fifth hour, when the stars have predicted he will die. Once he believes the danger has passed, we shall strike."

"My champion and I will be guarding the empress and the escape path as promised. Our two swords equal twenty, but the fewer you can keep from coming for us, Norbanus, the better."

"Understood." Norbanus' head turned between Manius and Jonathan. "Any more questions?"

"Yes." Jonathan moved his hand from his dagger to the grip of his sword, but did not draw it. Yet. He could feel every pair of eyes in the room on him, but watched only those of his half-brother. "Where is our father?"

Silence fell over the room.

Manius' expression twisted with all the incredulity Jonathan expected. "How dare you insult the House of Tarquinius." He shifted his chin to

Torren, but kept his gaze fixed on Jonathan. "I want his tongue cut from his head so he never utters such a sacrilege again. You're fortunate I don't have him killed this instant."

Fortunate? Fresh anger swept Jonathan's sword from its sheath. "Try it. But this time have the courage to do it yourself."

Norbanus drew his sword and stepped between them.

Torren drew his own sword and joined Jonathan's side. "Put that away. I'm not sure what's happening here, but if we try to solve it with swords, I assure you only Jonathan and I will be left standing."

Stephanus stepped away from them. He appeared unarmed. Manius was calculating. Jonathan could see it in his eyes, but there was no way he could draw that dagger and launch it before Jonathan reached him.

"I'll ask again. Where—is—my—father?"

"Are you going to allow this?" Manius shot a glare at Torren. "I'm ready to order you both from my villa this instant." He reached for his dagger, and Jonathan dropped into opening position.

"Stop." Torren moved between them, dropping his sword to the floor with a violent clatter of metal on stone. "Put the weapons down and remember who the real enemy is. Fighting among ourselves will destroy everything, including Rome."

"Gallego is right," Norbanus said, but his sword remained ready.

"Jonathan." Torren's gaze pleaded. "You would never make so bold a claim unless you believed it, but—"

Manius lunged, knocking Torren aside and into Jonathan's blade. Pulling the sword into position would wound Torren, so Jonathan dropped it and reached for his dagger. Too late. Manius slammed into him. Jonathan felt the wound rip into his forearm—close enough to his wrist that terror threatened to seize him as they struggled, crashing over the couch to the floor.

"Get the senator!" Torren screamed, and the light disappeared as the three men grabbed at them. Jonathan had one goal. Seize that dagger and slit Manius' throat. His half-brother had spent his chance at mercy. Manius tried to knee him, and someone had grabbed his arms, but he threw his weight into Manius and wrestled the dagger from his hand. He fought and shoved, their tunics ripping and knees and feet sliding on the smooth stone.

An arm grasped Jonathan's neck, jerking him back. He banged the back of his skull into the face of whoever had tackled his back, but the man held on.

"Let him go or I swear on Jupiter's throne I will kill her." Torren tightened his hold on Jonathan's throat. "I'll kill her."

Nessa. The shock of Torren's threat clubbed him and he dropped the knife.

Manius glared at him as he crawled away on his back, using his elbows to move him away from Jonathan. "Kill him!"

"No," Torren said, as Stephanus and Norbanus turned toward them.

"It wasn't a request." Manius massaged his throat as he struggled to his feet.

"I said no, Senator. We need his sword."

"Let me go." Jonathan grabbed Torren's strong arm still wrapped around his neck. He couldn't get to his feet with Torren holding him back on his knees.

The door flew open and a little girl ran in, no more than seven or eight years old, her black hair flying behind her. A woman ran in after her, skidding to a stop as her gaze swept the room. "Forgive us, Manius. She heard the shouting, and I couldn't contain her."

A daughter?

"Get her out of here, now," Manius ordered.

The woman's gaze went to Jonathan, and she gasped. "What's going on?"

Her face was familiar, but why? Torren tightened his hold so much Jonathan could hardly breathe.

Manius swept the girl up and thrust her toward the woman. "I said get her out of here *now*."

She held the child close, the little girl wrapping her arms and legs around her mother. The woman didn't look away from him. Instead she took a step closer. "Jonathan?"

He looked closer at her slim face and deepset eyes. Tried to imagine them ten years ago and see them in the woman before him. "Hadriana?" he rasped.

Her eyes widened and her gaze flew to Manius—who slapped her.

"Take my daughter to her chamber now," he yelled.

A growl tore from Jonathan's throat as he jerked against Torren's hold. He pulled free as the little girl cowered against her mother, who'd backed away, holding the side of her face. "Coward," Jonathan screamed, lunging for Manius, ready to rip his arms from his body with his bare hands.

This time Norbanus and Torren grabbed him, one on each arm, and Jonathan couldn't break free. Hadriana and her daughter fled the room and Manius shut the door behind them. Stephanus picked up the dropped dagger and withheld it when Manius held his hand out for it.

"I mean it, Jonathan." Torren's harsh whisper fanned heat on Jonathan's neck. "You will calm yourself and obey me, or I will have Nessa killed. You're leaving me no choice."

He wouldn't. Jonathan stilled to meet his gaze to be sure. What he saw there chilled his blood.

"Lest you think this a hollow threat or she's safe in Germania, remember the men in this room are about to assassinate the emperor of the Roman Empire. There is no one we can't reach, and you yourself told me the day we met there is no better way to compel you."

"I want him killed for this outrageous lie. I demand it or the alliance is broken." Manius wiped at blood coming from his nose beneath a glare that would melt steel.

"Enough, Tarquinius." Norbanus eased his hold on Jonathan's right arm. "I'm sure you do want him killed, but we all have eyes. He does favor you, and your father, gods rest him."

Father was dead. He'd always known that was a possibility, but the confirmation came like spears to his chest.

"Torren is right in that we need his sword," Stephanus said. "And you are too deep to back out now, and you know it. We all do."

Manius' bitter silence was acceptance. Jonathan turned to Torren. "You know I'm telling the truth. You can look at us and see it. Hadriana recognized me too. She was to be my betrothed. Manius tried to have me killed ten years ago, and thought he had. I was sold into slavery though I was a Roman citizen and a noble. Now that you know, you can't keep me enslaved, Torren. You can't."

"Is it true?" Norbanus asked.

"Yes," Manius answered. The hate in his eyes echoed in his voice. "As you all reminded me so eloquently, we're united in this. So to have my coin and the support of my followers in the senate, you will forget this ever transpired. Torren will keep his gladiator, I don't halve my rightful inheritance, and we install the new Caesar Rome is in dire need of. Everyone emerges a victor."

"Torren, you're a man of honor." Jonathan felt no desire to rise to his feet now. He was about to beg. "You know the truth now. I'm a Roman citizen. You face grave punishment to knowingly enslave me."

"He'd need me to prove it, Torren," Manius said, coming closer. "And I won't. Neither will my wife."

Torren was silent for a long time, though both he and Norbanus had long since ceased holding him down. Jonathan remained on his knees, waiting and praying. Torren met his gaze, and Jonathan knew it was over.

"I'm sorry. I am, but we must free Rome from Domitian, and we cannot do it without Senator Tarquinius or you. Sacrifices must be made for the greater good, Jonathan. I hope you can understand."

Understand. Jonathan hoped the venom in his chest would fill his voice. "I understand. I understand you are no better than Caius."

Torren's expression changed, Jonathan's arrows landing in the soft spot he'd hoped. He pulled free and rose to his feet, enjoying when Manius backed toward the door. Jonathan picked up a cushion from where it had fallen in the struggle and pressed the expensive silk to the wound on his arm before meeting Torren's gaze. "I will defend the empress with you as I would defend Nessa's life. Because it's the right thing to do, not because you threaten the woman I love."

He turned to Manius. "I can only pray that my father died without knowing the man you truly are. For the love I bore him, I will let you live. Not because you deserve it, but because you are also his son."

But Manius laughed. "You'll *let* me live?"

"Yes," Torren said, walking up behind Jonathan. "The past few moments, he could have reached his sword and severed your head from your body before Norbanus or I could have stopped him. You'd do well to remember that, Senator. We are in this together, as you said."

"I'll send word once Domitian is dead and we are ready to move," Torren said to Norbanus. "Have Nerva and the others ready so we do not face another year of four emperors." Torren picked up Jonathan's sword from the floor and grabbed Jonathan's elbow with his free hand. "We need to get that cleaned and wrapped before we get to the palace."

Jonathan met Manius' gaze. "This isn't over."

"I think it is," Manius said. "You can keep the cushion. You've ruined it with your slave blood."

"Manius, don't push him," Torren said.

Jonathan didn't need Torren to defend him. He needed him to go back to being the man he'd walked into this villa with. A man he respected and obeyed from loyalty and honor, not a man like Caius. As they left, the villa he remembered so well seemed darker, colder. Absent of hope. His father was dead. Torren had done the unthinkable. Manius remained corrupt, and Jonathan feared Nerva could be as well. Torren had just proven he'd do anything to accomplish his purpose, with impunity. So were the men he would lend his sword to tomorrow really so different from Caesar? Had he misunderstood God's leading that they were doing right for Rome and the greater good?

Outside, he couldn't look back. The steps felt longer, and as much as he wanted to look back at his old home, he couldn't. Torren walked beside him, but Jonathan kept trying to put distance between them. The streets were quiet as they approached the inn where they'd been staying. The night slave shot to his feet with bleary eyes when they entered.

"I need linen strips and warm wine," Torren said. "Bring them to our room."

Once inside, Jonathan could no longer avoid him. Torren lit the lamp and took the pillow from Jonathan's arm. The bleeding had stopped but a scab had yet to form.

"I don't need your help." Jonathan went to the palate he'd made himself on the floor the night before. He opened his pack, pulled his spare tunic from it, and used his dagger to start a tear in the hem. The ripping cloth tore the silence as well, and Torren watched with arms crossed from where he leaned against the wall.

"You should at least cleanse it," Torren said.

Jonathan folded a square of his garment and pressed it to the wound. It took some work to get the longer strip wrapped around it tightly with only one good hand and his teeth, but he managed. As he finished, the innkeeper's slave knocked on their door and gave Torren the cloths and pitcher of wine. Steam rose from the mouth of the vessel in the lamplight, and while it would probably taste and feel good, Jonathan lay down on his pallet and turned toward the wall, propping his wounded arm up beside his head on his small sleeping cushion.

The soft splash told him Torren had poured a cup of the wine. "You should drink this. You've lost blood."

Telling him to drown himself with it would be going too far, so Jonathan chose silence instead.

"Drink it."

Jonathan rolled back over and sat up. "Will you have Nessa killed if I don't?"

Torren frowned as he knelt to be at eye level. "Just drink it."

The cup was already warm to the touch when Jonathan took it. He downed the wine as fast as he could swallow and set the empty cup on the floor beside him, hard enough to crack them both. "Anything else?"

"Yes. Try to understand how important it is that we—"

"I said I understand. I will be your sword-wielding puppet, still wrongly-enslaved, doing what I'm ordered to with no regard to my birthright, my freedom, my beliefs, or my own mind. In exchange you won't kill the woman I love. Did I miss anything?"

"Yes. Why we're doing this."

"Nothing you can say to me is going to justify your threatening Nessa's life. Nothing." Jonathan lay back down and faced the wall. It was a long moment before Torren rose and walked to his bed. He blew out the lamp and Jonathan lay there in the dark.

He'd always known his father could already be dead. What he never thought he'd see die was the friendship he'd been foolish enough to allow between him and Torren, and he silently grieved them both—long into the night.

CHAPTER 40 – FORGIVE

Jonathan was never going to forgive him. Torren glanced at him again, riding beside him to the ludis. His face remained set in stone, as it had been since leaving Tarquinius' villa the night before. This should be a day to celebrate. Rome was free of Domitian. The assassination had gone perfectly but for the death of Stephanus. Torren would see that the others in the alliance contributed generously to the thousand sestercii he planned to send to the chamberlain's family. The many senators and wealthy targets of Domitian were breathing easier this day. All but Torren.

He drew the leather reins of his horse tight and brought the animal to a stop on the road. "I couldn't let you kill Tarquinius."

Jonathan pulled his mount to a stop but didn't turn to face him.

"I told you the only thing I knew would still your hand but I would never have hurt her, Jonathan."

Did it matter that was the truth? Torren would never harm Nessa. He'd sooner harm Caelina. Well, sometimes he was angry enough at her continued silence to consider it, but never Nessa. Otherwise, he wouldn't have put his other plan in place that should already be underway. If he could say with certainty it would be successful, he'd tell Jonathan everything. Right now. But he'd already disappointed his champion and wouldn't risk doing so a second time.

Torren's horse lowered its head, and he allowed the animal to crop some grass near the edge of the pavestones. He wasn't moving until they'd settled this. It was bad enough to have lost Caelina.

Jonathan surprised him when he leaned forward and slid from the saddle to the ground. He kept the reins in his hand, on the arm still bound tight with the pieces of his tunic, and stared up at Torren. "You ask me to believe that you were lying then?"

"I'm telling you the truth. I needed to stop you from tearing apart the alliance, and I didn't know how else to do that."

"Truth?" Jonathan stepped toward him. There was anger in his voice, and in his eyes. Even the horse felt it, for he raised his head. "If the truth mattered to anyone I wouldn't still be a slave. You saw. You heard. Manius confessed. So if truth is of any value, why am I still a slave?"

If only he could tell him.

Jonathan's gaze cut Torren like a frigid wind. "That's what I thought." He put his back to him, climbed back on his horse, and kicked the animal into a hard gallop.

Torren watched him go. Jonathan would never believe until he saw it for himself.

When Nerva's first games as emperor, the *Ludi Augustales,* came, the knife wound on Jonathan's arm from his half-brother's dagger was little more than a scab. Yet Torren had shocked them all by declaring him still unfit for contest. Jonathan grew angrier, counting on those winnings to begin replenishing his earnings for Nessa's freedom. When his restlessness would attack, he would feel God and Nessa both urge him to forgive Torren. And he wanted to, but every time he thought he had, he'd remember the absolute conviction in Torren's voice threatening to kill her.

He no longer possessed any reluctance about sparring viciously with Torren, which he did often. The others occasionally stared or commented, recognizing the rift between them, but Jonathan never told them the reason. There were still those in Rome who'd vowed to never be at peace until the conspirators were discovered and killed. No formal oath of secrecy had been required among the alliance. They all knew their lives depended on keeping silent.

The first games of the year were only two months away, and Jonathan hadn't convinced Torren he was in perfect fighting form yet. He still winded faster than he had before he'd nearly been killed with opium, but that was never going to go away, no matter how hard he trained.

He held his wooden training sword over his head and sank into a low squat, holding it until his legs trembled from the effort. Thankfully, he was alone in the training yard today, so none of his brothers were there to cast glances of pity his direction. That annoyed him, and on occasion he would step over to spar with the man to whom the mournful look belonged. He'd put his sword in his left hand, and then put the man on his back in short order. Although Prito was growing very good at defending against Jonathan's left-handed assault—almost as good as Torren. Would Tao have been able to? Had he earned his freedom or met his end in the arena? Part of Jonathan didn't want to know, so that he could live with the hope Tao was free—as he would never be.

A messenger on horseback entered through the ludis gates. Jonathan hoped he would bear a scroll from Quintus, and if not Quintus, then at least Caelina. He knew by the way Torren often stared from his window toward Rome that she hadn't returned. The longing in the man's eyes in those moments was unmistakable.

Again Jonathan heard Nessa's quiet voice. Justice or mercy. He couldn't have both. She would want Jonathan to forgive Torren. Even for threatening to kill her. He would find the strength to, for her, because even if she didn't know, God would know. When he and Torren trained next, Jonathan would try to find a way to set aside his bitterness. It couldn't be any harder than killing a lion with a pugil stick, and might give him back some of the joy that had been missing since that day he'd returned to his father's villa.

After a solid hour of forms and work at the pole, his wrists and elbows ached on both sides. He'd switched hands halfway through his exercises so his right arm would still be as good with a sword as his left. His breathing labored, and a few times he felt a little faint, but right now he felt strong. *Thank you, Lord.* After some watered wine from the kitchens, he'd return to the courtyard and practice simple blocks and thrusts. On the way, Cam entered from the peristyle carrying something he'd made with his clay. "What are you making this week, Cam?"

"An eagle in flight with a fish in its talons."

Jonathan turned his head several different angles, but no matter how he looked at the two shapes, he could only see something that resembled a bread loaf and a shape more elephant than eagle. "Have you ever thought about making bowls?"

"Why does everyone ask that?" Cam glared at him before walking away.

Jonathan chuckled and continued toward the kitchen, but Rufus stopped him in the hall.

"The master summons you." Rufus wouldn't meet Jonathan's gaze the entire walk to the study.

Torren stood behind his desk, waving Jonathan forward. The door shut behind him, leaving them alone, and Jonathan's unease grew.

Torren looked him over and frowned. "Why are you covered in sweat?"

"I was working the pole this morning."

"It's rest day," Torren snapped.

His foul mood suggested Caelina must be involved somehow. "Yes, but it's also our free day. I want to be in peak condition before the spring games."

Torren grinned, almost laughing as he rubbed his hair and turned around. "Sit down."

"I need to tell you something first, if I may."

A dark eyebrow rose as Torren nodded. "Of course."

"Nessa once told me I could have justice or mercy but not both." Jonathan laughed, picturing her round face, laughing eyes, and full smile. How he ached to hold her, smell her, hear her voice. He swallowed. "Lie or not, you were wrong to threaten her." Torren frowned, but Jonathan continued. "I have not always done the right thing. Much of my life I did not. But I will not add to my wrongs by refusing to forgive you yours."

Silence hung between them for a long time. So long Jonathan questioned whether he'd angered Torren, for his expression remained unreadable.

Finally a corner of Torren's mouth pulled up and he released a deep sigh. "Thank you."

Jonathan nodded, and a weight he hadn't known he'd carried fell from his chest. As forgiving as his Nessa was, it was little wonder she was perpetually joyful. It felt good. Jonathan seated himself on the couch while Torren circled his desk and poured two cups of wine. He handed Jonathan one before taking his own seat opposite him. "Did you know my father was a gladiator?"

"I did not." Jonathan raised the cup to his lips and the fragrant aroma tantalized his nose. His brow dipped in curiosity, until the moment the cool red wine rolled over his tongue. He savored it a moment before swallowing. "Falernian?"

Torren grinned. "Indeed. It was my father's favorite."

"It was my father's favorite as well." Another sip of the fine wine helped push the sadness away. Jonathan had known his father for over four years. A kind, honorable man, whose name he would always be proud to carry, even if only in his heart.

"It's no riddle why I'm a lanista. I became one like my father before me. He taught me a great many things, some of which he meant to." Torren's gaze moved toward a marble bust in the corner of the room. "I keep hoping that statue will speak one day. That my father will tell me he's proud of me from the afterlife. Something I never heard from him in this one."

Torren stared at the statue a long moment and the silence became uncomfortable. Jonathan knew he should say *something*, but didn't know what. Torren blinked, and his gaze returned to Jonathan with a rueful slant to his mouth. "Forgive me, my friend." He took a long pull at his wine before refilling their cups. "Tell me now of your father. How you went from a nobleman's son to a gladiator under that idiot Caius Pullus, and how you and Nessa both survived him."

"That's a long story, and not worthy to be told over so fine a vintage."

"Appease me."

Jonathan sighed and stared into his wine. Torren stood on the threshold of Jonathan's past, inviting himself in, and Jonathan wanted nothing more than to shut the door. He'd never told his story to anyone but Nessa. With her, he'd been able to leave out the work of the Lord's hand, because she would know it without explanation. Even when God had delivered him from Hulderic. He had no desire to relive all that pain again in the retelling.

But what if God had opened the door? Jonathan took a deep breath and a long drink of wine to prepare. "I was twelve years old the day I met my father. The same day my mother died. Instead of turning to God for comfort, I turned away. I didn't know it then, but that was the worst mistake of my life. To this day."

Torren hung on Jonathan's every word, and Jonathan missed nothing. From the slave cart bound for Capua, to finding Nessa violated, killing an innocent man, and how Caius broke him. He told of God's voice and strength that delivered him from the Final Shadow that day in the arena. He even shared his anger at Torren for taking his coin to free Ramses, and the moment of shame and repentance at having given in to temptation with Caelina in his brokenness because of it. He left out one detail—a private conversation with Prefect Norbanus prior to leaving Rome. A small but growing group of Christians met there in the palace in secret. Torren didn't need to know that, at least not yet. Faith in God Most High was alive and well in Rome, even in the palace of the men who claimed to be gods themselves. Jonathan finished and wet his throat with the last of his wine.

"And now, here I sit as a testament to the never-ending love and sovereignty of the one true God."

Torren stared at Jonathan like he'd never seen him before, the wine in his hand all but forgotten.

"Now that you know everything, what do you think of me?"

A knock at the door interrupted, and Rufus stuck his head in. "It's done, my lord."

Torren nodded to him, and Rufus closed the door again. "I think I am a man of coin and not words, though I've never been sorry for it until now." His hand came up to rub the back of his head as he frowned. "I hope what I'm about to give you tells you in the way my words cannot that since I've known you, you have taught me more about what it means to be a champion than anyone I have ever known, including my father. I envy you many things, Jonathan Tarquinius. Your noble name, the love of a woman more constant than the sun, but most of all, the way you are at peace with who you are."

Torren had used his full name, but Jonathan couldn't dwell on that now. "The peace of God can be yours through Jesus Christ. I can tell you how, if you wish."

"Another time, my friend. There is a gift I must give you first."

Jonathan grimaced as Torren stood and reached for a scroll on his desk. He wanted to tell Torren nothing could be more important, but instead he prayed the seeds of truth planted in the heart of his master would be watered by the Spirit of God.

Torren held the scroll out to him. There was no seal, so it couldn't be from the messenger he'd seen earlier. "Without you we couldn't have delivered Rome from the tyranny of Domitian and protected the lives of all in the alliance."

Jonathan chose not to tell Torren that God had given him peace and purpose for his part in assassinating Domitian. To honor both God and his master, he framed his response to acknowledge them both. "My hope is that one day the men who rule Rome will also worship the one, true God. At the very least, let those of us who do, do so freely, allowed to live free of fear and persecution."

"I know. I believe Nerva is such a man, incorruptible by power and if he isn't, well, he's too old to do much damage and will be our problem, not yours. Your work is finished. For Rome, for the alliance, and for me."

Torren extended the scroll to him once again, smiling from ear to ear. "Your freedom, Jonathan."

Breath ceased as Jonathan stared at the scroll in Torren's outstretched hand.

"Take it." Torren thrust the rolled scroll toward him again.

Jonathan's fingers trembled as he grasped the parchment. His vision blurred as his eyes filled with tears. He took the scroll and a deep breath—his first as a free man in eleven years.

"You can keep the mark of our house if you wish. Once a member of this familia gladitoria, it is an honor carried to death. We also always throw a feast whenever freedom is earned. I hope you'll stay and enjoy it with your brothers tonight."

"Of course." Jonathan forced the words out, no longer trying to fight the tears in his eyes or the weight of the gratitude he felt.

"This is also yours." Torren placed a heavy leather bag in Jonathan's other hand. "Enough coin for a good beginning wherever you choose to go from here. Even Germania."

Jonathan's gaze flew to Torren, who stood and smiled at him. "Take it to your room and put it away before any of your brothers are tempted to pilfer while your back is turned. Especially Wolf."

"I don't know what to say." And he didn't—to Torren or to God.

"You've already said it, my friend. Every day in the way you live. Now go. Put that away, and don't forget. Feast tonight. We must have our guest of honor present."

"I wouldn't miss it."

Torren grinned, and laughter danced in his eyes. "I'll remember you said that. Now go."

Jonathan loosened the ties on the leather pouch while he walked to his chamber. The coins inside were gold aureii, and there were too many to count without pouring them all out. He planned to do that as soon as he reached his table. He'd need to buy a good donkey, and hire a guide to get him to the legion camp in Germania, after inquiring at the palace if it was still in the same location. Maybe he should also hire a guard in case he ran into robbers along the way. An ex-gladiator, who would be an expert with a sword and used to harsh conditions. God help whoever dared to stand between him and Nessa ever again.

He opened his door, and a flash of color that didn't belong brought his head up. The pouch fell from his grip to the stone floor and gold coins scattered everywhere.

But he didn't care.

Nessa stood facing him from the center of his room. She wore a wool tunic and *stola* the color of new wine, held in place by a belt of beaded silver. Her dark brown hair was skillfully arranged to frame her face. Long tendrils hung near her cheeks beside that blush and smile that could only be hers. And her eyes—those deep, brown eyes met his.

She came toward him like in his dreams. Touched his face and whispered his name. He lowered his mouth to hers, tasted the nectar of her kiss, and knew with certainty this was no dream. And that his dreams had not done justice to the love between them.

When he felt the fire race through his veins that normally readied him for battle, he at last pulled back to look into her eyes again. "How are you here in answer to my every prayer?"

Her mouth curved, still shiny and damp from dancing with his. With the pad of her thumb, she stroked the scar on his cheek made by Caius' ring. "Because the Lord is faithful to all His promises and loving toward all He has made."

She ran her fingers through his short hair, sweeping it back in that gentle stroke of hers that owned him in a way no man ever had. "Torren Gallego sent word to Quintus under imperial escort, though I don't know how he managed that. The scroll they carried must have been very powerful, because the General released Quintus from service. After Quintus returned from speaking with him, Quintus freed me. We traveled under praetorian escort back to Rome. I'm a slave no longer."

"Nor am I. Torren gave me my freedom only moments ago." And a small fortune that still lay at their feet. Right now the coin didn't matter. They were free. They were together. Jonathan pulled her into his arms once again and held her as tight as he could. Gratitude to God he couldn't put into words poured from his heart in silence as he held his betrothed.

She rested her face against his chest and her hands warmed his back through the thin wool of his tunic. For a long moment he held her, savoring the feel of her in his arms, her hair brushing his skin and the heat of her breath against his heartbeat.

Her grip on him tightened and she pressed closer to him. "What are you thinking about?"

"Right now?"

"Yes."

She'd always been beautiful to him. Her spirit above all else, but seeing her attired as richly as she deserved stunned him. Her radiance would have his brothers, especially Styx, in an absolute frenzy at the feast tonight. "That my brothers will take one look at you and I'll have to fight them all right there for your favor."

She raised her head and sorrow filled her eyes. Her eyes grew damp as she traced the scar on his cheek again, this time with her fingertips. "You will never have to fight for me again. I'm yours for as long as I draw breath. Even after, God willing."

The promise in her eyes pierced his soul. He took her face between his hands and turned her head up until her gaze was chained to his. "I would endure every moment of every day that has passed a thousand times over to be here with you now."

Her mouth parted and a single tear fell from the corner of her eye. "As would I."

His brows knit together as he remembered the atrocity she suffered at the hands of Caius because of him and his gaze fell away.

She grasped his chin and raised it so his eyes returned to her. "As would I. Every moment."

Her simple words spoke of her love more than any others could. He pulled her close again, tucking her to him so his chin could rest on the crown of her head. "I'm unworthy of you."

"You are not." She squeezed him tighter in her embrace. "You are fearfully and wonderfully made in the image and likeness of the living God." She pulled back to look up at him again. "And I love you for that."

"And I love you."

"That's good, because you promised to marry me, in case you forgot." A mischievous smile rounded her cheeks as she pulled his mother's carving from inside the neckline of her dress and let it hang between them.

"I didn't forget." He kissed the tip of her nose. "I have someone in mind to marry us, but it will require a trip to the palace. There is much I need to tell you."

"Yes, there is. Quintus and I spent last night at the palace, and today two praetorians traveled here with us. One of them knows you."

"Is his name Norbanus?"

Her face scrunched for a long moment. "I can't remember his name. Ever since joining the legion, I've been terrible with names. There were too many."

"Does he look like an older, thinner Quintus, with black and silver hair under his helmet?"

Her eyes widened. "He does! I can't believe I didn't see that right away."

Lord, you are too good to me. "He's the man I wanted to marry us. But it seems God already knew that and how hard it would be for me to wait even a single day." Jonathan laughed as he watched that blush he loved color her face as deep as her stola. "I'm sure Torren won't mind if we make my celebration tonight a wedding feast. If you don't."

She answered him with another kiss, and Jonathan lost himself in the love of the woman in his arms and the God who'd given him back a life far richer than the one stolen from him all those years ago.

CHAPTER 41 – SURRENDER

Jonathan shut the door to his room—their room—and tried to temper the anxiety coursing through him as if he were about to enter the arena.

"I think I ate too much." Nessa clutched her stomach with both hands and smiled. "I can't remember the last time I saw so much food in one place that wasn't for a legion."

Jonathan pulled her into his arms and kissed her forehead. "I was too busy admiring my new wife to notice any food."

"That's not what the *garum* smell on your tongue says." Nessa chuckled, her laughter making her vibrate in his arms. "But I don't mind." Her gaze traveled the short distance from his eyes to his mouth. The smile fell from her face, replaced not by sadness, but a different kind of hunger.

He swallowed. "I know it's been a long day for you, but I'd like nothing more than to feel you beside me until morning." Her expression remained unchanged. He'd been hoping for relief, prepared for hesitation, but something to help steer him. He wanted her, but didn't want to rush her either, especially since it would be her first time since *him.*

"I'd like that, very much." She pulled away and moved toward the table, presumably to dim the lamps.

He approached his bed—their bed. His fingers trembled as he unbuckled his belt and hung it on the hook like always. It would have been easier to sit to take his sandals off but the thought of turning around and facing her terrified him. He kept his tunic on, thinking she would feel more comfortable that way.

"Jonathan."

He glanced over his shoulder. For a second he couldn't breathe. He couldn't think.

She wore nothing but lamplight. The beauty of her body in full view staggered him. The creamy glint of her skin was alabaster perfection—unblemished, unmarred, and beginning to blush as deep as her face. When his lungs finally remembered to breathe, his intake of breath was so swift it made an audible gasp. The flawlessness of her body made him keenly aware of every battle scar on his own. He swallowed against the fear rising inside him at the obvious inequity of their forms. She was Eve in the garden. He was unfit to even gaze upon her and looked away.

"I'm sorry," she stammered.

He looked up to try to explain, but she'd turned her back to him and reached for her discarded garment. He reached her in three strides, taking hold of her elbow gently. "Don't be." He tugged her lightly and she turned to face him again, keeping her eyes at her feet. "Nessa, look at me. Please." He fought the urge to tip her chin up. She was his wife now, and even before she was, he would never have forced her to do anything. Ever. "You are the most beautiful thing I have ever beheld. It makes me afraid."

Her eyes slowly rose and the look of uncertainty in their brown depths pierced him like a spear. "Of me?"

"No," he whispered, reaching to touch her face. "No, of course not."

She pressed her cheek into his palm. "Then what are you afraid of?"

He could feel his own face flushing and he bit his lower lip, trying to summon the courage to tell her the truth. He licked his lips, stared at the dip below her throat instead of her face. "Of not knowing how to please you. And my scars, they—I don't…" His throat closed and his breathing deepened.

Her hands moved from his back to his neck, tugging his head down to her shoulder. He closed his eyes as she cradled his head against her. The pad of her thumb traced the raised ridge on his cheekbone near his eye and she whispered in his ear, "Your scars are my scars."

She moved to kiss the skin her thumb had caressed. She pushed him away gently at the shoulders and before he could meet her eyes, she leaned up to kiss another on his shoulder.

"Your scars are beautiful. They are a part of you, just as I am." Her hands began to gather the fabric of his tunic with purpose. "Raise your arms," she commanded.

He did, and she slipped the cloth over his head in a deft motion and let it fall to the stone floor. Standing before her in only his cloth, her gaze traveled over him. Fear made his heart race. She had yet to see his back, what they'd done to him in her absence. He'd never seen them, the scars from the scourging, but he knew they were there. She caressed his shoulder as she moved past him and he held his breath.

Her gasp reached the far walls as her fingertips traced the skin of his back. He hung his head and closed his eyes.

"Did Torren do this?"

"No."

Her arms encircled him, her cheek resting against his backbone. "Who?"

"It doesn't matter now." He gripped her arms held around his stomach.

"I wish I'd been there to care for you."

"You were. More than you know." He turned to face her, saddened at the tears in her eyes. "I hope in time the sight of them isn't as hard to bear."

Nessa grasped his head between her hands and locked her eyes with his. "Listen to me. My tears are for the pain you suffered. No other reason. You are a treasure. Your body is a treasure, and made perfect in my love for you. I meant what I said. Your scars are beautiful. As are you. Inside, and out."

She pulled him down to her and kissed him again. Soon her hands played over his back, from neck to waist, her palms traveled every length of his scars while she kissed him until he could no longer stand under the cleansing tide of her acceptance. He pulled his lips from hers and she released him and moved toward the bed.

"Come lay with me," she said, her voice calm and assured.

He was neither calm, nor assured, but his love and desire propelled him forward. He'd never wanted to surrender more in his life than to his wife in their marriage bed.

Jonathan traced the line of Nessa's spine, up and down, ever so slowly, while she slept securely in the crook of his body. The steady rhythm of her breath on his skin had him wondering how he'd ever survived being apart from her.

"Are you cold?" she asked.

His hand stilled on her back. "You're awake."

"Yes." Her head rolled so that her chin rested on his chest and those fur brown eyes he adored peeked at him from beneath her lashes. "Are you cold?"

"No. Are you?"

"No. Every few minutes you tremble, as if you were cold. I want you to be comfortable."

"You always take care of me, don't you?" Jonathan moved his hand from her back to her head, admiring the way her hair was a tangled mess from their passion.

"I try." She smiled and slid her leg atop his knee beneath the blanket.

"I think you want to kiss me," he said, his cheeks hurting from how big his smile became.

"See, I was right. I knew you hadn't been hit in the head too many times like Quintus said."

Jonathan laughed, a vision of the heavyset and bald doctor laying waste the passion Nessa had stirred a moment ago. "Please don't ever mention Quintus while we're in bed, ever again." He laughed more, and Nessa joined him, her cheeks puffing as she reddened.

"I won't. I promise." She propped her head in her hand while her elbow dug into the mattress beside him and her expression turned serious. "But he will stay here, now that Torren Gallego employs him. Will we stay as well?"

Jonathan thought of his scroll and the bag of gold on the table. "I don't know."

"It's strange, isn't it?"

"What?"

"Deciding where you want to go. Who you want to see. All the things you can do without having to ask permission." Her eyes were filled with possibilities and Jonathan wanted nothing more than to give them all to her. But there were several things he needed to attend to first.

"Would you mind if we spent some time in the city? There's someone I need to try to find."

"Your father?"

"No." Jonathan swallowed and the sadness must have shown on his face, because Nessa absorbed it immediately.

She touched his cheek, then placed her palm against his jaw. "What's wrong?"

"My father is dead."

"Beloved, I'm so sorry."

"It's not your fault." It was Manius' fault. His fault Jonathan had not been at his father's side. And of course, he had unfinished matters in Capua with Caius Pullus and Valentina, but that could wait. "I want to try to find the woman who helped raise me, if I can. She's probably dead also, but I'd like to try."

"Of course. Anything you wish."

The love in her eyes told him she would follow him anywhere. He caressed the smooth skin of her shoulder and felt the corner of his mouth rise, along with his brow. "Anything?"

She looked him full in the face before raising two fingers between them. The last thing he saw before her lips claimed his again. Jonathan smiled against her kiss. That King Solomon knew what he was talking about. He who finds a wife finds a good thing.

CHAPTER 42 – FREE

The temples, baths, insulae buildings, street booths, all were the same. Yet the city looked different through a free man's eyes. It smelled different. Everything was different. A light rain fell but Jonathan didn't mind. The thick wool of Nessa's cloak would keep her dry, and if the rain picked up, he would cover her with his. When they passed through the shadow of the amphitheater, her grip on his hand tightened.

He pulled her hand to his lips and kissed the back. Though there were no games and no shouts of the crowd, and wouldn't be for weeks, this place would always affect him. As she always did, his wife could sense his unspoken need. She released his hand and slid her arm around his waist, pressing close to his side as they walked.

He slowed his pace when they reached the insulae he'd been looking for.

"Is this the building?" she asked.

He nodded, and stopped. Nessa didn't rush him, or ask more questions as he stared at the entry for a long time. Was it better not to know? To imagine her as he remembered?

A young woman passed him, carrying a basket laden with blackberries and a dark loaf of bread. She glanced at them, and he summoned the courage to begin. "I seek a woman named Deborah who once lived here."

The woman smiled. "I am Deborah. Should I know you?"

"No. The woman I seek would be many years older than you. She was from Jerusalem, in the Judean province, and—"

"You seek *YaYa* Deborah."

Grandmother? She'd been too old to have children when she'd taken in his mother.

The young woman's smile slipped and she clutched her basket close. "Who are you?"

"It's best if I tell her myself. Would that be permitted?" The sweat was already beading high on his back. What if it was her? What if it wasn't?

The woman's gaze cut to Nessa, and that seemed to ease her mind. Nessa had that effect on everyone. "Wait here." She disappeared into the insulae with her basket.

Nessa tugged him out of the doorway toward the plaster wall. Broken pottery and other trash littered the edges of the alcove. "Careful not to cut your feet," he told her.

She smiled and cupped his cheek in her hand. "Always taking care of me." She stroked his hair back from his forehead. It was becoming long enough he'd have to see a cutter or she would take his dagger to it soon.

"Don't be afraid," she whispered.

Easy for her to say. His heart was ready to ram its way free of his chest. If it was Deborah—his Deborah—he would have so much to tell her. The lives he'd taken. The bitter, broken man he'd become after the death of his mother. The reason he'd never returned to visit. So much of his life would disappoint her.

"Stranger," a woman called from behind him. He turned and found the young woman from earlier watching them in the doorway. "Yaya says to come inside. You and your companion."

"Don't be afraid," Nessa whispered one more time as she fell into step beside him and squeezed his hand. Perhaps they shouldn't have worn their best clothing. Perhaps he should have sent a scroll, but the likelihood of anyone here being able to read it was as small as a mustard seed. Perhaps he should have never come. The sweat gathering beneath his tunic agreed.

The woman stopped at a door he didn't remember, opened it, and beckoned them inside. This was the wrong room. It wasn't the one he and his mother had shared with Deborah. Nessa entered first, tugging him in with her. It was two rooms. The front area held a large table and four stools, shelves with jars and lamps and various cooking tools. And a boy about ten with wheat-colored hair staring at them with his arms crossed.

Another woman, older than the first, in a plain black tunic, came from the back room. Her gaze swept both Jonathan and Nessa before landing on the boy between them. "Jonathan, don't stare. It's unwelcoming. Offer our guests a cup of water."

The boy had his name? Nessa looked to him in question, but he had no answer for her.

"Would you like a cup of water?" the child asked, mistrust clear in his voice.

"No," Jonathan answered.

"No, thank you." Nessa squeezed Jonathan's hand again, and smiled at the boy.

"Deborah, will you take Jonathan for a walk to the fountain to refill the pitchers?"

"Yes." She took the boy's hand and slipped between Jonathan and the wall toward the door. "Come, Jonathan. The elders are going to discuss things they don't want us to hear," she mumbled.

Nessa chuckled beside him, and Jonathan would have grinned were he not so nervous. When the pair departed, the woman glanced over her shoulder behind her, and then approached them. "Can I ask how you know Deborah? I mean, the eldest Deborah?"

Jonathan did his best to match her hushed tone. "She helped raise me. My mother and I lived with her a long time ago."

The woman's ash-gray eyes searched his face a long moment and her hand crept to her mouth. "Jonathan? Is it really you?"

He tightened his thoughts, trying to place the face before him. "Do you know of me?"

"You gave me a denarius and sent me here, before my son was born. Deborah took me in also. My son is named for you." Her eyes shined with welling tears. "They told us you were dead. Your father came and he said—" She swallowed. "Is it really you?"

"It is." He could hear the huskiness in his own voice.

So could Nessa, for she slipped her hand from his to hold his upper arm. "Would you like me to wait here?"

"No." He couldn't do this without her. Without being able to draw from her strength.

"Yaya Deborah is blind. She has been for a few years now. She can hear, but you must speak loudly. Come."

His heart pounded faster as they followed the woman through the low doorway. Jonathan had to duck and be careful not to tangle Nessa. Blanket-covered straw pallets, five of them, lined one wall. A low couch rested in the corner, and on it, Deborah.

Her hair was the white of strong leather, still braided in a single strand at her neck. Her eyes were also white, where they had once been deep brown like his wife's. Dark spots of age covered her narrow face, and thin shoulders poked through a simple tunic. A wool blanket covered her lap and her hands were folded in prayer as he remembered.

"Deborah?" After their quiet conversation, the woman's loud voice jolted him.

"Yes." Her voice was the same. Jonathan closed his eyes a moment and let it wash through him.

"Who's there?" she asked, as demanding as he remembered. Age hadn't affected that.

"It's me. Jonathan." He watched her face, but it didn't move.

"Which one?"

"No, Yaya," the woman with them answered. She gave him and Nessa an apologetic smile and knelt by the woman's knee. "Not my Jonathan, or Julia's Jonathan. This man says that he is the Jonathan that sent us."

The woman scowled and leaned back against the plaster wall. "That Jonathan is dead."

"I was." The words fell from his mouth. "Manius meant to take my life and in many ways he did. But it is me." He turned to Nessa and put his fingers to his chest.

She cocked her head and he reached for the necklace inside her tunic. When she understood, she rushed to pull the leather cord over her head and hand him the small bone horse head. He knelt beside the woman at Deborah's feet.

"The first time you swatted me was for stealing two eggs from the market. You told my mother and she made me walk them back. Many nights she and I sat beside you much like this and listened to the stories of your people. Of King David and the prophets and the Messiah. My mother named me for your husband. The husband you lost in Jerusalem when Titus destroyed the city."

Deborah's milky eyes began to shine. "Jonathan? Livia's boy?"

"It's me." Jonathan placed the small carving in her frail hand.

Her bony fingers traced the horse head as the first of her tears fell. "Your father carved this for Livia when she was a little girl. I remember she always wore it around her neck, and that you would chew on it when your teeth were coming in." The tears fell faster now. "Where have you been?"

"Many places. Few of them my choosing, until now. I have a wife. She is here with me."

"A wife?"

"Yes. This is Nessa. She has a faith as deep as yours. As deep as you gave my mother."

Nessa touched his back, kneeling beside him. "It's an honor to know you, my lady."

"Nessa means miracle in the tongue of my people," Deborah said. "And the Lord has worked a great miracle, that you are here, my boy." She reached toward his face.

Jonathan took her hand and placed it on his cheek, hoping the stubble of his beard wouldn't hurt her silk-thin skin. Her fingers were frail, but these hands had held his mother's, stroked his back when the other boys mocked his lack of a father, and they touched him the same way now.

"The scroll," Deborah said. She pulled her hand from his face. "Octavia, on the tallest shelf there should be an alabaster box. Inside it is a scroll. Bring it to me."

The woman beside him rose and went into the other room. Nessa took Jonathan's hand again and settled beside him, tucking her legs beneath her and smiling reassuringly.

"Oh, my dear girl." Deborah held the carving out. "For Jonathan to have given it to you I know he must love you a great deal. I will also."

"Thank you." Nessa took it and slipped it back over her head.

The woman returned and settled on the couch beside Deborah. "I found it."

"Give it to Jonathan," Deborah said.

He took the small scroll. A thin leather cord held it closed.

"Can you read?" she asked.

"Yes. I learned in my father's house."

Deborah smiled. A smile so full of wisdom and beauty Jonathan wanted to carve it into his mind forever. "Then later, when you are alone, open it. Not now. I know now why the Lord had me keep it all these years."

She couldn't see, and he wanted to know what the scroll was. So did the younger Deborah and Nessa, the way they gazed intently at it. He pushed the cord to the end of the roll of parchment but Nessa stayed his hand with hers. She shook her head, admonishing him with her eyes. He slipped it into his belt and put his arm around her, breathing deep of her honey scent.

"Do you remember the feast we had your last day with me?" Deborah asked.

"Of course." He would never forget it. Back then a feast had been a piece of cheese the size of his fist and three honeyed raisin cakes.

"Tonight we feast again." Deborah shifted on the couch and spread her hands over her knees. "Octavia, gather the others. Tell them the news. I know they will want to meet Jonathan, especially Julia's boy."

"Nessa and I would enjoy that very much." He reached in his coin pouch and pulled out two gold aureii. He handed them to younger

Deborah, who took them, mouth agape. "Please let us help. If you can find green grapes for my wife, they are her favorite. Whatever else you, your son and the others enjoy best, think nothing of the cost."

"Spoken like a Tarquinius." Deborah chuckled. "Your father was always so generous. We mourned him, you know."

"Thank you."

In the other room, a door flew open and the boy from earlier came running in, a taller, darker boy behind him. Both were out of breath.

"Is it true," the shorter one rasped, "that you were a gladiator?"

"And that you're the gladiator that defeated the Final Shadow?" the older one asked. "And you fight with your sword in your left hand? And that we're named after you? And—"

"Boys," Octavia snapped.

Jonathan laughed, and pulled Nessa into his side. "Yes. All true."

Their young eyes widened and they dropped to the floor. "Tell us about the arena. I heard they have lions and elephants and spotted goats with necks as tall as the city walls."

"They're not goats, they're called giraffes. They come from the land of Carthage." Had he been this eager when Dionysius first began teaching him?

"Who cares about the goats? I want to know about the lions," the smaller one said.

"My Jonathan once killed a lion in the arena with only a stick," Nessa said, casting him a proud stare.

"Really?" the boys said in unison, each sitting up taller.

"Really. And he'll tell you all about it, won't you, Beloved?" She grinned at him and patted his knee as if he were one of the young boys sitting across from them.

"Tell us, Jonathan," Deborah said. "I want to know everything."

So he did. He left out the darker parts of his years as a slave, and over honeyed wine and food as fine as he'd known at his father's table, eaten from simple clay dishes on the floor, they talked well into the evening. He met Julia, whom he didn't remember sending to Deborah, and learned that younger Deborah's mother had died shortly after she'd been born. Julia and Octavia had raised her together with their sons. Nessa figured out before he did the older of the boys went by Jon so they could be told apart if called. Seeing her with the children and the women brought out such a different side of her, one that made him love her even more, though he would have sworn it impossible.

She'd been as reluctant to return to their inn as he was. They only escaped the boys by promising to visit again tomorrow. He'd visit the markets first with Nessa. She would be able to tell better than he what sizes of sandals and tunics the children wore. With the list of gifts and provisions he'd been making as they walked, they'd probably need a cart. The innkeeper could tell him where to hire one in the morning.

They'd entered their room and he set their coin pouch and cloaks beside their wineskins. Nessa watched as he took the scroll from his belt and set it on the small table with the basin and pitcher of water.

"Will you read it now?" she asked, sitting down on the edge of the sleeping couch.

"Not yet." It was an exercise in discipline, but more so an opportunity to show favor to his wife. "Take your sandals off."

She did, giving him a sheepish grin as she removed her tunic as well. But instead of following her leadings he filled the basin with water, took a towel from beneath the table, and knelt on the floor at her feet.

"Jonathan?"

He met her gaze but didn't answer her in words. Instead, he washed her feet.

She remained quiet, pensive as she watched him work. He'd meant it as a gift, though the adoration in her eyes when he finished felt like a gift in return. As did her kiss.

The scroll.

In the fervor of shared passion that intimacy with his wife always brought, he'd forgotten it. Jonathan slipped his arm from beneath Nessa's neck and kissed her forehead. She stirred beneath the blankets but didn't rouse. She was never more beautiful than when she slept beside him, trusting him completely. A trust he would spend a lifetime honoring.

The floor was cold on his bare feet as he picked up the small lamp from the table by the bed and moved to the far corner of the room. He found the scroll among his clothes, set the lamp down, and unrolled the parchment in the flickering light.

My son, there is much I would tell you, but scribes charge by the word. I know you will have grown to be a man as upright and honorable as your father. You are and will always be the very best part of my life.

When you find a woman who loves our God and loves you, treasure her and find delight in her alone as long as you both live. Be generous with the needy. Forgive those who wrong you. Let their transgressions be between them and our God. Knowing you will want for nothing in your father's house gives me great peace. It is a peace I want for you, always. So if sorrow should come, remember this.

Suffering is a pile of stones. You can carry them, let them lay upon the ground, throw them at others, or you can build an altar.

Build an altar, my son. Always.

Jonathan read his mother's words again before allowing the scroll to reroll and then tucking it beside their coin pouch. In the light from the single flame of the oil lamp, he studied his wife as she slept.

Only then did he understand the last part of his mother's letter.

Jonathan had floundered on the stones. He'd hurled them at others in his anger. He'd tried to carry them alone until they crushed him. It had taken Nessa to show him how to build an altar of the suffering they'd both known.

More stones would come. He knew enough of life to know that they would. He knew enough of God and himself this time to build the altars. A gladiator no more, but a warrior still. Jonathan extinguished the lamp and returned to his wife, praying the Lord's work for both of them would not be finished for a long, long time.

ACKNOWLEDGEMENTS

I'm blessed to be the one putting my name on the cover but Jonathan's story would never have made it to you the reader solely by my own efforts. Thank you to my family for your sacrifices and encouragement every step of the way. I owe immeasurable gratitude to Joan Deneve—best friend, critique partner, and tireless champion of both me and this story. Only God could have brought us together. To my colleagues in American Christian Fiction Writers and Writers on the Storm, thank you for your inspiration and encouragement. Special thanks to Whitney and Darren whose praise and encouragement chapter by chapter in those first days and draft gave me more courage than you know. Thank you to my editor, and now friend, Ellen Tarver for her finishing touches and passion for this story. To my fans the "K-Squad"—your love for Jonathan and my novels keeps me writing. Thank you.

There were many sources of research I gleaned from but I must formally acknowledge those that were indispensable to me: Fik Meijer's *The Gladiators: History's Most Deadly Sport*, the BBC Film *Colosseum - A Gladiator's Story*, and *Ancient Rome: A Complete History Of The Rise And Fall Of The Roman Empire* by Nigel Rodgers and Dr. Hazel Dodge. My deepest gratitude to renowned gladiatorial expert and Harvard University's James Loeb Professor of the Classics, Dr. Kathleen M. Coleman, for her generosity in providing me with requested offprints of her research. Jonathan is left-handed as a tribute to Dr. Coleman and her work to preserve and deepen our understanding of gladiator history.

Thank you to Chad Arnold, for graciously allowing me to take his words, "*Suffering is like a pile of rocks. You can choose to carry the load, throw them at someone, just let it lay there, or you can build an altar,*" and give them to Jonathan's mother in the final chapter. I first heard those two sentences of truth at a time I was facing that same choice, and was forever changed by them.

Lastly, to *T.* Your support and encouragement as I chased this dream down, and admonishment when I wanted to give it up, will forever echo in the victory.

Nancy Kimball
Ezekiel 36:33-36

NANCY KIMBALL
FICTION FROM THE ASHES

Author, avid reader, and shameless hero addict, Nancy Kimball loves books, Ancient Rome and all things gladiator. She makes her home in Houston, Texas and is the former president of her local American Christian Fiction Writers chapter, Writers on the Storm. Her industry accolades include a two-time ACFW Genesis finalist (Chasing the Lion – 2012 / Unseen Love – 2013), and a Romance Writers of America Lonestar finalist in the Inspirational Category (Adrift No More – 2013). In 2012, her best friend and critique partner bestowed Nancy with the nickname "Phoenix" after hearing her personal testimony. Nancy loved the name and adopted the Phoenix symbol to embody her life verse, Ezekiel 36:33-36. It later came to represent her brand, Fiction From the Ashes, symbolizing stories of characters that rise from brokenness to victory.

Visit Nancy at her website, http://www.nancykimball.com for more on Jonathan and Nancy.

Subscribe to her newsletter for reader appreciation giveaways, author news, and book fun.

New subscribers receive a deleted scene from Chasing the Lion..

18851210R00221

Made in the USA
Middletown, DE
26 March 2015